The powerful be
ground with a r

Grant was certain that if he hadn't moved, the hammering impact would have tested the non-Newtonian properties of his shadow suit.

The strength of the monstrosity before him was on a par with the impact force of his gun, but this thing could back its power with great claws. The Kongamato lunged out with its other winged arm, but Grant pushed himself on top of the thing, wrapping his brawny arms around it and tugging it off balance. Its beaklike muzzle jammed into the ground, propelled by Grant's weight. Giving it a savage twist, Grant heard joints and tendons pop inside the sinewy wing, and the beast unleashed its cry into the ground.

Other titles in this series:

James Axler
Outlanders®

WINGS OF DEATH

A GOLD EAGLE BOOK FROM
WORLDWIDE®

TORONTO • NEW YORK • LONDON
AMSTERDAM • PARIS • SYDNEY • HAMBURG
STOCKHOLM • ATHENS • TOKYO • MILAN
MADRID • WARSAW • BUDAPEST • AUCKLAND

Recycling programs
for this product may
not exist in your area.

First edition February 2014

ISBN-13: 978-0-373-63881-9

WINGS OF DEATH

Copyright © 2014 by Worldwide Library

Special thanks to Douglas Wojtowicz for his contribution to this work.

Printed in U.S.A.

A monster vile, whom God and man does hate:
Therefore I read beware. Fly fly (quoth then
The fearefull Dwarfe:) this is no place for living men.
—Edmund Spenser,
1552–1599

The Road to Outlands—
From Secret Government Files to the Future

Almost two hundred years after the global holocaust, Kane, a former Magistrate of Cobaltville, often thought the world had been lucky to survive at all after a nuclear device detonated in the Russian embassy in Washington, D.C. The aftermath—forever known as skydark—reshaped continents and turned civilization into ashes.

Nearly depopulated, America became the Deathlands—poisoned by radiation, home to chaos and mutated life forms. Feudal rule reappeared in the form of baronies, while remote outposts clung to a brutish existence.

What eventually helped shape this wasteland were the redoubts, the secret preholocaust military installations with stores of weapons, and the home of gateways, the locational matter-transfer facilities. Some of the redoubts hid clues that had once fed wild theories of government cover-ups and alien visitations.

Rearmed from redoubt stockpiles, the barons consolidated their power and reclaimed technology for the villes. Their power, supported by some invisible authority, extended beyond their fortified walls to what was now called the Outlands. It was here that the rootstock of humanity survived, living with hellzones and chemical storms, hounded by Magistrates.

In the villes, rigid laws were enforced—to atone for the sins of the past and prepare the way for a better future. That was the barons' public credo and their right-to-rule.

Kane, along with friend and fellow Magistrate Grant, had upheld that claim until a fateful Outlands expedition. A displaced piece of technology…a question to a keeper of the archives…a vague clue about alien masters—and their world shifted radically. Suddenly, Brigid Baptiste, the archivist, faced summary execution, and Grant a quick termination. For Kane there was forgiveness if he pledged his unquestioning allegiance to Baron Cobalt and his unknown masters and abandoned his friends.

But that allegiance would make him support a mysterious and alien power and deny loyalty and friends. Then what else was there?

Kane had been brought up solely to serve the ville. Brigid's only link with her family was her mother's red-gold hair, green eyes and supple form. Grant's clues to his lineage were his ebony skin and powerful physique. But Domi, she of the white hair, was an Outlander pressed into sexual servitude in Cobaltville. She at least knew her roots and was a reminder to the exiles that the outcasts belonged in the human family.

Parents, friends, community—the very rootedness of humanity was denied. With no continuity, there was no forward momentum to the future. And that was the crux—when Kane began to wonder if there was a future.

For Kane, it wouldn't do. So the only way was out—way, way out.

After their escape, they found shelter at the forgotten Cerberus redoubt headed by Lakesh, a scientist, Cobaltville's head archivist, and secret opponent of the barons.

With their past turned into a lie, their future threatened, only one thing was left to give meaning to the outcasts. The hunger for freedom, the will to resist the hostile influences. And perhaps, by opposing, end them.

Chapter 1

Nathan Longa's throat tightened and he clutched the staff he was carrying as he looked at the gully below, which was blocking his journey through the forest. It was teeming, alive, and if he dropped into it, he knew he would be doomed to an agonizing death. There was no mistaking the millions-strong horde of siafu ants, a bloodthirsty form of superorganism. Within minutes of landing in the gully, his skin would be gone. At the end of a day, he'd be bleached, picked-clean bones.

With a surge of energy, Nathan hurled himself off the crumbling slope, stretching out, striving to reach the far edge of the gully. When he landed on the other side, his knees buckled and gravity seized him, threatening to pull him down into the rustling force below. He threw his free hand out to stop his fall, and felt the scrape of sharp gravel on his palm, his fingernails bending as he clawed the mud. He finally got his feet beneath him and pushed himself upward, scrambling over the top of the bank. All the while, he kept the staff grasped in his fist.

The bottom of the strange weapon was tapered to a point that never blunted, no matter how many times Nathan, or his father, or his fathers before him, had plunged it into the earth. It wasn't a keen, arrow-sharp point, but Nathan and the Longa clan had driven it through the chest of many a bandit in its years, eons that stretched back to the dawn of man and the ages of Atlantis.

The top of the staff had two snakes winding around it

in a crisscrossing pattern, reminiscent of the old symbol of healing. And yet the raised heads of the twin serpents, their eyes protruding like engine nacelles, had an alien look.

The Longas had held on to the stick for at least four centuries, perhaps longer. Only a few other names had been linked to it: Suleiman, Solomon, Kane....

Nathan's father, Nelson Longa, had been near death, his throat torn by a creature who'd fled when Nathan appeared with his torch.

"This must go to the West, across the Atlantic," the dying man had gasped. "It must reach the hands of the one being who can wield it as a sword of justice. Take it!" he'd pleaded.

Nathan had grabbed the damned stick and started running.

There had been times when he wanted to take the black staff and break it across his knee, but the shaft never flexed, even with all his weight on one end, and the other levered against the hardest granite, wedged beneath boulders. It appeared to be wood, but would never shatter, its surface well-worn and smooth, despite the fact that Nathan couldn't scratch it with his knife.

The staff's remarkable nature had become apparent the first time he'd grasped it. It had its own inner warmth, even though it was hard as steel. The warmth trickled up his arm, a strange vibration that hummed through Nathan's blood, carrying a subtle communication that obviously came from some other consciousness. The staff, in fact, guided him. When he awoke in the morning, he knew the direction he had to go, how far. Instinct had taken him across the African continent, pushing him to the north.

And now he was being prodded to even swifter flight, to the point where he couldn't dare pause in the face of the gnawing, deadly mass of killer ants.

He was being pursued by something even more fearsome than the siafu. He set off running into the thick jungle.

Even as he raced, he heard the rustle and snap of branches, both behind and above.

Then he heard the crash of something falling into the gully he'd crossed, followed by a wild shriek. Whatever had been chasing him had a healthy set of lungs, and the tearing jaws of thousands of ants gave him plenty to howl about.

There was no time to stop, no time to slow down. Nathan charged on, headlong. He had to escape the hunters. Those that were higher up, seeming to bound from branch to branch, weren't going to be deterred by the slicing mandibles of ants.

He pushed himself harder, and with each step could feel the fibers in his burning thigh muscles stretch and snap. Nathan came from the two-centuries-old postapocalyptic metropolis of Harare. Before the megacull, Harare had been a sprawling place of more than two and a half-million souls. After the hellish weather caused by nuclear winters in the northern hemisphere, and the seismic surges caused by earthshaker bombs, it still held on to its status as a strong, thriving city-state, though imports and exports with the rest of the world had been sharply limited due to the rampant anarchy in surrounding regions of Zimbabwe.

Harare remained a peaceful place, having a large military and police presence, as well as sufficient infrastructure to weather the centuries since the northern continents went into a self-destructive war. Still, population numbers were down to a million and a half thanks to conflicts and disease—especially a rampant plague of HIV, which had taken the country to the limits of its medical abilities.

Striking out beyond the borders was an arduous ordeal. To the east and west were lands of lawless excess, where Harare's military battled all along the frontier, struggling to keep the wolves at bay and the populace secure. The south was tumultuous, much more so because of drought and the inability to produce food. Harare's northern location, and its relatively good water supplies and arable land, had allowed it to hold on as a civilization, even in the face of bandits and maniacs trying to invade.

Nathan didn't think that those following him were from the hunger lands, the frontiers of madness and war. He had run too hard, too far, and burned too many calories to be of interest to flesh-starved cannibals.

These were someone else.

Someone or something.

Nathan kept running. He'd crossed into Zambia this day, and already he could hear Mosi-oa-Tunya—the Smoke that Thundered—in the distance. The staff wanted to get there, was being drawn in, pulling Nathan along toward his destiny. Back in the age before skydark, Mosi-oa-Tunya had been also known as Victoria Falls, the highest waterfall in the world at 355 feet. The seismic shift caused by distant earthshaker bombs had upped that by twenty to fifty feet, according to Harare's trade partners to the northeast.

He could see a road up ahead through the trees, and knew that his chance of dodging his pursuers was growing thinner. At the same time, with the bellow of the falls, he realized he might actually be close to a settlement. He remembered that the Zambians shared a complex of preskydark power stations with Harare, electricity that was produced by the still-operational Victoria Falls Power Station. The two countries valued their independence from each other, but the shared resource was one that was inexhaustible. Attempting to fight over it would be foolish and needlessly destructive. There were other enemies for Zambia and Harare to stand against.

The road, when he reached it, seemed lonely, desolate. Even if he was close to the falls, that didn't mean he was near the power station and whichever city or town clung to the place. Nathan didn't stop to look at a map, but reached down, ripping the stubby but powerful little Detonics Combat Master from its holster. If he were out in the open, he would need to fight, and the staff of Suleiman might not be enough. Not from creatures that danced upon the boughs of a jungle canopy, stalking prey on the ground.

Nathan glanced around, pulling the hammer back with his thumb, ready to unleash a storm of .45-caliber slugs against whatever burst from the branches above. There were lights, electric lights, glowing, silhouetting a knoll covered with brush and long grasses at a curve in the winding road. It was unclear whether the lights were a part of the Victoria Falls Power Station, still in operation after two centuries, though only one of the substations and three of its original generators were still pumping out megawatts, with the assistance of three more jury-rigged generators.

Nathan took a deep breath, then set off again in long, loping strides. His finger was off the trigger, resting against the dustcover, outside the guard. This was one way to keep the gun from going off by accident. He didn't want to waste one of his vital first seven shots, didn't want to accidentally blast a hole in his foot. He also didn't want the sound of gunfire to break the silence and perhaps bring a dozen Zambian soldiers running to the defense of the power station, and perhaps riddle him with rifle fire.

That would be a distinct possibility, after all. While Harare and Zambia were trade partners, only the most naive of nations would be unconcerned about an armed traveler on the road late at night. Nathan hadn't called ahead, and wished with all his heart that he could have let them know he would be coming.

Judging from the rush of water, he was in the third gorge of Mosi-oa-Tunya, six hundred meters south from the top of the falls. But there was a whole kilometer-plus of river where the station could be. Victoria Falls was huge, and this was the rainy season, as opposed to the dry season, when it was a trickle. This was the time of year when the falls were at their most powerful.

There was a sudden flash of movement behind him, something he heard rather than saw. Nathan whirled, grimacing. He wouldn't be able to hold his fire, and would possibly have a threat from two fronts.

As he drew the little .45 up toward the figure hurtling at him in the darkness, he paused, eyes wide with horror.

The creature wasn't as tall as Nathan's six foot two, maybe a few inches short of six feet, even, but its arms were as long as its body, from its shoulder to the end of its "little finger," with bulbous, swelling biceps that flowed into a pack of chest muscles as large as melons. Nathan didn't even think to put his finger on the .45's trigger, and the creature slammed into him hard.

The gun went skittering across the hard-packed road, dirt interspersed with old crumbled tarmac. But before it landed, Nathan brought the staff of Suleiman up and across, the blackened "wood" of the stick catching a corner of a fang-filled mouth. The creature was horrible, alien. Its mouth extended from its face like some form of beak, but there were long canines jutting from beneath the decurved upper bill, just as others rose, gleaming and sharp, to close on the staff.

Nathan's instincts, or the staff itself, had saved his face and throat from being savaged by jaws filled with brutal weaponry. The creature grunted, snorted out mucus from its bill-mounted nostrils, and struggled, pushing against the unbreakable rod of Solomon. There was an ugly crunch as it flexed its jaw, and blood erupted from gums where the creature had wrenched its lower canines loose. It had hoped to bite through the stick, and instead only caused itself pain. Nathan winced, spit out the thing's blood, and shook off his shock.

He brought up his knees, pushed, kicked hard against his assailant's stomach. His boots held their traction on cobblestone-hard abdominal muscles, though the thing was surprisingly light for its bulk. The bat-winged creature toppled backward, crashing to the ground.

With a surge, Nathan lunged for the fallen pistol, scooping it up.

Zambian response be damned, this was an abomination, a horrific being that had no right.to occupy the border between two relatively peaceful nations. Nathan's fingers closed around the small grip of the handgun and he turned. The creature who'd lost fangs to the staff was scrambling to all fours, human-sized hind legs and gorillalike forelimbs spread on the ground, the incarnation of a giant bat, one designed with the head of a prehistoric reptile. Unfortunately for Nathan, it wasn't alone, and a second beast leaped from a branch toward him, a third and fourth bounding from the thicket at the side of the road.

Nathan fired, and his first .45-caliber slug struck the lunging bat monster in the chest. The thing grunted, and it actually looked stunned, but the young adventurer was fully aware that the thick musculature necessary for it to take flight would be backed up by a powerful breastbone that could anchor those muscles and withstand the forces necessary to lift a hundred fifty pounds of aerial predator off the ground. The creature veered off course and tumbled, crashing into the long grasses at the side of the road.

Nathan turned toward the other newcomers and reversed the staff in his hands, its sharp point lashing out like the tip of a spear. The creatures halted, scrambling to stay beyond the slashing arc. Nathan didn't know how smart the monsters were, but they certainly feared the weapon he held. Whether that was due to the strange nature of its material, or they just knew a big pointed stick could cause havoc in their lives, they hung back warily.

The one who'd lost teeth glared balefully toward Nathan. Yellowed eyes locked hard onto him, ignoring the gun, ignoring the stick. From the roadside, he heard the rustle of the creature he'd shot. It rose but seemed to favor its left foreleg. A quick glance showed that the beast had clamped its hand over the gunshot wound, which trickled blood.

"Round one to me, bastards," Nathan muttered. "The long run doesn't look so good."

Surprise and audacity had carried him this far. That wouldn't last. He needed to make a retreat, and that meant cutting a path. Nathan whirled toward the injured beast and aimed the Detonics. Instead of going for the muscle-and-bone-armored chest, easily capable of deflecting bullets along its sloped surface, he fired at the monster's face. It opened its mouth wide in a screech of defiance and aggression, which allowed the .45-caliber slug to enter the roof of its mouth and punch up into the brain pan

The bat-winged horror jerked, reflexes firing in a futile attempt to protect the central nervous system, but too late. The damage was done, a fat slug having torn its way into the brain. The monster toppled, crumpling on its four limbs.

Nathan spun back, lashing out with the staff of Suleiman, the shaft rebounding off of the beak of one of the trio of monstrosities penning him in on his other flank. The blow was glancing, but it caused the creature to recoil, to back off. The others feinted, but despite the glaring hatred in their yellow eyes, they didn't dare close in on a man who held the snake-entwined stick.

Nathan took this opportunity and spun, breaking into a wild run up the road. His legs hurt and all his limbs felt like lead, his energy sapped by the desperate chase through the forest. Still, he placed one foot in front of the other, each stride taking him closer to the bend, and hopefully, to the owners of the lights that faintly illuminated this deadly tableau.

He didn't hear the snap and flutter of leathery wings taking flight behind him, either, he heard the punch of knuckles into the crumbled tarmac and dirt. The things weren't interested in flying, or elsewere toying with him. A bullet to the chest wasn't enough for them to die, so they must have realized they were better off against him on the ground. Or maybe they needed speed and space to gain flight. He couldn't imagine that they had much room to fly through the trees or undergrowth; hence the bounding from branch to branch. Or maybe they were gliders, though the bulky muscle of their torsos and arms belied that notion.

Nathan cut into the jungle again, shouldering past bushes and branches, bounding over tall grass lest it snarl his legs and trip him up. He was cutting the corner, and hoped that would even the odds, slowing his enemies down. But the creatures stuck to the road, sounding like horses as they clopped along on their thick, armored knuckles.

They must have lost their taste for undergrowth during the chase.

Nathan had a glimmer of hope. There had originally been five of these things, but surely even their powerful muscles and hideous fangs couldn't deal with the onslaught of a siafu ant horde. It might not be much, but might be one way to kill them, beyond a bullet to the brain.

Exploding from the bushes, he saw a line of light poles. There was a guard tower in the distance, 150 yards away. He couldn't tell if it was manned, given the way the glare of bulbs cut into his night vision. It didn't matter; he swung hard and raced down the slope toward the tower. He was able to make out a ten-foot fence with a roll of concertina wire atop it.

The power plant, or a nearby guard post.

Either way, Nathan was now running toward Zambian guns, and he didn't know if they were going to open up on him. He gritted his teeth and kept pushing, lungs burning, each stride making it feel as if he'd hammered another nail into the soles of his feet, despite the heavy-treaded combat boots he wore. The snarls and shrieks of the winged things erupted just behind him, and Nathan fought the urge to look back, to see how close his enemies were to him.

His heart was a drum, hammering at his ears, the world fading to silence as his pulse raced, blood pumping to oxygen-starved muscles. Tears burned his eyes and rivulets of sweat stung his eyelids. Nathan had a goal, and he pushed toward it with all his might.

That pushing seemed to be for naught when one of the golden-brown monster bats galloped past him, roaring angrily. Nathan suddenly noticed that there was distant gunfire, momentarily drowned out by the roar of his pulse. The Zambians were shooting, but he didn't feel any fresh injuries. Indeed, he was tearing along just fine.

That's when he saw other creatures. There were more of those abominable things in the air, wings flapping. More than the three he was being hounded by. And the guard tower seemed to wear a crown of light, from the, muzzle-flashes burning in the night as riflemen cut loose against them.

Nathan skidded to a halt ten yards from the front gate. Gun in one hand, stave in the other, he saw that the three he'd been pursued by were only a fraction of the nightmare he'd spurred into pursuit. There must have been ten of them up there, plus two more that had just whipped past him on all fours, their odd loping gallop allowing them to cover two meters in a single stride. The chain-link fence buckled under their weight, and Nathan saw one, then two of the monstrosities crash to the ground as assault rifles overcame their alien flesh. Even so, Zambian men screeched in terror as they were grasped and punctured with three-inch fangs.

Those whose throats were bitten, torn out in a single mouthful of flesh, were the lucky ones. Nathan saw one of the creatures grab a man by his arms and extend its long, corded wing-limbs. Shoulders tore from their sockets, joints splitting and skin stretching before the torso between fell loose, toppling from the guard tower, only to be snatched up by a soaring bat-beast.

Nathan spied a rent in the fence torn by the insanely powerful arms of the bat creatures, and he pushed through, then dropped into a shoulder roll to avoid the charging slash of one of the winged horrors. Another pivoted on its wing and aimed at him, turning and diving. Nathan brought up the staff of Suleiman and lunged with it, using all his strength and weight. The snake-head sculptures, like the tines of a fork, speared the creature in the hollow of its throat, and for a moment, Nathan felt as if he'd missed, slashing only at empty air.

An instant later, a headless body struck the ground, tumbling end over end, a deflated, boneless sack of shredded meat flowing from the stump of its neck. Lucky shot? Nathan didn't care. He had a chance and he took it. There was an open door to a building. Zambian soldiers were shooting. One of them waved to him. It didn't matter who Nathan was. He was human, and he'd just attacked one of the beast invaders.

Nathan once again broke into a run.

These creatures didn't seem to mind assault rifle fire as much as a .45-caliber bullet through an open mouth. Just one more reason that Nathan was dead certain he'd struck at a decapitated body, not a living attacker.

Nathan reached the door, where hands grabbed him, hauled him in. He let out a rasp as he finally came to a halt, sucking oxygen into his burning lungs.

"Who are you?" one of the guards asked. The door, a steel one, was thrown shut, an iron bar sealing him in with the Zambians.

"Nathan Longa, of Harare…" he gasped.

There were three men in here with him, but the room was large enough for more. Nathan looked over a railing, saw a stairway descending below. There was a small armory down there, as well as briefing tables, benches. He looked back at the Zambians, whose faces were gaunt and glistening with sweat.

"What are those things?" the guard asked him.

"Nightmares," Nathan returned.

Another of the Zambians spoke up. "This is the wrong place for them."

"For what?" the first guard asked.

"Olitiau," the Zambian muttered.

"Never heard of that," Nathan replied.

"That's because you're even farther south than we are," the second man said. He blinked, then offered his hand. "I'm Shuka."

"South? What's that got to do with anything?" the first pressed. "I'm Jonas."

"The Olitiau are said to be from farther north, in Cameroon. And all the way to the Atlantic Coast," Shuka added. "They could also be kongamato, but those are smaller than the beasts out there…only supposed to be five to seven feet in wingspan."

"Those are fairy tales," Jonas grumbled, irritation making his words sound brittle.

Shuka gritted his teeth. "You were shooting at fairy tales, then. And they killed a dozen of our friends! That doesn't sound like fantasy to me!"

"Relax, you two," the third guard, an older man, ordered. He was cleanly shaved atop his skull, but wore a white frosting of beard that stood out in contrast to his ebony skin. "I'm Lomon. What are you doing here…now?"

"I'm trying to get to the Atlantic," Nathan admitted. "On a quest for my father."

Lomon narrowed his eyes, turning his attention to the

staff. "The Atlantic…where these things are obviously more common."

Nathan grimaced at the idea that his appearance here-witht the arrival of the olitiau was more than just a coincidence. "I don't know anything about them."

"I don't presume you do," Lomon stated. "But maybe they know that stick."

Nathan swallowed. "The stick."

"It's got a head, and doesn't look like any wood I've seen in Africa," Lomon told him. "That thing…"

"Sorry," Nathan returned. "I didn't know."

The older man shook his head. "Nobody could have predicted this. But I can predict that this door is not going to last long. You'll need more than a pistol, and we'll need more cover."

Nathan nodded. Already the steel door was shaking in its frame, emitting clouds of dust around its reinforced-concrete frame.

He remembered those gorilla arms, remembered how one of the beasts had dismembered a man with a single tug. With enough of them, they'd be able to hammer even that slab of steel off its heavy hinges, and get past the thick bar across it. The door frame wouldn't last long.

"I hope there's a way out the back," Nathan mused.

Lomon grimaced. "No, but there's a way down."

The hammering on the steel door, plus the concrete chips spilling, punctuated the urgency of that statement. The four men scrambled down the stairs.

Chapter 2

The thunderous blows on the steel door in its reinforced frame drowned out the clatter of boots as Nathan Longa, Lomon, Shuka and Jonas rushed to the power station's ready room. Jonas lunged past the others and unlocked one of the cabinets. He quickly drew a rifle from the locker and lobbed it to Nathan.

"That might do more than that tiny little popper of yours," the Zambian muttered. He grabbed some loaded magazines to replenish the ones he'd spent in fighting off the bat-winged monstrosities, then handed out spares to his compatriots before passing Nathan some.

"No offense," he added.

Nathan shook his head. "None taken. Bros before strangers."

Jonas smirked in response.

"This isn't going to be a good defensive position. Those things obviously can handle a bump from jumping thirty feet over a railing, as well as taking the stairs," Lomon mused as he reloaded his partially spent rifle. On a whim, he went to another locker and pulled out web gear. "Shuka, get out some of the machetes and garden stuff."

Shuka didn't pause for a moment, but immediately complied. "Rifles are having a hard time with them. What makes you think a few feet of sharp steel's going to work?" Despite his doubt, he drew a machete, gave it an expert twirl, then hooked it onto his belt, before handing others out. He paused when he got to Nathan, who was holding the bloody staff. "You need one?"

Nathan glanced at the dripping serpent heads tipping his rod. "They don't like it."

"So why are they chasing it down?" Jonas asked.

Nathan frowned. "To stop it from getting where it needs to go?" He shrugged. "All I know is that my father suffered a fatal mauling from some kind of creature. It ran away, but I sure as hell didn't get any glimpse of bat wings."

"It was dark, right?" Lomon muttered.

Nathan nodded.

Lomon nodded toward another set of doors, which Jonas opened. Beyond them was a stairwell that seemed to descend down into the cliff.

Nathan gazed around assessingly. "This is the power station, right?"

"We thought it was," Shuka stated.

There was a sudden crash. Nathan glanced up and saw claws skittering around a bent corner of the steel door. Cracks emanated from the brackets that held the draw bar in place.

"Thought it was?" Nathan repeated, distracted by the horrors above.

"Let's go!" Lomon shouted.

Jonas and Shuka unlocked the two big doors at the other side of the ready room, and Nathan peered into the cavernous tunnel behind them. He studied the doors themselves and noted that they looked to be thick, at least four inches deep. As soon as he and Lomon were through, the other two swung the doors shut, and they moved effortlessly on their hinges. There wasn't even the squeak of metal on metal, which meant that they must have been gliding, nearly weightlessly on oiled bearings.

The two doors slammed shut with a reverberating thunder. Latches were thrown and more draw bars pulled.

"Now we can talk," Lomon told him. "Those should be good for a while. Maybe even years."

"What is this tunnel?" Nathan asked.

"This is the Zambian National Storage for our charged batteries," Jonas told him. "Bank vault thick and tough."

"This is for batteries?" Nathan said doubtfully.

"It was built long ago. We're just using it for safe storage," Lomon returned. "And that safe storage is going to keep us alive, at least for a little bit."

"I don't think they're that strong," Shuka muttered. He still gripped the handle of his machete. "This was built originally as some kind of bomb shelter."

Nathan nodded. "Looks as much. But who'd need a bomb shelter *here?*"

Jonas shrugged. "We don't know. This place has been cleaned out for decades, maybe even the whole past two centuries since the northern hemisphere went boom."

"Cleaned out," Nathan repeated.

Lomon waved them along and they continued down the corridor. Nathan felt good in the company of armed Zambians, with the heavy vault doors at his back.

"Do we call for help?" Shuka asked. "I mean, we barely had a chance against them.... Could a patrol deal with those things?"

"Or would they even do more than pick up the pieces of our dead friends?" Jonas added. "Let alone possibly lead those bastards back to the city…leave them open for attack."

"I don't know," Lomon said. "But if we can get to the command center and take a look through the cameras, we'd at least have a chance to talk about it, to plan it out."

"So we came into a hole in the ground with no other exits, and an enemy at our back, with no plan?" Shuka asked.

Lomon glared at the younger guard. "Yes, because the other door wasn't doing so well. Remember?"

"So that we'd get to a secure area. One more defensible than outside," Jonas pointed out.

Nathan found himself nodding at the older man's assessment. He stopped the moment he realized it. He was an outsider here. A guest.

A refugee.

He didn't feel as if his opinion would have much worth with these three, even if they did trust him with a loaded gun. They outnumbered and surrounded him, and were certainly keeping their eyes on him, just in case he was an enemy, a spy. They didn't seem to believe he was a member of the winged horde of horrors, but Zambia and Harare were tentative friends. If there could be an advantage gotten, it would come through the efforts of spies and duplicity, but not to the point where the nations would go to war.

There were enough other forces in Africa that would be perfectly willing to take sides in a battle between two civilized societies and pick up the bloody pieces.

"We'll call back to home base," Lomon announced. "Warn them of a raider force. But tell them not to send reinforcements."

"If we did get help, chances are they might be jumped," Shuka muttered.

"You said that before," Jonas stated.

Shuka nodded. "Doesn't make it less true."

Jonas shook his head. "Nope."

"You two done?" Lomon asked.

They both nodded.

"And you," Lomon said to Nathan. "You might want to take that stick and get it out of here if and when those things clear out."

"I'll do my best," he answered.

With that, Lomon looked back toward the doors. They could hear the thump and echo of mighty blows against the heavy hatches, but they would hold.

Nathan desperately prayed that they would, at least.

THE SILENCE OF the observation room was disturbed only by the breathing of four men. Nathan, drained by his ordeals and lulled into a false sense of security by the soundless assault on the doors of the redoubt, allowed his eyelids to shut, lured by the temptation of sleep. Almost immediately, he felt himself start to fall. With a flash of movement, he shook himself, and realized that he was leaning on the black staff of Suleiman, and was on his feet, not slumped in a chair.

Nathan looked around and found the other three were asleep. The video screens were flickering, but his mind couldn't make sense of them. There were flashes of imagery, but instead of focusing on what should have shown the winged horrors hammering at the doors, he turned and walked through the exit.

Something hummed, a distant calling. It murmured at the back of his consciousness, slowly growing in strength. Nathan moved forward numbly, realizing only after he'd gone fifty yards along the twisting halls that the staff seemed to be directing him. Each step he took was accompanied by a lift of the stick, and then a push forward, as if it were dragging him along.

"So creepy," he muttered to the silent weapon. "Why can't you make things easier to understand?"

This had to be a dream, Nathan mused. Otherwise, there would have been someone awake in the security command center. They would have been too wired, too nervous about the heavily muscled creatures that had pounded through the inch-thick steel fire door into the complex, many of which had survived direct hits from rifles and kept on attacking, with the strength to rip arms from sockets.

The damned cryptic staff kept needling him, pushing him along. He gritted his teeth and realized the only thing he could do was relax and allow it to drag him along. Nathan was getting sick of the stick's stubborn will. He was about to curse the black, woodlike thing, but then remembered his father's insistence that he carry it.

He remembered the scene he'd come upon, with his father fallen beneath the shadowy form of another person. Nathan had turned on his flashlight and the stranger had fled, moving ahead of the light. The horror of his father's wounds had transfixed Nathan, slowing his pursuit of the killer. Nelson Longa had been still alive, though with every exhalation, air bubbled through the horrific wound in his throat, and blood sputtered over his lips.

There was one thing that Nathan knew, however. It wasn't one of the alien, misshapen things that had assaulted the Zambians, killing twelve heavily armed men with only their fangs and claws, who had assaunted his father. The figure had been too...human. Nthan couldn't make out details in the dark, although even now he could remember the rustle of a cloak.

He wanted to know who had killed his father, but the urge to bring the staff to its "rightful owner" was too strong.

The young African couldn't let his father down.

The door that stood before him was akin to the ones a hundred feet above that were holding back the swarm of winged beasts. It showed signs of damage, burns from where blowtorches had attempted to cut into it. Nathan reached out and touched the surface. The scars had long been cooled, so he couldn't tell when the damage had been done, but at least the door remained in place. The electronic panel to one side was a mess, wires dangling, for no apparent rhyme nor reason.

Nathan blinked.

He could feel the metal, the burned surface.

"What are you doing here?" a voice asked. Nathan jumped, whirling and bringing up the point of the staff. It was Lomon. Nathan's heart was going a mile a minute, and he lost his footing, toppling over and crashing against the burn-scarred door.

The scream that came from him was hardly one to be proud of, but as his head bounced against the steel of the strange door, he winced and slid to the floor.

When Lomon knelt over him, Nathan tried to speak, but his mouth was dry, cottony with shock.

"Dream…" he managed to sputter.

"Sleepwalking?" Lomon asked.

Nathan let go of the staff and sought the floor, gathering his strength to get up. Lomon, pistol in one hand, hooked his hand beneath Nathan's armpit, pulling on him, getting him to his feet.

"Stick," Nathan grunted. He hated not being able to speak clearly. He glared at the snake-entwined staff, which he thought had fallen to the floor, but was now leaning against the tangle of electrical wires poking from the dismantled security panel. It seemed to be watching him with those odd, carved eyes. He'd never noticed their ability to focus on him before, but now his brain was swimming. Was it a real phenomenon, or merely the result of his sudden jolt of panic at being jarred from walking in his sleep?

"I noticed you were missing," Lomon said. "You left your guns behind, and hadn't gone toward any of the storage areas."

Nathan looked up and saw a camera in the corner of the ceiling, pointed toward the entrance to the sealed chamber. "What is this place?"

He scraped his tongue with his teeth, trying to get saliva flowing so it would be easier to speak. It wasn't helping, and only reminding him of how much he needed a drink of water, or some food, or something else to keep him going.

He'd been on his trek for so long he didn't remember the last time he'd eaten. But with the flood of adrenaline while fighting against the olitiau, and in the tense minutes after getting to the control center, his exhaustion had been cast aside.

"According to the government, it's nothing," Lomon told him.

"What about according to you?" Nathan countered.

The eldest of the Zambian guards looked around. "It's something top secret. We thought maybe it had something to do with the nuclear reactor running this facility."

"Nuclear reactor. What about the hydroelectric power produced by the falls?" Nathan inquired.

Lomon glanced at him, then back to the doors. "Trust me, we've been trying to get into the grid. The reactors themselves are buried even deeper than this redoubt. We're safe from radiation exposure by dint of at least a hundred feet of granite."

Nathan looked at the door. "The control room for the reactor?"

The other man shook his head. "No. The government found that. And it's why we had a platoon of men guarding this place. We're trying to keep the nuclear power plant a secret, but since we can't even reach the fuel rods, there's no real worry about you finding this door. There's nothing on the other side, except for what looks like a computer laboratory."

"You've opened it?" Nathan asked.

Lomon nodded. "Just jiggle a couple of those wires together and…"

With that pronouncement, the snake-entwined staff started to shift. A spark flew as wires brushed each other, completing a circuit. With a hiss and groan, the door slid open.

Lomon's eyes went wide at the coincidence. He glared

at the snake-entwined staff, and frowned. "That stick is spooky."

"No shit," Nathan returned. He reached out and plucked the staff back into his hand. "But I was dreaming about it dragging me here…. It's been leading me to this place for days."

"Leading you?" Lomon asked. "As in talking to you?"

Nathan shook his head. "Nothing so easy."

Lomon took a moment to figure out his meaning. "I see."

Nathan stepped through the doorway. Motion-activated lights flickered on, revealing a hexagon-patterned set of glass walls around a base pad through another door. There were heavy computer systems off to the side. He walked to the entrance of the chamber, looking it over, curious, but keeping enough distance so he didn't accidentally step onto the pad, or even lean through the doorway.

"It's some kind of a laboratory, but we've run Geiger counters and all manner of tests on it," Lomon said. "*We* as in the scientists who might know something about what it could do. But there's no power to these consoles, and the GUI—graphical user interface—locks out any attempt at discerning what it actually does."

Nathan walked around to the consoles. "My father told me to follow the staff's lead. And to get it across the Atlantic."

"You've mentioned that," Lomon replied. "You think this might be a shortcut?"

He shrugged. "Why would I wake up and wander here?"

Lomon looked at the staff. "Crazy stick. Then again, that platform, the door, the computers…it reminds me of something."

"An old TV show?" Nathan asked.

Lomon nodded. "Stylistically, it's nothing like those old vids, but damned if this doesn't remind me of a transporter room."

"Step onto the transporter mat, punch in the coordinates, and zap. I'm there," Nathan mused. "But this doesn't look as if it works. You said the GUI locks out any attempts at exploring what it does."

Lomon looked at the consoles. "Yeah. And we're not completely without computer savvy...."

"I'm not doubting it," Nathan said. He spent a few moments looking over the thing, then glared at the twin robotic serpents on the staff. "Anytime you feel like giving me some supersecret pass code, I'm all ears."

"Has it ever answered a question put to it?" Lomon asked.

"Never," Nathan grumbled. "But you mentioned how to open the door, and it followed that suggestion."

"Coincidence," Lomon said. He almost looked as if he believed it.

Nathan shrugged. "Let's turn this thing on. Maybe we'll get lucky."

"Maybe we'll get lucky," the Zambian repeated. "Where a couple centuries of computer experts haven't been able to."

Nathan sighed. "Dumb luck, stick magic. Who knows what it'll take, but it's brought me this far."

The two men went to work at the console.

THE SHRIEK OF a creature slashed over Kane's head, and his gaze snapped up to it. For a moment, he mistook the thing for a bird, but the leathery expanse of wings wasn't avian. He remembered the pinwheeling, gliding forms of pterosaurs against the lava-tube glow of an underground kingdom's "roof" when he'd been down in the Dragon's Spine.

This wasn't underground, though. The sun was bright, the sky was blue and the air wasn't tainted with the stink of a heavy, overoxygenated atmosphere or the funk of grown saurians. Kane tried to remember how he'd gotten here, and wondered if he wasn't on Thunder Isle, the subject of a time-trawling experiment.

He looked down at himself, and noted he was wearing a T-shirt and blue jeans. He was barefoot, but at least his belt had a sheath for his foot-long fighting knife. Kane grimaced, wondering why he was in the forest of Thunder Isle all barefoot, like Domi on one of her feral field trips.

Maybe this wasn't the island, he mused. He wrapped his hand around the grip scales of the knife and felt reassured that he wasn't completely helpless. He'd have been a little more comfortable with the folding Sin Eater that was both the badge of office of a magistrate and a deadly weapon in his highly trained hands.

"Not so different from my time with Sky Dog's tribe," he said out loud. He felt the timbre of his voice, the vibration of his words, hoping he could tell the difference between reality and a dream. The checkers of the grip scales were real against his palm and finger pads. The air smelled wild and free; the sun tingled on his skin, promising tanning from exposure to UV rays.

Kane pursed his lips. He still didn't remember getting here, and dived deep into his thoughts, looking for hints and clues. Maybe he'd been deposited here, somewhere that pterosaurs took to the skies but was temperate enough for him to wander half-dressed and armed only with a foot of razor-sharp steel. He wouldn't put it past the technology of any of his enemies, the overlords, Sindri, Major Thrush, to scoop him up and leave him, amnesiac, at a battleground.

There'd be easier ways to kill him, but the overlords and Major Thrush were the type to engage in complicated, circuitous schemes to prove their superiority and cleverness. Sindri, though they had recently parted on slightly less than friendly terms, was prankster enough to dump Kane into a mess. There could be other explanations, too.

This could all be a fever dream from a bad mat-trans

jump. He'd encountered them before, transcendental experiences where he'd become privy to strips of secret history lost in the annals of time. Kane looked around, studying the trees, the grasses, checking for signs of life other than the lone, leather-winged shadow that had disappeared overhead.

"This feels familiar," he mused to himself. "I've been here."

He strode through the grasses, and so far, he could tell that they were different from those that grew in the shadows of the Bitterroot Mountains around Cerberus redoubt and the mountain it had been built into. This was vaguely familiar ground, but the trees were all wrong. He was familiar with the firs and pines of the forests around the redoubt, and these were different species. He might not have Brigid Baptiste's encyclopedic knowledge of scientific minutiae, but he could tell that this also wasn't the foliage on Thunder Isle. He was somewhere completely new.

Kane frowned, thinking of why this seemed so familiar.

The forests of India and China? No, those were different, too. This wasn't Europe, either.

"Throw me a bone here," Kane murmured, feeling frustrated at the hints that nibbled at the edges of his consciousness.

He brushed his jaw, and while he could feel the pintle leads surgically implanted for the Commtact, the plate that they would hold in place was gone. Again, the plate could have been removed, or he simply had been dropped here from sleep.

Trouble was, he didn't usually sleep with a belt knife at Cerberus. He found himself fighting off consternation, kneeling and looking for some sign of where he was.

He tried the earth, picking up a pinch of it. Dry and claylike.

If Brigid Baptiste were here, she would know where they were. He drew the knife and pressed the point to his fingertip. He felt the searing heat of the razor tip cutting into the pad of flesh. This couldn't be a dream, and yet...he remembered feeling the swords of his enemies, the chopping blades of the men who slew Cuchulain as he rose to the defense of Morrigan.

He returned the knife to its sheath, then took a slurp of the bead of blood drawn by the knife point. Rather than stand idly waiting for answers, he let his restless nature draw him to the tree line. Beyond the grove was a cliff overlooking the surrounding countryside. Once out of the open, away from the grassy field, he'd have a little better chance of figuring where he was, while feeling less exposed.

The sun was already starting to set by the time he reached the trees. Kane tried to get his bearings on the passage of time, but couldn't recall exactly what the azimuth of the sun had been when he'd started his march. But once there, he took out his knife and started chopping at thorny trees and bushes in the nearest thicket. The briar branches took some effort to gather, and when he'd finished, his hand was covered with pinpricks and stung.

Still, he was more than certain that this wasn't a dream, and began to feel as if he were in Africa somewhere. It didn't feel like the Congo, which he'd been to months ago when he sought out the treasure of Prestor John, but there were enough similarities in the foliage. He withdrew a flint from the hollow butt of the survival knife and scraped it against the crosspiece until he sparked a good camping flame. So far, he hadn't heard or seen wild animals, but that could easily change come the sunset. Nocturnal hunters were infamous in the African wilderness.

A fire, and a thick-trunked tree at his back, would provide him some measure of security, which would be enforced by his light sleep and keen senses.

With the campfire blazing, Kane took a seat, held the

knife in his grasp and waited for darkness to flow around the improvised camp.

He wondered what mysteries would come to him in the night.

Chapter 3

Kane's head started to droop beneath the tree branches that filtered out the full moon above. He was on the edge of the forest, so the canopy above him was thin enough that he could glimpse the relatively clear night sky, even as the ground seemed to ooze mist, rising up like ghosts from a graveyard. It was silent, but there was no eerie quality, no hushed desperation to the quiet.

Indeed, it seemed calm, free, loose. A gentle cloak of slumber wrapped about him like a blanket. The mist held no threat, no malice. As a result, he was starting to lose his struggle to stay awake and alert. The forest was seductive, charming, enchanting, drawing him into a state of relaxation he felt only when he was among the Lakota. As much as he didn't want to sleep, there was no conscious, logical reason for him to be on edge, except that he was most studiously not being threatened.

Finally, sleep drew him down, down, sent him tumbling into unconsciousness, until he felt fingers pluck up his wrist. Kane's eyes snapped open, and he found a tall man before him, dressed in the off-duty attire of a magistrate, complete with armored trench coat with the oversize sleeve to allow for the presence of the forearm holstered Sin Eater.

There was no fear, but Kane knew this man. It was Magistrate Thurmond, formerly of Cobaltville, the same megalithic city that Kane had served in when he was a pawn of the hybrid barons, a prior, near-human incarnation of the Annunaki. Back then, Baron Cobalt, the antecedent of

Overlord Marduk, had sent Thurmond on an expedition to Europe to recover technology he had scarcely remembered. Kane had known Thurmond only briefly, encountering him years later when he, Brigid, Grant and Domi had gone in search of clues about a possible civil war between the scattered overlords.

In Greece, Kane had found Thurmond, as well as Dr. Helena Garthwaite and Magistrate Danton. The three of them had discovered robotic technology-gear skeletons that replaced the limbs of amputees and granted them the physical strength and power of a walking tank. Thurmond and Helena had set themselves up as leaders of the society called New Olympus, while Danton made use of another ancient Annunaki technology, clone vats, to create the threat necessary to turn New Olympus into an efficient government.

Even though Thurmond had been initially in on the con, having gone by the pilot code name Z005, he grew to love the people of New Olympus, making the other pilots of the gear skeletons his family. When Helena Garthwaite, rechristened Hera, went mad with power thanks to the interference of Marduk himself, Thurmond not only fought tooth and nail to drive back the forces of the Annunaki overlord, but died stopping Hera's murderous rampage, sacrificing himself for the sake of his fellow New Olympians.

Seeing Thurmond tall and healthy, with his own legs intact, not lost to the necessary amputation required in becoming a gear skeleton pilot, Kane wasn't confused or frightened; he was filled with awe.

"You died," he said, offering a hand. Thurmond drew him to his feet, then passed his fellow ex-magistrate a boxy object. It was a folded Sin Eater machine pistol, in its holster.

"It's time to get up," Thurmond responded. "The hounds of hell are on the prowl, and you'll need your weapon."

Kane strapped on the Sin Eater. He accepted a pair of

20-round magazines for the weapon, pushing them into the pockets of his jeans. He repeated Thurmond's warning. "Hounds of hell."

"They are hunters in the darkness. The living exemplars of the foul creatures Danton, Helena and I tried to summon in our deception against New Olympus," Thurmond said. His voice sounded pained as he recalled those events. "They are blood hungry, and they travel by night, seeking death and destruction everywhere they go. They are aware of you, Kane."

"Why?" he asked. He flexed his forearm and the Sin Eater jumped into his grasp.

Thurmond pointed toward the tree that Kane had been sleeping against. Kane blinked for a moment, then saw a black staff, seven feet from the top of its twin carved serpents to the point at its other end. He felt a tingling in his arm, and his palm recalled the odd, almost living warmth of its jet-black wood when he'd gripped it, the weight of it that he'd used on multiple occasions to fight off the forces of darkness, to parry the hungry spear points of killers and to inflict wounds upon those things that not even the sharpest Spanish steel could dent. Those twin serpents seemed entwined in a familiar pattern that Kane had seen on medpacks, but they were metallic, and brought to mind a chilling similarity: the ASP conduits that the Nephilim wore on their forearms, the cobralike heads spitting energized fire with deadly heat and efficiency.

Despite that resemblance to an alien weapon, this staff was far more familiar. It was almost like a lost piece of his right arm, something he'd spent years leaning his weight upon as he crossed wildernesses. He was about to reach for it when Thurmond gripped him by the shoulder.

"Not now," the ex-magistrate told him, his deep voice almost desperate. "Strong wings push through the night sky, and bloodstained claws press into the mud, driving their owners our way. They want to stop the staff, and they wish to take your head."

Kane nodded, and in addition to the Sin Eater in his grasp, he drew the foot-long fighting knife from its sheath to supplement his fighting power. He glanced back to the tree, but the snake-entwined stick was gone, another phantom in the night.

He had no time to think about the staff's disappearance, because a loud wail suddenly arose, the fury of a hundred agonized throats opening up at once. Kane tensed, but didn't need to look around to realize that the little clearing where he'd set up was relatively well defended from the approaching threat. He'd hacked his way into the briar bushes and created the fire pit, with a circle of thorny branches left in place. Those would likely be broken by the very first attackers, but unless an entire army was bearing down on them, those thickets of thorny, stabbing branches would limit avenues of assault, making defense easier.

In a moment, the first figure burst into view, snagging on branches that stuck to his skin. Its features were odd, alien, terrifying, but Kane brought up the Sin Eater and dispatched it with a single shot, its face disappearing in a cloud of blood and gore, even as Thurmond lashed out with his combat knife, its wicked long blade slashing through a heavily muscled chest. A kicking foot skidded into the fire, eliciting a growl of pain from an odd, alien throat, and Kane whirled.

This *had* to be a dream. Thurmond had died. And these things were vague shapes, wrapped in cloaks, their faces odd and translucent, features indistinct behind gelatinous skin and muscle. Kane grimaced and lunged, plunging his knife into the belly of another attacker, but he felt the weight, the presence of the opponent he speared even as he hefted it back into a tangle of thorns.

He whirled at the arrival of other cloaked figures, firing the Sin Eater on single-shot, ripping off three rounds into three different targets. Two collapsed instantly, cored by the heavyweight 9 mm slugs fired by the high-tech machine pistol. The third staggered, wounded by an off-center shot, but Kane stepped in close, bringing the foot-long battle knife across its throat and slashing through skin and flesh. The thing's head was torn loose, bouncing onto the ground, a skull floating in semiviscous ooze, a face whose teeth were malformed, each one a filed dagger designed to puncture meat. With mouths like that, their attackers must be dedicated carnivores, well armed to slash and tear, leaving brutal wounds in their wake.

Kane grimaced at the sight and pivoted. He brought the steel frame of the folding Sin Eater against another face, watching the skull crack beneath its semitransparent covering, dagger teeth snapping under the force of Kane's brutal blow. He followed the pistol-whip with the lunging sweep of his knife, plunging it deep into the guts of his attacker, ripping the steel from its abdomen in such a violent fashion that loops of intestine poured out, semiclear organs slipping from their moorings and splashing on the dirt of the battleground.

Kane felt forceful fingers grab his shoulders, two sets of hands pulling him off his feet, and he kicked at empty air, trying to get traction and leverage against the two attackers.

Thurmond whirled and opened fire, a single 9 mm slug smashing the assailant to his left, and swift as a cobra, Kane drew his knees in tight to his chest and levered himself into the other one. His weight came down hard on this enemy, and fetid breath exploded past Kane's ear. With a surge, he rolled off the downed foe. He could see two new sets of legs approaching as he rose to his knees.

With well-honed hip-firing reflexes, he triggered the Sin Eater, his slugs stopping the two enemies' advance, one catching a round in the chest, the other folding over a bullet to the belly. Kane surged to his feet, then paused to look at the fallen, wormlike wrestler. He lashed out, his heel taking the creature by the jaw, and all of Kane's weight, strength and fury splitting the mandible and popping it from its moorings. Ugly pinkish discharge gushed over the thing's lips and across Kane's naked foot, but the translucent attacker didn't move.

The creature blasted in the belly stood up, holding its ruined guts, its pale, albino-pink eyes glaring hatefully at him. Dimly reminded of Domi, Kane pressed forward, wishing that the feral Outlander girl was fighting by his side. He stabbed his combat knife through the man-thing's face, splitting and smashing the bone between its eye sockets. The blade stuck for an instant, but Kane gave the handle a sharp twist, then whirled, using the dead creature's own momentum and weight to wrench it off the knife.

In the dim firelight, Kane could see his bare arms, knotted like oak, flexing with each gunshot, each slash of the knife. When the translucent horrors rose to attack, even with vicious, debilitating wounds, the former magistrate struck back. Bones broke, semiclear flesh tore, pink gelatinous ooze spilled from ravaging cuts. Steel and lead, fire and blade ruled this bloody, horrible fight, and in a manner reminiscent of a dream, the battle passed rapidly.

Whether they were dead or fleeing from the trampled clearing, Kane was soon abandoned by his attackers. He turned and looked for Thurmond, but already, as if this were the sequel to another half-remembered dream, he knew that no man would be standing there to take an offered hand of thanks.

Kane, the Cerberus rebel, the former magistrate, was alone among the bodies of dead, wormy men.

He then heard a familiar voice snap into his thoughts.

"What the hell are you doing here with that knife, Kane?" Donald Bry asked.

Kane blinked, his eyes focused on a strange African copse of trees and thorn bushes just before they closed. And when he opened them he stood in the mat-trans chamber of Cerberus redoubt. For a moment, he feared that he had been sleepwalking, acting out his strange nightmare with naked steel flashing in his fist. But he was dressed in a T-shirt and jeans, barefoot, his only adornment a belt-sheathed combat knife in a cross draw on his hip.

He looked down at himself. In the dream, he'd become caked in bloodlike discharge and greasy with sweat and dirt, but here, he was clean and fresh, stirred awake from a nightmare.

"Would you believe that it was a bad dream?" Kane asked Bry.

The red-haired master of technology for Cerberus redoubt looked him over. Bry himself was small, slender, with a sardonic smirk and hints of freckles on his face. By weight, he was half of Kane, and a half a foot shorter than the former magistrate, who carried much of his muscle mass in his upper chest and shoulders. Where Bry was wiry, with an almost impish demeanor, Kane resembled a wolf recast as a man, right down to his grizzled brown mane and predatory, focused blue eyes.

Bry shrugged. "Considering some of the shit you've been through, I'm just glad you kept your sword in its sheath."

Kane frowned. "I must have been sleepwalking."

Bry studied Kane's face for a sign of joking, perhaps a prank gone wrong, or ill thought out. But he could see the confusion in the man's features. "Damn. You're serious."

"What the hell is wrong with me?" Kane muttered. Bry pointed to a nearby chair at one of the control consoles, and he took it, flopping down and resting both hands between his thighs. "I had a vivid dream. Like something out of one of the older mat-trans deliriums."

With that, Kane explained what he thought had happened in the dream, especially his eventual deduction that he was wandering around in Africa.

"There haven't been many of those since we've gotten the control algorithms straightened out," Bry mused. "So it can't be leftover trauma."

"No," Kane agreed. He allowed himself to go deep into thought. This time, knowing he was awake, he felt sure he would have more control of his brain. There were familiar images, things he *knew* from his dream of Africa, that meant there was some element of truth within the entire adventure. Also, he could *feel* pain, the touch of the clear breeze, the heat of the fire, the sharp thorns and the impact of blows against his flesh. This was more than just a dream; it had been a real occurrence, but maybe not one his current body, his current life had experienced.

He remembered only glimpses, hints of other lifetimes that had been opened to him through the psychic meddling of beings like Fand and Balam, or via the dimension-punching properties of the mat trans, which gave him brief views of other universes and histories far-flung, different from the reality he existed in. These were "casements," alternate dimensions, with warps in history, and events that cast him in other roles, both as hero and villain, savior and marauder, colliding worlds that could be better or far worse than the one he'd been born into.

The mat trans had proved to be both a blessing and a curse. Without the wondrous transporter, he and the others wouldn't have had the ability to traverse the globe, even get to other worlds within the solar system, seeking the materials necessary to fight the overlords and improve the lot of the human race. But the mat trans had also burdened Kane with visions of other lives, other deaths he'd experienced, other loves lost as he was cast about as a pawn of the universe.

He checked the chronometer on the wall. It was midmorning, and Kane wondered at the lateness of his slumber. But then he thought of the dream itself, its reality, its hold, the sharpness of thorns stabbing into his palms.

There was one person up now, available, who might be able to make sense out of things.

"I'm going to talk to Baptiste," he told Bry. "Unless there's something up here."

Bry looked at the screen. "Nope, everything's still quiet enough that I could entertain you and your sleepwalking ways."

He snorted. "Thanks."

As soon as Kane walked out of the control center, Bry caught a beep on his console. He turned back, and pulled up what had caused the alert on the system.

"New station on line," he muttered. "Location, Victoria Falls."

Bry wasn't a geography buff, but he knew damn well that Victoria Falls was in Africa.

Exactly where Kane claimed his dream had occurred.

Bry leaned back. "What the hell?"

He glanced to the door.

Bry decided to take a closer look at the new linkup. He wasn't going to run after Kane in the hall, not until he'd found out everything he could about the new location on the mat-trans circuit.

BRIGID BAPTISTE SAT on her bench at her desk. She wasn't wearing her duty uniform, but was in black stirrup pants with no socks or shoes, plus a long-sleeved turtleneck sweater light enough that she wouldn't be too warm in the controlled environment, but heavy enough for a brief step outside in the brisk fall day. She wore her reading glasses, and as Kane interrupted her, she was poring over a new hardback book that Domi had discovered in her far ranging wanderings in the woods. Brigid's flame-gold hair was pulled back with a scrunchie, making her look even more like the librarian he'd originally pegged her as.

Right now, with her in her day-off wear, toes wriggling at the end of the bench, and one knee drawn up to her chest, the other folded at a right angle, her foot beneath her butt, Kane couldn't see the person she'd hardened into over years of struggle against tyranny and threats both domestic and from other dimensions.

But beneath the snug-fitting pants and sweater, Kane knew, her body was toned with muscle. And just above her hairline there was a scar from when she'd been struck by a wrench, a trauma that had put her into a sickbed for several days, leaving her more vulnerable to the eyestrain that necessitated those reading glasses. She'd started out as an archivist, a brilliant young woman who collected and collated the facts of the world from before the terrible destruction of civilization, a nuclear war instigated by the subterfuge of the alien cabal of schemers now known as the overlords. The nuclear megacull had been intended to bring humanity down to more manageable, controllable numbers, but there was one great weakness in the Annunaki's thinking.

Humankind was too strong-willed, too free and too hungry for knowledge to remain under a dictatorial thumb for long. Even Kane himself, a member of Baron Cobalt's own elite magistrates, indoctrinated and separated from mere humanity as much as possible, had found the cause of freedom irresistible. And he wasn't the only one. Others had rebelled, and many had joined the ranks of those willing to fight for freedom against the overlords, despite measures designed to rob them of their individuality, removing all but their family name, and hiding them behind shells of polycarbonate, to be recast into identical, ominous storm troopers.

Now, Brigid had gone from scholar to defender of the world, saver of lives. She wasn't a master of combat, like Kane and Grant, nor was she a feral package of wild strength and rage like Domi, but her intellect, courage and experience made her worth a whole platoon of local militia.

Though she seemed almost bored at the moment, curling and flexing her toes as she sat on the bench, only a fool would have mistaken her for being off in a wistful flight of fancy, ignoring the world about her. She was deep in thought, her eidetic memory peering through the collected wisdom of mankind, looking for similarities in Kane's recollection of the waking dream. Her emerald-green eyes flashed with fire over each correlation she constructed in her mind, and slowly her lips began to curve into a smile as her conclusions were solidified.

Kane simply folded his arms, waiting for her to speak. She'd been like this for only a minute, but even when he'd told her about his "incident" she was already at work. If there was one thing that had impressed him about her, it was her ability to take data and extrapolate on it, all the while avoiding flights of fancy that would steer her toward a wrong conclusion. It didn't hurt that she had that eidetic memory, a steel-trap brain that could instantly summon up every bit of data she'd ever learned, every image she'd seen, every sound, every smell. It was a frightening, almost mutant ability, but Kane was endlessly thankful for it when she could use her intellect to defang a threat just by thinking.

"So?" he asked as she finally rose from her bench. She went to a small coffee machine she kept in the kitchenette in her quarters and poured two mugs, one for herself, one for the other.

"One question. Have you read the poem *The Return of Sir Richard Grenville?*" she asked him.

"Can't say that I have. I'm not much for poetry," Kane replied.

Brigid nodded. "It is a tale of the ghost of a friend and fellow warrior awakening his brother in arms. The events took place in Africa, as you guessed in your dreamlike wanderings. I would have to say from the thorns that harried you, you were dealing with acacia trees and bushes."

"Who was Sir Richard Grenville?" Kane asked.

Brigid regarded him. "He was a sea captain who, on behalf of England, battled the Spanish Armada. He died in the effort in 1591."

"Off of Africa?" Kane asked.

"No," Brigid responded. "He was in the New World."

Kane drew his lips tight, trying to suppress a wave of annoyance. "So what does he have to do with Africa?"

"Because of the man who owned the strange staff you described from your dream," Brigid responded.

"The staff," Kane repeated. "What the hell was that about?"

"That was an ancient artifact once owned, presumably, by a man named Solomon Kane," Brigid responded. "Indeed, the events of your encounter with Thurmond closely echo the encounter between Solomon Kane and his fellow fighter against the Spanish—"

"Grenville." Kane cut her off. "Who the hell was Solomon Kane? And was there any relationship between him and me?"

"According to the fictionalized accounts of his life, he never had any sons, nor nephews or nieces that I could recall. He was a strictly religious man, lived a life of celibacy and self-denial to a level adhered to by few other Puritans."

Kane chuckled. "Celibacy. So, not a great-grandfather, and we don't have *that* in common."

Brigid smiled. "No. And I'm still waiting for a blue-eyed little papoose to show up in that village."

Kane cleared his throat. "Other than the surname, we don't seem to have much at all in common." He smirked as he caught a look of irritation on Brigid's face. "And he owned that staff."

"Kane's adventures in Africa were heavily detailed by author Robert E. Howard," Baptiste added. "Whether they were true or not…"

"So far, we've encountered myths aplenty," Kane mused. "Remember, Remus claimed to have been a close friend of Edgar Rice Burroughs…."

Brigid nodded.

"The thing that gets me is that stick looked like it had an ASP unit attached to it," Kane added. "So we're looking at a man who wandered around with the equivalent of an energy rocket launcher, and yet never fired it."

"It would be worth investigation," Brigid responded. "The staff, and the name similarity between you and Solomon Kane, the Puritan, definitely piques my interest."

"What is so special about the stick?" Kane asked.

"I've been doing some research, and allegedly, it was the staff of wonders that Moses used to perform miracles in Egypt," Brigid told him. "Its proper name is Nehushtan."

"Gesundheit," Kane returned.

She rolled her eyes. "It also was the Scepter of Israel, wielded by King Solomon. He used it to combat magicians and to dispel demons."

She pulled out a photo. Certainly enough, it was a staff with crisscrossed serpents, except made of brass, not coated in dull black. And the serpent heads faced each other, instead of looking up and forward, as in his dream. Then again, Kane remembered how the serpentine aspects of the ASPs wound around the forearms of the Nephilim as they donned their armor.

"Dispel demons," Kane repeated. "Like Archons?"

"I've been doing a lot of work to correlate demonic and godly mythology into what we know about the Annunaki and others, such as the Tuatha de Danann or Kakusa," Brigid told him.

"So, a staff owned by Solomon ends up in the hands of

a man named Solomon Kane, and now the damned stick ends up in my dreams," he mused. "Think we're off to Africa soon?"

Brigid was about to speak when the comm-link on her desk beeped to life. "This is Bry. You and Kane better get here."

She motioned for Kane to put his plate on. Bry repeated his message.

"What's up?" Kane asked.

"A new mat-trans station opened up on our grid," Bry told them. "And get this...."

"It's in Africa?" Kane interjected.

"Spoilsport," Bry replied. "Get down here."

Kane smirked. "Time to suit up, Baptiste. We're going traveling."

Chapter 4

Lomon had managed to reroute the video feed from the security cameras to the teleporter chamber so that he and Nathan Longa wouldn't need to worry about being surprised by a sudden breakthrough. As strong as the horrific olitiau seemed to be, they were barely doing any damage to the thick double doors that sealed off the underground quarters of the base. They were frustrated, and had been joined by at least four new creatures, who showed no signs of having incurred small-arms fire.

While Lomon did this, Nathan perused the various electronics on the consoles, discovering an intercom in the process. He examined it, not certain whether getting on the horn would actually bring help or expose them to new problems and horrors. As it was, he didn't touch a dial. If he opened communication, especially without conferring with Lomon, chances were he'd catch a headful of bullets.

"I've found a communication link," Nathan said. "Not radio based…"

"Probably through the central computer system on this," Lomon replied. "The GUI front page hints that this is on a much larger network."

Nathan nodded. Communications were limited. Hard land lines were vulnerable to sabotage, and the earthquakes of the megacull in 2001 had shaken the whole planet, isolating large regions. Zambia and Harare were relatively well off because the border they shared was uninterrupted. The rest of the continent of Africa might have been scoured from the surface of the Earth for all they knew. Indeed, except for waves of broken mountains and barren wilderness, there was little to see in the territories held by roving bands of maniacs.

"It hints at a larger network, but are we still connected?" Nathan asked. "Otherwise, we turn on the radio, we'll just end up talking to nothing."

Lomon frowned. "Then coming down here was a waste of time, and I don't think that your stick is a time waster."

Nathan looked at the staff. "You've got a point."

The controls on the intercom blinked, catching their attention.

"Incoming signal," Lomon murmured. "Did you turn anything on?"

"Nope. But they could know that we're here simply because you've tried to access the interface for the transporter," Nathan suggested.

"Fair enough," Lomon said. "You want to take this?"

"You're in charge here," he conceded.

Lomon picked up the microphone. "This is Captain Aaron Lomon, Zambian militia. Who's calling?"

"My name is Donald Bry of Cerberus redoubt," a voice answered. "We detected your station coming online"

"How long have you been debating talking to us?" Lomon asked.

There was a chuckle. "Long enough to make first contact."

"Who is 'we,' pardon my grammar," Lomon pressed.

"Cerberus redoubt is a fairly good sized facility with a large staff," Bry responded. "What inspired you to start the computers?"

"We're pretty desperate," Lomon told him. "The upper levels of this facility are under siege by…an unusual enemy. I was hoping for a back door, and my friend here stumbled on this chamber."

"How many people are there with you?" Bry asked.

"Myself and three others," Lomon said. "And there's about seven to twelve outside."

"What exactly are outside?" Bry inquired.

"Can you take a look at the video feed?" Nathan asked, leaning in toward the microphone. "Because if we described it, you'd think we were nuts."

"Give me a minute," Bry answered.

Lomon nodded to the newcomer from Harare. "Good idea, Nathan."

A moment later, they heard the hiss of Bry's reaction to the olitiau at the door.

"Okay, you don't see that every day," he said aloud.

"Got any help for us?" Nathan pleaded.

"All right, give me one minute," he responded. "I'm synchronizing your mat trans to ours, since you don't appear to have a working pass code into the system."

"You pulling us out?" Lomon asked. "If so, I'm going to call the rest of my men in here."

"We're sending a support team to you," Bry replied. He leaned away for a moment, then returned. "Three people will be coming through."

"There used to be over a dozen of us," Lomon stressed. "You won't even be doubling our forces."

A new voice broke over the line. "Trust me, we'll be ready for whatever those things are."

With those words, Nathan went stiff, eyes wide.

Lomon leaned back and looked to the younger man. "What?"

"That voice. I know it," Nathan said numbly. "Or maybe the staff knows it."

Within moments, the hexagonal plates on the floor of the chamber, the mat trans as Bry had called it, began to power up. A mist began building up in the chamber, a plasma-like spill of energy that represented the power of a nuclear reactor splitting open a channel through time and space.

"That stick better have picked a goddamned superhero," Lomon muttered. Even so, he edged closer to the big wood-and-steel rifle leaning against the control console. "Otherwise, we're opening the doors to a nightmare."

As the energy wave built up, three figures appeared within the mist. All were tall, the shortest of them eye to eye with the nearly six foot Lomon, the other two even larger. Nathan's vision cleared, or the trio sharpened more into reality, and he saw that the largest of the three was a black man, lighter in skin tone than Lomon and his fellow Zambians, well over six feet tall, with his brawny frame squeezed into a body-hugging black top and matching cargo pants.

The second man was a couple inches taller than Lomon, approximately six-one, and while strong looking, was composed of lean, packed muscle denoting grace, as well as strength. Steely blue-gray eyes immediately sized up Lomon and Nathan, then locked on to the blackened staff. Whereas Nathan had felt stricken when'd he heard that voice, this man shared the same horrified recognition of the odd object.

The last of the three, in terms of height, was a beautiful woman with hair the colors of a blazing sunset, and sharp emerald eyes that scanned the room as if she were memorizing the world about her, seeking out every nuance, drinking in her environment. Both the second man and the woman were whites, not rare on the African continent, but given the relative lightness of the largest man's skin, none of them hailed from this side of an ocean.

All three were dressed alike. The skintight tops seemed to move and flex like second skins, and disappeared down into the waistbands of battle dress uniform pants festooned with pockets. The two men had strange devices on their right forearms, slender and relatively low profile, but carrying an edge of deadly menace. Lomon could make out the blunt noses of barely exposed firearms barrels, as opposed to the woman with her more traditionally holstered pistol. The three all carried futuristic-looking but compact submachine guns, but these were slung and out of the way.

When they arrived, they had all made certain to show up with empty hands, palms raised politely and shown to the defenders of the Victoria Falls facility. They went to the door of the chamber and opened it. It hissed with the sound of its seal breaking, and the three people were soon among them. Lomon had joked about summoning a superhero. The three of them in their second-skin tops and gloves and belts of equipment reminded the Zambian national guardsman of an old vid of a well-equipped hero in black armor.

"Did someone have an infestation problem?" The black man spoke up, his voice deep, rumbling, with a hint of humor to allay any fears.

"Yes," Lomon replied. "I'm Aaron Lomon. This is Nathan Longa."

Grant nodded as he stepped forward, offering his hand. "I'm Grant. This is Kane. That is Brigid Baptiste."

Kane stared at Nathan and the staff, his attention rapt. Nathan returned the scrutiny. Both of them looked incredulous, as if they wondered if they had stumbled back into a dream despite being awake.

"Just the three of you for the monsters outside?" Lomon asked, turning his attention to the more loquacious arrivals, Grant and Brigid.

The red-haired woman walked to the monitor displaying the creatures gathered about the doors. She leaned in close, unfurling a pair of wire-framed glasses to peer more clearly at them. "Given the firepower that Kane and Grant bring along, we've been able to hold our own against most menaces."

"Most menaces," Lomon repeated. "Like six-foot winged gorillas?"

Grant peered over Brigid's shoulder. The droop of his gunslinger's mustache increased the pensive quality of his frown as he studied the creatures. "Sure as hell ain't no pterodactyl or pteranodon."

Brigid shook her head. "They definitely have a more mammalian vibe to them. Any idea what provoked them?"

Nathan Longa finally broke his silence, his voice soft and shy at first. "This probably did."

Lomon, Grant and Brigid turned toward him, and noted the staff he held in his hand.

"Is that Nehushtan?" Kane finally asked. "It doesn't look as if it's made of brass."

"Brass was also the alleged color of orichalcum, the wonder metal of Atlantis," Brigid replied. She took a step toward it. "This could be like the secondary alloys derived from it."

"The stable stuff that doesn't blow up when sunlight hits it," Kane mused. "But this is all black."

"So…you're the rightful owner of this stick," Nathan said. He didn't look as if he was ready to surrender the staff, and Kane didn't seem in a hurry to take it up.

"Except for a dream or vision, I never even knew this existed," Kane returned. "Why…don't you just hang on to it for a bit?"

Nathan looked from him to the pair of snake heads. "Sounds fair."

"Really?" Brigid asked. "You're not curious?"

"I've had an ancient artifact or two entrusted to me before, remember," Kane replied. "Not really that keen on them. Almost more trouble than they're worth."

"What's going on? Holy…" said a voice from the doorway.

Lomon had to respect the calm with which Grant and

Kane reacted to the arrival of Jonas and Shuka. His two fellow guards had shown up, and while the newcomers from Cerberus had appeared to notice them even in the hall, neither showed surprise at their arrival. The nonchalance they displayed was almost welcoming, though they kept wary eyes on them.

"We found a back door," Lomon told the pair. "Meet Shuka and Jonas, he said to the others."

The two guards nodded a greeting. Kane and Grant shook their hands, while Brigid seemed torn between observing the creatures on the video feed and the staff itself. She touched it, and Nathan allowed her to hold it.

"Lightweight alloy," she mused. "The coating is dark. Some sort of carbon that's scratch resistant. Like an insulation around the staff itself."

"What is orichalcum?" Nathan asked.

"It's either a true element on its own, or an alloy of some type. You know about the heavier metals, the radioactive ores?" Brigid asked.

He nodded.

"Orichalcum itself, according to legend, is a mystical metal forged by the gods," Brigid continued. "One can assume the magic involved is actually the technology of either the Annunaki or the Tuatha de Danann, or they both discovered it."

"The gods are real?" Shuka asked in surprise, his attention drawn from the introductions just completed. "Oh, you said Annunaki. I thought you meant Anansi."

"I wouldn't be surprised if Nancy were real, either," Grant interjected.

"Anansi," Shuka repeated. "He is son of Nyame, the god of the sky, and he owns all stories."

"Are those doors holding?" Jonas asked. He gripped his rifle a little tighter, his knuckles whitening with his tension. "I'd hate to interrupt mythology 101 for actually solving our problems."

"He's right," Kane agreed. "Grant, Baptiste—"

"Take a look here," Brigid interrupted.

The three from Cerberus huddled over the monitors, speaking in low tones to each other, three close allies who were used to each other's counsel and conversation as they examined the demeanor of their foes.

"What are these things called?" Brigid stopped to ask.

Shuka spoke up. "Those things are new as hell to us, but they resemble mythic creatures known as the olitiau, great man-eating bats."

"Olitiau," Brigid mused. Her emerald eyes sparkled with recognition of the obscure term. "Wouldn't those…"

"Yes. Allegedly from Cameroon, much farther north," Shuka answered. "But who is to say that these things never migrated?"

"I'd have thought that Zambians would identify those creatures as kongamato," Brigid replied.

He shrugged. "The past couple hundred years have given us time to do some exploration of the swamps it was supposed to inhabit. People who investigated sightings determined that they were saddle-billed storks."

"So, you figured that the olitiau are imports," she said, getting a nod of agreement from Shuka.

"Or weren't manufactured on the spot," Kane added.

"Manufactured?" Lomon inquired.

"We've dealt with more than a few foes who've utilized biological engineering, or even stored specimens, to create foot soldiers," Grant explained. "These could have been whipped up in some lab."

"Shades of Frankenstein," Nathan murmured. "Custom-built monsters."

"How would you know what the olitiau are?" Shuka

asked. "I only remember because my grandfather told me the stories of old, and he traveled far."

Brigid turned her attention back to Shuka. "I have an eidetic memory and remember reading about them. It was in the writings of Ivan T. Sanderson, the man who first encountered the creatures. He coined the term cryptozoology and went on to seek out both real and legendary creatures."

Shuka nodded. "Makes sense. What exactly are they? Winged apes? Dinosaurs?"

Grant shook his head. "No. Definitely not dinosaurs. Pterosaurs and pteranodons are not technically dinosaurs. And the jaws of those things are just a little too blunt even for pteranodons, which have teeth." Grant looked to Shuka and shrugged. "My girlfriend lives close to an island inhabited by dinosaurs."

Lomon raised an eyebrow at that, as Grant unzipped a large war bag and removed a massive weapon with a large telescope mounted on top. A small canvas satchel hung off of the side of the brutal-looking firearm. Grant opened a hatch, made sure that the belt of ammunition coming from the canvas sack was centered on the feed tray, then closed it. He gestured toward the piece. "A light machine gun."

Grant nodded. "I didn't think that a Copperhead had enough punch to deal with these things. I can use this as a rifle, and firing short bursts, I can engage a target flying as far away as nine hundred meters. Up close, this will punch through even the musculature of one of those monsters."

"I'm trying to decide whether we wait these things out or confront them," Kane mused aloud. "Baptiste…is there a parallax point outside, near enough?"

"Either a parallax point, or I could drop in with a Manta," Grant suggested. "We hop back to Cerberus…."

"One of these days, we're going to have to put gun pods onto a Manta," Kane murmured. "Hang on. The creatures are moving away. Why didn't you radio for closer reinforcements?"

Lomon spoke up again. "We had a platoon of armed men guarding this facility. Those creatures came down and wiped out trained fighters. We barely managed to withdraw to the upper levels of this facility, and it was my call."

"You didn't want to risk the lives of anyone else," Kane said.

Lomon nodded.

Kane clapped him on the shoulder. "Good man. Can't have been an easy choice."

"We're tucked into a vault," Lomon said. He worked through the monitor settings, showing new camera views. The winged horrors did seem to be leaving, but his brow furrowed with concern. "Are they really retreating?"

"They probably expended too many calories trying to break in," Grant suggested. He pointed to the camera views of blood smears, ominously absent of corpses. "Four fresh bodies isn't going to make up for the energy exerted on breaking those doors. Typical predator behavior."

"They seemed a lot smarter than run-of-the-mill predators," Nathan mused. "But…it could have been that they were chasing me. Relentlessly."

"The area beyond the vault door is clear, though," Kane said. "I'm going to take a step outside."

"What about me?" Grant asked.

"Stay back and be ready to open the door if they come after me," Kane answered.

"Do you want the machine gun?" Grant pressed, but didn't hold it out. He simply watched Kane shake his head.

"I'll need mobility," Kane responded. "You can run around with that thing as if it was a rifle. I can't."

"Be careful," Grant told him.

Kane gave his friend a one percent salute, a touch to the bridge of his nose—shorthand for the deep, brotherly and complex loyalty that the two men held for each other when they faced overwhelming odds. "Is there a closer place to watch the monitors?"

"We'll take you there," Jonas said. "I want to come with you."

"I've got protective clothing," Kane responded. "This isn't a T-shirt. It's a shadow suit. Might not be much, but it absorbs impacts and is resistant to cutting. You're not armored for outside."

Brigid rummaged through her pack. "Take this with you."

Kane looked down and saw that she'd withdrawn a small square object that hung from a neck lanyard. It was a digital camera, part of the equipment that the Cerberus explorers had started using on their journeys out into the dangerous world of postapocalyptic Earth.

"This will give us a closer look at the things, and a much clearer view than the security cameras. It's already running, so you don't have to fiddle with it," Brigid told him.

Kane looped it over his neck, and a small electroadhesive patch on the back of the camera sealed it to his chest. The lanyard was simply extra support, and Kane, given the adventures he'd been on, knew that wasn't an unnecessary precaution.

"Thanks, Baptiste," he said.

At the vault doors, Kane stood for a moment. His long, lean limbs were loose, and his every instinct was attuned, from his five normal senses to his point-man's instinct— a nearly preternatural awareness of danger and ambush. Something felt wrong about the big doors, the new quiet with their arrival at the Victoria Falls facility. Even so, he had his gear, and he had Grant as backup, standing ready to manipulate the huge, heavy redoubt doors.

"Baptiste?" Kane asked over the Commtact, the jaw-bone-mounted communicator plate.

"The lobby is clear," she responded.

With that, Grant and Kane unhooked one of the doors and slid it open. It felt as light as a feather, but that was an illusion provided by the hinges. Both men had seen similar doors at Cerberus redoubt, and these were heavy, designed to hermetically seal the underground installations and withstand attacks of weapons at large as a small nuclear warhead.

Once the door was open just enough for Kane to walk through, he darted into the lobby, Grant swiftly hurling his strength into sealing the bank-vault-sized doors. There was a deep, metallic thump, the rumble of heavy locking bars fitting into their nesting spots.

Kane glanced over his shoulder and saw that the surface was dotted with bloody prints where fists had hammered at it. Whether the blood came from the olitiau's split knuckles or palms, or were bloody leftovers of the Zambians they had slain, was difficult to discern. Either way, there were small dents in the surface. The things were strong, perhaps as strong as an Annunaki itself.

Which, in Kane's experience, was more than sufficient.

"Are you reading me?" he asked over the Commtact.

Grant and Brigid spoke in unison. "Loud and clear."

"Great," Kane responded. They were on the opposite side of heavy, armored doors, meant to keep out the horrors of a nukecaust. Getting to him if he was overwhelmed would be a bad idea. Kane had a plan for superior enemy odds—a series of grenades hooked to his belt. As strong as these creatures might be, they were mortal enough. During the walk to the vault doors, he'd been informed that the creatures would fall to concentrated rifle fire.

So they're only as dangerous as an enraged dinosaur, he thought. Kane and his allies had survived that kind of opposition before.

It was not the best of circumstances, and he'd taken

plenty of beatings from those kinds of foes. This still felt like a risk, Kane had to admit.

He didn't like the staff. It was proof that some of the dreams he had during mat-trans jumps were more than just delusions, the overactive workings of a mind besieged by transdimensional space. Out here, he was free and out of claustrophobic confinement with an alien thing that murmured into his subconscious. With the actions of beings such as Balam, Kakusa, Ullikummis and other psychics touching his mind, he was growing sensitive, aware of the odd mental radiations around him when they were in use.

The staff had that kind of "feel."

Better to go toe to toe with monstrous creatures that he could touch, rather than be mentally manhandled by an artifact that was nothing more than a hunk of metal.

"Back on the clock," he whispered to himself.

The doorway above had been peeled open, the reinforced concrete frame smashed and cratered as steel folded and finally yielded to their attack. The door itself was down here in what the other men had called "the ready room." Eyeballing the bent wreckage, he figured the thing must have weighed four hundred pounds, and the olitiau or the kongamato or whatever they really were they had used only their bare fists to destroy it.

Kane had the Copperhead grasped in both hands, taking cautious steps, avoiding a footfall that would betray his presence. He climbed the stairs, scanning the doorway, gauging every step of advance, looking for any of the creatures outside.

"Kane, the cameras out in the courtyard are out of commission," Brigid said. "They just went down."

Kane paused. He hadn't heard any sounds, but then, if the olitiau were intelligent, they'd know enough to smother the device with their wings, or just sever video cables with their claws. Either way, someone knew he was coming.

Any element of surprise he had on his side was an illusion.

There was movement in the doorway and Kane froze, then dropped low as he spotted a hulking shadow. He hadn't ducked below the stairs before being seen, and the figure jerked to cover as well.

First contact was going to be hard. Hard as bullets.

Chapter 5

Kane snapped the Copperhead to his shoulder, peering through the low-powered scope of the submachine gun, seeking out the shadowy figure that lurched back from the door, even as Brigid Baptiste, in contact with him through their Commtact, announced that more cameras had blinked off line.

"Kane...we're blind out there!" Her voice was taut with urgency.

Kane advanced toward the door, eyes flitting left and right, ears peeled, listening for any breath, a scrape of a claw, the flap of a leathery, deadly wing. He spoke low, only loud enough for the surgically implanted transreceiver of the Commtact to translate vibrations into crystal-clear words. "You are. I'm not."

Suddenly, the signal transmitted through the small cybernetic device released a squeal of feedback, and Kane jolted as if he'd been struck in the face with a hammer. With a tap of the plate, he killed the sound, but his ears were left ringing, and his head was swimming from the sonic shock. The feedback blast was strong, and more than enough to stop him cold and make him shut his eyes, if only for a moment.

When they opened, he saw the flickering motion of a braided length of leather snagging the Copperhead in his hands. A powerful tug pulled the already staggered Kane off balance, and he released the gun in order to grab the stairway rail with one hand. His other hand instantly filled with his Sin Eater as the holster shot the weapon into his palm.

The whip cracked again, a shock wave burst of pressure released from the clacker at the end of the weapon, missing Kane's face by inches. But the sonic boom forced him to blink again, blinding him for another moment. A hand grasped his gun arm and raised it to the ceiling. Kane was about to swing a fist up into the man's ribs when his eyes opened.

He recognized Fargo North immediately, and paused for an instant.

"Hold on, Kane," the man said.

Kane ignored the plea and fired off a short knuckle punch that struck his adversary just above the floating rib. Air exploded from North's mouth and nose, and he flopped unceremoniously on the floor at the top of the steps. Kane swung his Sin Eater toward the man, someone he had first met as a millennialist operative attempting to break into the city of Garuda, the home of the Nagah. While the man was a classic double dealer, without the sabotage bombs that North had planted, Kane would have fallen before the vastly upgraded Prince Durga.

As such, while Fargo North had helped the Nagah, and gained them a chance at a new ally, he had also earned intense scorn.

Kane sneered at the fallen archaeologist, then flexed his forearm, retracting the Sin Eater back into its folded position. He then reached down, grabbing two big handfuls of North's battered leather jacket, and hauled him to his feet. Expending a little more frustration at the two-timing adventurer, he bounced North up against the concrete wall, pinning him there with a forearm across the throat.

Kane glanced toward the door. "Did you see anything outside?"

"You mean the flock of creatures with three-yard

wingspans?" North asked. "Yes. That's why I approached slowly."

Kane turned and glared into his eyes. "You're the one who turned off the cameras. You've got a skull full of those nanomachines."

"Technically, they're all throughout my nervous system at this point," North replied. "But I—"

Kane took a deep breath, then flexed his fist, driving the man's head harder into the wall. "You messed with the Commtacts."

North blinked, then rasped, "Yes."

"Why?" Kane asked.

"I'm trying to keep a low profile here," North returned. "Could you let me go?"

Kane leaned in close. "Let's see. You sneak around the door of a redoubt under siege. You knock out the cameras that could tell us if we're being attacked. Then you not only cut me off from my allies, but hit me with feedback and a whip. Why should I let you free?"

"Because I never struck you with my whip," North said.

Kane grimaced. "Then I would be one of the first you haven't abused."

"You'd be surprised," the man replied.

"Kane?" Grant bellowed from the vault doors.

"I'm here," Kane grunted in reply. "Turn off the jamming. Now."

"All you had to do—" North began. Kane applied more pressure to his throat, turning his words to a wet crackle past a constricted windpipe.

"Ask?" Kane growled. "No. Now."

"The Commtacts are clear now," Grant and North said in unison, the stereo between Kane's ears and the cybernetic implant adding an odd, almost ghostly double intonation.

Kane backed off of North. "Watch this asshole."

Grant stayed where he was, but shouldered the machine gun, lining up North in the scope. "Done."

Kane took his time checking the perimeter of the Victoria Falls substation. There was little left of either man or beast. He found a few gnawed bones that were too large to crunch and swallow, pelvises and lower vertebrae. The winged horrors must have had jaws like hyenas, able to crush through bone to slurp out the marrow, or just digest the whole thing as bonemeal. That meant they had more than just fangs; they had bone-crushing molars.

What Kane *did* find was spatters of blood and piles of empty shell casings befitting a battle of life or death. The place smelled of death, gunpowder and coagulation. The monsters that had struck were cruelly efficient, leaving neither their own, nor their victims behind, at least in parts larger than gnawed bones.

The forest beyond the tall fence and its concertina wire was empty. Kane scanned the branches of the canopy just to be certain, but he doubted there were any of the creatures remaining behind. Already birds and small mammals were visible on the boughs. Were there a semihumanoid predator present, it would have been out of sight, hiding. The African jungle had returned to a semblance of normalcy as wildlife frittered to and fro, seeking food or shelter.

He glanced toward the station house. There was a second level above the bunker house that led down to the vault doors. It had been constructed of wood and corrugated metal, but that had been smashed with unfettered violence. Mangled panels of sheet metal had been collapsed by hammer blows, and from the spray of blood across them, Kane knew that one of the Zambian guards had fought his last up there.

Kane returned to the door to see Grant still guarding North.

"They're gone?" Grant asked.

Kane nodded. He turned toward the other man. "Why didn't you get any attention from them?"

"The kongamato?" North asked. "I don't know. The boat breakers had moved on, so I made my entrance."

"Boat breakers?" Grant asked. "These things are aquatic?"

"I'd surmise so," North responded. "They didn't retreat into the forest, but into the rapids."

Kane sized up North, wondering if the man was telling the truth. He recalled that Shuka had mentioned the name North referred to, the kongamato. The one thing Kane didn't care for was the archaeologist's arrival so swiftly on the heels of their attack. "Why are you here?"

"The same reason you are, I presume," North said. "I sensed the awakening of the Nehushtan."

Kane's lips drew into a thin, bloodless line. "I swear, if you're behind those monsters attacking this place…"

"No. I'm not," North replied. "But an old, mutual adversary is."

"The Millennium Consortium? Enlil?" Kane pressed.

"Durga is in Africa," North explained. "As well as the consortium."

Grant and Kane shared a shocked glance.

"My bombs were more than enough to strip away Durga's added biomass. He was left a cripple.…" North began.

"We know," Grant interjected. "A while back, we returned to Garuda for a brief stopover. His people are still at work trying to destabilize Hannah's administration and increase tensions between transformed Nagah and the human population."

"I presume he also left a message that he was looking for a means of returning to his full strength," North replied.

Kane nodded. "The bastard also forced his DNA matrix onto Hannah's unborn children."

North's lip curled. "Will she be all right?"

"Manticor is still willing to raise them both as his own," Kane replied.

North's disgust faded. "Let us pray that nurture is more than sufficient to make good people out of Durga's seed."

"How did you know that Durga is in Africa?" Grant inquired.

"The matrix that the cobra baths inserted into my brain has picked up on Durga's communications. He mentioned seeking out the key to the Mines of Solomon," North answered. "That key, in short, is the staff Nehushtan."

"Yeah. I got the lowdown on Moses's brass stick. Thing is, it's not here," Kane lied.

"Oh, it is. I can sense it," North told him. "I just didn't know *you* were here until I caught a glimpse of you a moment ago."

"A conveniently constructed story," Grant murmured. "Why the hell should we roll out the welcome mat for you?"

"I'm just here to make certain that Durga does not open that mine," North said. "It is full of things that man was not meant to deal with. That is why, after millennia, it is still listed as missing."

"Things," Kane repeated. "Anything like Kakusa?"

North seemed confused by that reference. "Explain."

"Kakusa was a creature that was being kept off of Florida, in an undersea science station known as the Tongue of the Ocean, or TOTO," Kane stated. "He was a collection of creatures which, when their cells were attached to another, would take control of them."

"Oh." North thought for a moment, searching through the lore of Enki. Even as he did so, he frowned. "That. The Faceless One. Did you exterminate it?"

"Hopefully," Kane replied. "And yes, I know that if even one cell survived..."

"Not necessarily," North replied. "When the Annunaki imprisoned it, they broke one of the command sequences in its DNA. It cannot reproduce itself. Then they implanted it into a mindless, controllable organism. One of their hopes was to utilize it as a punishment device."

"Punishment?" Grant asked. He frowned. "That explains the despondence of those separated from its cell structure."

"They committed suicide," North surmised.

"Right," Grant said.

The vault doors opened below, and Brigid, Natha, and the three surviving Zambians appeared in the ready room.

North's eyes narrowed as he spied the staff that Nathan carried. "I said Nehushtan was here."

"That's not Moses's brass stick," Kane returned.

North gritted his teeth. "How many times do you have to encounter orichalcum to realize that it needs to be kept from sunlight? It's a highly unstable isotope as well as a dense, powerful metal. Obviously, the black coating is for the protection of those who manipulate it, and those around it."

"Enki's database is up there, so you have all the answers," Kane said, tapping North's forehead. "Then how about you take the staff?"

"No. That would be bad," he responded. "I am simply here to make certain that Durga does not receive that key to the mine. As you had mentioned Kakusa, there are other horrors imprisoned within those tombs. Things that cannot be forever killed, but wait dead, ever dreaming of their freedom."

"Then we destroy the stick," Kane said. "Nobody gets it."

"The destruction of Nehushtan would take most of this continent with it," North said. "You're blunt, crude and pragmatic, but I truly doubt that you're willing to take millions of innocent lives."

"That bad," Kane muttered.

"Far worse than you could ever imagine," North told him. "Orichalcum is highly destructive on its own. But the staff's configuration amplifies its power. You have no concept of how powerful a weapon it could be."

"You do," Kane countered.

He nodded. "Such is the burden of the knowledge I sought all my life."

Nathan looked at the staff in his hand, and Kane could see the young man's sudden discomfort, almost as if Nehushtan was reacting to their conversation, growing agitated. That, more than ever, made Kane reluctant to touch the damned thing. If it had proved able to imprison creatures that even the Annunaki could not kill, then certainly, it was a terrible object by any stretch of the imagination.

Kane looked sideways toward North. "Did Durga mention anything about waking up some creatures?"

"Like, perhaps, the kongamato?" North offered.

Kane nodded. "Because Nathan told me about the things chasing him, but unwilling to be touched by it."

North frowned. "It is likely."

Nathan paled as he stepped closer. "I hear the two of you, even heard you behind the blast doors. The staff is transmitting to me."

Kane touched his Commtact, then looked to the young man.

"It sounded a bit like a radio," Nathan said, not even waiting for Kane's upcoming question.

"Both Grant and I could listen in over our Commtact units as well," Brigid interjected. "Kane, you have to touch the staff. I'm dying to know—"

"No," he growled, and unceremoniously took a step away from it. Nathan didn't look as if he was in a hurry to cede ownership of the snake-entwined staff, either.

"Durga is onto the presence of Nehushtan," North explained. "He will want to get it out of your hands, young man. And keep it from you, Kane. That alone is cause—"

"No." Nathan and Kane spoke in unison. Nathan tugged

the staff closer to his side, his knuckles lightening as he clutched it tightly. Kane felt a sense of relief at the African's stubbornness matching his own.

"Can you read the markings on its surface?" Brigid asked.

North tried to lean in close, but Kane noted that standing this near to the object seemed to fill him with discomfort. "I presume that I could, if Nehushtan weren't determined to protect its secrets."

"It's sentient," Brigid mused.

North nodded. "That is as good a term as any for its nature. It is programmed, and it is not interested in letting my matrix close to it."

Nathan took a step back, and the relief the archaeologist felt showed on his features.

"I spent my life seeking out the greatest mysteries of this world, and here is living mythology, living *history,* and like its owner, Moses himself, I am denied entry to the promised land," North lamented. "Perhaps you can decipher some of its mysteries, Ms. Baptiste?"

Brigid looked from Kane to Nathan. "I could certainly try."

"Go right ahead, Baptiste," Kane grumbled curtly. "But if you say one more thing—"

"Like how you could just touch it, and you'd know all we need to?" Brigid interrupted.

Kane grimaced. "Exactly like that."

"I'll make a mental note of it," she responded.

Lomon and the others had brought out a spare radio unit, as the comm equipment in the ready room had been turned to electronic garbage by the raiding kongamato. While Jonas was busy dialing home base, the other two joined the Cerberus explorers, Nathan and North.

"So what are your plans, Kane?" Lomon asked.

Kane spent a few minutes going over the gist of the

conversation he'd had with the former millennialist, regarding Durga, the staff and the creatures.

"Kongamato," Shuka interjected upon North's naming of the things. "Yes, we did call them boat breakers. They seemed perfectly at home in the air, on the land and in the water. In fact, during the Zambian expedition to determine the origin of the myth, one of the strongest candidates for the creature's true identity was a species of freshwater stingray."

"They are none of those. Rather, they are genetic constructs, chimeras if you will, designed to protect the privacy and secrecy of the First Folk and other entities," North explained.

"You know this much, doesn't it ruin things for you?" Shuka asked. "You were a seeker of knowledge, and now you've got a filing cabinet in your head full of everything you wanted to learn."

"It is not that easy, and my knowledge of Nehushtan has only come to the forefront because of the imminent threat," North said. "The database of Enki is not omniscience in any sense."

"So, that matrix tells you what they are, but it doesn't give you anything as to where they come from?" Kane asked.

North nodded. "It would be easy, wouldn't it?"

"And convenient," Kane added. "But since your knowledge base is more trivia than practical information, who knows how many people Durga could menace with the kongamato…."

"We do know," Jonas said, running breathlessly to join them. "Livingstone had a sighting of these creatures while we were trapped underground. There were no casualties, but they put the fear of God into the town. The national guard had to button down the capital, Lusaka, Mongu, and of course, Livingstone."

Brigid narrowed her eyes in concentration. Kane could tell that she was using her eidetic memory to construct a map of the movements of the creatures. "Livingstone is six miles to the north of the falls. However, Mongu and Lusaka are much farther away."

"The sightings there might have just been rumors and species misidentification," Shuka suggested. "After all, once it hits the news that olitiau or kongamato have been sighted…much like UFOs in the late twentieth century… others end up seeing what may not be there."

"Or even one or two appearing that far afield could give the impression to the population that there are more present," Brigid added. "Whichever the case, those sightings elsewhere will have any military response buttoned down and away from us."

"Any news from Harare?" Nathan asked.

Jonas shook his head. "Nothing on the radio, but they sent out a distress call to us here. We responded with news of the losses we took."

Brigid tilted her head. "Zimbabwe renamed itself?"

"Unlike Zambia, which managed to weather the apocalypse as a contiguous nation, Harare had to set up its own city state," Nathan replied. "Most of the districts around what is now the nation are fallen to chaos and barbarism. It didn't help that the nuclear holocaust in the northern hemisphere took place during a time of famine and drought, nor that the earthquakes that shook Africa caused a lot of upheaval."

"Interesting," Brigid noted. "But Zimbabwe was where the staff originated."

Nathan nodded. "Northwestern sector of Harare. About fifty miles southeast of here."

"Then I'm going to have to take a closer look at that staff. I doubt that Durga would increase military and police operations in a sector he's operating within, no matter what kind of force he's awakened," Brigid said.

"Back to Harare? Or maybe one of the outlaw sections?" Kane asked.

Nathan pursed his lips. "Harare itself is pretty outlaw already. It's why everyone has at least one gun and a knife. Things have improved, but it's still rough. Zambia keeps us as a buffer between them and the harder parts of what used to be Zimbabwe."

"We'll know our destination soon enough," Brigid replied. "May I?"

Nathan ceded possession of the staff to the red-haired woman. Kane avoided her as she took the ancient artifact back down into the redoubt.

Kane just wished that she would find those answers quickly, before Durga and his minions laid waste to this section of Africa.

WITH A RASPY breath, Durga reached out for the radio handset offered to him by his hulking aide, Makoba. Makoba was an African, but he was also a member of the Millennium Consortium, chosen to be Durga's bodyguard and caretaker, literally the fallen prince's hands and voice. This was the call that the exiled prince expected, and Makoba brought the phone to Durga's ear.

"Speak," Durga said. Each word that came from his scaled lips felt like glass pushed up through his throat. It was only his will, his insatiable desire to be whole again, that allowed him to speak, to stumble along on crutches despite the raw sensation of his own weight pressing on the arm pads. Even giving out his written orders was an exercise in self-torture, as his explosion-ravaged body was still weak, still healing. Had it not been for the injection of nanomachines from Enki's stores and the interface with his body, the detonation of the Garuda monument, and the fuel-air explosion afterward, would have slain him. As it was, his recovery was slow. The microscopic robots that had once given him insane superhuman strength expended the last of their power, restoring him to the minimum possible functions to keep him alive.

That was all right. Durga was nothing if not patient. The brief taste of godhood had shown him that quick and easy solutions were only a quicker means to downfall.

"The son of Longa has reached the Victoria Falls redoubt," answered Thurpa. "We tried to retrieve the Nehushtan, but even our winged warriors have not the strength to burst into a nuclear-proof bunker."

Durga nodded, then released a single name, his voice dragged over sandpaper. "Kane?"

"He came outside," Thurpa responded. "Grant and Brigid Baptiste were seen on the grounds, as well. Also, there was another white man, one who crossed the jungle, on Nathan Longa's heels."

"Who?" Durga asked.

Knowing every word was an effort, Thurpa was swift in describing the white man, his battered leather jacket, wide-brimmed hat, and the coiled whip at his hip. Durga's upper lip twitched in reaction. His eye, the one Fargo North had struck with that same weapon of leather and cruelty, was in constant pain, and provided only milky, blurry vision since his reconstruction.

"Shall I send in the kongamato again?" Thurpa asked.

"Wait," Durga ordered. His fury, his hatred for both Kane, the former magistrate, and North, the conniving millennialist lackey, deadened any feeling of pain in his body. "We shall come there. Draw them here to Kariba. But do so carefully. I want to see them suffer for what they have done."

Durga could see Makoba's reaction to such sustained

speech. Thurpa, on the other end, must have been equally shocked.

So be it, Durga thought. Each spasm of pain that shot through his throat would only make the destruction of the Cerberus interlopers and Fargo North that much sweeter.

Chapter 6

If there was one thing that Kane could do while Brigid Baptiste was applying her considerable mental faculties to translating dead languages, it was to look for physical evidence of the path of the kongamato. Going by what he'd seen of them on the video monitors, which had been plenty, and judging by the depth of the knuckle and claw prints left in the dirt as they'd landed, he could get a gauge of their true weight and power.

"Grant, take a step there."

"Why?" the larger ex-magistrate asked.

"I know the mass of you and that gear off the top of my head. I want to see how these things measure up to you," Kane returned.

Grant nodded, took a step into the spot indicated, then withdrew his boot. Kane knelt next to the imprint. He reached into his pocket and withdrew a set of folding pliers. On one of the handle pieces a small ruler was imprinted. "What's the story, Kane? Do I have to go on a diet again?"

Kane glanced up at his friend after studying the depth comparison. "You're heavier than one of those things, despite all that muscle they seem to be carrying."

"Which means they're not hauling around a war bag full of grens and spare belts of machine gun ammunition," Grant offered. "And they also probably have hollow bone structures."

"Hollow bones and yet they can hammer thick steel like that?" Kane asked.

"Hollow bones doesn't mean fragile. It means, however, that the skeletal structure is highly efficient," Grant returned. "The so-called air pockets are hexagonal supports, meant to absorb a lot of physical stress. They're then reinforced by lighter-than-bone muscle tissue and blood, which, being mostly fluid, is incompressible and thus difficult to break."

Kane stared at Grant for a long, silent moment.

"I can't help it. The creatures of Thunder Isle are fascinating," Grant finally said. "Plus, Brigid's been hogging all the fun to herself."

Kane raised an eyebrow.

"Yeah, lecturing other people is fun. Fun as hell," Grant continued.

Kane smirked.

"You don't mind learning this stuff from us," Grant mused.

"All the specifics might not stick, but I do learn something," Kane admitted. "All right, so these things are strong, even more so because their bones are inured against pressure and abuse."

"That makes them especially dangerous," Grant returned. "They also appeared to be able to absorb a lot of damage before going down."

"Let me guess on that one," Kane offered.

"All right, how are they so hard to kill?" Grant asked.

Kane reached down and began drawing in the dirt with a screwdriver head from his folding tool. "The wings. Most of that is membrane."

"So, that makes them bulletproof?" Grant wondered.

Kane shook his head. "No, but it alters the shape of the target. You think you're hitting center mass, but what you're really doing is hitting skin with a bunch of ice picks. And since the membrane is elastic…"

"You think you're putting a whole mag into a target, but

all you're doing is pissing it off with a bunch of pinprick injuries," Grant mused.

"That, plus thick muscle and strong bones around the vital organs, makes them harder to kill, but not impossible," Kane added. "The damnedest part of it is that in the middle of combat, when you're shooting at something, you don't have a lot of time to adjust for shooting heads or chests instead of wings or cloaks."

"That's why those swashbucklers wore capes," Grant mused.

Kane nodded. "The simple art of misdirection."

"Fight smarter, not harder," Grant said. "Or, in our case, fight smarter *and* harder."

"Given the crap we have to stop, yeah," Kane muttered. "All right. So we have an idea how to better deal with these creatures. And they went right to the river."

"Given that they're terrestrial, they probably aren't water breathers," Grant suggested. "But, with enough lung tissue, and maybe pockets in their skeletons, they can hold their breath fairly well. Penguins can actively hunt underwater for twenty minutes without taking a breath, and alligators or crocodiles can stay for hours on a river bottom."

"That's all well and good, but this gorge is full of whitewater," Kane returned. "If they're staying put anywhere, it's not going to be at this part of the river."

Grant frowned as he looked at the water. "There could be runoff ponds here and there along the river, but those would only be able to harbor one or two creatures."

"That's assuming they'd stay put underwater," Kane replied. "Nathan said that these creatures chased him through the forest."

"Why are you so against taking up Nehushtan?" Grant asked, springing the question in his usual blunt manner.

"You're going to start on me with that shit?" Kane snapped back.

Grant took a deep breath. "It's an ancient weapon. According to Brigid, that thing was able to imprison demons. And if it imprisoned demons, it either was used to battle creatures like the Annunaki, or their enemies, like Kakusa."

"Big deal," Kane grumbled. "We've done well enough without it."

His friend folded his arms.

"You want to have this conversation here? In a forest potentially full of amphibious flying bat horrors?" Kane asked.

"Why?" Grant pressed. "Why can't you pick up the stick and do some magic with it?"

Kane grimaced. "Because I've seen what happens with people who get sucked up into this technology. These ancient powers are left hidden for a reason. I don't want to grab it, and have myself shredded. I mean, look at what happened to North!"

"What did happen?" Grant asked. "He's almost human now."

"And before, he was the biggest asshole around," Kane declared. "You saw the human flesh he had on his whip, and he'd cleaned it. Before he had those nanites in his skull, he set up a bomb that could have murdered thousands in the town square, rather than cripple a demigod like Durga had become."

"You're actually buying that North turned over a new leaf," Grant stated.

Kane nodded, and then in spat in frustration and kicked a rock into the turgid river. "I'm not going to be a meat puppet, even if a good guy's pulling the strings."

"Back to Lakesh," Grant murmured. "He was directing you, needling you to the discoveries you made, which got us kicked out of Cobaltville."

Kane nodded. "It was all for the best cause, the freedom of the human race. But damn it…"

"You don't like being manipulated," Grant said. "None of us do. But…that stick is a tool. It's to be used."

"It's already dragged me across the planet to Africa," Kane returned. "And it's brought you and Baptiste along, right into another dangerous situation.

"Give it a touch, what could it hurt?" Grant asked.

Kane's lip curled. "How much did you enjoy your trip into the past?"

Grant frowned.

"When you were no longer yourself. When you were something different, torn from your body, split into multiple pieces? How about when we were in the casements?" Kane pressed. "You weren't yourself."

Grant said, "But I'm still here. I'm still me, even after all those switches. So are you, after all of those casements. We are the line in the sand, and I've never seen you skittish about taking a risk."

"Death's one thing. Injuries can heal. But losing myself…" Kane shook his head. "I don't want to lose my *self*. It's a petty thing, perhaps…."

"Trust me," Grant told him. "We got home from those other casements. You dragged me back from the slip between time and other dimensions. If anyone can survive even an Annunaki war stick, it'll be you."

Kane looked up at his friend. "Forgive me if I'm not in too much of a hurry—"

"Kane! Grant!"

The two men turned, to see Nathan Longa approaching again. He didn't have the staff with him, meaning it was most likely back with Brigid Baptiste, who was studying it. Longa still had the rifle that the Zambians had lent him, and his personal handgun on his hip.

"This is a dangerous place," Kane admonished. "You sure you want to be out here without the staff?"

"I'm not sure of anything anymore," Nathan returned.

"But I was getting claustrophobic in there. Any progress on finding where our winged friends took off to?"

Kane shook his head again. "We've had a hard time tracking them. It doesn't help that they don't even have to fly, just leap and glide, to break up their footprint trail, or coast down that whitewater."

Nathan nodded, coming closer. He kept his eyes skyward, on the branches.

"We're keeping an eye on things upstairs, too," Grant mentioned.

"I know. But I've had these things chase me. They still have me paranoid," Nathan replied.

Grant tipped his head toward Kane. "It isn't paranoia if they really are hunting you. But don't worry, Kane's sharp. Nothing is going to sneak up on us."

"Don't make it seem so cut and dried," his friend muttered, bristling at the sudden pressure put on him. "Things have hit us in the past, even when I was at my most alert."

Nathan took special care to look around at the forest canopy near them, almost as if Kane and Grant were daring the gods. "Nothing yet…thank goodness."

Grant smirked and rapped his knuckles against a tree trunk. "Not to be too superstitious, but given what we've run into…"

A rustle of leaves suddenly sliced through the big ex-magistrate's mood. In a heartbeat, both Kane's and his Sin Eaters snapped into their hands, launched on pure reflex. Even with all that speed, the hurtling forms of three kongamato were upon them in the space of instants.

Kane's reflexes were the fastest of the three people, his Sin Eater up and barking, but even as the first slugs ripped out of the barrel of his machine pistol, the bat-winged kongamato brought up its hind feet and kicked him to the ground. The creature landed, hot blood splashing across Kane's face, as the Sin Eater's slugs had opened it up. Even wounded, though, the creature was big, strong and heavy, levering one long forearm across Kane's throat, pressing down.

The Cerberus champion's gun arm was pinned by one taloned, three-fingered hand, the other finger being an extended spine for the kongamato's wing membrane. Kane grimaced and pulled the foot-long fighting knife from its sheath. With a mighty heave, he upset the creature's balance atop him, left hand punching into its abdomen. The point of the blade went through much more easily than Kane's center-of-mass gunshots, which had been slowed by thick, ropey muscle and keel-shaped breastbone that deflected bullets from the heart. Flesh and sinew parted around the point of the blade, and with a savage whip of his wrist, Kane found his stomach painted with kongamato blood and gore. Rubbery loops of intestines burst from the wicked, savage wound he'd torn, and the monster let loose an ear-splitting shriek.

Kane felt as if a bomb had gone off in his face, but the pressure of the monster's mass was gone, and he clenched the Sin Eater back in his hand. His head rang like a bell in the aftermath of the batlike creature's sonic assault, but he could see his opponent, one claw shoveling in loosened bowels inefficiently, eyes wild with pain. The ambushing kongamato was on the defensive now, and Kane didn't think it would prove to be a threat. He had to assist Grant and Nathan in their battles. He turned away from the wounded beast, and instants later, the whiplike snap and whisper of the dactyl claw at the end of its wing brushed across his shoulder.

Smart polymers split, allowing only a minor scratch on Kane's skin, but the shadow suits were designed to redistribute impact and provide protection fromenvironmental hazards. Powerful weapons could cleave through the non-Newtonian materials, or at least transmit trauma through fabric that hardened into a shell on impact. Cutting it was something Kane had seen in only rare instances, warning him that the wing claws of these creatures were deadly, and gave the kongamato a threat radius of at least eight feet.

He whirled as his opponent's wing flashed out once more, the flickering hook of the talon whistling through the air over his head with murderous speed and intent. Had Kane not stepped back a foot, his throat would have been opened up, probably to the vertebrae.

He cut loose with the Sin Eater, snapping it to eye level and firing the gun on full auto. Heavy slugs tore the kongamato's streamlined skull asunder, the extended rudder point on the back of its head flopping to the ground.

In the same moment that Kane faced his initial attack, Grant cursed that his reflexes were only a slight bit slower, enough of a delay that the big man's kongamato had been able to bat aside Grant's machine pistol before he could get a shot off. The squat, densely packed mound of mutant muscle collided with the tall, powerfully built human, and found itself bouncing off an immovable object, not quite the irresistible force it imagined itself as.

Grant was glad for the protective qualities of his shadow suit's fluidlike polymers, which flowed and stretched, conforming to his physique without restriction. That, combined with his strength and greater mass, enabled him to withstand the onslaught.

The creature toppled backward, and Grant moved in toward it. The kongamato flipped up one winged arm, and though Grant was inside the arc of its dactyl claw, the force of the whole extended limb struck hard enough to push him off balance, bowling him to the ground. Grant let out a grunt, but even in midfall, twisted his lithe, muscular form, avoiding a subsequent swat by the kongamato's wing.

The second slash of the powerful beast's limb struck the ground with a thump that resounded like a drumbeat, pounding a foot-deep divot into the dirt. Grant was certain that if he hadn't moved, the hammering impact would have tested the protective properties of his shadow suit.

The strength of the monstrosity before him was on the scale of impact force that the gun possessed, but this thing could back its power with claws of great strength. The kongamato lunged out with its other winged arm, and Grant pushed himself atop the limb, wrapping his brawny arms around it and tugging it off balance. The thing's beaklike muzzle was jammed into the ground, and when Grant gave a savage twist, he heard joints and tendons pop inside the sinewy wing, while the beast unleashed a cry of pain into the earth.

Using all his strength and agility, Grant held on to the captive wing and threw himself across the broad, muscular back of the kongamato, wrenching its shoulder out of its socket. The idea of being able to capture one of these monstrosities alive for study was foremost in his mind, as was more than a little anger at being jumped, and knocked around so easily. He heard the thunder of Kane's Sin Eater, and watched as the monster who'd attacked his friend fell, mostly headless, bits of it falling to the ground in ugly chunks.

"Go help Nathan," Grant snarled when something wet and sticky splashed into his face.

Nathan Longa was the last of the three men to react to the assault of the kongamato, and he was bowled backward, knocked down by the speed and power of the winged predator. It was only Nathan's reflexes and stubborn toughness that kept him from being hurled into a tangle of insensate limbs as he wrapped one arm around the conical skull rudder on the monster's head. His rifle had been jarred from numbed hands by the creature's tackle, but he quickly whipped out the tiny .45 from its holster and pressed it against the closest flat section of flesh he could find. A thumb back to the hammer, a press of the trigger, and the Detonics roared, sending blood flying from the creature's back.

Nathan's injured opponent dumped him into the long grass below while it hurtled through the air, blood and screams trailing behind. Nathan scurried to his feet, looking back to see the kongamato tumbling through the underbrush, then landing with a crash. The assault rifle was a dozen feet away, and Nathan whirled and charged toward it, knowing that it would provide a better account than his handgun.

Even as he neared the fallen rifle, he whirled and saw that the beast had gathered itself back up to all fours, one of its shoulders drooping, thanks to the damage of a .45-caliber slug. The kongamato's eyes were red rimmed with anger, and it surged forward in a gallop. Nathan lunged and somersaulted, grabbing his rifle as he tumbled.

He spun and brought up the weapon, squeezing the trigger. The rifle chattered, spitting out lead when he spotted the thing within ten feet. Even as slugs struck the attacking creature, creating blossoms of blood across its upper chest, the thing's wing slashed forward. Nathan hadn't encountered the dactyl claw, the wicked carving blade at the end of the creature's extended "pinkie." At least not until it struck him across the chest, opening up muscle and slipping between ribs. The fabric of Nathan's shirt was nothing compared to the shadow suits, providing no protection against the deadly hooked blade.

The kongamato shuddered violently in death, gunfire tearing through its heavy muscle and breaking its ribs, but its flickering claw had scored a brutal, vital hit upon the young man from Harare. Even as it collapsed in upon itself, furious glare dulling, it knew that there would be little way for the humans to preserve its enemy's life, given the bright spray of oxygenated blood gushing from the wicked chest wound.

Nathan Longa's life blood gushed, spattering into Grant's face, his strength abandoning him. His legs folded, he reached out, letting the rifle fall away.

The cold darkness of death was brushing its fingers along Nathan's spine as he gazed into the shocked faces of Grant and Kane. Then his eyes rolled up and he toppled backward.

Grant looked down at the creature he had pinned, then at Kane. "Get back to the redoubt!"

"What?" he asked.

Grant gave a mighty surge, feeling the neck bones of the kongamato in his grasp shatter. "I can stabilize him, but there's no way we can deal with a deep lung laceration without a full-fledged med bay. No oxygen tanks, no surgical tools…"

He let the lifeless creature slump on the ground and immediately took out a wad of gauze and applied direct pressure to Nathan's chest. "There's only one thing within miles that can save this man's life."

Kane grimaced as he watched Grant staunch the flow of blood. Even though he was doing an admirable job of preventing the hemorrhage spewing from the cut, there was no doubt the young man's thoracic cavity was starting to fill with blood.

"Nehushtan," Kane answered.

And with that, without pause, he spun and raced toward the power station.

All concern for his "self" was thrown to the wind.

A very real life was in danger, and the ancient staff was the only tool with the conceptual ability to stop a needless death.

Chapter 7

Brigid Baptiste had spent years studying the secret history of the Earth, and in that time, she'd come across multiple dead languages. In some cases, deciphering them was relatively easy, utilizing the local languages of humans in the same region. In the case of the Annunaki, she had taken a slow, difficult road. The symbology was dense, difficult, and many of the concepts "written" about were alien to the point of abstraction, even for her level of intellect.

The markings in the black coating on Nehushtan were of this sort. Some things flickered, danced on the end of recognition, vague echoes of reminders that frustrated the flame-haired woman. She had a photographic memory, a command of every experience she'd ever felt, every article she'd ever read, every object she'd ever seen. Some people considered her nearly supernatural in nature, in that she was able to retrace steps across a featureless desert to locate a well-hidden cache of supplies.

Brigid had her glasses on, thick black frames resting on her nose as she peered closely at the carvings on the odd staff. She couldn't tell if the thing's black coating had an effect on the original runes, or if they were an entirely new layer of impressions. At times it looked as if symbols were bleeding into each other, but in every instance of trying to get a bas-relief, rubbing a pencil and paper across the surface, she came up with a different result.

The staff didn't feel as if it was changing, but the results that showed on the paper were incontrovertible. This was something solid, but just as Nathan said, it felt warm, alive.

Perhaps the coating was in some way animated. Or maybe the orichalcum beneath was in constant flux.

Either way, progress in deciphering the markings on the surface was nigh impossible. It was as if Nehushtan were truly alive, and sentient enough to stymie any attempt at delving into its mysteries. Just as it broadcast a low-level signal that caused North's brain to buzz uncomfortably, it was taunting, tantalizing Brigid with new language, new secrets.

She leaned away from the object, turning to look at the archaeologist, who remained at a distance, repelled by Nehushtan as it produced a signal that caused a painful reaction in his enhanced brain. He glared, bristling at the secretive nature of this relic of a world history he'd devoted his life to uncovering.

North's obsession with history and archeology had been so great that he'd allied himself with unsavory types as he hunted treasures and mysteries around the globe. One group had been the Millennium Consortium, currently among the most unrelenting opponents that the heroes of Cerberus had to deal with. Where the overlords had physical power, technology and Nephilim minions, the millennialists were insidious, able to infiltrate the postapocalyptic societies, luring them to their side by either force and blackmail or promises of safety and security.

Where Brigid and her allies sought out knowledge in order to improve the lot of mankind in a world stripped of its technological wonders and hope, North sought knowledge for the sake of his insatiable lust. He didn't want power, though he had garnered enough to seek revenge with the millennialists. It had been a while, so the man may have changed, but the ire written across his features was an indication that he still relished the acquisition of secrets. He was jealous, on edge, wanting to pry the staff from her and delve into its mysteries on his own.

Of course, that could have merely been supposition on Brigid's part, but she wouldn't put it past North, if only Nehushtan wasn't protecting itself from his hands....

The staff gave a sudden lurch on the table where it lay. Brigid looked down at it, but there was no one near who could have disturbed it, and it was far too heavy to have been shifted by a breeze, if there had been one. She reached toward Nehushtan, and it shook, trembling like a nervous animal. Brigid had a brief mental image of an elongated puppy, its tail wagging with excitement at having its master return. The conjuration was a slap in the face, cold water splashing all over her, giving her a chill of surprise.

Brigid extended her hand once more. Nehushtan seemed awake now. Alive.

There was only one reason for that.

"Kane's coming for the staff!" she called out to North.

As if on cue, the moment she mentioned that, Nehushtan jerked from the table into her hand. It was a short hop, but something that should have been impossible for an inanimate staff, even if it was made from an ancient alien alloy.

But this was a legendary item, a relic of ages before mankind, a tool that had been utilized by biblical figures. Moses had utilized it to command miracles and summon plagues, and Solomon himself had battled the demons of hell, driving them from his kingdom into the depths of Africa.

If anything had a spark, a bit of a soul, it had to have been this staff, this odd walking stick whose pedigree allegedly stretched back to Atlantis, or whatever the Annunaki or Tuatha de Danann equivalent was.

Then one thought surged through her mind.

"Go!"

With that impulse, Brigid whirled and barreled straight past North, nearly running him over, the proximity of

Nehushtan to the archaeologist causing him to stumble backward as if blasted full in the face with pepper spray. Brigid didn't care about North. He had brought this upon himself, for no matter how much he appeared to be on the side of angels now, he had been a devil before. Let him suffer, let him writhe in pain for what crimes he had committed unto others in the past.

Brigid ran, her long legs carrying her in ground-eating strides. Even as she reached the heavy doors of the underground redoubt, the massive vault barrier meant to repel the forces of an atomic blast, she was receiving the first buzz of communication from Kane's Commtact.

"Baptiste! Baptiste! I need the stick now! Nathan's been injured!" Kane's voice cut through her skull, his words a shout that made the implanted nodes in her jaw vibrate powerfully with the thunder of his urgency.

"I'm on my way," she replied. "Nehushtan knew you needed it!"

"What?" Kane grunted.

Brigid hurtled up the stairs, taking them three at a time, using strength she'd never realized she possessed, power and agility surging through her from the warm, throbbing contact she had with the staff. She glanced down at it even as she reached the door to the power station, looking out toward the fence, and the forest beyond, where Kane, Grant and Nathan Longa had been exploring. For Nathan to have been injured, it had to have been an attack by the kongamato. For Grant to be apart from Kane, he had to be applying first aid to the injured young African.

And for Nehushtan to respond, unbidden, to Kane's thoughts and sudden acceptance of the need for it, the conclusion was obvious. The staff had a mind of its own, either of a living spirit, or perhaps some form of strange artificial intelligence, something built into it by the alien hands of the Annunaki. The concept of living technology was not unknown to the explorers of Cerberus. The Annunaki blurred the line between biological and machine, with their smart metal armors and ASPs, and the great ship *Leviathan*, which had come to Earth and awakened the overlords from their centuries-long slumber inside the genetic patterns of the humanoid barons.

The life and power within the staff itself seemed to transmit through her, and her brain hummed, abuzz with dozens of fluttering, racing thoughts that dashed across axons and neurons too fast for her to even contemplate. Images flickered across her mind's eye, even as she raced to the fence, her feet moving deftly, avoiding hazards even as her concentration was occupied by the incredible surge of pictures assailing her.

She realized that she was through the gates and bounding through the forest with the swiftness of a gazelle, her legs pumping as she leaped over tangling shrubs and long grasses. This must have been what it felt to be someone like Fand—possessed of more than human ability in mind and body.

And then she extended Nehushtan in her hand, holding it out.

Another took the staff.

In a moment, Brigid crashed back to normal. She'd been touching the might of the gods, and now she was once more limited to a mere human shell. Even her amazing eidetic memory couldn't make out a tenth of the events that had been played across the screen of her mind's eye. She dropped to her knees, not that she was gasping for breath. Her lungs and muscles didn't want for oxygen, not when she'd possessed the staff, or rather, it possessed her. She'd run, she'd raced along in the space of seconds.

"Baptiste?" Kane asked, looking down at her.

"Go," she whispered. "Nathan needs you."

"I didn't get fifty yards since I called you," Kane remarked.

Brigid looked up and saw Nathan on his back, Grant applying direct pressure to his chest. She blinked, eyes welling up with tears at the realization that Nehushtan hadn't hesitated once it felt the call. The first reaction, the sudden jump. That was the staff's realization of its owner's wound. The rest had been a response to Kane.

There was a new weight within her mind, a concentration of thoughts and ideas, jumbled and snarled so that even her intellect couldn't unkink it, make it intelligible.

However, that jumble settled, sinking into a miasma of muddled confusion. Brigid prided herself on her flawless memory, but the staff had given, and now it had taken away.

Frustration at forgetting something was a new experience, and she hated it. But Nehushtan had its reasons. The one thing she'd pulled from her brief contact with it, its momentary control of her body and senses, was that it *was* indeed alive, something that existed and knew and felt.

Kane's eyes seemed to glaze over for a second as the staff pressed into his grasp. It was only a momentary lapse, as if Kane were taken away, pulled elsewhere. And then he was back, running toward Nathan Longa and pressing the head of the snake-entwined staff against the side of the young adventurer.

Brigid Baptiste would have given anything to be in Kane's head for that brief moment before he jolted into vital activity.

KANE WAS A fast man, one of the fastest runners in the Cerberus redoubt. So when he broke into a run toward the Zambian power station, he expected to be halfway there before the Commtact could penetrate the bunker and pass the low-level radio interference that accompanied Nehushtan. The underground African redoubt, inured against nuclear assault and the radiation and fallout released, was naturally going to resist a radio signal.

But even as he made the decision to take up the staff, maybe a few moments of hesitation afterward, he heard Baptiste's frantic breathing come over the cybernetic implant.

"Baptiste! Baptiste! I need the stick now! Nathan's been injured!" Kane called. She might have taken a brief respite from examining the staff, grabbing a gulp of fresh air. If he could urge her on, he could cut down on the amount of time it would take to retrieve Nehushtan. This was an instance where seconds mattered. Grant was good at first aid, but a deep lung laceration was a nightmare of an injury to deal with. A man could do only so much with direct pressure to control the bleeding, especially if a brachial artery had been severed.

No, there was no if in this instance. The bright blood bubbling on Nathan's lips was unmistakable. He was bleeding fresh arterial blood, and he was coughing it up. The young man had minutes, and every moment was one step closer to death, either through fluid building up in his chest cavity or a loss of oxygen as the lung was no longer able to infuse the blood with the life-giving gas.

Kane's worry for Nathan's well-being was interrupted by Brigid's breathless response.

"I'm on my way," she cried. "Nehushtan knew you needed it!"

"What?" Kane grunted.

He paused a half step as the woman, seemingly breathless, spoke to him. The staff *knew* that Kane and Nathan needed it? His decision to use the stick and tap into its legendary healing powers couldn't have been broadcast, not if Brigid was still underground and Nehushtan producing a signal with which to repel Fargo North. They'd learned of the staff's radio interference capabilities when the archaeologist had drawn closer to the relic. Their Commtacts picked up the signal, obviously operating on a similar frequency to that of the cybernetic nanomachines that North had picked up in Garuda, the city of the Nagah.

But now Brigid was coming in loud and clear. Kane couldn't imagine that she had Nehushtan in her hand, but didn't wait for proof, and continued racing on. After ten seconds and over fifty yards of all-out racing, he spotted a shape bounding toward him along the trail to the power station. At first he thought it was another assault from the kongamato, but as soon as his eyes focused on her, he recognized Brigid Baptiste, moving with a speed and agility that he'd never seen before in any human, let alone the lithe, toned archivist. She had improved in her physique, her athleticism since her initial exile from Cobaltville, but no human could make five-yard strides or spring from tree trunk to tree trunk like a bouncing ball.

When the woman came to a halt, she held out the staff. Kane paused, stunned at the sudden surge of strength and speed that she'd displayed. He grabbed up Nehushtan as she offered it, her eyes blank, distant, as if she didn't even notice his presence.

Judging by his fear of the staff, she probably didn't. Even as he took the stick, he could feel a warmth, a living pulse within the wood, or maybe it was just his own heartbeat throbbing in the palm of his hand, amplified against the hardness of the staff.

"Baptiste?" Kane asked, looking down at her.

"Go," she whispered. "Nathan needs you."

"I didn't get fifty yards since I called you," Kane returned.

Brigid looked around, dazed, as if she'd been awakened from a dream. And then the world seemed to melt around him.

"Every time this happens," Kane heard a voice say.

"Every time we meet, there is an uncomfortable moment. Sometimes it lasts even as we're together for years. Other times, it is mercifully short."

And with that, Kane was in Africa, but gone was his Sin Eater and the skintight shadow suit. His jaw was bare of the cybernetic pintles that made the Commtact possible. He was clad in rough, grime-black clothing, his slouch hat covering his eyes against the harsh sun of an open field in the dark continent. An ornately handled Spanish sword, complete with a basket to protect his knuckles, rested in a belt sheath, while a simple cloth sash provided support for a pair of heavy, single-shot black powder pistols, the bottoms of their butts thick and round, like primitive clubs, perfect for use in smashing faces or breaking skulls when their powder and lead were spent, and even his had fallen by the wayside in battle.

He looked upon a man very similar to Nathan, an almost identical twin, though he was clad in a wrap that tucked up over one shoulder, his face lined with more years in the harsh African wilderness than the young man Kane had met. This person's facial features seemed wizened, his skin lined endlessly, sallow and gaunt. But judging from his physique, the decades bled off, for his arms and chest were corded and taut, his limbs lean and muscled. The stranger had a timeless quality about him.

"Nay, N'Longa," Kane heard himself say. He realized that he was a phantom, a fly on the wall of his own skull, a mere audience, not a participant. "I will not truck with your black arts. I am a man of faith, and neither I nor my Lord will suffer witchcraft."

"I insist, Solomon," N'Longa returned. It didn't escape Kane's notice that he shared Nathan's family name. This made sense, and perhaps it answered some of the questions he had about this sudden psychic episode and the doubts he felt about the staff. "The juju of this walking stick comes not from below, but from on high."

His hand reached for the haft of the staff. And once more he was jolted, hurled backward down the corridors of time.

Then he was in a cloak, a leather breastplate of armor, a metal band replacing the slouch hat. Again the staff was in his hands, but it was warm, and he felt an unending dread of the device. Once more there was a man resembling Nathan.

"But, sire…this is your staff. This is your standard!"

Kane blinked, looking at it. "It is too powerful for the hand of any one man."

"Then why give it to me, Suleiman?" Nathan's doppelgänger asked.

Kane watched himself rest his hand on the younger man's shoulder. "Because I know you. Your heart is good. And if any man knows how to use power, it is he who was without it."

Nathan's ancestor took the staff, cautiously. "But what of you? What of your needs?"

Kane looked around. There was smoke rising from a distant battlefield. Odd creatures lay twisted, scorched.

"Should I need this again, I will know where it is," he heard his voice say. "But what has been done this day…"

He turned away from the younger man, casting his eyes over the carnage strewed for miles.

"I need to get to Nathan," Kane interrupted.

"This has already happened. Here, in your mind, it unfolds at a seeming leisurely pace," Nehushtan told him, using his own voice. "But this is only an instant. You have the time necessary to save Nathan Longa's life."

With that, Kane snapped out of it. Nehushtan was in his grasp, and he was by Grant's side.

On instinct, he reached down, took Nathan's hand, and with both of them holding the staff, there was a sudden surge of warmth through the ancient tool.

Grant looked from Kane to the young man he was tending, then removed his hands from the deadly laceration. Already he could see little golden embers of light shining within the rent flesh, stretching out and bridging the deadly gash.

Kane grimaced, his body racked with the same pain that Nathan must have felt, or maybe it was something worse. Energy was being channeled through him, and he felt as if his whole body were a pair of hands clamped tightly around a rope, friction burning flesh across every cubic inch. Tears stung his eyes as the agonizing action of his body filtering untold power held him stone still, insensate to anything except the force that surged through him.

And then the pain was gone, and Kane toppled backward, landing in the dirt beside Nathan.

"Kane?" Grant asked nervously.

"I'll live. Nathan?" he croaked.

"His wound is closed," Grant answered. "And right now, he's hacking up whatever blood was in his windpipe."

"That's what that wonderful sound is," Kane grumbled.

"How do you feel?" Brigid asked.

"Like a human tea bag," Kane responded. He sat up. Nothing hurt at the moment, but the memory of the trauma, the searing fire slicing through his nerves, was fresh and raw.

For now, that didn't matter.

Kane—and Nehushtan—had saved the life of a brave young man.

But Kane couldn't forget the horror that he'd seen from the life two steps back. The horrible wreckage, the carnage, the dread of "Suleiman" as he gazed upon the remnants of a war. And that the only soldiers on the fields of the dead were himself, Nathan's ancestor and utterly destroyed alien monstrosities.

The fear of Nehushtan was not something new. It had

been with Kane through prior lives, and the fact that the staff remembered him only made him feel chilled under the hot African sun. Something that terrified one of his former incarnations, something worse than whatever army he chased to Africa and destroyed, had raised an alarm, summoning Kane to war with a terrible relic of a weapon.

Chapter 8

Nathan Longa and Kane were subjected to the incessant worries of the others for about an hour, which was about thirty minutes after they stopped feeling the last tremors of their predicaments. Nathan wiped anxiously at the corners of his mouth, still feeling the flakes of dried blood and spittle, despite having cleaned them off.

Kane, on the other hand, was still a little off balance. He tried to reconcile what he'd seen of the staff. He'd been shown the last two changing of hands in the space of a heartbeat, played out as if in a dream. The world was a better place for those transfers. More hints, more flashes of memory invaded his fevered brow, splayed there like a vid against the screen of his mind's eye. The details were hazy, half remembered, carrying with them the wild incredulity of a waking nightmare. If he could relate half of what he imagined... No, this wasn't imagination. This was Nehushtan, an ancient staff, wielded by god-kings and wayward champions.

It had split seas and engaged in battle against other weird weapons of its ilk. And it had picked Kane, chosen him, sifted through the thousands upon thousands of minds on Earth, choosing him as its wielder.

But the fear he held of it had changed. Kane's mind, Kane's being was still his own. The damned stick hadn't swallowed him, casting him into oblivion, uprooting him from his body and hurling him along the line to another identity, another organism in another dimension. He had recognized glimpses of other casements, other eras, ones that could not have existed within this world, at least as far as he could tell.

The real fear was of what he could become. Kane hadn't touched the staff since he'd healed Nathan of his injuries. He didn't want to know what he could be capable of with it in his hands. It was more than just another tool, as he'd imagined. It was an amazing weapon.

Wielding it, a man could be considered a god, or the right hand of said god. There were times when Kane had wanted to possess such power, as when he'd fought face-to-face with Enlil and his alien brethren. Kane tried to reason with himself, regarding the Sin Eater on his forearm.

As a magistrate, one of the first things he'd been drilled on was the discipline needed to carry the deadly folding submachine gun in its hydraulic forearm holster. With a simple motion, a twitch of his wrist, the Sin Eater would shoot into his hand. Without a trigger guard, the gun would fire immediately upon striking his hooked index finger. Kane had learned how to control that impulse, learned the discipline, the restraint necessary to prevent an unnecessary reaction. A magistrate in training needed to wear the holster and gun, unloaded, for six months before being trusted with ammunition for the weapon.

Just like the deadly firearm that could kill at a mere twitch and reflex, Nehushtan was something that required discipline. If Kane couldn't trust himself with the ancient staff, then he shouldn't trust himself with a less powerful gun. He'd fought for the world, and gladly placed himself into the line of fire between those who would maim indiscriminately and those who could barely protect themselves. He was the living line in the sand between predators and prey.

As such, Nehushtan, despite the power it demonstrated in Kane's memory, should not be so terrifying to him.

"Are you back with us?" Grant asked him.

"Never left," Kane answered.

"And grouchy as ever. Good. It didn't steal your soul."

Kane used his middle finger to wipe his lower eyelid, getting some dried seepage out of the way, another answer, half mocking, half serious, to Grant's diagnosis of his mental condition.

Neither Grant nor Brigid missed the implication, but they smiled.

"Welcome back," Brigid said. "What did you learn from Nehushtan?"

Kane narrowed his eyes. "Who said it talked to me?"

She frowned. "I was carrying it. It transmitted all manner of thoughts to me as I was bringing it to you…but I couldn't make anything out."

"Really?" Kane asked. If anything could surprise him, it was the knowledge that Brigid Baptiste, with her brilliant intellect and quick working mind, could be left befuddled by any instance. That Nehushtan's communications were gibberish only went further toward his realization that the ancient relic had some truly remarkable abilities.

Brigid shook her head, and her smooth brow wrinkled as she understood the source of Kane's question. "What did it tell you?"

"It didn't tell as much as it related memories," he answered. "I was viewing the world through the eyes of my predecessors. It told me that this wasn't the first time I was resistant to wielding it."

"Told you. As in spoke?" Brigid wondered.

"Remember our first incident with the Nagah at Garuda? When I was in telepathic congress with Enlil?" Kane asked.

"It occurred at the speed of thought. One moment you were drifting off, the next you were floored by what appeared to be a heart attack," Grant said.

"This occurred at that kind of time frame. I didn't realize

it at first," Kane muttered. "I just knew that I had to save Nathan's life, and didn't want to waste a single moment."

"You were able to interact with the device," Brigid mused. "Meanwhile, I seemed to have been more pulled along than anything else."

"It manipulated you?" Grant asked. The big man frowned, his gunfighter mustache emphasizing the expression.

Kane didn't know what caused Grant's discomfort at first, but then remembered the efforts of Enlil's son, the mad god Ullikummis, and his attempt to break Brigid Baptiste's spirit, turning her into his right-hand man. It had been a daring ploy by the stone-skinned Annunaki, but Brigid had found a way to fight against his brainwashing, storing her true identity away in her brain, allowing the appearance of servitude to shield her from further soul-breaking. She'd allowed Ullikummis to construct a shell that she had named Brigid Haight, and the brilliant archivist had proved herself an unwavering part of the rocky demon's crusade to conquer the world. Only at the last moment had she shed the false identity, and assisted Kane and Grant in defeating him.

That Nehushtan could work her over, make her into a puppet and courier for its transportation to Kane's hand showed that there was even more power to the artifact.

"So, we're all of the same opinion on Nehushtan," Kane stated. "It's a damned scary stick."

"No kidding," Brigid returned. "I'm just glad that you can handle it."

"Me, too," Kane muttered.

He spent the next half hour describing to them the sights he had seen. Battles in jungle tombs with gelatinous beings, wars with all manner of demonic soldiers who left scars upon the world, walks in ancient Atlantis, and journeys across barren, inhospitable deserts. Brigid seemed to brighten at mention of individual incidents, as if something had sparked within her memory.

If anything, that made Kane only more uncomfortable. It was as if Nehushtan had given the woman hints, but was still playing it close to the vest. The staff was allowing her glimpses into things it had fed into her mind, seeming to unlock them only with the proper reference from Kane himself. She remained quiet on this point, which proved unsettling. At least she was able to provide references for some of the things that Kane had observed, thanks to the staff.

While they talked, North, Lomon and Jonas were busy going over the creatures that Grant, Kane and Nathan had killed. It was North who did the majority of the postmortem examination of the creatures, while Lomon and Jonas provided security. Shuka was in the redoubt with the newly healed Nathan and the three travelers from Cerberus.

Finally, the two Zambians and the archaeologist returned from their investigation.

"Any sign of other kongamato?" Brigid asked as they arrived.

North shook his head. "No. Just the three of them, gutted. We took care of the bodies, dumping them in the river, but we found this." He held out a plastic bag that seems to be full of wet garbage.

North reached into the sack and pulled out a bloody, torn uniform fragment. There was a badge on the chest, and Nathan took a closer look.

"Lomon and Jonas already confirmed that it's a Harare military uniform," North stated. "And the badge shows that they're stationed at the power station on Harare's side of the river."

"Kariba to be exact," Lomon added.

Brigid looked closely at the torn scrap of uniform. "This was in the creature's guts?"

North nodded.

She examined it. Sure enough, there was a small sewn-on badge stating it was from a militia member protecting the Kariba station. She bit her lower lip, immediately turning her thoughts to the map of the region provided by Cerberus's computers and satellites. Kariba Dam was shared between the two territories of Zambia and Harare, a balance that had been in existence since Harare was known as Zimbabwe. The very hydroelectric dams and power stations that allowed the two nations to maintain twentieth-century living standards, with some improvements over the two hundred years in skydark's wake, had its terminus at the dam and the massive gorge it had been named after.

The Harare station was mirrored in Zambia to the north, across the Zambezi River, though the south station was the first of them built, Brigid recalled from her quick brush up. If they were in the Harare section of the Kariba gorge, it would explain why Nathan had been chased to the Zambezi, and why the Zambians had been taken by surprise. Nathan hadn't seen any details of the ominous shadow that had slain his father, but with the brutality of the kongamato, it was unlikely that the winged beasts would have been warned off by the arrival of a young man.

Then Brigid recalled the surge she had felt when she had been given power by Nehushtan. She also remembered that Nathan had described his own encounter with the creatures, and their unwillingness to come in contact with him or the staff as he swung it as a weapon. Him being relatively untouched in comparison to heavily armed soldiers had to be due to the protection Nehushtan provided.

"This means we're going exploring," Kane mused as he listened to Brigid's assessment of the new evidence. "Do you know anything about the Kariba station? I mean, we just came from one that had a redoubt hidden beneath it…."

"I'll conference with Bry. We'll look at records on the dam," Brigid said. "If there's nothing from Africa about it, there might be in some European databases, as this was designed by an Italian firm, which means that this could have been a front for the Totality Concept."

"Two redoubts, right across the river from each other?" Grant asked.

"It seems unlikely, I agree," Brigid responded. "But there might be a connecting tunnel, somewhere beneath the river. Most redoubts have their nuclear generators buried underneath enough bedrock to block their radioactive output, not only limiting the danger to people living within them, but lowering their profile for any outside source seeking it by radiation signature."

"Makes sense," Kane mused. "Do you have any direct communications with Kariba?"

Lomon rubbed his chin with his thumb. "Usually. And they should have called if they had come under attack…."

"We also didn't get a chance to send out our own distress call when those things struck," Jonas added. "And they were in a more blatant mood to intercept Nathan."

Nathan looked around at his new friends. His quest had brought all six people into perilous conflict with an inhuman foe. Lomon, Jonas and Shuka had lost a dozen compatriots to the kongamato, and Nathan himself had nearly died, costing Grant and Kane the opportunity to take one of the beasts alive and possibly speaking. However, neither group seemed to be flinching from the fact that they needed to head to the Harare nation's Kariba station to seek out the main body of the winged horrors.

"I know that I didn't do a good job…." Nathan spoke up at last.

Kane held up his hand. "It was a lucky strike by the kongamato."

"That's the problem. It wasn't a chance hit. This time, I wasn't under the protection of the staff," Nathan countered. "I'm pretty good with it…."

"Do we really want to bring him along?" Shuka asked.

Lomon shot a harsh glare at the younger Zambian. "This young man braved the frontier between his home city and the Zambezi River. Whether it was the staff or not, he has proved himself a man. If he wishes to join us in our fight… we simply do not have the manpower to reject anyone."

Lomon then looked toward Brigid, and nodded to her. "Would you turn aside her assistance, as well?"

Shuka glanced toward the flame-haired woman. Brigid Baptiste was tall, and the shadow suit she wore only emphasized her physique. She still had curves, but after years of battling the barons and their magistrate shock troopers, fighting pirates and conspirators, challenging godlings and other alien menaces, she was lean and fit. Shuka could see from the way her muscles moved beneath the black high-tech polymers, and could tell from the TP-9 pistol resting in its holster, and other assorted battle gear, that she was no stranger to conflict and danger. The exclamation point to his quick perusal of her worth as a fellow fighter was the sharpness of her emerald eyes, bright with defiance and confidence.

Shuka turned back to Nathan, who had the same resolve to join in this quest. "Seven against Kariba?" Shuka mused. "And the gods know how many kongamato are present there."

"I was thinking six," Kane offered. "No offense, Lomon."

The eldest of the Zambian soldiers nodded. "You want someone manning this base."

"In case reinforcements free up from the search for the beasts, I'd rather have a Zambian officer present to greet them. I'd also like you to keep in contact with Cerberus base. If something does show up banging at the door, a second team will arrive within moments," Kane stated.

"Similarly accoutered as you," Lomon added.

"CAT Beta," Grant explained. "Cerberus Away Teams. For when we need backup."

"I wouldn't be averse to having them come over now," Lomon mused. "I'd be outnumbered, but honestly, the three of you have the body armor and the technology to have overpowered us already if you wanted to."

"Then let's get in contact with Cerberus," Brigid offered. "I'll confer with Bry about the presence of plans and layouts for the Kariba Dam and its complex, and we'll have Domi and the others hop over."

With that, the seven people returned to the mat-trans control room.

Durga sat in silence as he listened to the report from Thurpa, his scout. One thing shared between the subcontinent of India and the continent of Africa was the presence of the hooded elapids known as cobras. As such, the presence of a Nagah humanoid in Africa was akin to the arrival of the Spaniards in Mexico. The Spaniards resembled their god, another serpent, the feathered Quetzalcoatl in human form, and thus, the Aztecs accepted the armed, technologically superior Spanish conquistadors into their city. Only the fighting skills of the Spaniards had kept them from being slaughtered by the Aztecs.

While the nations of Zambia and Harare were at relative peace with each other, and thanks to that state of equality, able to maintain higher standards of education as well as technology, the wastelands, stricken by famine and barbarians, were not so enlightened.

With powerful weapons culled from the stash that Enlil had shared with him, Durga's scout had impressed a militia, who assumed that Thurpa and his millennialist allies were, though not gods themselves, impressive enough to join. Once Durga's other men had found the cloning facilities for the kongamato, Thurpa had pointed out the added power these creatures would bring to their militia. So enabled, Durga's local forces were growing.

Makoba, a millennialist, from the Ivory Coast, interpreted the exiled prince's head motions as he conveyed Durga's satisfaction to Thurpa. Then Makoba seemed a bit confused.

"He wants to speak directly to you," Makoba said.

Durga blinked, then nodded, almost imperceptibly. The communicator was put to Durga's ear.

"Sir, there is one thing you must know above all others. When the young man was attacked, he was mortally wounded.

"So?" Durga rasped. His earlier speech had left him weak, but his annoyance was growing at the delay of this "vital news."

"In less than a minute, the red-haired human woman arrived with the walking stick that Nathan Longa had possessed. Kane then took the staff and healed him," Thurpa said.

Durga grunted.

"There was a powerful glow, and the youth no longer required direct pressure on a deep lung injury. His clothes were a mess, but I could see his wound through my scope. The skin was closed."

Durga swallowed.

"I know you wanted to draw Kane and his allies into a trap, but it was Kane who used the rod to heal Longa," Thurpa said. "Perhaps…"

"Yes," Durga responded.

"What is the plan?" Thurpa asked.

Durga's upper lip curled. Speech and movement were difficult things, so that even writing instructions was a laborious task. However, now that Kane possessed the artifact, one Durga already desired as a weapon of enormous power, and one that could open the hidden doors to a trove of power placed there during the days before the Great Flood, filled with alien devices and organisms beyond the wildest imagination of mere humans, he was motivated to action.

"Wait for me," Durga ordered.

With that, he nodded slightly, and Makoba took the comm back from his ear.

"We're going to Kariba?" the millennialist inferred.

Durga nodded.

"I shall get the Threshold, then," he stated.

Rather than be loaded into a chair for an arduous cross-country trek, Durga was glad to have discovered an ancient Annunaki Threshold, a gemlike artifact that could open up gateways, akin to how the mat trans and the interphaser of Cerberus redoubt did. It would take only instants, the alien device zipping him through hyperspace, along a network of lines of electromagnetic force that naturally crisscrossed the surface of the Earth.

Humanity had eventually learned how to duplicate the process, but it required massive bases to house nuclear power plants to generate the necessary energy to open temporary wormholes. The Threshold was actually attuned to a more readily available font of energy, receiving its power from an ancient Annunaki source that could transmit from a central generator to anywhere within a vast radius. Before the fall of *Tiamat,* Enlil's personal starship, Durga had assumed that the Threshold operated off of power from the bowels of the massive space cruiser. Since her near total destruction, Durga wasn't so certain, but considering Leviathan might not actually be dead, but in some hibernation state, his original hypothesis could have been correct. However, the Annunaki and their Tuatha de Danann counterparts likely had other sources of energy on Earth, for *Tiamat* had been away for aeons.

Whatever the means of generating the wormholes, the

Threshold had been necessary to get him from the Indian subcontinent to Africa, and to take Durga from parallax point to parallax point, cutting down on effort and peril in his search for the rumored location of King Solomon's mines, which were not only rumored to be a source of vast wealth in the form of gold and precious gems, but may have been the storage place of artifacts both wondrous and terrible.

Durga had never contemplated that the item he required to become whole and healthy again might be in the hands of the man who had left him a cripple before.

With grim resolve, he was going to meet Kane face-to-face, and somehow trick the man into bringing him back to life as something more than a storm of bitterness trapped in the shell of a broken body.

When that happened, woe unto all who stood in the Nagah prince's path.

His prize would be far more valuable than simply India. Africa was a vast continent, home to many secrets, and nearly limitless resources more than sufficient to be the stepping stone to global conquest.

All he needed was revitalization from the very stick he'd sent Thurpa and the kongamato to capture.

Chapter 9

Thurpa looked in derision at the mammals as they milled along the small trail. They were wary, alert that they were heading into a potential trap, but he was getting sick of their presence in his world. He took a grenade off his harness, savoring the weight of the tiny explosive device before arming it.

With a lob, he sent the egg-shaped blaster into the midst of the mammals who thought they were being so stealthy as they tried to move around Thurpa and his bodyguards.

When the grenade went off, the small pack of meerkats were reduced to shredded flesh and pulped bone. Fur and gore flew everywhere, and all but a couple of the millennialists and militiamen with Thurpa ducked at the sudden detonation.

Thurpa's chief lieutenant, Magruder, chuckled at the carnage wrought upon the tiny, ferretlike creatures by the hand gren. The mess left in the wake of the blast was horrific, and the gren had blown a huge crater in the ditch beside the road.

"Nice shot," he told Thurpa.

Thurpa regarded the millennialist, whose skull seemed too large for his slender body, made even more bulbous in appearance due to his bald head and large ears. His scalp, however, was the only part of him devoid of hair, as he had bushy eyebrows and a thick black goatee. Beneath the cuffs of his sleeves, long hair stretched from wrist to knuckles, making him seem more at home dressed in a leopard-print wrap and carrying a club, rather than carrying a high-tech rifle, a vest full of munitions and magazines, and a belt accoutered with plenty of electronics.

"Those chittering mammals outlived my patience for them," Thurpa grumbled. He glanced to Magruder. "Keep that in mind, Mac."

"Oh, I know," Magruder responded. The two men had managed to keep an amicable working relationship, but the millennialist's initial unease with the cobralike Thurpa was still simmering just beneath the surface. The "chittering mammals" remark couldn't have been more pointedly directed at Magruder and the rest of the humans in this patrol if he'd flexed those venom-filled fangs for emphasis.

Still, Magruder had one advantage over the mercenaries and militiamen who were in Thurpa's contingent. The millennialist knew just the right things to say to stay on the Nagah's good side, all the while keeping up promises of support that would go beyond any from Thurpa and his master Durga's prior benefactor, the Annunaki overlord Enlil. The Millennium Consortium had widespread influence in the postapocalyptic world, but the would-be technocracy was woefully underequipped in the face of technological prodigies such as Cerberus's Mohandas Lakesh Singh or former baronial dragon queen Erica Van Sloane, let alone standing up in the face of even the most scattered forces of the verlords themselves.

Durga had long ago hoped for the technological support of the extant Annunaki, but aside from the presence of a few ships and some Nephilim, the involvement of Enlil had been only cursory, merely sufficient to raise Durga's insurrection to the level of widespread chaos and carnage. The Nagah nation had suffered great losses among their leadership, and even to this day, believers in the cause of the "pure bloods" kept up attacks and mayhem.

Gamal, the leader of the militia that Durga had recruited

in Africa, had noted Thurpa's annoyance at the small creatures, so he had been expecting a vulgar display of force. Still, he gave a glare of admonishment, in full view of his soldiers, in order to keep their respect. Anything more, however, would entail some messy, and unnecessary, violence.

"I will warn your men the next time I have to exterminate some pests," Thurpa said by way of an apology that also didn't make him seem weak.

It was a delicate balance among the three parties. The Millennium Consortium expedition needed assistance and wanted power, so they had to acquiesce to the desires of their partners, yet not seem like leeches. Thurpa had some of the technology that Durga had uncovered and retained, and he truly needed manpower, but he was still an alien in a world that looked upon him with fright and suspicion. And Gamal was on his home turf, but the millennialists and the Nagah representative had abilities and resources that could be quite valuable. That required sitting and eating a bit of shit from these newcomers, provided they wanted to share, and not completely nuke his force.

"Thanks," Gamal replied. "So why are we no longer in a stealth profile?"

Thurpa looked the man over. "Because the plan has changed. The strangers who showed up have a resource that we could really utilize, but only if we can finesse them."

"What resource?" Gamal asked.

"How much do you know your Bible?" Thurpa countered.

"Which one? The Christian?" Gamal replied. "I know all of the big stories."

"Remember Moses?"

Gamal nodded. "Started Israel. Had a heart-to-heart with flaming shrubbery. Split a sea."

"The stick that Moses carried is a powerful instrument,"

Thurpa explained. "With that staff, he divided the Red Sea long enough for thousands of his people to cross it. Then he tapped it again, and the sea closed in, drowning the pharaoh and his forces who were in hot pursuit."

"The stick had magical powers?" Gamal asked.

"It was supposedly delivered unto him by God, when they first conversed," Magruder interjected. "There's some speculation that when these biblical stories were written, it was by primitive people trying to interpret the strange and unusual. The staff might have been an artifact, a conduit for extraterrestrial powers. And we have proof of extraterrestrial interference in the history of Earth."

Gamal tilted his head, then looked back to Thurpa. "He does know that you're a humanoid cobra, right?"

Thurpa snorted, amused at Magruder's lack of obvious proof standing right next to him.

"Hey, he could be a mutie." Magruder spoke up in defense of himself.

Gamal shrugged. "Really, I don't think there are too many recessive cobra genes in human DNA. No, Thurpa, you are a designed creature. And while it might be two centuries since the last people in the northern atmosphere published articles about these experiments, I don't think there are too many scientists advancing genetic manipulation. Not on a scale where Thurpa has a bunch of friends. In sum, aliens put the Nagah together."

Thurpa smiled.

Gamal leaned closer to Magruder. "While we poor Negroids in the dark continent appreciate your helping us rise from the stone age, we ain't stupid."

Magruder nodded, ashamed of the dress-down. Thurpa's sensitivity to heat, aided by IR-sensitive pits near his nostrils, detected that the millennialist's ears were growing warmer from embarrassment Thurpa made a mental note to keep a close eye on the man. Such a clash of wills would inevitably lead to a moment where Magruder wanted to get even. If that happened, Thurpa didn't want to get caught in the crossfire between the consortium and Gamal's militia.

"All right, gentlemen," Thurpa said, trying to disarm the tension of the exchange.

"So, this is an alien artifact." Gamal spoke up. "Why not keep to our plan of killing the people holding on to it?"

"Because there's evidence that the staff will only demonstrate its abilities in the right hands," Thurpa explained. "The stick might not work without the proper DNA signature, or even the proper mind in contact with it."

"It's telepathic?" Gamal asked.

Thurpa shrugged. "Whichever, we cannot risk an armed conflict. Not until we are sure we can use the power of the artifact."

"And what about the rest of the group with the staff?" Gamal asked.

"Leverage," Thurpa offered.

Gamal nodded. "We can do leverage."

Thurpa watched the smile grow across the man's face. There was ruthless delight shining in his big brown eyes. It was close to the same expression he'd seen in his liege, Prince Durga, as he plotted his vengeance. Thurpa could respect that kind of ruthlessness. It was something to watch out for, fearfully. But utilized on his side, it could be a useful weapon in his quiver, especially in the face of threats other than Gamal and his militia.

"Right now, we want you to lie low. Disappear into the terrain. We need to look as if we are besieged by the kongamato," Thurpa stated. "This way, we'll look as if we're in more of a position to need their help, rather than be an intimidating force."

Gamal smirked. "But once they show up, we can move in and surround them. Catch them between two us."

"Only on my signal," Thurpa said. "Chances are, you might not be needed. Not if we can use other means."

Gamal's smirk faded. "Hopefully, I guess."

There was a crackle of ionized air in the distance, and the three leaders turned their attention toward it. Gamal and Magruder appeared confused, but Thurpa had been expecting this arrival.

"Gentlemen, I would like to introduce you both to my sovereign," he announced. "He is the prince of the true blood, born of the regal cobra lineage, and a warrior of the realm. He was brought low by Kane only through trickery and high explosives, and yet even that could not slay him. I present to you Durga, the future king of Garuda and the fist of Enlil."

And then Durga appeared, being carried down the access road on a platform born by six strong men. One of his arms was draped almost lazily over the back of the reclining couch, and his other limbs were stretched out carefully. The only thing that wasn't relaxed and sedate were his eyes. They were black, yet the glint of sunlight off them seemed to be like the fires of hell burning within his skull, attempting to break out.

Durga's carriers wore the same gray jumpsuits as the rest of the Millennium Consortium, and each had his Calico pistol hanging low at his waist, dangling on a shoulder sling. They didn't seem to mind carrying the prince, perhaps because there were six of them. They remained quiet, looking straight ahead, not even acknowledging Magruder's presence, nor his small coterie assembled with Thurpa.

"This is your king," Gamal said aloud, looking the cobra man over as he regarded the assembled humans with that sizzling, simmering ire.

"Yes," Durga responded, matching Gamal's gaze. "You... warlord."

Gamal smiled. "I am a warlord of the Panthers of Manosha. One of four."

Durga nodded.

"It is for you that we must retrieve this staff," Gamal stated.

"Rewarding." Durga's voice crackled.

Gamal bowed his head. "You refused to die when you were blown up. And that was how long ago?"

"Months," he responded.

Gamal stepped closer. "You still have your fangs."

Durga smiled, tight-lipped.

"And even if I tried to kill you here and now, you would make me pay for it. Not your men, but you," Gamal added.

"Venom," he said simply.

"I would see you at your strongest, my prince," Gamal said. Then he turned back to Thurpa. "I need a comm to keep in touch with you."

Thurpa motioned to Magruder, who produced one from his belt.

"Good luck, Durga," Gamal stated.

With that, he gave the hand signal for the Panthers of Manosha to disappear into the forest.

Thurpa was impressed with the speed and professionalism of the militia as they took to hiding, fading from view within a minute.

"Soon," Durga croaked.

He looked back to his prince.

"Vengeance," Durga added.

"We will have it. Kane and his allies have conducted autopsies on the kongamato we sent after them. They discovered the contents of their stomachs," Thurpa said. "Then they all went down below. I can presume that they're calling in reinforcements."

Durga nodded in assent. "Kariba," he ordered.

With that, Thurpa, Magruder and the millennialists gathered up their gear and began the march toward the Kariba power station. Thurpa noted that the skies above were dotted with the winged kongamato, soaring and gliding upon air currents, forming aereal cover for the procession.

Thurpa remained quiet, but he was worried about Gamal's posturing. Yes, Durga still had his fangs, and most importantly, his venom sacs, which could project streams of burning, blinding toxins into the face of any who attacked him. Thurpa had even seen Durga punish an insolent follower without warning. There was nothing preventing the prince from blinding Gamal, possibly for life, if the African militiaman was intent on causing harm.

By the same token, that venom would do nothing to save Durga in a violent conflict between man and Nagah. He would maim his murderer, but the spray of venom was not a shield. Still, he had not flinched at the closeness of Gamal. There was a defiance in Durga's eyes. The Nagah prince would perhaps die, but he would not back down. There was no fear in him, not after suffering the pains of hell for months and months.

Of course, the situation would have turned to shit for Thurpa if the two came down to it. The millennialists and Thurpa were heavily outnumbered. Even without Gamal at their head, the Panthers would have overwhelmed the group, slaughtering them.

"You doubt your master?" A woman's voice cut into his thoughts.

Thurpa whirled, taken completely off guard. The speaker, over six feet in height, had a sharp-featured face, pointy chin and pert, upturned nose, plus an odd, russet-red tint to her skin. Her eyes were brilliant beacons of emerald that suddenly held the Nagah's attention. He stopped walking, jaw slack, as he studied the vision before him.

"Who…?" he began.

"Queen," Durga stated.

Thurpa pulled his attention from the unusual, bewitching woman before him. He couldn't believe he had just become enraptured by a human female. Sure, he could find unenhanced women attractive, but he always felt as if his truest desire was for the cool, shimmering scales of a fellow Nagah, the genetic product of an ancient god's tampering with the genome of mankind. Yet the crimson woman drew him, anchoring his thoughts upon her.

And how in the hell did she know what he was thinking?

"There is a reason why Durga has taken a shine to me," she stated softly, striding close to him on tiptoe. "My talents are many," she whispered in his ear.

"Neekra," Durga said. Thurpa immediately knew it was her name, when those emerald eyes glimmered.

The woman gave off an air of seduction, but as much as Thurpa felt his manhood stir, something dark touched him as well. If anything, the dull dread he felt only enhanced her enchantment. It was as if she were dangling raw, fresh bait in front of him, still alive and kicking, much like how the more feral and manly of the young punk Nagah loved to experiment. Thurpa and his friends used to huddle in caverns and engage in swallowing live rodents, aping the actions of a red-jumpsuited race of alien reptiles from an old television miniseries.

Thurpa remembered the sensation of having a living mouse in his throat, at once disgusting and exhilarating. He'd been defying convention, while engaging in the needless suffering of a living mammal. He'd enjoyed the thrill and the rush, which had overcome the nauseating feeling of having that, twisting thing stuck down his esophagus. It was wrong, horrible, but it had felt good.

Neekra had that same forbidden flavor, tantalizing enough to make him ignore the alien, gut-churning notions that went along with her presence.

And then Thurpa was free of that heady rush of seductive decadence as she made her way to Durga's side. She ran one long, talon-nailed finger along his scaled chest, and Durga smirked at her.

"And you are the new queen?" Thurpa asked, shaking himself out of his dazed state.

"Not of you and your kind, not yet. But the time comes," Neekra said. "My kingdom is farther away. It will take us a brief journey to reach it, and to awaken it."

"Prize," Durga said softly.

Her kingdom was the elusive prize Durga had sought. But Thurpa hadn't heard anything about the arrival of this "queen." Where exactly did she come from?

"Questions, questions. You possess too many to answer, at least at this time," she murmured, again plumbing Thurpa's thoughts as easily as if he had spoken aloud. It was becoming frustrating, but he knew that Durga must have allied himself with her for a reason. Thurpa would wait and listen for answers from his prince.

She smiled at that decision.

"I must away, handsome one," Neekra said to the fallen prince. She leaned in close to him, her lips brushing his cheek easily, as she was taller than the men carrying him. "Be well."

"Yes," Durga responded.

With that, the red-skinned woman turned and stepped into the brush. Thurpa expected to follow her movements, given the sheen of her flesh, but within moments, she, too, had disappeared.

"I'm starting to get a little tired of how easily these people can fade into the jungle," Thurpa grumbled.

"Goddess," Durga interjected. He waved one of his clawed fingers toward the stretch of forest where the woman had faded.

Thurpa glanced to Magruder and then Makoba, who

had remained quiet during the whole exchange. "Can we trust her?"

Durga locked eyes with his minion. "Must."

Of course we have to, Thurpa thought. The woman was a mind reader.

Any attempts at duplicity against her would be seen through almost instantly. Thurpa made the choice to go along with her, to project nothing but confidence in her relationship with Durga. Anything else would be tantamount to suicide should she discover his true feelings about her.

And again he had that sensation in the pit of his stomach. Neekra was a dangerous woman, but her beauty and grace, the succulent tones of her voice, were almost hypnotic. Legends said that cobras could enchant their prey, freeze them with something beyond fear, to produce the kind of heat and light that would draw in victims like moths. This woman, this queen of Africa, possessed those abilities and then some. He could easily envision her as a snake charmer.

Neekra.

"Enough," Durga spit.

"I apologize," Thurpa responded.

"To Kariba," Durga ordered.

Thurpa glanced sidelong toward Makoba, who remained stony-faced. Whatever he thought about Neekra seemed as if it would stay deeply buried. Maybe beneath enough layers that the woman couldn't get to it.

Thurpa realized that he was pondering way too much about this. He had to shut down his thinking. Too many doubts would be hard to hide, make him vulnerable if Neekra was a true danger, able to turn him into her prey.

There were enough dangers in Africa to be concerned about. And one of those dangers was approaching with a staff of ancient power, the only tool that could bring his liege back to full life and strength.

Chapter 10

The decision of who was going to be on the exploration team seemed smart and simple in the end, but the discussion about it had gone on for a couple hours, until Kane felt as if he were on the verge of shooting out a window and bounding into the jungle by himself.

Domi and Nathan would be joining them on this excursion, leaving Sela Sinclair in charge of the Cerberus delegation staying behind at the Victoria Falls redoubt. Sinclair was a black woman, which might make things more diplomatic, and with a background as a United States Air Force officer, she was as good a leader as any. Colonel Sinclair and the hulking former Magistrate Edwards would prove to be worth a small army, given the Cerberus redoubt weaponry that they had brought, and Sinclair's African-American features would make the culture shock of newcomers less jolting should Zambian reinforcements arrive to bolster Lomon, Jonas and Shuka.

Kane also felt better with a smaller troupe. Fargo North would be tagging along, which was something Kane didn't enjoy, but if they were overrun by kongamato, Domi was a good fighter to have on hand. While Lakesh often spoke of the efficacy of the trinity of Kane, Grant and Brigid Baptiste, the Cerberus explorer was fully aware of the value of the feral little albino woman. Her senses, her ferocity and her instinctive wits had helped to balance nearly impossible odds before. If Lakesh envisioned Kane, Grant and Brigid as the Three Musketeers, then Domi was their D'Artagnan.

She had grown from the wild child who went from illiterate wilderness waif, stuck in a hell pit where she was forced to sell her sex, to a girl who'd learned how to read, and was willing to risk her life for the safety of others.

With Lakesh and Brigid as her teachers, Domi's education could expand. In five years, she'd developed plenty, but her future, thanks to those two, would be phenomenal.

Right now, she was crouched next to the unmistakable depression of a grenade blast crater. Her nose was wrinkled with disgust.

"Grenade blast. Was it a battle?" Kane asked. So far, they'd been following the tracks of a procession of men. By first count, it seemed as if there were at least forty of them, but up ahead, the group seemed to diminish in size. Since the foot traffic showed no sign of any backtracking, Kane was certain that the force had split into two. One was continuing on toward the Kariba power station, while the rest had broken off and melted into the jungle around them.

"Not a battle. Just cruelty," Domi answered. She held up a tuft of bloody fur. "Gren blew up rodents."

Kane nodded, suddenly aware why her nose was wrinkled in disdain. Someone had utilized a hand grenade to eliminate a pest for no other reason than to blow it up. A grenade toss wasn't the ideal means of taking meat for the night's cooking pot. There would be more fragments than actual chunks of flesh. The small creatures had been blasted into confetti. He looked around, and was certain that the act must have been done by newcomers to this region. There was little sign that the bandit hordes that surrounded the city-state of Harare had the resources to eliminate rats with precious weaponry, and the millennialists that Kane suspected North was still allied with were similarly stingy about their high explosives.

The cruelty of using the grenade and the "freedom" of wasting it pointed toward one force: Durga, or one of his people, had destroyed the small rodents. Kane was acutely aware of the Nagah prince's penchant for referring to humans derisively as mammals. It wasn't too far removed to extrapolate that spite for mammals to one of his followers.

"Good woodsmen," Domi mentioned. "Disappeared quick. No tracks."

"Up until this point, they didn't care if anyone noticed them," Kane agreed. "But something happened just after that gren went off."

"Started talking. And look." Domi pointed toward the earth. Kane, with his point man's instinct, was able to notice the depression there and a disturbance in the long grasses leading from a copse of trees. It was a faint trail, nothing like the trampling of forty sets of feet on a dirt road, but he was certain there were few who could have picked up the subtle difference and variations as well as either he or Domi. At times Kane thought the albino girl was half wildcat, as much of a hunter as any of Sky Dog's tribe. Kane had already been a great tracker during his time as a magistrate for Cobaltville, and only sharpened those skills among the Lakota.

"Someone new arrived," he mused.

The millennialists must have encountered some of their own allies. Thus reunited, they could have sent the other group, likely a local militia, off to form a secure perimeter for whichever trap was being set. Kariba station was too obvious a location for the kongamato to not be some sort of bait. Anything the Millennium Consortium was involved with stank to high hell, part of the reason why he had such loathing for Fargo North.

The technocrats had little concern for human life, only that they had subjects to rule.

"Should I go hunting?" Domi asked. Her hand rested on the rubberized handle of her knife. Though she had a suppressed Copperhead, the feral albino girl was by far one of the deadliest human beings alive with a length of sharpened steel. Granted, Kane was certain that Shizuka won in pure swordsmanship, but he'd seen Domi handle multiple opponents, grown men easily twice her weight, and take them down brutally.

Kane was fully aware of the explosive violence that she was capable of, and he often was glad for that razor-sharp precision of hers. But this wasn't the time to split the group. Five people were already a small enough force tactically. Further dividing them on a hunt for a potential group of trappers that might or might not be hiding out would be dangerous.

Especially considering that it would be Domi fighting against vastly superior odds, and against men with massive firepower. She would have to keep from making a single mistake, and they would turn on her in a flash.

Kane didn't want to risk her on such a dangerous side mission, not when they had their ace in the hole back at the Victoria redoubt. If a local militia did surface, Kane would activate his Commtact, and Edwards, Sinclair and the Zambians would take them hard and fast.

It was a ruthless tactic, but Kane and Domi had confirmed that at least twenty-five men had dispersed into the woods. Those kinds of numbers were plain deadly.

And that wasn't counting the predatory kongamato.

"No. No hunting," Kane said. "In fact…"

"Calling Sela and Edwards," Domi finished for him.

KANE WAITED UNTIL Brigid, Grant, Nathan and North caught up with them. Kariba station was still a couple miles away, and they had the cover of the intervening forest. Kane kept his eyes and ears peeled for signs of the militiamen who were in the brush, but their leader probably was too smart to leave his force close enough to the dirt road to be noticed except by the sharpest of eyes. Both Kane and Domi made an effort to trail the soldiers, but they were good.

Too good.

Given some of the rifles that Kane saw available, they could be three to four hundred yards distant, cushioned from discovery even by his and Domi's razor-keen senses, yet still visible targets to those snipers.

"So, what did you two little scouts find out poking in the dirt?" Grant asked.

"I found out that you're in no big hurry when it's up to us to look for trouble," Kane said.

Grant smirked. "Did you see any bat-winged horrors swoop down on you?"

Kane's lips curled, and he squinted one eye. "No."

"You are welcome," his friend answered.

Kane rolled his eyes at his joking. There were times when the two men actually did get on each other's nerves. But they had been together for so long that Brigid likened them to an old married couple. "Fine. I'll give you the rundown."

With that, Kane gave his partners a quick summary of what he and Domi had tracked and recovered from prints on the dirt road. The presence of a split force and a rendezvous with another, smaller group brought looks of concern to all present, except for North, which Kane had expected. However, contrary to his belief that North was still a patsy of the consortium, the archaeologist's face was screwed into a mask of pissy annoyance.

Kane made a mental note to decide whether he cared at all about North's ire. As it was, it was a sign that the man was at cross-purposes with the millennialists. However, Kane was fully aware that North had played fast and loose with his alliances during their first encounter at Garuda. Maybe the sudden onset of grumpiness could be attributed to his disgust at their incompetence, or to the sharp senses of Kane and Domi in detecting the group. Either way, Kane wasn't going to ease up on him.

"I told you, Durga was with the consortium," North said.

"And I told you that sounded like a convenient story," Grant snapped. "Just because it has elements of truth doesn't mean shit."

North bristled at the insinuation, and Kane wondered if the slightest notion of violence on the untrustworthy archaeologist's part would summon a ham-sized fist into his face. So far, Kane and Grant had been playing with kid gloves in regards to the man, but North's history of maiming and murder was long and gruesome. Though he claimed to have turned over a new leaf, this "blossom" before them was grown in soil soaked with blood and pain. The sins of his past bore a heavy cost, and if there was one thing that the explorers of Cerberus redoubt believed in, it was justice for all, even those they had never met.

"I am warning the two of you." North spoke slowly. "I am fully aware of who I was when we first met. I am tolerating your low opinion of me. But I am not your enemy. Durga is. And if it comes to defending myself, when I have to, there will be no second chance for either of you to cause me harm. Ever."

"We've heard that plenty of times," Kane said. "We're still here."

North didn't say anything more, but Kane's bravado was only halfhearted. He knew that he and his partners were up to many challenges, but there had also been times when they had gotten through on blind luck and by the skin of their teeth.

Given the knowledge and power that North had obtained from the Nanite Matrix beneath Garuda, they could well be dealing with someone on the same scale as Maccan or Enlil. He was tolerating their abuse, maybe because whatever they were throwing at him glanced off him like raindrops against a Sandcat's hull. North's glaring eyes held menace and crackled with hatred. If he had been a cruel and vindictive scoundrel before his brain's "upgrade," what kind of a horror would he be if he cut loose and unleashed that power?

Every instinct in Kane told him that he should just raise the Sin Eater, press the barrel against the man's forehead and blast it into a million pieces, emptying magazine after magazine into the splattered brain until not even pulpy, quivering bits of gray matter remained. He held off on that urge, if only for the fact that if the first shot didn't work against North, there was no telling what kind of wrathful genie would be released.

"We'll keep trusting you," Kane said. "But that doesn't mean we won't be wary."

"Trust me," North repeated. "You should. Because if I wanted it, you would have been a corpse a thousand times over."

Kane looked toward Nathan, who held the staff Nehushtan. The stick seemed to repel North, but he'd found a distance from it that he could tolerate, about eight feet. Nathan decided to save the day by stepping close to Kane's side. North winced, backing away from the ancient stick.

"Behave. Both of you," Nathan said, with an authority beyond his nineteen years.

Kane nodded. This was no time for squabbling. Grant had brought up a major threat that could strike from above, and there were likely militiamen in the woods, and an armed party of millennialists at the Kariba Dam power station.

Nathan looked especially at Kane and Grant. "Both sides, actually. No manhandling...unless you're throwing me out of the path of a rampaging kongamato. Then toss me like a beanbag."

Grant smirked. "You got it, Nathan."

"Are we going to stand around all day yakking?" Brigid asked, impatience clinging to each word.

"No, we've got people to do, things to kill," Kane replied.

North nodded. "We can't give Durga a chance to explore any farther in Africa. The mines he seeks are where Suleiman imprisoned demons. The kongamato are the smallest, least powerful of those creatures. Considering that Suleiman was armed with an Annunaki artifact to drive them into their cells tells much about the horrors entombed within."

Kane fought the urge to sneer, to engage in another pissing contest with the millennialist archaeologist. Something was nagging at him. North might have been granted the powers of the ultimate badass powerhouse, but the way he acted was just not right. Even before, North had done his best to keep himself ingratiated with the Cerberus explorers. This time he was rattling sabers just for the sake of getting on Kane's nerves.

Was this part of some secret plan? Again, there were so many things around them, all manner of dangers, that taking the time to pick this apart would be stone-cold deadly.

"Let's get going," Kane said, agreeing with Brigid. As usual, the brainy, beautiful woman was the voice of reason. He would trust his instincts when it came to sudden, nearby threats, but not when he was sure that those senses were being tugged at for the sake of making him hair-triggered to go off half-cocked. There were people who needed help. The blood on the Kariba uniforms was real enough. Humans had died and parts of them had ended up in the bellies of the kongamato.

North, sinner or saint, would have to wait for his ultimate judgment.

Right now, there was a flock of carnivores with inhuman strength and the ability to fly threatening the countryside between Harare and Zambia. They had to be stopped, even if Kane had to tolerate the presence of the devil in his very own camp.

DOMI LOOKED BACK and saw that the others had caught up with Kane. She was itching to get moving. Standing around and talking, especially in enemy territory, was not her favorite activity in the world. The feral girl regarded North with a deep-down loathing based on their first encounter. North had been entirely too smooth and buttery in his first speech, tossing out compliments and condescension thick enough to drown in.

The man had been tangle-brained then, willing to whip the skin off the backs of innocent men and women in order to find trinkets from worlds dead for thousands of years. Now, he *felt* different to her, but it didn't make her more or less comfortable around him. There was something unnatural about him, more than human. He had this strange, eerie calm. His eyes didn't dart from face to face as someone was talking. He didn't react to outside stimulus, and yet it seemed as though he missed nothing.

North claimed that the tiny bugs within his brain—nanites, Brigid Baptiste had called them—had enhanced his intellect and his senses. Kane said that the man was able to jam their communications, seemingly at will. Domi tried to put her finger on what unsettled her, but even as she tried, the thought was elusive. He just didn't seem... human anymore.

Certainly, he sounded that way. He spoke normally. He walked, he breathed. But his head remained still. He didn't tilt it, didn't turn his gaze to speak to anyone face-to-face, to *look* at them. It was as if he was blind, and yet he navigated the world perfectly, never stumbling, never tripping, always aware of every movement about him.

It was creepy.

"All right," Sela Sinclair said on the other end. "Lomon just told me that there was a Zambian company of soldiers about six hours from the station. If you don't run into trouble before, we'll come out and meet you then."

"And if not?" Domi asked.

"We drop everything except our guns and come smack that militia right in the ass," Sinclair concluded.

Edwards's chuckle reverberated through her skull. "Provided you leave anything for us to smack."

"Could be bad. Soldiers might have bat things on their side," Domi said.

She immediately caught the sudden change in her diction. She'd begun dropping prepositions, speaking more primitively. That happened when she was tense and on edge.

Fargo North was a good candidate for her unease.

And then there were the kongamato, presumably under the control of the Millennium Consortium.

Throw in a local militia who had a reputation for spitting their prisoners alive and roasting them for a feast, at least according to the Zambian guards at Victoria Falls redoubt, and Domi was surprised she wasn't reduced to monosyllabic grunts.

Finally, there was Durga.

The last time she had seen him, he was close to twenty feet long, a writhing half man, half stony python with the strength to smash through rocky walls as if they were made of cardboard. He was ruthless, bulletproof, and had the reflexes to catch her and hurl her like a rag doll. She still ached some from that encounter.

If Durga himself wasn't enough of a menace, she also remembered the last time she'd gone up against a couple of his followers, two full-transformed Nagah. They were strong, and their venom had left her blinded temporarily. If not for their battle being in waist-deep sewage, she'd have suffered even worse, but her fight against the two of them had nearly killed her.

Domi had little fear of any opponent, no matter how strong, but to date, her battles against the worst the Nagah had to offer had been true tests of her strength and courage.

Yes, she was on edge. But that was good. Fear made her smarter, stronger, faster. If her elocution dropped to grunts and snarls, then too bad. If she had to fight, she wasn't going to talk anyone to death.

She switched channels back to Kane's almost instantly, spotting movement up ahead.

"Trouble," she whispered.

He didn't have to answer; she already heard him coming to her side, though she had to stretch to hear his approach. He moved quickly, but walking heel to toe, finally kneeling by her side, his breath smooth and shallow, falling into silence. The two people, obscured by the long grass, watched as a tall figure moved in the foliage off to the side of the dirt road.

It was a man, but as he struggled into view, they could see that he was not in good shape. Blood dripped off him, and farther into the trees something large and strong was on the move.

Without a thought, Domi was on her feet, long strides taking her closer to the wounded man. Almost as an afterthought, she realized that the figure before her was other than human. She could tell by the thick muscled hood that connected the sides of his head to his shoulders and the glimmering, iridescent scales twinkling in the sunlight. Blood poured over cracked lips, and frightened eyes looked up and behind him.

Kane had moved with her, and she heard the hydraulic snap of his holster launching the Sin Eater into his palm.

The Nagah on the road collapsed, his arms no longer able to hold up his weight.

Out of the thick forest, a kongamato appeared, screeching its predator cry so loudly that Domi felt her ears would burst.

She turned toward the attacking monster.

It didn't matter that the Nagah could be one of the same murderous monsters that had slain innocent nurses back in Garuda, the powerful bruisers who had nearly killed her in that sewer fight.

Domi had grown, had learned much.

And most of all, she'd learned that the strong rose to the defense of the weak and the injured.

The feral girl unleashed her own savage cry.

Chapter 11

Thurpa clutched his chest. He'd never thought that anything could cut the thick scales running down the front of his torso so easily, but the hard, almost armor-plate shell had been split easily by the cruel talons of the kongamato. He struggled forward, gasping for breath, spitting from split lips that oozed blood into his mouth so that he nearly choked with every inhalation. He was in deep trouble.

How the hell had he gotten himself into this situation?

That didn't matter. All he could do was run, knowing that beasts were on his trail, hounding him, hunting him down to rip him limb from limb. Those things were on the warpath, and he'd barely survived first contact. Those kongamato weren't fooling around, and if he stopped, if he stumbled, he could count the remainder of his life in seconds.

But now the trees and bushes that had hindered the progress of the winged horrors on his heels were gone, and he had nothing to cover him. He crashed to his knees, still clutching his wounded chest, blood spilling from broken lips and a torn cheek. He could barely think, his head was reeling so badly. Even with his fingernails sinking into the dirt of the roadside ditch, the ground seemed to sway. He kept his elbow straight, fought for balance, but the world spun about him.

Blood loss? Head trauma?

Branches snapped. Leaves rustled. Something thick and solid and fearsome was coming closer. Thurpa wished that he hadn't dropped his sidearm, but he was battered, bleeding. He could barely keep his balance while on one hand and both knees. The breaking of a branch as loud as a gunshot made him whirl around, and with that, all hope left him. His eyes widened as he saw the apelike creature, its ugly, conical skull counterbalancing a fang-filled beak floating between bulbous shoulders and above chest muscles that were like pulsing boulders on its furry chest. As it balanced on its half-sized, almost comical hind legs, its long, freakish arms reached out, trailing leathery membranes from its waist to the end of a wickedly clawed, impossibly long finger.

The wounded Nagah let out a groan. "Why, Durga…"

And with that, his arm folded beneath him and he crashed against the side of the ditch. Strength gone, the kongamato wailing its brain-spearing sonic wail, Thurpa felt himself slipping from consciousness, the contents of his skull starting to liquefy. He just hoped that the end was quick….

But then a woman's voice rose to a screech in defiance against the kongamato's. There was a crash of bodies just above him and Thurpa rolled over to see a lithe, almost catlike shape lunging into the winged frame of the hell beast that was chasing him.

DOMI DIDN'T HAVE a lot of time to consider her tactical options. The kongamato was nearly atop the wounded Nagah, and she didn't dare let the battle drop on top of him, for fear of exacerbating his injuries. With all her strength, she launched herself like a human missile, intercepting the winged predator from the side. She knew that she didn't have the size and power to stop the creature's forward momentum cold with a head-on tackle, but even her hundred pounds of weight could deflect the beast from its deadly course.

Domi didn't think of this in terms of physics, in mass or momentum, or conservation of energy. Rather, she thought of it in a practical manner, just as she had experienced it in the Outlands. She remembered how she'd seen a coyote bring down a pronghorn antelope, which was faster and a little bigger, tackling it from the side, catching it off guard with a blindside attack. Coyotes didn't do mathematical equations in planning their moved, and neither did the feral Domi, and yet the end result was the same. Both the hunting canine and the albino girl managed to bring down a larger, faster, stronger enemy using tactics rather than brute force. She hit the kongamato at a right angle, arms snaking around its neck, feeling the incredible musculature shifting beneath the creature's skin.

Domi herself was no slouch in the department of deceptive strength. A life of hardship in wilderness and urban war zones had hardened her to toughness beyond what a twentieth-century albino would have had. If she'd been born before skydark, she would have been frail, her pale flesh far too weak to withstand harsh sunlight, eyes easily burned out by the brightest days. But Domi, in spite of or even thanks to her difference, fought harder. She refused to die. She didn't possess bulging muscles, and yet they were tightly corded, taut against bones that had been banged around in multiple combats, strengthened by stress. Because of this, she was able to dig deeper into her reserves, last longer, hold on harder, move faster than others her size. Domi and the predator both slammed into the berm alongside the road. The creature's beaked snout took the brunt of their combined impact with a sickening crunch, the kongamato stuck with Domi hanging around its neck, perched between its broad shoulders, at its back.

The winged beast wrenched itself upward, twisting in a blind effort to dislodge the small woman who had denied it the kill of the Nagah. Domi kept one of her sinewy legs wrapped around the thing's side, pinning a wing down. Blood frothed from its shattered nostrils, and teeth spilled from crushed lips and its broken jaw. Pain made it wild and confused, so that it didn't even think to pause and hurl itself onto its back, to grind Domi against the earth with its weight. Rather, it slapped at its own chest and shoulders, killer wing claw flicking at empty air, as she was in too close for it to slash at her. The Outlander girl had drawn her knife even as she'd raced to the Nagah's aid, and now she twisted her wrist around and stabbed deep, just above the creature's clavicle, avoiding the ribs and heavy muscle of the beast's chest. The razor-sharp blade carved through windpipe and blood vessels feeding the thing's brain, and the kongamato's cries of rage and terror faded swiftly to sputtering, useless sprays of lifeblood. In a moment, the predator's struggles were over forever.

Unfortunately for Domi, hers were just beginning.

The albino girl whirled as a fresh blast of shrieks was directed at her from another monster breaking from the tree line. High cries laced with infrasonic vibrations shook her brains until she felt her eyeballs begin to throb in their sockets. The creature's screech was a stunning tool, and it left her flat-footed enough that she didn't have the forethought to raise her knife to meet her next attacker. It struck her, and Domi was carried through the air until she was on the opposite side of the dirt road, some fifteen feet wide. Even tangle-brained by the beast's yell, she managed to draw her knees up against the thing's chest, and when they struck the ground, her feet hit first, and transferred that impact force against the heavy keel bone of the winged menace's chest.

That knocked the breath from the kongamato, and it tumbled over her, ass over head, into the scrub. Domi had been spared from the crushing force of the fall by her shadow suit. But she wasn't wearing head protection, and could already feel the abrasion at the back trickling blood where her scalp was ground against the dirt road. It smarted, and didn't make getting up any easier, but she rolled, knife in hand, toward the off-balance predator. It scrambled to get to all fours, but Domi's blade was aiming for home. She jabbed at the struggling, bat-winged horror. The blade's point carved through tough muscle and stopped as she struck solid bone.

The kongamato released another roar and gave a powerful shrug with one wing. The backhand blow scooped Domi off her back and tossed her into the ditch, twenty feet away, where she'd slain the first of the African nightmares. She managed to twist in midflight and push her feet in front of her, and the shadow suit's non-Newtonian nature once again helped redistribute the impact of the landing. With a sidestep, she was back and balanced on both feet, turning to face the kongamato across the road.

Domi had recovered just in time, and now her knife was up and ready to respond to the beast's attack. It sliced out to meet the killing finger-claw on the creature's wing, the impossibly long digit stretching out seven feet to slash through her throat if she hadn't been on the defensive. With the strength of her response working against the power of her opponent's movement, she cut through bone, muscle and wing membrane. The already bloodied thing let out a wail at the loss of one of its weapons.

Suddenly the unmistakable cracking of a Sin Eater accompanied the beast's violent shudders. Both combatants had been so focused on each other that they hadn't noticed that Kane had taken down two more kongamato with his guns, and now his unerring bullets had blasted this one to the jungle floor.

Domi glanced back and saw that Kane had a few scuffs on his face, and his shadow suit was caked with dust and spattered with blood, meaning he hadn't had the easiest time of it. Even so, he'd dispatched both his foes and moved in to settle Domi's battle for her. It may not have been part of the rules of a duel, coming to the aid of another, but this was the jungle, and Domi's ears were ringing from her head smacking the ground and the earsplitting screeches of the winged predators. Chances were even that if the battle had gone on longer, she would either be too wounded to be useful, or dead. The shadow suit had shielded most of her from injury, but when she put her hand to the back of her head, it came away smeared with blood.

Already Brigid and Grant were on the scene, weapons scanning for any new threats, even as Kane tended to Domi's injuries.

"Fine," she said tersely. "Brain rattled."

"So, you're perfectly normal," Kane said with a wink, tilting her head and looking at the bleeding.

Domi pointed toward the Nagah who had burst from the forest. She wasn't in the mood to spar verbally with Kane, not at the moment. She'd risked her life for the snake man, even moments after worrying about how tough it would be to battle one. He was covered with blood and lying in the roadside ditch, chest heaving, more blood pouring over one hand. "Nagah."

"I know what he is," Kane answered. "But you count more to me."

Domi smiled through the pain as he handed her some gauze with surgical tape on it. "Okay. Thanks."

With Domi affixing her dressing to the back of her head, Kane was free to check on the newcomer.

The cobra man had a bad laceration across his chest, and his face had taken a hammering, but as he panted deeply, no flecks of blood sprayed from his nostrils. That was a good sign that the cut by the killer claw was nasty, but hadn't penetrated his lungs. Even so, the Nagah's cheek was torn, and his mouth was full of blood that he kept coughing and hacking out. It was amazing how the thick chest scales of the reptilian had provided so little protection. Kane realized that the man had been lucky.

Kane sprinkled coagulant powder into the chest wound, the powder soaking up blood and turning into a gelatinous mass that closed off the minor blood vessels severed by the predator's wing claw. Kane took a few moments to put gauze pads across the cut scales, then tape them in place. He wasn't certain how many nerves were active in the chest plates of a Nagah, but the gauze would provide some padding. The coagulant powder would be absorbed by the body. There would be a scar remaining, but at least the wound wouldn't cause more blood loss, or allow infection to enter his body.

Nathan showed up and rushed to Kane's side, holding the staff Nehushtan, concerned over the health of whoever was getting first aid. The sight of the cobra man, however, stopped the young Harare man cold, eyes wide as he gaped at him.

"What's your name?" Kane asked, nonchalantly. This was to check to see if his patient was all right, but also to add an element of humanity, for Nathan's sake. Kane was used to the reptilian race, unlike the young African.

"Burba," the cobra man answered, voice slurred, lips and front teeth dripping blood, mouth swollen.

"You can tell me later," Kane said.

The Nagah nodded. "Okabe."

Kane reached into his medical kit and took out a sealed ice pack, slapping it hard to let the two chemicals mix and produce an endothermic reaction. Thurpa accepted the pack and pressed it to his battered mouth to bring down the swelling.

Kane then glanced toward Nathan and the staff, and shook his head. This wasn't the time to go broadcasting the capabilities of Nehushtan to strangers. Thurpa's injuries weren't as life threatening as Nathan's had been, and chances were this could have been a trick of Durga's to plant a spy in the Cerberus explorers' camp.

"This…this is one of Durga's people?" Nathan asked.

Thurpa nodded, but his eyes held confusion. "Ibe a Nagah. But Ibe not sure ib Ibe with Durga abby-more."

Thurpa pressed the cold pack to his mouth again, realizing how silly he sounded.

Kane looked at the cobra man and could see genuine confusion and betrayal in his eyes. "So you came here with Durga?"

Thurpa nodded slowly, as if admitting to a great sin. The injuries he had suffered were brutal. If Kane hadn't had a means of clotting his chest wounds, the Nagah would have been in big trouble in the space of half an hour, if not from major blood loss, then from pathogens getting into his body. Durga was a ruthless, clever enemy, but the kongamato didn't strike Kane as being so surgical with their claws that they could nearly kill a man, yet leave him alive enough to be saved.

Even if that were the case, Kane wasn't certain of how fanatical Thurpa was. Would he risk his own life? Or would he even think he was doing so? Kane thought about how he'd saved Nathan before. It was out in the open, and a good stalker could have spied upon the staff and seen its powers.

Kane put those questions aside and continued talking to his patient. "Do you know why the kongamatos attacked you?"

Thurpa shook his head. "Just went wild."

"Was Durga controlling them?" he pressed.

The cobra man nodded. "I thought he was. But he told me to find you, Kane. You are Kane, right?"

"Right," Kane confirmed.

The Nagah took the cold pack from his lips again. "The name is Thurpa."

He had to exaggerate for clarity, but this time, didn't

sound as if he was burbling. He returned the cold pack to his mouth. He looked toward Domi, then nodded toward her. "Thank you."

"No problem," she answered. "Where is Durga?"

"He was going to the Kariba power station, the last time I talked to him. That was about an hour ago, before the winged freaks went nuts," Thurpa replied.

"And what is at Kariba?" Nathan inquired.

"He was looking for a means to restore his health and strength," Thurpa explained. "He's heard that somewhere in this area is a redoubt, and given the lack of high-tech facilities, except when it comes to hydroelectric dams…"

"Well, he's off by a bit if he's going to Kariba," Nathan said. "Did he unleash those winged things?"

Thurpa nodded. "He and the millennialists found a cloning facility where he was able to make them."

"How could he do that? Those creatures are huge," Grant said.

"Actually, studying some of Hera's notes from when she was running the Tartarus vats in Greece, I was able to put something together on how she got rapidly aged drones," Brigid interjected. Kane was glad to see her, hoping maybe she could come up with something. "These aren't living creatures per se, They're actually reprogrammed biomass."

"Biomass?" Kane asked.

"It's a blank slate set of material. Stem cells, actually, which do not have any programming from DNA. Thus, when they are mixed into another organism, they take on the attributes of the cellular tissue they are in contact with," Brigid explained. "At one time, it was thought that stem cell research would provide the means of grafting new nerve tissue into people to help the paralyzed walk once more, or burn victims to grow new skin. Unfortunately, at the time, the religious dogma of certain political parties prevented stem cell research, stating that the sources of these cells were from aborted fetuses."

Domi glared at Brigid. "Aborted? What?"

"Abortion was a means of ending a perilous or unwanted pregnancy, but that had nothing to do with the stem cell sources," she answered.

Domi looked stunned at the concept of ending a pregnancy, but she came from an era where childbirth was a difficult thing unless one had access to great medical technology. Where she had been raised, most pregnancies were hit-or-miss, due to food and water shortages, exposure to radioactivity, or just plain injuries and hardship. It took her a moment to realize that Brigid was speaking of a time when billions of humans had teemed across the planet, breeding with abandon.

"So, the Annunaki have somehow found a way to grow and store masses of stem cells?" Grant inquired.

North spoke up now. "The growth and storage is relatively easy. The stem cells have very little need for nutrition and don't have any aging factor to them. So a nutrient bath and a sealed set of canisters allows for storage of literally tons of biomass to grow anything from mindless troops to replacement body parts for an injured craft like *Tiamat*. All you need is the proper genetic code sequence injected into the material, and you can create a good duplicate for anything you need. It'll look the same, move the same, but it won't think the same, not without a proper program in its brain."

"Like Erica's SQUID technology," Brigid mused.

North narrowed his eyes. "Oh…you're on a first-name basis with her?"

Erica Van Sloane had been a part of the Cerberus group's cadre of foes and allies of necessity since their first exile into the hell of the Deathlands. One of her inventions was an electronic webbing that sapped the will of whichever minions she wanted, and placed them under her unwavering control. Of course, this was an echo of similar devices, nodules in fact, that Enlil and the other Annunaki utilized to take command of the Nephilim, Enlil's lobotomized version of the lower caste of the race, the Igigi.

The kongamato were strong enough and took enough bullets and cutting to kill that this made them even more worrisome. If they were under Durga's mental command, then they could at least be contained by the Cerberus team taking out the Nagah prince. But now, unfettered by any control modules and still lashing out brutally, the winged mutants were a deadly force of nature, impossible to stop by anything other than straight-out genocide.

"We're going to have a lot of work ahead if that's right," Grant mused.

"What do you mean, if?" Thurpa asked. "Those things tried to kill me."

"It could have been a sacrifice play. Something to get you on our side," Grant told him. He looked over to North. "Either to discredit this asshole or to sneak him a message, or maybe just to kill him if Durga doesn't like him anymore."

"Not too trustworthy, are we?" North asked.

"No, you aren't," Grant snapped at him. "And I'm sorry, Thurpa, but this is too damned convenient. You might not know that you're bait in a trap, which is why I'm feeling sorry for you."

"If I am, then to hell with Durga," Thurpa responded.

Kane, Brigid and Domi were all observing him closely. With their sharp senses and observational skills, they were keeping watch for tells of lies. It would be difficult, considering the facial and skin structure of a Nagah male, but if anyone could make an accurate observation, it was going to be those three. However, even Grant, with all his years of police work as a magistrate in Cobaltville, was picking up a strong case of veracity on Thurpa's part.

Even so, this could have been part of Durga's plan. They were dealing with a cunning opponent, one who'd managed to wreck Hannah and Manticor's chances of having a child that was theirs genetically.

Grant hated the pun, but Durga was a true snake in the grass, and no amount of duplicity would be too great for him.

But for now, Thurpa looked as if he could be trusted.

Kane offered his hand to the Nagah expatriate, helping him to his feet. "Welcome to the party, Thurpa," he said. "I just hope for your sake that you're really on our side."

The Nagah looked at the dead kongamato around them. "I hope so, too."

Chapter 12

The rest of the trek toward Kariba station was done in silence, but not in calm. The group had grown to seven in size, but the Cerberus quartet could trust only each other, though Nathan Longa had proved himself a good man.

Thurpa had been part of Durga's rebellious cabal, a group that believed in "genetic purity" among the castes of the Nagah nation, and as such, even if he hadn't committed murder here in Africa, he had been part of a bigoted agenda back in Garuda. He was damaged goods, not nearly so bad as North had been in the past, but he was still an unknown quantity. The four travelers from Cerberus, fortunately, had been on dozens of quests around the world, and while they generally tried to be cordial with those seeking to be friendly, they had quickly developed instincts as to who was dangerous and who wasn't. Right now, Thurpa demonstrated enough loyalty and thankfulness for the rescue and first aid that he was sticking with them. He seemed to be more interested in the tree line and the skies above, where more kongamato might appear, than in looking for weaknesses among the group.

Whatever Durga had done, it had turned Thurpa into a convert.

If that lasted, Kane thought, then so much the better.

"Thurpa, you don't seem to have much trouble throwing in with humans," he began. "So why join a bigot like Durga?"

Brigid tossed Kane a glare. Things had been quiet so

far, and now that they were just a few hundred yards from the Kariba power station, she presumed that he was going to cause trouble. Needless trouble, on the doorstep of the very enemy they were stalking.

"He didn't come off as a bigot. His original message, the one that made me align with him, was of truth to oneself," Thurpa responded. "The Nagah are a constructed species. Mere humans with additions grafted to our genetic structure. And a lot of the inclusiveness in Nagah society seems to be along the lines of pounding square pegs into round holes. Why should humans have to literally change their skin to fit in with us? It seemed the only way to get high status in Garuda was to give up normal humanity and mess with your genetic structure. And much of the time, what came out? Piebald freaks who were mosaics of human and cobra, or even worse, Nagah who were forced by a cruel genetic joke to live in a wheelchair or drag themselves along on their elbows because their legs were taken from them."

Kane remembered how easily Manticor was able to adapt to life in a wheelchair after his legs had been crippled in battle with Durga's minions. Because of the nature of the cobra baths, sometimes the changes from human to Nagah did result in people who were, for all intents and purposes, paraplegic or quadriplegic, their legs and even their arms fused together or to their torsos, turning them into living, limbless snake analogs.

"Sure, Matron Yun alleviated the stigma of their disability, calling them the chosen of the great cobra, but it still wouldn't have happened if people weren't so willing to trade one identity for a little bit of status and equality," Thurpa returned. "I have nothing against humans, or even Nagah descended from humans. But it's a dangerous game, made even more so by the severe losses suffered upon Durga's open revolt. The technology used to make these changes is finite, and growing ever more fallible with each change. Sooner or later, someone going into the cobra baths is going to come out dead."

"So that helps you to ignore the terrorism for this cause?" Kane asked.

"Not all of his followers agree with the violence, and Durga assured us that it was a fanatic few responsible for those attacks," Thurpa answered. "Now, though...we're working with a militia of Mashona. And they look pretty ruthless. And Magruder... Granted, I felt good being on their side, because they were dangerous."

"Magruder. He's with the consortium?" Brigid inquired.

Thurpa nodded. "We're in a dangerous place, Miss Baptiste. I'd rather have the most dangerous people on my side, thank you very much."

"Hence your throwing in with us so quickly," Grant said. "We tore the hell out of that pack of kongas on your ass."

Thurpa smiled. "You know it."

"Makes sense enough to me," Grant replied. "Just remember, if we could do that to a bunch of mutie beasts, what we could do to a lone asshole or two."

The cobra man chuckled, trying to cover for a sudden attack of nerves, but the rapid flutter of his laugh was sign enough that Grant's warning had been noted. "I am not stupid."

"Good." Grant placed a big, reassuring hand on the Nagah's shoulder.

"So, what is our plan to get in there, now that you're done marking your territory around the newbie?" North asked.

Kane and Grant both gave the archaeologist a hairy eyeball for that crack, but Kane at least felt he should answer. "What we are going to do is to leave Nathan and that stick back here. Grant, I love you like a brother, but when it comes to sneaking..."

"I make a better babysitter for the guy with the magic

staff," Grant returned. He gave Kane his one percent salute. "You and Domi will go on ahead."

"We call it clear, you come up," Domi added. "Plus, be
good if you had our backs."

She nodded toward the obscenely big rifle that the huge
ex-magistrate carried slung across his back. Normally, the
big .50-caliber Barrett was hardly the kind of weapon that
an exploratory group would bring with them, but Grant
was aware of mutant beasts on the rampage in Africa, and
the same monstrous rifle that could kill such a beast with
one shot was also pretty good at dealing with regular mal-
contents, such as millennialists, bandits and militia. Even
so, of late, Grant had been also used to dealing with creatures that required even more effort to kill than normal,
human-sized foe

"I never would have thought of that," he said with a
wink. "I have your back, always."

Kane suppressed a chuckle, and he and Domi split up
and advanced toward the Kariba station. The area had been
cleared from the fence perimeter to a hundred yards out,
but now that the sun had gone down, there was enough
knee-high grass and ground clutter in the forms of shrubs
to give the skillful pair a good path of approach. Granted,
things would be difficult, as the Millennium Consortium
had night-vision goggles. But with the lights on within the
compound, Kane and Domi would see any observers at the
fence backlit, and anyone farther in would have his light-
amplification devices overwhelmed by the lamps. There
were no towers, unlike at the Victoria Falls station, at least
none they could readily see.

"Grant," Kane muttered into his Commtact.

"Checking the roof. Camp lighting is pretty harsh, even
through my daylight scope," Grant replied.

"Keep us appraised," he returned.

"Got it," Grant responded.

With that, Kane went silent. His ears were peeled, as were his eyes. For now, he moved along in a crouch, walking smoothly, quietly, heel to toe so as not to stumble if he stepped on uneven ground, and to feel ahead for any twigs or trip wires that would give him away. Domi had her own catlike movements, and the pair of them advanced relatively quickly across the field, looking toward the perimeter only occasionally for signs of someone watching them, while concentrating on avoiding booby traps or alarm systems while crossing the partially cleared field.

All the while they traversed the darkened grounds, they were keenly aware that every moment their friends sat still, they were targets for whatever force wanted to ambush them, be it the Mashona militia Thurpa had told them of, or the kongamato. It was a fine edge between rushing into Kariba half-blind, or being alert and certain of the presence of danger within the compound. No matter if Thurpa had been betrayed or simply had the bad luck to be present when Durga lost control of the cloned creatures, the odds of there being something deadly inside the Harare station were high. So far they'd been lucky to avoid any security measures belonging to either Harare or to Durga.

Kane and Domi finally met at the perimeter fence, and Kane signaled to the others to move up.

The field was clear of trouble, and the group once more assembled. They found the gate, and it was open.

"Come into my parlor, said the cobra to the flies," Brigid murmured.

Thurpa cast a guilty glance toward her.

"Durga. Not you," she amended.

"No, I was just worried if you're going to shoot me first if something goes wrong," Thurpa said. "Maybe I should just take point."

"Go eat worms in the corner on your own time," Brigid

replied. "Besides, you've got nothing on these two." She nodded toward Kane and Domi.

"No scat smell," Domi noted. "Things aren't nesting here."

"No signs of bodies or blood spilled, so there's no kongamato present," Kane mused. "But Durga's people could have swept or cleaned up after shooting the Harare staff in the head."

Nathan frowned. "I don't know how many worked at this particular facility. I wish I could help."

"Chances are the numbers weren't much different from those in Zambia," North interjected. "And according to the duty roster I accessed…"

"You read their roster? When?" Brigid asked.

"I went into their computer check-in," North said. He tapped his skull. "I can wirelessly access those things."

"That can be done?" Grant asked.

"It was called Wi-Fi. It was a popular trend for notebook computers starting in 1999," Brigid responded. "Before it became part of the public consciousness, it was making inroads to military and business usage. We have some of that technology back at the redoubt, and I'm sure that some of it found its way to Africa either before or just after."

"We're not a desert wasteland here," Nathan told her. "The thing is, it takes a lot of precious metals to assemble that kind of circuitry, so it's still fairly rare, but we have it. Two centuries of development, mining and such, and not wasted frivolously in coffeehouses."

"I never thought that," Brigid said. "You've done a lot better than most areas of this world. Especially without a reunification program."

"Enough jawing," North muttered. "There's not a lick of computer access in there, and I'm even going outside of wireless connectivity."

Brigid noted that the archaeologist was standing next

to one of the floodlights that illuminated the courtyard. "You're hacking into the circuits that power the lights out here."

He nodded. "Back in the twentieth century, there were ideas of using the electrical system of buildings to convey computer information. My nanites are reading through the back door of the computer power systems." He glared toward Kane. "Or don't you trust me?"

Kane shrugged. "I believe you. But Durga and the Millennium Consortium don't really do a lot of sneaking and peeking electronically. They're more come in, trickl folks, or just plain shoot who they can't snow."

Nathan blinked. "Snow?"

"Fool," Kane corrected.

"We don't get a lot of fluffy white stuff here in Harare," Nathan said with a chuckle, "so we don't use the word much."

"Made enough noise. Get inside," Domi muttered, opening the door to one of the buildings. She had her .45 in hand, her ruby-red eyes peeled, picking up light much better than a nonalbino. Normally, bright daylight would have been a terror to her, if not for her melaninless skin, but she'd turned her sensitive eyes into an asset. She dealt with the pain of a hot sun searing her untannable flesh. She survived.

And with those photosensitive eyes, she was able to scan shadows deeper than her friends could. She seemed as if she were suffering from tics as her gaze was drawn toward each sound. It may have seemed paranoid, but that level of alertness had kept her and her companions alive for years.

Kane, behind her, was also feeling for threats lurking in the darkness. He was one of the few humans in the world who paid the same attention to his peripheral senses as to what was right in front of him. When people said that he had the build of a wolf, Domi was puzzled, but the man definitely had the predatory alertness of the lupine hunter.

She wasn't surprised when he put a hand on her shoulder, noticing something that she'd missed. The figure on the ground was badly mauled, but recognizably human. Domi skittered closer, then went on watch while Kane examined the form.

"Dead," Kane pronounced. "Something tore his arms from their sockets." He gave the corpse a quick scan with a small LED flashlight. Domi stole a glance and noticed that he was wearing the traditional gray overalls of the consortium. She bit her lower lip, seeing the horror in the dead man's bulging eyes. He'd died slow and hard. Chunks of his belly and chest were gone.

"Let's see if Thurpa recognizes him," Kane suggested.

Domi let out a short whistle to summon the others from their position at the door. So far, the only other occupant of this building was a dead man, and she'd made certain to look up into the rafters. Even without seeing anything, she knew that no bat things were asleep up there. She didn't pick up a whiff of urine or feces in the entire building. Domi had spent enough time in bat caves to know that when those things slept, they tended to excrete wherever they hung.

It was safe in here.

Thurpa approached the dead body and looked at its face, illuminated by Kane's pocket torch.

"That's one of Magruder's men. I think he was Jacobs," Thurpa replied. He realized how lucky he had been and suppressed a shudder at the sight. "He was with the group that was coming with me to meet you."

"Magruder, as well?" Brigid inquired.

Thurpa nodded. He couldn't tear his gaze away from the corpse for long monents, but then looked around. "Not a lot of blood for all those injuries."

"He was brought here as food. I didn't see any arms here, either," Kane added.

"Why drop the body here and not guard it?" Grant asked.

"Bait," Domi mused. She pointed toward a high window with a catwalk in front of it. The glass had been broken out, and the opening was obviously large enough for one of those creatures to slip through. "They could have been hanging out one of the windows."

"I looked. There was nothing. Remember, I fought these things, too, and I was specifically looking for them," Grant said.

"We'd best take leave of this building," North stated.

"But…" Thurpa began, looking at the dead man. He could barely imagine how, earlier in the day, he had been so callous in linking the destruction of a group of meerkats to how he would have liked to deal with the consortium members and their incessant grumbling. Now, Jacobs was lying here, torn apart and gutted, and reality smacked Thurpa in the face like a brick. "We're leaving him here?"

"If he's bait, they'll know if we've touched him or moved him," Kane replied. He'd been studiously careful not to disturb the form on the ground.

"Next building," Grant said, leading the way back to the door. He took point on the route out, simply because he wanted to be the front man in case they needed a breakout. No telling what kind of trap those winged monsters could assemble, but so far, they'd attacked with raw, brute force twice. Maybe the third time they'd go for something a little more strategic and stealthy.

Grant set up just outside the exit and waited for the others to emerge. He might not have had a point man's instinct, like Kane, but he had some keen senses and situational awareness. Not preternatural or feral, like Kane's or Domi's, but serving as a magistrate required being more than just an insensate lump of meat whose only instincts were to pound on troublemakers. Sure, it was one of the things that Baron Cobalt had really loved about his magistrate corps, but the day-to-day life Grant had led was one where he had to be a community peacekeeper. Straight up brute force always took second place to keen observation and awareness of dangers, to intercept them and disarm them.

He didn't see any of the creatures, but he didn't let up on his paranoia about their presence. This whole situation stank. He was further distracted and on edge from the presence of two former enemies, North and Thurpa. Though he'd never come into conflict with Thurpa himself, Grant *had* seen the kind of brutality North was capable of, including setting bombs that would have turned a crowded public square in the city of Garuda into an inferno of death and destruction, all to provide chaos that would assist the Millennium Consortium to move in and conquer the underground realm.

The night sky was a clear backdrop, with stars sprinkled across it like grains of sand spilled on black velvet. He caught glimpses of night birds fluttering to and fro, as well as insects, but there was nothing larger than his fist up in the air.

That didn't make Grant feel any better. He'd rather know exactly where the enemy was. Waiting was hardly his favorite thing to do, especially when the payoff for that patience was a fanged and clawed creature trying to tear him open and feast on his entrails.

Grant waved for Kane to make a quick dash toward the next building. This one looked more like administrative offices, and the windows, at least on the two sides he'd already observed, were all intact. There was still the half he didn't see, windows that would allow plenty of access to kongamato. The building looked like a maze, but fortunately, was only five stories tall.

"We'll stick to the lobby," Kane said over his Commtact. "Going room-to-room to clear the place just screams trouble. We'll either get too caught up to notice militia or Durga arriving, or we'll end up stuck in a hallway with kongamato pushing in from either side."

"Check," Grant returned.

North seemed to have drifted off into a trance. His eyes were closed, even as he walked. Yet he didn't stumble once, but kept pace with the rest of the group.

Grant rapped his knuckle against North's forehead. "Rise and shine, digger boy," he grunted.

North opened his eyes, his features gone from placid calm to open disdain. "I'm scanning for communications."

"You'll trip over your damned feet if you keep walking like that," Grant told him.

North rolled his eyes. "If I did, what would you care?"

"Like it or not, I'd have to pick your stupid ass off the ground," he replied.

The archaeologist shook his head. "I wouldn't trip. I've memorized every inch of this terrain. I'm using my optical nerves for something more useful."

"Fine," Grant answered.

North blew out a sigh, then looked to Brigid. "Is he always this dense?"

"Dense is being snotty to someone who's looking out for your safety," Brigid replied. "But hey, nobody's perfect, except for you."

North grimaced.

"Did you pick anything up?" she asked.

He shook his head. "No. That's what's so disconcerting. The lights are working, but there's not a soul in sight."

"Maybe some people just know how to shut the hell up and not attract attention to themselves," Nathan offered.

"All of this waiting is eating at what nerves I've got left," Thurpa mused. Kane waved, and the cobra man was the first to jog toward the lobby of the office building. Grant and Brigid hung back to make certain they weren't being shadowed by creatures stealthily gliding on high.

When they finally followed the others into the lobby, they noted that Domi quickly signaled for them to shush. Someone had rushed through, knocking over chairs and tables, spilling papers and mugs across the floor. Kane pointed to a splotch on the wall next to a fire door. Grant and Brigid had seen enough aftereffects of violence to realize that someone had been shot. There was no pool on the floor, which meant that the person hit had at least gotten through the doorway before succumbing.

But there was no telling who that had been.

"Do we go?" Brigid asked.

"I'll go," Kane offered. "You guys take care of our guests and keep an eye out for trouble up here."

"Sure?" Domi asked. Kane could tell that she was itching to come along with him.

"The fewer we leave behind up here means the harder it will be to protect the lobby if someone comes at us," Kane returned. "Trust me, if there's a trap down there, I'll spring it loud and clear. Then you can come down and help."

Grant gave his friend another one percent salute. Kane returned it.

Sin Eater slapped into the palm of his hand, he opened the door and entered adark stairwell leading to the basement. The click of the shutting door resounded through him, running a tingle of dread throughout his body.

With the closing of the door, the stairway was pitch-black. Even after a few moments of his eyes adjusting to the darkness, there was not a hint of illumination that he could pick up. Turning on his pocket torch, he saw a dribble of blood droplets on the steps, and followed it downward.

Chapter 13

The blue-white beam from his flashlight preceded Kane as he descended to the lower levels of the building. The setup of the Kariba facility was much different from the one they'd encountered upriver at Victoria Falls, but even as he walked down the steps, his peripheral vision was starting to pick up similarities in architecture. Normally, Kane didn't think of building style or design, and even if he did, he recalled Brigid's mention of an Italian firm doing both the design and construction of the facilities along the river.

However, the similarities were far more than just flashes of familiarity from recent surroundings. Kane paused and knelt, checking the stairs. He'd seen some like them back at Cerberus, which only added to the growing suspicions he held that the power stations all along the river had been built as a cover for Project Overwhisper and its redoubts. Considering that the same firm had worked on both sides of the river, and the border between then Zimbabwe and Zambia, it made sense that they might have dug a whole network of tunnels along and possibly under the river, connecting a number of buildings.

Kane continued downward, keeping his beam on the droplets of blood leaking from the gunshot victim, not on his surroundings. The stairwell was a rectangular spiral, and while there were doors breaking off every twenty feet, leading to various basement floors, he could check that out on the way back up. The blood trail was the vital thing, and there was no sign of the victim pausing, loitering, as a companion stopped off at one of those doors.

But Kane would stop as soon as he saw evidence of that. The last thing he needed was an ambush cutting him off from his friends upstairs. So far, his instincts were dead-on about stumbling into these kinds of traps, a combination of his natural alertness and years of experience giving him a nearly supernatural intuition about trouble.

He paused again when he reached a landing where many droplets had assembled, creating a small puddle. The wounded man had stopped here for a while. Kane glanced toward a nearby door and clicked off the light. Once more, the velvety darkness descended upon him, and he waited a few moments to allow his eyes to adjust.

He walked to the door and gently opened it, trying to make as little sound as possible. Even as he did so, despite the inky darkness smothering his vision, his ears and other senses were keen, picking up on the slightest of cues. The sound of the door was only a few clicks of the handle and latch, but there was also a quick, almost imperceptible intake of breath. And a spray of light that was doused at the same moment the shadowy figure gasped. It was only a momentary glimmer, but it had silhouetted the stranger, and gave Kane a perfect target.

Rather than go for the Sin Eater, he slashed out with a straight knife hand, rigid fingers spearing into the chest of the man and rewarding Kane with a spray of fetid breath and spittle. An instant later, he brought up the pocket light, keeping the lens far forward from his eyes, and hit the switch. A blaze of white-blue light caught his breathless opponent right in the face, the beam burning harshly into his wide-open eyes.

Kane released the toggle switch and the hallway was cast into darkness once more. Even if his opponent turned on his own light, there wouldn't be much he could see anymore, thanks to the sudden blast of LED-powered illumination in the face. Kane wanted to know who was working with Durga, and how they controlled the winged horrors on the rampage. Thus, he needed someone to ask.

The man who had appeared in the brief flash of the pocket light had a bald pate, completely clean and shiny from the eyebrows up. But from the eyebrows on down he sported a sheen of long hair, concealed only by gray coveralls. His hands and wrists were equally as furry, even to the knuckles. If it hadn't been for the gleam of his bald dome, Kane could have confused him with a wolf man from an ancient vid, but this was just a particularly hirsute member of the Millennium Consortium.

Kane reached out, hooking the man by the neck with curved fingers, and leaned back, pivoting around to slam him facefirst into the closing door behind him.

The millennialist's head bounced of the edge of the door, and once more Kane felt a rain of spittle, and perhaps blood, released by the impact. Another grab and he shoved the tumbling fur ball backward to the floor, planting him there with a grunt. Kane stepped on the fallen man's shoulder, eliciting a groan.

He turned on the flashlight again, glaring down at him. "Who was shot?"

"Ma-Makoba," the man sputtered. His beard was covered with bloody saliva from his lips, and blood seeped from a split eyebrow.

"How badly is he hurt?" Kane asked.

"Bullet went through and through," his captive answered. "Why ask?"

"Because I came into this stairwell looking for a wounded person to help, if I could," Kane responded. "I still want to help, but you seemed as if you wanted to ambush me."

"How…"

"I have some good instincts," Kane said. "You must be Magruder. Thurpa described you. I'm Kane, of Cerberus redoubt."

"You're him?" Magruder mumbled, recognition setting in.

He nodded. "So, you survived the kongamato attack?"

Magruder brightened at the inference. "Thurpa's alive?"

"Yes," Kane returned. "So why did you hang back?"

"This floor, I was told that there were medical supplies here, to help Makoba," he responded.

Kane frowned. He scanned around and found a small basket of materials strewn on the floor. There was gauze, tape, sutures, even some disinfectant and clot powder. "Gather that stuff up."

Magruder was able to move now that Kane was no longer stepping on his shoulder. He gave a cough, and Kane actually knelt to help him collect the medical supplies. Kane opened one packet of gauze and pressed it to Magruder's oozing brow.

"Thanks...."

"You're bleeding all over," Kane told him. "Remember that if you try to jump me again."

"All I can see is a big golden blur in the middle of my vision," Magruder muttered. "What did you hit me with?"

"Just an ordinary flashlight," Kane returned. "And then a door."

Kane had his Commtact transmitting, so that the others could at least hear half the conversation with Magruder That kind of information would let them know what was going on with him, and that he'd made contact with potential enemies.

Surprisingly, during Kane's examination, he'd discovered that the millennialist was apparently unarmed. In a dangerous situation like this, it either meant that Durga and his crew were disarmed, or that they'd sent Magruder up without a weapon, another piece of bait to hook the Cerberus explorers. And all Kane could think of was the trophy up in the lobby, the orichalcum staff, Nehushtan, and its uncanny abilities.

And now it was time to follow Magruder to the wounded man. Kane let the millennialist take the lead. This was feeling more and more like a trap, but he'd established that he was easily as dangerous as any group he was set to encounter. He also had the consortium thug in his sights, and more than a little rattled. The banging he'd just taken would be more than sufficient to impair any rapid response Magruder could summon up. Sure, the man could still walk, but Kane had gauged his strike so that it wouldn't have been fatal, but definitely concussion inducing. The drunken stagger as they descended the steps was proof of Kane's ability and the success of his tactic.

Magruder opened the door. "Makoba? Durga?"

"Here," said a hoarse voice that Kane recognized immediately.

"I found Kane," Magruder called back.

"Hurry," Durga rasped.

Kane took Magruder by the arm, hustling him along, but all the while keeping his right hand free, his forearm holster ready to snap the Sin Eater into his palm and begin blasting. His neck hairs stood up as he drew closer. Durga looked like hell, sprawled on a piece of fabric that connected two wooden bars, his yellow eyes glimmering like hot embers in the light cast by a small lantern.

Makoba was a large black man, easily as tall as Grant, but about fifty pounds heavier, his thick, bulging muscles covered by a layer of fat that softened his silhouette. He looked waxen and pale, clearly suffering from blood loss. Magruder went to work, as did a couple of men who had stayed there. They two had been hovering near Durga's gurney, but immediately went to work, helping their leader, who glared at Kane.

"You look like shit," Kane offered.

Durga smirked. He was balanced on one elbow, but relying mostly on the wall behind him to keep him from being prone. "Feel it. Thank you."

"I seem to recall you had something to do with this situation," Kane answered.

Durga glared, then looked to Makoba. The consortium men had already started an IV of saline solution to help with his blood loss. In the meantime, Makoba's arm was being administered to, gauze sopping away drying, clotting blood before packets of coagulant went into the wound, front and back. Makoba's eyes were glazed and unfocused, but when he was requested to shift position to make his treatment easier, he responded.

"So who shot him?" Kane asked.

Durga turned back to him. "Traitor."

"That narrows it down," Kane joked.

"Every word that he speaks is an effort," Magruder interjected. "When you destroyed his enhanced body, you crippled him."

"And this is why you're wandering around Africa—looking for a cure? Or a way to become snakezilla again?" Kane asked.

"Walk again," Durga admitted. After a couple breaths, he sounded exhausted, and resigned to his condition. It seemed genuine, at least at first blush, but Durga's acting skills had disarmed Kane's suspicions once before. "No more."

"How is he doing?" Kane asked. He was fighting the urge to simply pull the Sin Eater and put a bullet through each of these beings here. He'd been in open conflict with the Millennium Consortium on several occasions, and Durga's machinations had harmed Hannah and Manticor badly. There wasn't a single friend here, and yet things looked so desperate, his humanity got the better of him. Even so, he kept a wary eye on his surroundings, making certain he knew where everyone present was positioned at all times.

"He'll live," Magruder said. "But his pulse is weak. He'd lost a lot of blood, and I'm pretty certain that the rifle round that went through his shoulder smashed the joint to splinters."

Kane grimaced. "So, he'll lose the use of that arm, maybe for months, if not longer."

"Cripples, easy prey." Durga spoke up. "Two. Useless. Men."

"You can drop the pretense about being ignorant of what's with our group," Kane said.

"No lie," Durga replied. "Know it."

Kane remained silent. This group had only one gun among the five of them, but having been down here for at least half an hour, they could have had plenty of opportunity to stash more weapons away. As well, a fully healthy Durga had his natural Nagah fangs, deadly teeth that could tear through a human throat, inject a very lethal venom or spit burning poison that blinded.

And Makoba was big enough that his ham-sized fists could be utilized as hammers. Kane had fought opponents of his size before, and had the blows from their fists rock him to the core. It would take speed and strategy to survive a battle with Makoba. Even a glancing punch could stun Kane enough to leave him a sitting duck for a rain of subsequent and ultimately lethal impacts.

And yet with all those doubts, he knew there was a horde of winged predators on the rampage, having gone as far as the outskirts of the nearest Zambian city, and wreaking havoc upon local men who were simply doing their jobs in protecting the power stations. The more fighting men Kane could assemble against the legendary horrors, the better.

"Doubt me. No blame," Durga sputtered. Every word came slow and painfully, with a contortion of his reptilian features. "But we are all meat."

"Baptiste?" Kane muttered under his breath, the Commtact picking up the vibrations of his vocal cords through his jawbone.

"We've got movement outside the doors. Even if we don't heal him, we definitely need to get down that stairwell," Brigid responded. "Sooner or later, a kongamato is going to take a poke at the lobby doors."

"My friends are coming down," Kane announced promptly. He added an aside to Magruder. "Thurpa is with them."

"We figured you didn't come here alone," another of the men said. Kane got a better look at him and spotted scuff marks and cuts on his face. He recognized that kind of beating, having had to run and leap through a thick forest himself. Being chased at high speed through trees and brush tended to hammer a person pretty hard.

These men had quite literally been running for their lives, pursued by the kongamato, or some other opponent.

"So who was the traitor?" Kane asked.

"It was one of our own, a member of our party by the name of Jacobs. He took the control helm for the kongamato, shooting Makoba for emphasis," the man replied. "I'm Gibbons. That's Davis."

Kane nodded in acknowledgment. They wore the uniform of the consortium, but had been sticking close to Durga. From the emergency gurney he lay upon, Kane could quite easily take them both for being bearers of the incapacitated prince. However, he didn't think that the former Nagah monarch would have deigned to ride on a blanket tied to sticks. Somewhere along the way, things had gone south.

"We found Jacobs. He was torn open by the creatures he wanted to control," Kane said.

"Helm?" Durga asked.

"Nowhere to be seen," Kane responded. "But it's possible that one of them could have shredded it, or even swallowed it."

"Shit," Durga cursed.

"So we have nothing to control those things with," Makoba said, slurring, sounding almost drunken, but looking a bit more animated now.

The door opened, and Grant led the way, big rifle out, but aimed at the floor. The intent was unmistakable. The Cerberus warriors came armed to the teeth, so any surprise was going to be blown in half by one of the largest portable firearms on the planet. Anyone causing that surprise was going to get cleaned up by Brigid and Domi, each gripping their Copperhead submachine guns. They were backed up by Nathan with his borrowed Zambian rifle, as well as Nehushtan over one shoulder. But he was there mainly to keep North in line, and train his attention on Thurpa, just in case.

Kane looked back to Durga.

"Please," the slumped, fallen prince said. "Hate…broken…body."

"You remember how badly it hurt when you healed me," Nathan offered, keeping his distance from North and Thurpa.

"Heard 'em hit lobby doors," Domi said. She was on full alert, speaking tersely, dropping her articles and pronouns. "Just testing."

"It was difficult to surmise if they were aware of our presence. We'd killed the lights, and the doors were closed," Brigid added. "By sight and sound, we were very low profile, but it depends on how good their other senses are. If they have an acute sense of smell…"

"We'll keep our ears open for them." Davis spoke up. "We've got a comm outside the door."

"Yeah, but we didn't hear *him*," Gibbons argued.

"You weren't supposed to," Kane countered.

"Don't worry about that," Magruder interrupted. "When those winged bastards come down, they'll make a hell of a lot of noise tearing the doors off the stairwell."

Durga looked at the staff on Nathan's back, then toward Kane. The Nagah prince seemed as if he was going to break into tears. Kane knew that if he ever gave such a kindness to Durga, it would likely end in suffering and torment. Even so…

"Stop looking like a kicked puppy," Kane growled. "Nathan…?"

Brigid glared at Kane. "Really? You're going to risk your life and health for…for that?"

Kane clenched his jaw. "And Makoba."

"How many have died because of him?" Brigid pressed. "And you don't have to answer that. I remember every detail of what he has done."

"And do you remember the kongamato? And the presence of a militia?" Kane countered.

Grant grumbled, then patted the big Barrett rifle. "Lay some healin' on that asshole. I've got my own five feet of magic to take away whatever health he abuses trying to kill us."

"Have…advant…age," Durga sputtered.

Nathan looked askance at Brigid Baptiste. She had been the voice of dissent in giving the Nagah prince a chance to walk, to stand, to fight alongside them. This was an instance, however, where expedience depended on every person present being able to resist the monsters assembled outside. Nathan handed Nehushtan to Kane.

The Cerberus explorer held the ancient staff, feeling the tingle of electricity running up his arm, flowing into his chest, warming him from within. Kane took a deep breath, and that inhalation seemed to make him surge even more with strength and confidence. He glanced toward Durga, holding out his other hand.

"Just remember, Durga. This can take what it bestows," he said, as if the thought had just been kicked loose from the tip of his tongue.

Durga paused before forcing his hand to meet Kane's. At the brush of their fingertips, the world suddenly sparked, lightning crackling around the pair of them.

The blue flames that engulfed Kane and Durga seemed to burn through every nerve in both their bodies. One writhing tentacle of energy spit between their foreheads, a pulsing, churning hell of heat and agony that made Kane feel as if he were being pulled and stretched as thin as wire.

Molten copper poured through his veins, and he could see the same within Durga. For that moment, they were one entity, combined by the odd energies stored within Nehushtan.

As soon as they were connected, Kane felt his opponent suddenly rampaging in his mind. The two beings were gripped by rage and confusion, their deepest emotions bubbling to the surface. Kane could feel his fingers stabbing into Durga's throat, and the Nagah's pointed nails sliced Kane's skin at his neck.

Both men's faces were twisted, contorted, and their bodies seemed to be hanging weightless in space, neither of them able to gain the leverage to crush the opponent in his grasp. It was a sudden, all-out physical war, giving Kane a surge of strength and energy, while at the same time disorienting him.

"Durga! Last I remember, I was trying to heal your ungrateful ass!" Kane bellowed. His breathing didn't seem hindered by the clutches of the Nagah prince.

The Nagah's eyes blazed with anger and rage. "Only after…"

Suddenly the raging electrical storm enveloping the two men seemed to fade, as though gravity had still not taken hold. The two looked around at the space they hung in. They were looking down upon their bodies, and the rest of the group who had been assembled. Time stood still as they hovered in the air.

"Out-of-body experience," Durga grumbled.

Kane remembered that Durga had been in telepathic conference with Enlil on a couple of occasions. Kane's own psychically caressed mind had picked up the whispers, the tingles in the background of his thoughts when the two had conversed, and the Annunaki overlord had very nearly slain Kane with a psionic assault. Only CPR by his allies had been able to restart his heart after Enlil's mental death blow. He gave Durga a glare, but couldn't hold the words in.

"You'd be familiar, wouldn't you?" Kane asked.

"We're on the mental plane," his opponent growled. "Keeping your surface thoughts hidden is nigh impossible!"

Kane kept his eye on Durga. "So, if you're plotting something, I'll know it."

The Nagah prince's lip curled as his eyes gleamed like black pearls. "You may believe what you wish, fool."

"Or you've learned discipline while dealing with Enlil," Kane mused.

Durga looked as if he'd just punched him in the gut.

"Is this a trap?" Kane snarled. "I can undo—"

"No, you cannot," Durga responded. "It's not my trap."

Kane paused. "You said *your* trap."

"Jacobs," Durga said. "Or whomever he was working with."

Kane immediately looked to North. The man was null,

empty space in an otherwise normal room. Nehushtan was unable to "see" him. Kane presumed, because both Kane and Durga were projected into astral forms by the staff. He turned back to Durga.

"I do not trust that ape," Durga growled, pointing to the spot where North should have been.

Kane frowned, a sudden realization striking him. "He said that Nehushtan was transmitting a signal to repel him from it."

"And yet he is gone, disappeared from our view, if we truly are here because of the manipulations of the old staff of Solomon," Durga responded.

Kane shot a glance at him. "So what do we do to get back into our bodies?"

"Return to them?" he replied with a shrug.

The two men turned toward their bodies, then tried to swim through the empty air toward their frozen forms.

That was when North's void form shifted, spread. Cold red eyes glowed within that gray shape.

"Oh no, Kane, Durga," the figure said. It sure as hell didn't sound like North. It was something different. Metallic. Resonant. "You are not going to ruin this."

With that, the creature lifted its hand, and Kane and Durga were tossed about like leaves in the wind.

Kane roared in impotent rage as he was hurled away from his body and into the void.

Chapter 14

Brigid Baptiste watched Kane place Durga's hand on the staff, and then a moment later, both men collapsed to the floor. She immediately wondered if Kane had gone to the well one too many times, utilizing the staff's healing abilities, but neither man looked as if he had been put through agony, not like when Kane first sealed Nathan's deadly claw wound. No, this instance made it seem as if they were marionettes with their strings severed. Alarm filled the Cerberus archivist, and she rushed to cradle Kane's head, checking for vital signs.

She let out a sigh of relief that he had a pulse, still breathed, still was warm to the touch. However, that relief chilled and shattered like icicles when she saw his eyes, open, blank, soulless.

"Kane?" she asked.

No response. He didn't even blink when she touched her finger to his eyeball. Dread supplanted any gratitude that Kane's heart and lungs worked.

"What happened? Are they dead?" Thurpa asked. He was as confused by this as the rest.

"It could be the staff." North spoke up. "Kane tried to revive Durga…and if Nehushtan wanted little to do with me, then…"

"So it killed them both?" Grant asked.

"They're alive, physically," Brigid returned. "But there is nobody home in there."

Grant looked at his friend, then to Durga. "You sure it was the stick?"

"What else could it be?" Makoba asked. He struggled to his feet, a little unsteady, but he no longer seemed to be oozing blood. His arm no longer sported a bullet hole. He looked down, surprised to have been returned to health. "Why didn't I become catatonic, as well?"

"Because you weren't in physical contact?" Nathan suggested. He looked at the staff, then picked it up. Brigid watched for any change in his demeanor or health, or any response from Kane or Durga.

Unfortunately, nothing happened to the pair of comatose men. She gave her bottom lip a chew, then heard the thunder of the stairwell door being hammered off of its hinges at lobby level. There was an immediate echo down by Davis, with his radio. The look on his face confirmed her suspicions. "There's no back way out. We're going to have to hold the doorway."

Grant opened his war bag. "I've got a few charges that can slow them down."

Gibbons pulled out a duffel from a hiding spot by the wall. "We might have a way out...."

With that, he dug into the bag, tossing aside a couple Calicos, both of which were retrieved by Davis and Makoba. Finally, Gibbons came out with a large jewel, and something that made the blood drain from Brigid's already pale features.

"Where did Durga get a Threshold?" Brigid asked.

Gibbons looked at her. "How do..." He thought the better of debating it. "Durga never said."

Thurpa swallowed. "That was how we got from India to Africa. A hell of a lot safer than riding the Indian Ocean."

Brigid glanced toward Thurpa. "Did he inform you how to operate it. Did he inform any of you?"

From the pause and blank expressions on the faces of

those present, none of them needed to speak. While she had seen a Threshold before on a couple of occasions, and had even been ferried about by one with Ullikummis as Brigid Haight, she didn't have the personal knowledge of how to operate the device. Since much of Annunaki technology tended to operate on mental interface, she presumed that if she had the proper instructions, she could open a portal, but just holding the thing and making wishes would be counterproductive.

Reluctantly, she turned toward Fargo North. "Give the Threshold to him."

North glanced at the jewel-like ancient artifact. "You presume that—"

Brigid's icy glare, accompanied by the curl of her upper lip, cut him off. "We do not have time for your duplicity. Operate the Threshold or we will all perish."

North narrowed his eyes. "I thought that you'd want to do your hero thing...."

"We're outnumbered, and in a death trap basement," Grant growled as he packed explosives into the ceiling in front of the door. He stabbed radio detonators into them. The plan was simple, yet canny, Brigid decided. The explosives weren't able to produce a lot of concussive or shrapnel damage to intercept kongamato crashing through the door, but in the arc that Grant was setting them in, he'd drop the ceiling atop the marauders, crushing them, hopefully.

Brigid returned her attention to North. "Unless you part with some of your ill-gotten knowledge, we are all going to be ripped to shreds."

The renegade archaeologist reached out and grasped the Threshold. North peered into the facets of the Annunaki artifact, handling it and observing it almost as if it were a newborn babe. He ran his hands across its surface, lips silently moving, like a prayer to Enlil himself. The whole acquaintanceship with the Threshold unnerved

Brigid, making the hairs on her neck stand up straight. She scanned the room, and noticed that even the comatose Kane's neck hairs were erect. There was static energy in the atmosphere of this subterranean chamber, and then the Threshold released beams of laser light, sheetlike plasma clouds undulating off rays.

"Gather them!" North commanded, pointing to Kane and Durga.

Gibbons and Makoba grabbed the Nagah prince, and Domi and Brigid both seized Kane by the shoulders. The whole sensation was not dissimilar to the way that the mat trans would crack open the walls of reality in her experience, but this was much more outré, even wider and more unreal than her first times standing in the presence of the interphaser. There was something primal about how this gemlike construct pulsed and unleashed its energies to open its wormhole, something that normally required the effort of nuclear generators to power.

Then again, there were many aspects of Annunaki technology and culture that made Brigid's skin crawl, things she couldn't forget, and cruelties that she could not excise from her memory. These things were living, if not in the sense of how a human lives, but not nearly as inert as a plant. The Threshold was simply another aspect of a society with a running thread of decadence and cruelty, one rife with the enslavement of "lesser beings."

All this flashed through her mind as the rest of the universe simply ceased to exist for a moment. Then, instants later, things were back in order, and they were in the "break room" back at the Zambian power station.

North seemed drunken as he set down the Threshold, then collapsed into a nearby chair. He put his hand to his forehead, eyes closed in obvious discomfort. Brigid made a quick count, and everyone was present, a little more bewildered than they had been back in the Harare installation. Makoba guided the insensate Durga toward a chair where he could sit. Brigid noticed that with a little push, the comatose Nagah could move his feet, and support his own weight.

Brigid gently urged Kane to walk toward another chair, and helped him to sit.

"Everything working," Domi noted. "Just no Kane."

"Something happened with Nehushtan," Brigid mused. She looked to Nathan, who still wielded the staff.

"Should we touch him with it?" the young man asked.

"I don't think that's too smart. It left Kane a vegetable," Grant muttered. "What if the next contact kills him? Because this stuff has been getting progressively worse."

"It's a dilemma that I truly do not care to ponder. The only seeming cure is the staff, which to date has shown the ability to take Kane no matter what. However, it seems not to have any detriment to either Nathan nor myself," Brigid mused. She twirled a lock of hair around one finger, thinking about this. "There was something present this time that was not accountable during the first use."

"Kane looked as if he'd been run over with a Sandcat the time he used the stick to heal Nathan," Grant mused. He thought about it. "But you're right. It wasn't the staff's fault. This had been his first time channeling that kind of power. He wasn't used to it."

"Which means the persons present…"

"What the hell are you people doing here?" Lomon bellowed, interjecting his voice into the conversation. "Good grief, more of those snake people."

"We had to beat a hasty retreat from Kariba station," Nathan explained. "We were under siege by the kongamato."

"One moment this place was empty, the next, the room is full of people," Lomon told them. "How did you get here so fast?"

"Alien technology," Brigid answered. "Courtesy of…it's

a long story. Let's get behind those vault doors first, before our enemy figures out that we left them."

Lomon hit the radio for downstairs and more men appeared, not just Shuka, Jonas and the CAT team.

"These are the rest of my people," Sinclair said as they arrived. "Plus some guests. Is that…"

"It's Durga. Comatose, just like Kane," Grant concluded for her.

"What happened?" Sinclair pressed, even as she helped guide people to the vault doors.

"We made contact with the kongamato, recovering this one." Brigid pointed toward Thurpa, who was assisting Durga alongside Makoba, having taken Gibbons's place. "And then we found the Kariba station, where these fools had their monsters turn on them."

"The fate of all mad scientists," Sinclair muttered. As if to punctuate her observation, she noticed North handling the Threshold. It was not a surprise to see him, but it was a slap in the face considering the memories of her youth. North had styled himself, and still did, after a daredevil movie hero she'd had a crush on as a girl. The truth that he was a conniving man who'd murdered and bullied left a bitter taste in her mouth. It had been made even worse because she'd been the one to debrief him, to try to get inside his mind when he'd first arrived on scene.

It had been hoped that a little flirtation would help him slip up, loosen some words so that the others could observe him more deeply, get a better handle on who and what he was. Even so, the forensic evidence on the man's whip, full of blood and muscle tissue, had been enough to paint the picture of him as nothing less than a coldhearted snake.

Being the target of his interest made her feel dirty in retrospect. It was her hope to avoid him, but he was there, and he glanced at her, cheeks darkening in a blush at a reaction to her glare.

Sinclair fought the urge to look more closely at him, to study him, uncertain of whether she was harboring a crush on this man, and thus seeing things that weren't there, or if his "blush" was something more sinister. After all, after the terrible war in Garuda city, North had been "gifted" with an interface with one of Enki's old computer networks, an accessible storage grid of information that, of late, also allowed him to jam communication signals.

Sinclair wasn't a fool. North might have been in intensive concentration, doing something untoward. Perhaps even his brain's enhancement was behind the fate of Kane and Durga. If she continued to pay attention to him, then she might get his attention, draw his suspicions. No, she'd tell Brigid and Grant later on about what was amiss.

She'd do that in private, and they'd have their Commtacts off, because if North could jam communications, then he could also spy upon those radio frequencies.

Sinclair, as an officer in the United States Air Force, studiously followed operational procedure, sharing no more over radio comms than necessary, and being almost paranoid in watching for slips of vital information that could endanger her team.

As it was, she had her hands full, literally, with Kane as they guided the small troupe behind the redoubt's doors.

She glanced back as the heavy panels swung closed once more, thick steel bars extending within, forming the hinged doors into one solid, continuous piece, capable of withstanding all but a direct nuclear explosion.

And now, with North among them, Sinclair wondered if they were protected, or trapped in a killing box.

KANE AND DURGA had no physical bodies at the moment, but that didn't take away from the aches that they suffered. If Kane had not been on the horrific journey that the void being had sent them on, he would have thought the situation impossible. As it was, he could only liken the "terrain" where they landed as being akin to a tumbling nightmare of confusion. There were eerie, almost living outcroppings and paths stretching for miles and miles, often interconnecting, some segments simply floating in the air. There were spheres and globes that shimmered against a space-like purple background, giving the impression to Kane that some were planets, while others floated close to him, no larger than a ball, yet covered with clouds, continents and water.

The scene was oddly familiar, but Kane could not concisely recall the last time he'd been godlike in size and stature against such a backdrop of planetoids. He fought to keep his mind focused as the paths shifted about him, some seeming as fluid as spilling water, yet looking as firm and stony as the steepest of cliffs. Here and there he could spot tangling tentacles of some living creatures, and branches and briars rustling at the corners of his vision.

There was also Durga. While outwardly he held his original form as a tall, youthful cobra man, there were blurs and smears of other figures dragging along in his wake, as if Kane could peer through aeons of history, seeing what bodies and lives Durga had been born into.

Kane recalled the fever dreams that stayed with him after he had been squirted into a place between universes as he and Brigid Baptiste had sought Grant, lost in time, on an earlier mission. The details were fuzzy, but he now remembered the odd, uneven reality that had enveloped the two of them. He tried to concentrate, remembering what he could of that excursion.

"Where the hell did he throw us?" Kane asked.

"North?" Durga suggested.

"The void that was where he was supposed to have been," Kane responded. "I'm not certain that he was controlling that thing. After all, why would it disguise itself when it tossed us to our deaths?"

"Our deaths?" Durga countered. "You and I are very much alive."

"We are?" Kane asked. "We might as well be dead. We're phantoms. This isn't reality. We are lost, and probably millions of miles, if not universes, away from our bodies."

Durga looked around. He reached out for one of the hovering balls, fingers splaying to grasp the object. Kane moved in front of him, preventing him from touching it.

"What?" Durga growled.

"That is a world," Kane answered.

"All the more reason to examine it," the Nagah responded. "Or are you squeamish?"

"It looks as if it has liquid water on it. If that's the case, it might have life," Kane said. "And if it has life, I'm not letting you screw with it."

Durga's eyes gleamed with anger at this sudden act of defiance. "We'll never return to our bodies if you continue to stymie my curiosity."

"My life for a living world?" Kane asked. "Not a big trade. And your life? I wouldn't rate it as worth a slice of a microscopic planet like that."

Durga held Kane's gaze. "You try my patience."

"The feeling is mutual, scale face," he snapped. "But like it or not, we need each other."

"But you're going to be in that scaly face," Durga growled back. "Even if I have an idea that might aid us."

"How about living by the doctrine of 'first, do no harm,' for a few hours?" Kane asked. "Would it kill you?"

"You never know, Kane," he responded. "I'm loath to take that risk."

Kane couldn't help but smirk at his slithering response. "At least you're keeping a sense of humor about this."

"Who was joking?" Durga asked, blinking innocently.

Kane pointed up one of the paths. "As far as I can figure, we flew from that direction."

Durga glanced that way, then looked back at the man. As much as Kane would have loved to dig into the Nagah traitor, his allies were out there, somewhere, without his aid. As much as it galled him to think of himself as truly important, he *was* one-third of a remarkable team that had prevailed against menaces from simple cold hearts to armies to gods themselves.

Even if his presence weren't a part of Lakesh's alleged "confluence of circumstance" that allowed them to be so lucky, Kane knew that three sets of eyes were better than two, and he had years of experience watching their backs. Sure, Domi and the rest of CAT Beta were with them, as well as Durga's men, Nathan and the Zambians, but Kane felt derelict in duty.

He protected his friends, and they protected him. Kane needed to get back to them to feel whole again.

He'd been afraid of Nehushtan and its potential to strip him of his personal identity. But now it had been something else that had wrenched him from his skin, tossed him across a universe, stranded him with a man who was once his enemy and far from those he considered his family as they were about to come under siege from an army of unholy beasts.

It didn't escape Kane's notice that these same monsters had been awakened by Durga.

"There's something about the physics of this realm that I'm trying to remember," Kane said.

"Such as?" Durga asked. "Even if we are moving at the speed of thought, there is no indication that we could reach our home, our bodies, anytime before the apocalyptic end of the kongamato assault."

Kane frowned. "Yes. Thanks for that."

"I sought to control those creatures," the cobra man said apologetically.

"Control," Kane repeated. "You set them loose, and they killed and assaulted Zambians who had nothing to do with you or your quest."

Durga sneered. "And you've never fired on savages who you came across."

"Only when they attacked," Kane replied. "And two things. The Zambians are a civilized culture with at least as much modern technology as the Nagah. And you were hanging around with a group of raiders who survive by pillage and murder. If they didn't try to kill you, then sure as hell, normal Zambians wouldn't have reacted violently to your presence."

"You have not crossed Africa," Durga countered.

"I have. In the past," Kane answered. "And yes, there are pockets of violence, and there are pockets of people trying to survive day to day, and yet are able to show compassion for both neighbors and wayward travelers. Whatever you encountered, you were the instigator of violence."

"Of course," Durga said. "And the Millennium Consortium is innocent."

"That's another reason why I don't trust your protests," Kane snarled. "The consortium share the same kind of prejudices you seem to. Africa is full of savages to be enslaved, exploited or exterminated. It's their way. And yours."

"Your bleeding heart touches me," Durga returned. "I will consent to leave these tiny planets be. But I refuse to listen to any more of your sanctimonious preaching."

"Fine," Kane grumbled. "We're going to have to learn how to fly."

"Fly?" Durga asked. "You must be kidding."

"No. I remember this place. I've been here, once in my past. It was a time when I was deliberately slipped between dimensions. This is a realm where will is power itself," Kane said. "Our imagination can move us, if we can."

"We can fly," Durga repeated. "Think a happy thought and a little pixie dust…"

"What?" Kane asked.

"Sorry. Something from an old animated motion picture," he explained. "It was how a group of children learned to fly."

"Well, we're not going to grind any pixies into dust," Kane warned.

Durga rolled his eyes, then spread his arms. "If you said will is power…" Gravity seemed to release the Nagah prince. He rose, gliding slowly upward. "…I was one whose will was the equal of Enlil himself."

"Good for you," Kane said with a sneer. "You can float." He turned his attention toward the horizon. "Try to keep up."

And in a flicker of time, Kane was a living rocket, hurtling through this nether space, following his instincts along a thin thread back to his loved ones.

He tried not to smile too much as Durga grunted in an effort to keep up.

Chapter 15

Though Brigid Baptiste was not the kind of woman to go overboard with all manner of military security and secrecy, she and Grant both agreed to the logic in Sela Sinclair's handwritten message to turn off their Commtacts when they met with CAT Beta. With Fargo North in the redoubt, there was little telling the full extent of his abilities to hack into and control technology. They wouldn't put it past North to attempt to listen to whatever was being said about him.

Sinclair gave her briefing about her beliefs that North had been concentrating on something while they were assembling back in the Victoria Falls redoubt, including the doubts that crowded her mind during the confusion of their sudden arrival.

Once that was done, the Cerberus adventurers put their minds to the challenge of what this could have meant.

Grant frowned beneath his mustache. "As much as I'd love for North to be guilty, so we could beat him like a rug and get Kane back, I'm going to express some doubt. He just interfaced with the Annunaki artifact, and we were all left off balance by it teleporting us back to this station."

Brigid Baptiste nodded, obviously feeling distaste for an explanation that would let North off the hook. "That is a valid point, but I still can't deny that North's presence and proximity to Nehushtan might have been a catalyst for the odd behavior of the staff."

Domi wrinkled one lip. "Lemme talk to him."

"We do that, there won't be much left for answers," Brigid countered.

"That's a downside?" Grant asked. Brigid was sure he wasn't being serious, but she still hit him with a glare of admonishment.

"The barons used to punish on the slightest of rumors," she retorted.

He nodded. "I remember. I used to be part of that."

"Same here," Edwards agreed, his tone glum and somber. "I know we're taking precautions by turning off our Commtacts, but what if North's abilities aren't just limited to radio communications?"

"Thought reading?" Brigid asked.

Edwards nodded.

"If that were the case, then undoubtedly he could have arranged for a system hiccup that would have delayed this meeting," Brigid surmised. "It's safe to speculate that our thoughts are still our own, for the time being."

"Time being," Sinclair repeated. "In other words, North might be on track to mind reading."

"He's exploring the world, and traveling the same path Durga had been on. Durga, we've determined, came here initially in search of a means of restoring his body to full health," Brigid explained. "Now, it has happened, but his mind is…elsewhere."

"That still does not solve our major problem here," Sinclair offered. "It'll be nice to have Kane back with us, but even if he gets back—"

"*Will* get back," Grant grumbled, his gaze flinty and hard as he regarded her.

"When he gets back," Sinclair amended, realizing that she'd touched a raw nerve. "We've still got a group of out-of-control kongamato on the loose. They've attacked one city to the north and two of the installations along the Zambezi River."

"I noticed how you stressed 'out of control,'" Brigid said.

"Things acting too smart," Domi agreed. "Hit and run. Herding us."

"They hit the force sent to the redoubt. It was two companies of Zambian troops, but only three platoons survived," Sinclair summarized. "So, things are a little more crowded down here."

"Not too much," Domi noted.

"The attack on the relief force might have been a random act, but they were far too swift," Sinclair said. "It was a deadly ambush. That meant the kongamato had to be organized."

Brigid and Grant nodded.

"The creatures left bait for us, drew us into the same hole in the ground as Durga. He claimed to have lost the control matrix for them," Brigid stated. She grimaced. "*That* could have been what North was concentrating on."

"Sending new instructions to his pets," Edwards mused. "After all, it'll take them some time to get from there to here, even flying."

"But was it him or was it Durga?" Domi asked.

"If the Nagah prince had them under his control, that would have broken the moment he went comatose," Brigid offered. "But what if he isn't completely insensate?"

"Smaller words, please," Edwards grunted.

"What if Durga's in that state because part of him is hard at work coordinating the kongamato?" Brigid asked.

"So, he shuts down everything except the bare minimum to survive, and he's riding in those things' hive minds," Grant suggested.

Brigid tapped her nose, indicating to him that he'd picked up on her train of thought.

"One problem. How does that explain Kane?" Grant asked.

"It doesn't," she returned. "Maybe the two of them connected through Nehushtan's influence, and they attacked each other."

"Durga overpowered Kane's mind. So, he's out cold?" Sinclair asked.

Brigid looked at her *anam chara,* dearest friend and soul mate, who sat straight in his chair. But there was no light in his eyes, no reaction to sound. He breathed. His eyes blinked as they grew dry. But other than that, he was a lifeless manikin, a semblance of a human being. The thought that Durga had telepathically incapacitated him, having done harm to his soul, chilled her. Ever since fleeing Cobaltville, they had stood side by side, taking any and every threat against them.

Now, he was gone. That left a cold void in her world. It was as if a leg had been kicked out from beneath the table that held her reality level. Things were sliding, collapsing off to one side.

She was inches away from completely toppling. The thought of Kane dead would have at least given her closure. The thought of him captured at least provided the hope for rescue or vengeance. But Kane was here…and yet *not.* She had never felt so helpless, so impotent. Despite all her fantastic mental skills, all she could do was make certain that Kane didn't topple over and hurt himself. She dreaded how bad it would be if she had to spoon-feed the vacant body.

North and Durga were both likely suspects, but there could have been other factors at work. Durga had arrived in Africa utilizing Annunaki technology, so the potential for one of the overlords assisting the fallen prince was a given. If it were Enlil or Marduk, then Brigid could understand the targeting of Kane for this odd, comatose state. Kane had battled and blunted Marduk's plans, both when he was Baron Cobalt, Kane's former commander in chief, and after his awakening into his near-godly form.

Enlil, the head of the pantheon of terror, hated Kane

even more, and in the past had nearly murdered him during a telepathic conference. Perhaps this time Enlil's assault was more focused, leaving Kane's autonomic system alone, rather than subjecting him to stresses that nearly drove him into cardiac arrest.

And mental attacks weren't simply the realm of Enlil or Annunaki technology. Erica Van Sloane, currently an associate of the Millennium Consortium, had perfected SQUID technology, a mind-control net that had made men into her slaves when she controlled the Xian pyramid in China. Rebuilding the technology would be simple with the proper resources, especially working alongside the consortium, or tapping a technological storehouse, such as an unattended redoubt in Africa.

Narrowing down the cause of these troubles would be difficult.

"Brigid?" Grant's voice cut in on her thoughts.

She realized that she'd been off in a trance for a moment, running lines of causality and relationship between opponents, technology and abilities in a mind's-eye diagram. It was a web of possibilities, and she'd been running the odds of each situation. Things were trimming down nicely, but even if she managed to narrow this list, there was another side of her that was thinking knowing *who* was not going to help. She needed to know *how*. Kane had been left dumbstruck.

"Sorry, just going over our history and the available variations on mental attacks, which could steer us toward the originator of Kane's symptoms. Once we figure out who caused this, we can then concentrate on reversing the process," she explained.

"Yeah. For like, oh, ten seconds, your eyes were lit up. You're usually not glazed over and lost in thought. When you think…it's faster," Grant said.

Domi frowned. "Not hopeful."

Brigid looked to Domi. The feral girl was concise in her observation. Brigid left with her mental wheels spinning was never a good sign. When it came to mental challenges, Domi knew that Brigid was second to none. With her eidetic memory, she was able to access hundreds of years of history, thousands upon thousands of hours of science and data that would offer some kernel of information relevant to the situation at hand. If she was stymied, then Domi was worried.

Brigid was at a loss for words. Kane was not a drooling mess, but he wasn't far from a vegetable. And right now, they were trapped in a stripped-bare redoubt, waiting for a siege of horrific beats from African myth to make their assault.

"We'll let you concentrate on that," Grant said. "The rest of us will put our more 'blunt instrument' skills together toward dealing with the muties."

Brigid nodded, a little too numbly and quickly for her own comfort. She suppressed a grimace and a bout of self-reproach over that. She had mental hoops to leap through, her "murder board" to examine on the wall of her mind's eye.

DURGA KEPT PACE with Kane as they soared spaceways that resembled the fragmented nightmares of a surrealist painter. They had crossed what must have been light years, but the two of them weren't at all certain of the passage of time. There was no sun in the sky, and they had no technology with them, not even Kane's cybernetically implanted Commtact.

And so they flew, moving along in grim silence as the psychic realm about them shifted and changed.

"Are we even moving?" Durga asked.

Kane didn't answer. He didn't want to think of the possibility that they could simply be spinning their wheels in a hallucinogenic star scape. With no real means of propulsion, nor any gauge of where they were going, they could have simply been deluded into stretching themselves out. The only sliver of hope was a faint, shimmering thread that spiraled out ahead of him, one that corkscrewed as he accelerated along it.

Kane had done some reading and research on psychic phenomena, as he'd been growing more and more sensitive to its presence in his life. He didn't have any telepathy or other doomsayer abilities, but ever since his first close contact with Balam, there seemed to have been a switch flipped in his mind, one that could pick up on the subtle vibrations of realms outside the senses he normally paid attention to.

"Kane, are we doing anything?" Durga snapped.

"I know you're getting on my nerves," he replied, barely controlling that errant thought.

Durga stopped, one hand grasping Kane and nearly jerking his shoulder out of its socket. There was reality here in this realm, physical sensation of gravity and breeze in what should have been an endless, featureless void. Amid the warmth and hospitality of this mind-bent dimension, both men had encountered things they could touch and handle.

But were those sensations also illusions?

Kane squeezed his shoulder, just as certainly as if he'd been in an actual body. "That hasn't changed," he muttered.

"What hasn't?" Durga asked.

"Our ability to interact with each other," he responded. "But is that merely our minds playing tricks on us?"

"That's your worry?" the Nagah asked. "We've been hurled across a universe or two, and it may take aeons for us to return home."

"I've been in this situation before. Well, a similar one to this."

Durga rolled his amber eyes. "So tell me of your great wisdom."

Kane thought of it, and as if by magic, a screen appeared beside him, showing the details he'd seen, or at least remembered as described by others. He recalled the attack on Thunder Isle, and Grant being sucked into a wormhole opened by the damaged time trawl.

There was the incident with the ghostly shadow of Grant, his memories trapped in the present, literally a fraction of himself, pure memories sans corpus, separated from another "shadow"—a tesseract body that had been trapped in ancient times, with spirit, but no memory. And both essences were in themselves only illusions of the real thing, Grant as an entity trapped in the void between time and spacial dimensions, in the membranes of reality where he was neither dead nor alive.

Finally, Durga was able to observe Kane's traverse of the dimensions as he and Brigid Baptiste were sent there, thanks to arcane algorithms that enabled them to puncture the confines of even the wormhole channels opened by the time trawl or the mat trans. Kane, seeing himself, his own shadows, an existence stretching across multiple human lifetimes, as well as the entity that had battled alongside Sir Richard Grenville originally, his translated dream shown in contrast.

Back in his physical body, trapped in the fetters of cold, hard three-dimensional physics, Kane couldn't remember. But here, he was not human, not limited by the nature of his mental chemistry or biological senses, so he could stretch out his awareness. As a being of pure thought, he could connect to the time worm that each living entity was, an undulating organism that spanned eternity and infinity, connecting Kane to earlier incarnations in this universe and others.

Durga's amber-hued eyes widened as he watched the branching threads of Kane's life explode into stark relief against the background of the multiverse.

"Time and space are not linear," Durga murmured. "The brane theory is correct."

"Brane theory?" Kane repeated.

Durga explained that the reality they observed was simply one of many, something Kane agreed with, having been sent to other universes, which he, Lakesh and the other Outlanders called "casements." These "branes" were short for membranes, elastic universes, layered together like onion skin, but very rarely touching each other. When those membranes did touch, things like mat trans and psychic doomsayer powers were able to make use of resulting universal bumps. There had been theories in the twentieth century that sightings of ghosts and UFOs were not paranormal, but glimpses of neighboring dimensions viewed when the branes bumped against each other.

Certainly enough, Grant's tesseract was evidence that hinted toward that truth.

"How did you return to your body last time?" Durga asked.

Kane frowned. "When you go through a mat trans or a time trawl, you're broken down into a wave form that has a specific frequency, which can be picked up by the transmitter. In the mat-trans network, the other end is set to receive that, but the trawl, as it sent us between the branes, as you called it, put out a carrier signal that our waves could home in on," he responded.

"So what signal are you following?" Durga asked.

"To me, it looks like a silver thread," Kane told him. "It trails off that way."

Durga squinted, and Kane concentrated, fanning the glow within the connection. Durga's eyes went wide again.

"So, we have a route back. Know how?" Durga asked.

"Maybe it's Nehushtan," Kane offered. "Or maybe it's just that this is semifamiliar terrain. Or maybe it's a mix."

"I can...I can nearly see my own thread," Durga replied.

Kane looked and saw it. He reached for Durga's tether, but the Nagah prince bared his fangs.

"I'm not going to harm you. I risked a lot trying to get you to stand once more," Kane reminded him.

Durga frowned. "And yet you assumed I'd crush a world?"

Kane shook his head. "You seemed to have a gleeful gleam in your eye when you saw an entire planet you could crush."

Durga grimaced. "Well…you might not have been far off from my intent."

"That's the difference between us. You think I'm like you," Kane accused.

Durga sighed. "We're in this together. You kind of know the way home, and I do owe you. But we both know each other's past. You haven't always been Saint Kane, noble hero."

Kane sneered. "Why do you think I'm trying so hard? I took my job as a magistrate seriously. I thought the world needed what I'd been doing. And then the scales finally fell from my eyes. I see a world desperately in need of so much. You had a city where you were a *prince*."

Durga glared. "You'll never understand power…."

Kane snatched at Durga's thread. "Power? You mean the ability to decide life and death on a whim? The same power I wielded over everyone as per the orders of Baron Cobalt? You forget. I was the fist of royalty. I *was* power. I understood that rush. That prestige. And I also was smart enough to understand when it was being abused, when it was too cruel. That's why I fought against it. Because power isn't worth anything unless it's used to dig the whole out of a hole."

Durga looked at the angry man clutching the thread that linked the Nagah to his body.

"You had gifts. You had a beautiful wife-to-be. And you

had a mother, a family," Kane spit with a grimace. "And you had a father."

Kane let go of the silver thread. "You had things I didn't. And what did you do? You murdered both your parents. You threw away the love of your people. You destroyed it, along with your city."

"That's your problem with me? Your own daddy issues, Kane?" Durga asked.

"My problem is that you had so much you didn't need to be greedy. You didn't need to be insane. You didn't need to murder," Kane retorted.

Durga looked down at the silver string stretching from him into the depths of infinity. He'd felt the constricting, strangling grasp as Kane had clutched it, knowing he'd felt Kane's steely fingers around his throat in prior battles. If anything, this felt worse, as if Kane had tried to rip his soul out by the roots, a twisting, tortuous strangulation that made Durga feel as if he had been dragged through a rock-strewn wilderness.

"We get home, and we won't remember this, not when we get there," Kane rasped. "But we will have some feelings, and maybe some flashes of recognition and epiphany in dreams, though once our eyes open, all this will be dashed against rocks. It happened in the casements. It happened when I sought out Grant. And it'll happen with this. But here and now, you'll know why I consider you the lowest of the low, a belly-crawling coward, a bottom feeder whose blindness took the closest thing to a utopia and turned it back into a third world nation ripped by civil war and greed," he growled. "Garuda was a beautiful realm. A place where human and posthuman were able to live in the same society, where prejudice wasn't the norm, where blind hatred was pushed aside to create a prosperous, advanced realm. Now, the tools that could have rebuilt a country are scrap metal. And even then…"

"And even then, my vengeance against Hannah and Manticor is blunted because they can't hate the seeds I planted in her," Durga said, disgust mixing with defeat. "You forget how much hope has survived in that damned hole in the ground. How much those people forgive. Forgive rotten genetics and being forced to live as worms beneath feet, not dragons across the sky."

"Poor you," Kane mock whimpered.

"You never were a second-class citizen, were you?" Durga asked. "We were the children of a lesser god, Enki. And then we were hidden in the catacombs when man rose and burned this world."

"Sins of the past," Kane growled. "We tried to undo that history, but it didn't work."

"The history where this planet was destroyed? Sure. Because it was just you naked apes at stake. You didn't know who you shared this mud ball with," Durga said.

"We didn't care who we saved," Kane said. "Just like I didn't care about saving you because maybe, just maybe, you'd have been a bit of help to protect my friends and all those people stuck with them. I don't care that you're not 'human.' You're someone who could do something to redeem yourself, or at least do me a solid for getting your damned feet back under you."

Durga curled his upper lip. "Fine. But don't ever touch my thread again. It felt as if you were killing me."

Kane nodded. "I won't. Now, if you can see your line, maybe we can get back a little faster."

"Maybe," Durga said. He looked around at the ersatz starscape around them. "But I think we've got miles to go before we're back in our heads."

Kane accelerated, Durga rushing to keep up as the weird universe swirled about them. The two men, divided by wrongs real and imagined, traveled along the spiral trails that they hoped would bring them back to reality.

Chapter 16

Grant grimaced as he looked over the layout of the redoubt. The kongamato were strong, but he couldn't see them succeeding in a direct assault against the vaultlike doors, designed to turn the underground installation into an impregnable fortress. He and Edwards had examined the outside doors, and saw that the creatures had somehow managed to put dents in the half-inch-thick outer later of steel, but that must have been after hours of effort.

Quite simply, it would take something far more powerful to cut through those barriers. Unfortunately, there was the reality that the vat-bred creatures were not on their own. They had a controlling force, one that might be directed by someone within their own ranks. Grant almost wanted to blame Kane not just for abandoning him, but for leaving him with a plethora of potential traitors.

He didn't mind teaming up with the Zambians or Nathan Longa. Those men had been under attack, and were not likely to turn on them. Grant's observation of the haggard, battered state of the reinforcements also gave that group a proper "vetting" in his eyes, especially with the assistance of Sinclair and Edwards, who were also both good judges of character and had done triage on some of the injured.

The millennialists were a group that Grant could have easily seen stumble toward extinction by their own hand, if not for the fact that they were extra bodies that would help against the final numbers. According to their local commander, Makoba, Durga's resurrection of the kongamato had taken place in a facility that was miles away, downstream, in the thickest jungles and beyond turbulent rapids. The Annunaki facility he'd opened was remote and well-hidden, but also had the ability to put out hundreds of the creatures in the space of a few days. Makoba hadn't had an exact count of what had been produced, but Durga was not going to allow himself to be overwhelmed by any force.

"Two hundred a day," Grant mused.

"And what if they're making more today?" Edwards asked.

Grant nodded. "Fighting one or two was tough, and that was with guns. I can see how these things attacked armed troops and inflicted heavy losses."

"We've got firepower, but the thing is, they're not just savage in their attacks. They're mobile. They're quick on all fours, moving like a gorilla as they run, and they can leap or glide, allowing them more angles of attack," Sinclair added. "If there were a means of limiting their mobility… Well, there is."

"Fighting them inside," Grant concluded. He folded his brawny arms, looking at the layout. "They're not going to come down on us from above, anyway."

"You think that the other facility has a tunnel leading here?" Sinclair asked.

"Makes sense," Edwards said. "They were built by the same company, and this is all one extended facility, designed to provide electricity to the whole region."

"There's no sign of a conduit from this redoubt to another across the river, though," Sinclair observed, her brow wrinkling with concern. "At least, nothing on paper."

"It also took them over a century to open the mat-trans chamber," Grant said. "These are post skydark plans, assembled by the Zambians. There are notes about locked doors in lower levels, doors that are sealed thanks to an outside power source."

"Like the nuclear generators that run the redoubts," Domi murmured. "Maybe I should look."

"Don't go alone," Grant ordered. He glanced to the brawny Edwards. "Cover her."

"And who knows, I might even spot something, as well," Edwards grumbled.

He nodded. CAT Beta might not have been the "magical" threesome that Lakesh viewed Grant, Kane and Brigid as, but the three of them did their best to make certain that Cerberus's other Away Team wasn't a group of second-rate warriors.

Edwards was large and brawny, a paler version of Grant, but just because he was a "big lug" did not mean he was mentally deficient. As a magistrate, he'd received the same training as Kane and Grant, and as such, was swifter than his bulk appeared. Plus he was skilled in unarmed combat, was wicked with a blade, and a far-above-average shot, as well as having the skills to operate all manner of communication devices and transport and combat vehicles. While his senses weren't anything beyond normal human, as Domi's feral instincts or Kane's point man instincts were, Edwards had spent enough time as a magistrate to have developed canny observational skills and a well-tuned bullshit filter.

Sinclair was a "freezie"—a survivor from centuries past who had been placed in suspended animation. She was an air force veteran, another member of the Cerberus group who had some facility with aircraft, although her specialty had been with security and espionage. Sinclair's instincts and observational abilities were on par with Edwards's, and she was in fine athletic condition. Technically and physically, she was bright and adaptable, and had brought late-twentieth-century law enforcement methods that, on more than one occasion, had proved the difference between needless bloodshed and the takedown of a person who was a danger both to himself and to the Cerberus explorers.

And then there was Domi. She had been with Kane, Grant and Brigid since the very beginning, changing from a feral child of the wilderness, hardened in the urban apocalypse of the Tartarus slums, into something more. She'd grown in education, in experience and in mental and emotional maturity. What had once been an illiterate, throat-slitting denizen of the slums had stood up in the face of gods and monsters, and had done so with compassion and the ability to connect with other humans, though never surrendering the savage talents that allowed her to fight so effectively that even Edwards, at three times her size, couldn't defeat her.

All things told, though, Grant wished he had Kane himself back, instead of a mindless husk.

All this also informed Grant that he was seriously alone. Brigid was left pondering the mystery of Kane's mental crippling, where he could have been attacked, whether he was alive and imprisoned in his own flesh, or if he were separated from his body.

If anyone could figure out the metaphysics of Kane's condition, it would be Brigid Baptiste. After all, she and Kane had sought out Grant's original self, trapped in a zone between dimensions. But that was with access to the time trawl, and with the assistance of some incredible mathematicians and quantum physicists, including Mohandas Lakesh Singh. The mat trans here didn't have access to temporal wave distortion, and Lakesh and the others *could* be working on it back at Cerberus. But one of the mathematicians who'd helped Kane and Brigid survive between dimensions and home in on Grant's multiversal location was dead, one of too many victims of Ullikummis's assault on the redoubt.

"This is eating at you," Sinclair noted.

Grant nodded. "It's one thing to go toe to toe with an Annunaki overlord, or a fifteen-foot robot. It's a whole other thing to sit by and be impotent when you're not even sure what happened to your friend. I want to help Brigid...."

"Do you remember anything of your time through the wormhole?" Sinclair asked.

He shook his head. "I asked Brigid if it was something wrong with my brain. She said it was a problem with everyone's brain."

"What does that mean?" Sinclair asked.

"We're stuck in a world ruled by three-dimensional physics and chemistry. The entity that I became when I was transmitted between worlds was something completely alien," Grant replied. "Oh, sure, the shadows it cast were recognizable as myself. But there are things 'visible' in that realm that just don't translate into human experience."

Sinclair blinked. "So..."

"Basically, I can't remember it because it's not memorable by the human mind," Grant said. "At least as Brigid explained it."

"Jeez," Sinclair muttered. "Just like when Bones asked what death was like..."

"What?" Grant asked.

She shrugged. "I'd have to be lost just like you'd been to have a common point of view."

He smirked. "And even then we couldn't bring that common point of view back from the other side to communicate it properly here."

Sinclair winced, trying to wrap her mind around that thought. "So we do what we can. And what will we do?"

"I'm going to give North a little bit of a poke," Grant said. More than he'd have liked. He brushed the Commtact plate against his jaw, even though it was already off, making them relatively invisible to North if he were listening in on their communications. "I've already demonstrated distrust of the asshole, so when I confront him, he'll be expecting some bullying, without implicating the rest of you."

"But that means he could try to kill you," Sinclair offered.

Grant smirked. "He's welcome to try."

GRANT ENTERED THE room that North had claimed for himself, finding the man sitting, eyes glazed, humming lowly, tunelessly, almost an unconscious trill.

"If you're thinking of making an attack upon me, Grant, I'll have you know the nanocomputers installed in my frontal lobes have already calculated every single one of your moves and informed me of them. I've summarized a response to over a million different battles between us, and in 78.04 percent of all instances, it ends with you bleeding and crying on the floor, drooling in your own spittle," the archaeologist said.

Grant snorted, then exploded into a laugh. "That's the reason I don't try to kill you on first sight. You always say funny shit."

North's vision focused on Grant. "Really?"

"Well, enough of the time to keep me from just up and doing some serious damage to you," Grant added. "You do know that I've held my own against you in the past, right?"

"Yes," North responded. "Is that why you're here? So we can unzip and measure ourselves against each other?"

"Nah," Grant said. He had a couple cans of soda with him, and lobbed one gently to North. "I came to talk."

The other man caught the can with a bit of fumbling, putting the lie to his boast of combat prowess. Or was he as clumsy as he seemed? Grant wondered. He could be playing, lulling his enemies into a false sense of security.

If there was one thing former magistrate Grant knew, cockiness was the quickest ticket to a world of pain and suffering. For as skilled as he was in combat, as physically powerful, Grant's flesh was no more durable than a normal man's, and his limits were still those of humanity. He'd seen what the nanites had done to Durga before Kane blew him up with a fuel-air explosion. The creature the Nagah prince had become was a giant, bulletproof and strong enough to ignore implosion grenades and bullets straight to the head, all while tearing through bricks and cave walls as if they were tissue paper. Whatever tricks North could hold might not be so vulgar in terms of might, not when the man's mind was plugged into its own personal computer.

"So, did you do something to Kane and Durga?" Grant pressed.

"You mean when they went mentally bye-bye?" North returned.

He nodded.

North opened his soda, took a sip.

"Well?" Grant asked.

"If I knew, I'd be gloating," the archaeologist answered.

Grant wrinkled his nose. "So you say."

"What made you think I've got some involvement in this?" North asked.

"Because the last time Kane used the stick to heal someone, he went through just fine," Grant responded. "But you were with us in that basement. And you claim that Nehushtan is producing some form of signal that prevents you from getting too close."

"I'm not claiming," North said. "It's what is happening to me."

Grant frowned.

"You don't trust me. I get it. But why in particular are you coming to bother me?" North asked.

"Because Brigid's busy determining other causes and solutions to the loss of Kane and the worm," Grant said. "And CAT Beta is battening down the hatches against a possible incursion by the kongamato."

"So, being the smartest of the remnants, you decided to

engage in a battle of wits with the guy and his nanite-enhanced brain," North concluded.

He nodded. "You know I wasn't born yesterday. For the past few years I've been dealing left, right and center with all kinds of manipulators."

"I don't doubt it," North admitted. "But this isn't your strongest suit. You're a blunt instrument."

Grant remained quiet, punctuating North's statement with the opening of his soda can. The crack-fizz of the opening beverage sounded especially harsh and loud in the quiet of the room. His lack of facial expression was all the condemnation that Grant required for North's attempted insult.

"Not rising to the challenge?" the other man asked.

"I'm waiting for the challenge," Grant answered.

North grimaced. "I've noticed that the lot of you from Cerberus have been very quiet on your radios."

Grant raised an eyebrow. "Oh dear. I thought you'd never have figured that out."

North smirked. "Playing dumb...more of a strength."

"You see these muscles. You don't think of what's between the ears," Grant told him.

"Who really got on to me?" North asked. "Brigid Baptiste? The girl with the movie hero fixation?"

Grant folded his arms. "You're the smart one."

North rolled his eyes. "Screw it. I'll talk to something more on my mental level." He studied his beverage can. "So, how are you doing today?"

Grant chuckled.

"Tell me why I shouldn't kick you out of my quarters," North finally asked, after a minute of silence and Grant's brief bit of amusement.

"Because this isn't your facility," he answered. "The Zambians own it."

"They don't know what they have. What they still have," North said.

"They figured out the mat trans's general user interface enough to call around the globe," Grant countered. "And that was after only about a half hour of looking at it without a manual."

North rolled his eyes. "Big deal."

"You're pretty good at considering people beneath you. Me. The Zambians," Grant mused. "Or is it just black people?"

"Give me a break. I look down on everyone," North replied. "You less than most others."

"Pin a medal on you," Grant retorted.

"For what?" North asked. "Realizing that Africans aren't backward and primitive? Just looking at how they haven't fallen into the kind of barbarism that North America collapsed into is proof enough. Then again, the collapse of civilization was in the planning for millennia."

"What is your goal here?" Grant asked. "What was so important that you needed to come to Africa?"

"It's a vast continent, full of history, myths and gods," North replied. "There are mysteries throughout this land."

"And the first mystery that you pop in upon happens to put you in the same neighborhood as Durga and us," Grant returned.

"Which I warned you of…"

"Yeah. You warned us he was present. That he was up to something," Grant replied. "Even that he had something to do with the kongamato…and yet—"

"And yet what?" North interrupted.

"Durga's control of the kongamato went south immediately, and now he and Kane are catatonic wrecks," Grant snapped.

"I don't have a personal problem with Durga," North replied. "If anything, he has a problem with me because of what I did to him. First I wrecked his face, and then it was my bomb that turned him into a cripple."

"So you wouldn't take advantage of this situation?" Grant asked.

"If I had the room and opportunity to take advantage of this, you know full well I would," North answered. "Durga's damned scary and dangerous. You wouldn't have stepped on him when he was helpless?"

"He's helpless now," Grant said. "What's stopping you from cutting the head off that snake?"

"Aside from Thurpa and the millennialists? And you do-gooders?" North retorted.

"Ah." Grant grunted.

"Yep," North agreed. "Morally, you're a damned idiot for not just killing him and putting out the consortium goon squad to be picked apart by kongamato."

"Morals. Killing the unarmed and helpless," Grant repeated.

"They're not unarmed now," North argued. "Not after getting into the Zambian's armory. They can fight for their own survival."

"Against creatures who took out a larger group of trained soldiers?" Grant asked.

"Your self-righteous attitude is starting to eat at my patience," North muttered.

Grant smirked. "Then I'm doing my job well."

"I thought you Cerberus people would be a lot more practical," North growled.

"Practical, or acting like barbarians who just scalp people for a can of creamed corn? Because sometimes, practical is doing the right thing, no matter what."

"You're kidding me," North exclaimed. "The right thing would be hunting down and exterminating every single millennialist that's ever been born. They're a heartless group of technocrats whose only goal is making themselves comfortable, no matter who they have to enslave."

"Trust me, nothing would make life easier for us, but take a look at the group of ragtag losers we have here. They're beaten. Whipped hard. Shell-shocked survivors. And their attitude is different now. They've changed," Grant said.

"And yet you still don't give me any slack despite *my* changes," North argued.

"They're powerless and frightened at this moment," Grant continued.

"Powerless, with the rifles you handed them," North reminded him.

"Shows you their essential good nature. They're hanging with us, not plotting against us," Grant insisted.

"So you assume," North said. "And you know the old saying."

"When you make an assumption, you make an ass out of you and umption," Grant countered. "A little trust goes a bit of a way, but we're not completely stupid."

North's eyes narrowed.

"Oh, you want to know if we're spying on the consortium, and how," Grant stated. "That we've come up with some pearl, some stratagem that gives us the advantage over those survivors."

North squinted even more, and sure enough, he tuned out momentarily. Whatever technological abilities he had, he was accessing them, and Grant simply waited.

Suddenly, the archaeologist's gaze locked back on him. "They're staying quiet. No communication with the band of marauders they've hooked up with. The same goes for Thurpa's comms. They're…"

Even as the man's voice trailed off, Grant remained impassive. Inwardly, he was surprised at how easily North had fallen for this ruse.

"Son of a bitch," he growled.

"Consider yourself vetted, too," Grant stated. "You legitimately checked on them to keep an eye out *for* us. Shows that you're genuinely trying to work alongside us."

"How do you know I wouldn't fabricate a lie?" North asked.

"Because you acted too spur-of-the-moment. Those nanites might increase your sensitivity, they might give you access to a huge database, but they can't improve your acting ability," Grant told him. "Getting pissed off at me right now also clinched it."

"Expect you to play dumb, and I end up the idiot," North growled.

"Come on, let's go check with the others and see what they've found out about whatever is linking this station with Kariba," Grant suggested.

"You think that the complex of power stations along the Zambezi River is all interconnected?"

"If you've got data showing otherwise, I'd love to know," Grant returned.

North dipped into his knowledge base, though not having to scan frequencies, his concentration didn't waver. It took only a few moments for his features to change expression, and realization give way to fear.

"Damn it. Damn it!" he growled.

"What?" Grant asked.

"The facility…this was supposed to be a supercenter," he said. "A one-stop shop. The mat trans, a time trawl and cloning facilities."

"Cloning…" Grant repeated. He activated his Commtact. "Command override power-off. Domi?"

"They're in!" he heard the feral girl shout, moments before he lost contact with her.

Grant's Sin Eater snapped into his grasp, and he took off running.

Chapter 17

Domi and Edwards moved easily through the halls. One of many things that the Zambians had done with this facility was take good care of it. The floors were clear of clutter, dust and other impediments to movement. The lights were well-regulated, making it easy to navigate and maneuver, even in the underutilized depths of the redoubt.

"So, what do you think Grant's gonna do with North?" Edwards asked.

"Talk to him," Domi answered. "Until it's time not to talk."

"In other words, 'shut up, Edwards,'" the big magistrate veteran replied.

"Nah." Domi shook her head. "Grant's not gonna attack someone not hurting him, or anyone else he's protecting. It'll be up to North to make the first mistake."

Edwards smirked.

"Listen, just because I walked to Kariba with the others doesn't mean I think you and Sela are second rate as a team. In fact…"

"Don't worry about it," Edwards returned. "And this ain't a woman's "don't worry" where you have to spend the rest of your days looking for the mines she buried. This is just a one-moment-I-thought-shit-was-up, but now I know it isn't."

Domi smirked. "You know I'm not that kind of a woman."

"The answer is probably yes, but do you smell that?"

"Dead body," she muttered.

Edwards grimaced.

Domi pulled her pistol, as did the big man. She had been steadily leading them toward the scent of rot down the hallway. "You picked up on it quick. I've only smelled it for a minute."

The two continued down the hallway in silence, their senses peeled, keen for any signs of opposition in the depths of the facility. Conversation now would only make it harder to anticipate the presence of opposition. The four of them—Grant, Domi, Sinclair and Edwards—had been correct about the potential of an underground path between the redoubts along the river. The thing that kept them on edge was whether it had been the kongamato who had created the corpse, or some other faction. And would the nonhuman monsters be able to track the scent of the deceased all the way here.

Domi and Edwards finally stopped, finding the source of the odor. It was a body wedged in a door, bullet holes in its chest. The corpse was of a millennialist, his jumpsuit and insignia prevalent despite bloodstains and tears on his uniform.

Domi pointed to the gunshots and Edwards took a closer look. As a magistrate, he had been at the scene of many a murder in the Tartarus. He'd be able to tell the difference between the kinds of wounds, at least in terms of the gear most Millennium Consortium men had, versus the locals.

"Not shot by his buddies. These aren't pistol rounds," Edwards said softly as he probed one bullet hole. "This is a rifle round. You can see the fractures in the skin around the entrance wound. The rifle noses are smaller than pistol bullet noses, but when they hit flesh and bone, they upset more, stretching the skin inward into the crater blown by metal expanding or fragmenting in soft tissue."

"Zambians or Harare?" Domi asked.

"Could be," Edwards said. "But I don't think so. The military folks here use full-powered battle rifle rounds from Heckler & Koch G3s or FN FALs, in the same caliber as the SIG AMTs we have with us. These entrance and exit wounds look a bit smaller. Like AK rounds, same caliber, but a smaller charge so they don't move as fast and hit as hard."

"And since we haven't seen anything bigger among the locals, he was shot by…bandits," Domi surmised.

Edwards nodded. "I spent some time asking what the militia and marauders were carrying, just for reference. The Zambians told me that they use old AK rifles in a lighter .30 caliber. The bigger bullets are meant to make poaching easier, and they don't have to worry as much about the quality of the bullets to get a punch. The Zambian military and police have a factory that can churn out good ammunition, as does Harare, so they go with the lighter, but more accurate ammunition."

Domi quirked her lips. "Left body here. Bait."

Edwards nodded in agreement.

She went around and took the corpse's feet. Edwards hauled the body off the ground by the armpits. The two of them walked it down the corridor, letting the door shut behind them.

"Should we turn on one of our Commtacts?" Edwards asked.

"Not yet," Domi said. "Grant'll override and turn us on."

"Great," Edwards grumbled. He glanced back at the door leading to the Zambians' redoubt. "So what should we do until he contacts us?"

"Look deeper," Domi replied. "And kill any of the beasts we find in these corridors."

"Good plan," Edwards returned. "I'll take point."

Domi nodded as he paused long enough to make certain the door was secured. He punched in the security code, then used a screwdriver to remove the keypad. Now, the only way they could get back in was by calling for help before getting to that door. It wasn't a vault like the one up above, so every bit of security would be needed. Edwards added some cable ties to further secure it, but short of getting out a welder, there wasn't much more he could do.

Once that was finished, he joined Domi in their advance.

Going back wasn't an option, but the hallway seemed to be leading to other facilities via an underground conduit. This was an emergency subterranean access. Edwards paused and pointed to a vent with a ladder symbol.

"We can get out of the way, if necessary," he said softly.

Domi nodded. "Pull them in there, too." She opened the door and looked up. "Tight fit for you."

"If we've got a dozen kongamato running at us, I can suck it in and get up that ladder," Edwards stated. "If not, I'll make a good clog in the drain. They won't get past me, or any of their buds that try catching up to me before I run out of ammo."

Domi smirked.

Just to be certain, Edwards went in and checked how quickly he could climb a few rungs. He wasn't impaired by the tightness of the escape tunnel, and he found that he could turn on the ladder and face down to fight. Domi caught a glimmer of glee in his eyes, a smile dancing across his lips.

"We got this," he declared.

Domi smirked again. "We got it?"

"We got it by the ass," Edwards said.

She chuckled, remembering that line from an old vid that Sinclair had shared with them. "You sure you want to say that?"

"Why not? I'm not a shrimp," Edwards returned.

Domi chuckled, feeling a little more relaxed. The two settled back into a state of grim readiness, having loosened up some. Being pulled emotionally taut was a quick road to ruin, as worries and scenarios clouded the mind. Domi had heard Grant's beloved, Shizuka, say a Japanese term that expressed the epitome of the samurai warrior woman's general being, and something Domi had never had the vocabulary to share.

Zanshin. Relaxed alertness The remaining mind. It was a state where the extraneous "what-ifs" were put aside, and the moment was experienced as it happened. Acting thoughtlessly was a good way to end up dead, but operating with too much thought was a way to distract yourself. Domi had lived that way for years, her keen senses and instincts operating, while the higher levels of her mind went into a more relaxed mode.

Her reflexes were honed and tuned to that, which was why her diction became more simple and primitive. Only things necessary to survival were paid attention to. She lived in the moment, focused on what was about her, not what had been or what could be.

It was enough to get her through the toughest of times. And sometimes the means of getting to that mental state was a simple thought, usually accompanied by a laugh. If there was one thing Domi cherished, it was the little laughs, the brief moments.

Right now she was at once focused and unfocused. Nothing put her senses into a tunnel, another bit of irony, as she herself was in one. Her ears picked up each crunch of dust beneath the boots she and Edwards wore, each drip of condensation, each buzz of a light fixture.

The two of them paused as they reached an intersection. It was more than a four-way. Domi was able to count nine tunnels spreading out from the center hub. She checked her watch, actually a readout screen on the forearm of her shadow suit, and found that they had traveled at least four thousand feet.

She was tempted to activate her Commtact and inform Grant about this linkage, and the potential for at least seven more unknown facilities being attached to the one the Zambians controlled, but depending on North, this information may have already come out. And if not…

Domi fought her mind, pushing the "what-ifs" away. Something had niggled at the edge of her hearing, and she started looking down the halls branching off from this central hub. Edwards picked up on her change in demeanor, and began taking up the slack. Certainly, there wasn't any threat coming from the tunnel they'd followed, so the two of them scanned the others.

The angry, batlike shriek of one of the creatures was faint, but it tripped Domi's survival instincts.

At that moment, the Commtacts came on.

"Domi?" Grant's voice cut in.

"They're in!" Domi answered. She had to make a decision now. She and Edwards could run back the way they'd came, but undoing the door would take too long, and it would bring an angry horde into the depths of the Zambian redoubt. There was little doubt that enough of those creatures could hammer the door off its hinges.

She looked to the left and picked one of those tunnels, pointing it out to Edwards, who was busy setting two grens along the way back "home."

"Why?" Domi asked.

"Animals don't want to risk injuring themselves going the same route others wanted to," he said. "If a gren blows every time they take that tunnel…"

Domi nodded. She pulled her knife and nicked the back of her wrist, drawing a small trickle of blood, smearing it along the way she intended to go. "Giving them a fresher trail to follow."

"Smart," Edwards returned. He was done setting his

booby traps, and now the creatures' sounds were growing louder.

The two people picked Domi's corridor and hurtled down it.

She quickly activated her Commtact and apprised Grant of the plan.

DURGA LET OUT a scream of frustration. It felt as if the two of them had been traveling for years. Behind them, the universe spun away, still showing the wild spiral of their back trail, the space they'd churned through looking like the wake wash of a fast-moving motorboat, except instead of white-water foam, it was some kind of black-and-purple diamond-faceted ripple that made Durga nauseated.

"What's wrong now?" Kane asked.

"We're getting nowhere. And we're taking forever to do it," Durga responded. "We just keep following this thread. How do we even know it's the right way?"

Kane remained silent as he weighed Durga's question. Neither of them seemed to be making any progress, and he had been under the assumption that the presence of the thread was a way home. He thought back to his prior experience, but this was different. This was…

Now Kane could understand the frustration. When last he'd been "betwixt realms," as Brigid had so poetically called it, he didn't remember details, but knew that unless he was grounded *in* a reality, such as when he'd landed at the entrance to Hades, and spoke with two familiar seeming entities, he hadn't *felt* the passage of time, nor space.

Here was something different. *Here* actually felt like a place.

"We weren't thrown across the multiverse by that void," Kane said.

"That's what I was starting to think. It's as if we're running on a treadmill," Durga replied.

Kane grimaced. "That's the thing. Memories in this place… Have we really been here as long as it seems?"

"Without any proper sensory stimulus, we could have been trying to escape for just a few seconds," Durga murmured. "And it's not as if we have a body to pick up the information of time's passage. I learned from some Nagah physicists that humans believe time is a biological illusion as much as anything else."

"Biological illusion…" Kane repeated.

"You've got something?" Durga asked.

"I'm thinking it out. What if *this* is a biological illusion? Something feeding us epiphanies, like we experience while dreaming, but when we awaken, we realize that a brilliant answer was nothing but gibberish."

"Where did you get that?" Durga asked.

"Skeptical articles on so-called psychic phenomena," Kane replied. "When Balam began poking around, communicating to me telepathically, I realized that I'd better educate myself about the field. I'm as far from an expert as you can get, but some things stuck with me, especially the means of debunking those phenomena."

"Debunking telepathy, when obviously we're in a telepathic trap," Durga murmured. Kane felt his neck hairs bristle at the Nagah prince's doubts, but held his tongue.

"Debunking is verifying what is and what isn't possible," Kane countered, keeping the taut impatience from his voice, but only barely. "Not being taken in by an illusion one way or another. It's looking for facts, not jumping to assumptions. And that's what I've been doing."

"Jumping to assumptions," Durga repeated.

"We're probably still with our bodies," Kane said. "But when we make contact with each other…"

"We feel it," the cobra man concluded. "So there is that much reality present."

Kane nodded.

"So…we're floating in imagination," Durga mused. "The only realities here are ourselves. But I felt your death grip on that silver thread connecting me to the distance."

Kane looked down at his own. He touched it, trying to get some sensation of it. He had presumed that this thread, now that he realized he wasn't on an astral plane, was just another illusion. But it had no depth, no texture, no weight. He couldn't feel it himself.

"Grab the thread," Kane said.

Durga narrowed his eyes.

"My thread," Kane clarified. "I thought these were tethers that could lead us back to our bodies, but what if the opposite is true?"

"That they're anchors keeping us here, and not in our normal forms," Durga mused aloud.

Kane nodded.

Durga clasped his, or at least tried to. As soon as he did so it became ephemeral, his long-nailed fingers grasping only free flowing mist.

"The only way to break these is to attack the others," Kane said. "I saw the pain you felt when I grabbed yours."

"It felt as if you were strangling me to death," Durga responded. "Unbearable pain."

"But once I let go, the pain was gone, right?"

Durga nodded. "Which means we have to inflict agony upon each other. You'd have thought that our opponent would have come up with a far more clever fate."

"You think? There's no guarantee that the trauma we'll inflict upon each other would be survivable," Kane said. "And there's no guarantee that we'd sit still to have someone else inflict torture on us."

"Oh, but I'd be so willing to bite through this umbilicus to hear your screams," Durga declared. "Especially if the result is my freedom."

"What would keep us here if we were to cut the tie for the other?" Kane wondered, then paused in thought.

"So…we can't enjoy the suffering of our foes," Durga concluded.

He nodded. "Maybe."

Durga's eyes narrowed.

"Like I said, this is supposition, but it's not as if we have a lot of time to experiment. We'd have to sever each other's tethers at the same instant," Kane said. "And there's nothing we can use as tools."

The Nagah prince frowned. "Except ourselves. We'll really have to bite through each other's umbilicus."

Kane nodded again.

"That's if our teeth actually work," Durga added. "Remember, our physical selves seem real here, but that could still be an illusion."

"I know," Kane returned. "But what choice have we got?"

Durga grimaced. "I should never have let Enlil into my head," he muttered.

Kane drew a breath. "Things would have been much easier, but that's the past. It's immutable. The only thing we can do now is keep moving forward."

Durga nodded. He grasped the silver thread holding him. This time, it didn't fade away. He kept it still and floated closer to Kane, who had similarly wrangled his tether. Both paused, knowing full well that they were placing their lives in each others' hands.

The psychic terrain around them shifted suddenly. The voidlike being that had enveloped North in their initial shared telepathic contact was suddenly present, and grasped both of the silvery umbilical cords attached to the disembodied men.

"You've grown far too clever," that distorted voice said. It hadn't come from the null-creature's "body," but reverberated all about them, a thunderous proclamation by an omnipresent god. With a sudden surge, the gigantic void being tugged on their silver threads, and it was as if Kane and Durga were toys, hurled about by a fitful child.

Kane grunted, feeling as if his bones crunched as his form crashed into Durga's, the violent impact bringing the taste of blood to his mouth.

"You must learn your places, children." The entity spoke again, while the two of them dangled, hanging by their psychic leashes, both looking battered after their brutal treatment by the giant who had trapped them here.

"Learn my place?" Kane asked. He was surprised at how difficult it was to speak. Again he tasted blood, could feel his lips split from where he'd smashed face-first into Durga. Kane tried to reach up, but his left shoulder refused to move any higher than halfway before injured ligaments barked a warning and his limb froze.

He was lifted until he was face-to-face with an ebon image, a mouse hung by its tail before the world's largest black cat. Kane sensed the purr of self-satisfaction from the entity.

"Yes, Kane. You must learn your place in my world order." The booming, everywhere-present voice assaulted him again. His eardrums twisted and groaned at the thunderous sound, the pressure of each syllable like the shock wave of an implosion grenade, even through his old black polycarbonate magistrate armor.

"What the hell are you?" Kane sputtered. His throat was raw, raspy. Given the control that this entity had over him, he now knew what a marionette felt like. The tether wasn't a link to his body; it wasn't the path back to reality. It was a noose, and this unknown foe gripped him tortuously. Each shake sent racking, body-twisting pain through him. Kane found himself wishing that he could die, even as a cosmic heartbeat pulsed between his ears.

"I am now your god. You have denied me for so long.…"

"Gods aren't bullies," Kane spit.

"You've been hanging around with the wrong crowd," the entity answered with a chuckle.

With a flick, Kane was once more hanging at Durga's level, except he felt the tether draw taut with a whip crack sound. The momentum he'd generated folded him physically in half, and breath exploded from his lungs. What had once been his lifeline was now a hook, and a cruel fisherman was bouncing him up and down on it, driving pain deeper and deeper into his flesh.

"The crowd…" he began, then didn't have much more strength than to breath in and out.

"Yes. The crowd that you've encountered has informed you of the behavior of want-to-be gods. Enlil and his ilk, pathetic pretenders to my throne," the entity said.

Kane gulped down another breath. This thing sounded familiar, not in terms of the voice itself, but the type of statements it was making.

Another had voiced similar feelings, he assumed. But was this real, or just another of those epiphanies that come to you in a dream, and with the cold light of logic are revealed to be the garbage math of a subconscious mind babbling out a mirror to the known world?

The tether yanked again, and he gagged.

"Kane…stop fighting!" Durga hissed. "The more you piss it off, the more it hurts the both of us!"

The Cerberus explorer was about to say something, but his will finally failed him.

A man can dance on the end of a noose for only so long before his strength gives out.…

Chapter 18

Brigid Baptiste was distracted from her efforts at breaking the conundrum about Kane and Durga by the sudden activation of her Commtact.

"Domi and Edwards spotted the kongamato in the tunnels beneath the redoubt," Grant's voice announced. "Everyone to battle stations."

The general signal cut off, and now Grant sounded much more intimate over the jaw plate communicator. "Brigid, any news on Kane or Durga?"

"They both still appear to be comatose," she answered. "Where do you need me?"

"Protecting them," Grant responded. "Two more men may or may not give us an edge, but right now we've got a lot of fighters, so you get your brains on what our problems are stemming from."

Brigid grimaced. "I've been contemplating for too long, and just feel as if I'm spinning my wheels."

"It may not feel as if you're doing something, but we're stretching things thin up here with the Zambians, the remains of Durga's group and Sinclair and I," Grant said.

"Stretching it?" Brigid asked.

"We're three different forces, with different tactics and training," he answered. "I can anticipate where you and Kane would be in a wild melee, but right now, the differences of our groups means we have to keep separate so we don't accidentally stumble into each other's lines of fire."

"Unit integrity," Brigid responded. "The theory that a

piecemeal force is less efficient than a small group who know each other's strategies and tactics intimately."

"Bingo," Grant said. "I'm keeping North and Nathan close."

"North? You're trusting him now?" Brigid asked.

"Just as far as I can reach, but he already knows that," Grant explained.

"Do you need Nathan?" Brigid asked.

"You want him, or just the staff?"

"Both," Brigid responded. "You haven't…"

"No," Grant said. "I'm sending him to you now."

Brigid heard the Commtact break off, and she looked at Kane. He'd gone from an emotionless mannequin to being in distress. His brow was wrinkled and his breathing belabored.

"Sure, now you start acting up, once we're under attack," Brigid muttered. She gave him a gentle shake, hoping to stir him from his stupor, but his response to stimulus seemed to be merely internal.

"Come on, *anam chara,* wake up. We need your help," she whispered.

Kane remained still, not even his eyeballs moving beneath their lids to show he was dreaming. Brigid feared that he might truly be lost, but she fought that off.

He had battled against nearly impossible odds before. Though he might be trapped now, he was still a warrior, a man driven to make the world a better place. The only thing that would keep Kane from coming back would be death itself.

THE ALERT SOUNDED by Domi and Edwards had put all the defenders in the Zambian redoubt on full alert. Nathan Longa, holding both Nehushtan and a borrowed rifle, felt out of his depth in all of this. What had been a small, intimate group had suddenly become a full-fledged military operation, but Nathan didn't begrudge the Zambian soldiers their professionalism and rough readiness.

He'd seen what the kongamato could do, and realized, after watching how Brigid Baptiste had rushed to his aid, that had it not been for the serpent-adorned staff, he would have been among the dead, as well. Even with all their guns, their training and their teamwork, the Zambian defenders had come through the deadly horde, battered, two-thirds of their number dead, and running in full retreat from the fearsome predators. Nathan wished he knew better how to wield the power of Nehushtan, wished that he could simply wave it as a wand and direct thunderbolts and lightning to shatter the savage mutates, but such dramatics seemed out of his reach.

And so Grant sent him to assist Brigid Baptiste in raising the long-limbed, wolf-muscled warrior, Kane. The man had utilized Nehushtan to bring Nathan back from the verge of death, and now he had a chance to return the favor, if only he could figure out how to activate the staff's healing abilities.

If I could figure it out, he thought. That was the staff's whim, not his own. Nehushtan had provided for Nathan. It had guided him across the countryside with dreams. It had boosted his strength and speed in hand-to-hand combat against the kongamato. It had repaired his deep lung laceration, mending severed blood vessels and restoring 100 percent function to his brachial passages.

Nehushtan made the decisions, not Nathan.

He squeezed the damned stick tighter.

Listen, Nehushtan. You need to stop jerking me around like a puppet and start healing Kane, and perhaps kicking mutant ass.

Nathan wondered if he "sounded" too tough in his thoughts, but realized it stemmed from pure frustration. The staff was a powerful artifact. His father and grandfather had told stories of how it had laid demons low and imprisoned the dark, old gods in tombs beneath Africa, entities that had shuffled upon the Earth's surface long before the squirming little hairless apes were even long-tailed rodent-sized puffballs. Then came Brigid Baptiste with her tales of the Annunaki, and enemies that even they had feared, or deemed potentially useful as future slaves—something that Nathan suspected the kongamato truly were.

Those "future slaves" were more like an invading army, relentless and as cruel as the siafu ants that he'd leaped over in sheer terror…was it really only two days ago? Nathan realized how out of his element he was.

And yet he'd survived for this long, met up with heroes, fought alongside them, earned their trust.

He just didn't relish the idea that he was going to have to fight against the entity who'd created the monsters.

Nathan kept going and found the small conference room where Brigid watched over Kane and their once-enemy, Durga. That the newcomers had risked so much for an opponent was a sign of their basic human goodness. They could have simply allowed the man to remain a cripple, a prisoner in his own whithered body, especially for his past murders.

Durga was a criminal, a killer who'd brought suffering on many for nothing more than his own political expediency. He'd already had all the benefits of royalty, including the admiration and love of his people, and yet he'd pushed for more, making deals with devils, both human and monstrous. Hell, the bastard had unleashed the very mutants who were terrorizing the frontier between Zambia and Harare, causing the deaths of dozens of Zambian soldiers and inspiring terror in smaller outskirt towns. Nathan didn't doubt that Kane and his people would have stood idly by when a healthy Durga was dragged away to be lynched by an angry force of people mourning and displaced.

Maybe that was why they'd offered to help him. The execution of a helpless man wouldn't have sat well with them, no matter what the crimes committed.

Again, that basic "human decency," even toward those who barely looked human, and had rarely shown any decency to others in the past.

He entered the room, and saw that Brigid was paying close attention to Kane, who seemed in a state of distress. Nathan immediately rushed to her side, and she jerked upright at the sudden intrusion.

"I brought the staff," he said. "How is Kane?"

"He seems to be engaged in some sort of conflict," Brigid responded. "There's some stimuli causing his autonomic systems to react, which means that he's in there somewhere. But he's unable to reach all the way out here."

"What?" Nathan asked.

"It's the only logical explanation," she explained. "If Kane's essence were somehow severed from his body, he wouldn't be experiencing spikes in heartbeat and respiration, as well as body temperature."

"So he isn't an empty shell," Nathan surmised. "But Durga doesn't look distressed."

Brigid turned and looked toward the immobile Nagah prince.

"Keep an eye on Kane," she ordered Nathan. She moved over to the cobra man and took his pulse, probing both his throat and his wrist.

Even as she did, she paused, looking down the length of his body. She remained silent, but her widened eyes told a story of surprise. Nathan reached out and touched her shoulder, and she turned away.

"What's wrong?" he asked her.

"I certainly didn't need to know that about Durga's anatomy," the woman responded. "He's all right?"

Nathan looked back and noticed that Durga seemed to

have a serpent writhing in his pants. After a moment, Nathan realized what he was looking at, and turned away, blushing.

"Alien sex," he muttered.

"Something I didn't need to know about, like I said," Brigid returned. "And in my case, 'what has been seen cannot be unseen' is the gospel truth." Her face reddened.

"Kane's being distressed and Durga's...being romanced?" Nathan asked.

"I hope that doesn't mean what I think it does," she murmured.

Nathan's eyes went wide. "Durga is psychically raping Kane? Would he do that?"

"Hannah, Kane's bride-to-be, had described Durga as a sexual predator and an abuser," Brigid said. "If he's in a position to commit violence against someone else, it's not below, or above him, to inflict violence on Kane. And it's not a sexual action. It's an infliction of his will, his anger and revenge."

"Killing a man doesn't make him suffer," Nathan mused. "But this doesn't seem right. Not that I think Durga would be homophobic enough to *not* engage in a psychic rape, but I just don't see a link. They've been kept together, and then separated. Whatever is happening is independent of each other. There's no link, no stray signals."

"Nothing that could be picked up on radio," Brigid corrected. She looked from the fallen Durga to the comatose Kane. Her brow wrinkled with concentration as she ran permutations through her mind. "You're right, these look very different in the light of logic. Durga is in sexual release, and rape is not about arousal, it's about punishment. And Durga wouldn't get all erect over damaging Kane."

She looked at her friend again, worry on her face. "You're right," she repeated.

She gave Kane's matted hair a quick brush with her

fingers, then turned to the staff. "I'm going to need Nehushtan."

Nathan nodded and handed it to her.

Even as she grasped the haft, her flame-gold hair began to float, to rise as if a sudden wind had whipped through the underground room.

The light released by the artifact forced Nathan to squeeze his eyes shut and turn away from her.

When he looked back, she was gone, and the staff lay on the floor.

An electric buzz of fear cut through the conference room as Kane's breath quickened.

BRIGID BAPTISTE FELT herself torn asunder, a sensation not unlike the stimuli she recalled when she was hurtled through time and space by either the mat trans or the Threshold. Nehushtan was gone, and suddenly the Cerberus archivist was in the middle of a forest, alone. The sky was dark, and the hair on her neck stood on end.

She realized that she'd left her Copperhead behind, but was glad that she'd remembered to keep her pistol in its holster on her thigh. She gritted her teeth and immediately turned on her Commtact.

"Grant," she whispered.

"What?" asked the big man.

"I'm outside of the redoubt," she answered. "I picked up Nehushtan, and suddenly I was gone."

"What?" he exclaimed. "Do you know where you are?"

"Looks like jungle," Brigid responded, keeping her voice low. There was a sudden rush of movement in the air, and she whirled toward it. It was a flock of birds quickly taking flight. Something bounded through the forest, and she recognized the long, slender limbs of an antelope. It wasn't alone, and was in full run, dark eyes wide with fear.

She heard the distant shriek of a kongamato, its very un-batlike howl piercing the darkness.

"Scratch that. I'm between the mutants and the redoubt," Brigid amended. "I'm on my way."

She turned and took off as fast as her long, athletic legs could push her. For a moment, she regretted having lost Nehushtan, missing the brief surge of strength and grace it had granted her as it allowed her to cross half a mile in a few moments. Practicality took over, though, and she realized that her mental energies were better directed toward navigating in the dark forest.

Already she found herself skidding on the ground, having hit some slick, matted leaves that offered no traction. Her escape nearly ended right then and there as she slid, knee-first, into a tree trunk, but the shadow suit shielded her patella and joint upon impact. What could have been a leg-breaking tumble turned into an uncomfortable rebound, but even so, Brigid landed face-first on hard-packed dirt.

She grimaced as she slid, but quickly sank her fingers into the soil and slowed her progress enough to gather her knees beneath her. Digging in her heels, she shot back to her feet and continued onward, quickly drawing the shadow suit's hood from within a utility pocket. With a tug, she found her head enclosed, but most importantly, the faceplate was in place, improving her night vision dramatically.

The shadow suits had been designed on the Mantoux moon base by a group of technical geniuses, and were meant to be the prototype of an advanced space suit—a second skin that allowed unlimited agility and prowess, while shielding the wearer from extremes of temperature and radiation. Additional design features in the hoods allowed for vastly improved visual acuity and air filtration.

The faceplate was a marvel of optics, and already Brigid was getting a real-time map of the terrain she was crossing. Moon-kissed highlights on branches and rocks became all the illumination she required, and as she glanced into the distance, tiny microlenses locked onto the object of her attention and magnified the image.

"Commtact tracking has you approximately two kilometers to the north of us, Brigid," Grant stated. "Did you put—"

"My hood is on and the faceplate adhered to it," she responded.

Brigid hustled along, cutting between bushes and skirting trees as she locked on to the position of the redoubt as it was located on the faceplate's head's-up display. She was receiving real-time information from the satellites as well as the mainframe up at the moon base. That database gave them full global positioning intelligence when necessary. The only drawback was having to be fully enclosed within the confines of the hood.

The data overload could have been unnerving to most people, but luckily, Brigid's mind was on a higher level, capable of processing incoming data at remarkable speeds, and keeping it in place, perfectly stored so that she could pluck an item of information at whim. The monsters in the forest shrieked behind her, but she maintained her calm, pausing only once to glance back.

The light amplification of the shadow suit picked up four shapes, and she immediately recognized them as the lumbering hulks of gorilla-sized kongamato, their broad shoulders and powerful arms allowing them to swing themselves along the ground as swiftly as they could maneuver through the air. Here in the forest, that had been a necessary adaptation, especially as there was little room for them to spread their wings and catch currents of air. Gliding would be difficult, and full-out flapping of those mighty limbs would have been impossible given all the branches and trunks.

And so the kongamato loped along on all fours, though Brigid knew there would be others, both in the jungle canopy and the dark, starlit skies above, that would be taking advantage of other means of locomotion. Even as she looked upward, she could pick up an inset on her screen, where infrared satellites picked up the presence of more kongamato.

According to the readout at the bottom, there were 117 of them currently in the forest, and they were making their way toward the Victoria Falls station, where Grant and the others had taken refuge.

She grimaced at the thought of being so unceremoniously expelled from the redoubt just as she'd taken hold of the artifact they'd come to know as Nehushtan. A brief flicker of energy had surged through her as she'd touched the staff, but just as soon as that initial contact was made, she was gone, scooped up by energies similar to those of a Threshold, and deposited two kilometers away.

Brigid felt glad that whoever had caused this hadn't gone to the effort of transmitting her into a solid object.

And then she remembered a flicker, a tinge of electric current as she'd felt herself almost materialize.

Nehushtan hadn't been able to protect her from the external forces teleporting her, but it had kept her in plasma wave form while she landed on the ground, then was guided up into the air.

It was a brief moment, and she wasn't even fully human at the time, merely a notion, a concept traveling on waves of magnetic force. But as soon as she'd thought about the Threshold manipulation, she'd been reminded.

Nehushtan provides, but first you have to ask the question, she thought with no small amount of irritation. The impulses that it had communicated with were elusive, so that even her thoughts could scarcely contain their mercurial whimsy. She was wondering what else the ancient artifact had left with her, when she saw something crash to the ground ahead of her.

It was a kongamato, and even as her attention was divided between navigating the midnight jungle and determining how she'd been transported away, she maintained enough awareness to realize that the monstrosity hadn't caught up with her, but had dropped thirty feet from above, landing with a thunderous crash.

Brigid pulled the TP-9 and aimed it at the creature, even as one part of her mind wondered how a "hollow-boned" creature could have survived such a plummet. Already her intellect was providing multiple responses, from the parachutelike effect of the creature's leathery wing membranes, to the fact that hollow-boned animals replaced very dense calcium material with pliant, cushioning muscle and blood vessels that kept their skeletons from being too brittle.

The kongamato had landed and was immediately able to whirl and present itself as a threat to Brigid Baptiste.

She fired off two quick shots, but the sudden flash of a wing buffeted her off her feet and hurled her through the air. The cushioning qualities of the shadow suit saved her as she rebounded off a tree trunk and crashed to the ground. Even so, the launch left her unnerved. Fortunately, she'd gripped the handle of her TP-9 so tightly, it remained in her grasp.

The hulking kongamato glared at her with cold detachment, light amplification providing Brigid with a detailed view of its expression. This wasn't a creature like the ones who had attacked before. This thing possessed intellect and malice, not animalistic rage. The suit's optics showed where she'd struck the creature center of mass, just as she'd been trained. The muscular chest and keel-like breastbone, however, rendered her 9 mm slugs as little more than nasty thorns in its side.

Seeing its bulk up close, Brigid also doubted whether the Copperhead and its 4.85 mm slugs would have acquitted itself any better. She regretted leaving her big .45-caliber

SIG-Sauer with the Copperhead as she'd been on "thinking duty."

Fortunately, if she survived this conflict, she would never again assume that even the thickest of walls were a guarantee of safety.

Before she could kick herself for disregarding the presence of the Threshold, and the potential of another party within the redoubt capable of utilizing it, Brigid saw the kongamato surge forward. Every ounce of her speed and intellect combined into a less-than-graceful lunge to the side, 250 pounds of vat-bred muscle rushing past her like a freight train. She winced as a tree trunk exploded under the sledgehammer fist of the African myth, the top portion of the tree sliding off the bottom and crashing into the dirt.

Brigid scrambled out of its path tucking in her legs just in time as hundreds of pounds of wood landed where she had been a moment before. Shadow suit or not, if she hadn't curled up, the fallen tree would have amputated her lower limbs, crudely, painfully.

She rolled to her knees, heartbeat racing, eyes focusing on the horror that had almost killed her by dropping a towering tree on top of her.

An icy chill raced through her as she saw the monster's mouth turn up, as if in a self-satisfied smile.

The animal before her was merely a puppet, and the entity in control was far more intelligent than the creatures they had fought before.

Chapter 19

Anam chara, wake up. A woman's voice reverberated inside of Kane's skull. He couldn't make out who it was; the world about him was a slurry of blackness, pain and disorientation. He wasn't even certain that his eyes were open. Halos with stringy tails kept floating around him in the oblivion before his eyeballs.

We need your help, the voice added.

"Got news for you, honey," Kane grumbled. "I'm first in line for as much help as there is."

Even speaking felt agonizing. His ribs had taken punch after punch, so that each intake of breath felt as if he were swallowing a bag of broken razor blades. His feet couldn't move, attached to each other as they were, with, a long spear running the length of him, and pinioned between his ankles. His arms were spread, and he could tell that they were still attached to his shoulders, and that one hands was pierced. He couldn't see, but could feel, and imagined a set of jagged iron jaws clamped over his wrist, their saw-toothed edge grinding on the bones of his forearm with each twitch, each bump of his pulse. His other hand was just plain gone, though if he concentrated enough to focus on his sense of smell, he could detect the stink of cooking pork, a sign that something had roasted him, considering the amorphous agony gnawing at the stump where his other hand should have been.

"Durga!" he croaked. "Durga, you stinking worm, maybe together we can pull out of this."

Nothing. Even as he spoke, the words were swallowed. He couldn't hear the pulse of his own voice. No vibrations. Nothing.

Kane flexed his muscles, drawing himself together.

This was a psychic plane, or maybe his own mind, but he couldn't believe that the bits of himself seemingly destroyed were gone forever. After all, he wasn't suffocating despite the sheer agony in his ribs. He was alone in a soundless void, and yet there was air, and his blood didn't boil.

The mutilations racking his form on this plane were all in his mind.

"Durga!"

Quiet.

"Been wondering where the hell you'd gone to," Kane growled.

Stop running your voice for at least a moment.

Kane grimaced, but kept his mind clear. Something was…wrong.

"Who is this?"

A pox upon my house that a descendant should have a tongue which wags endlessly!

Kane tried to focus his gaze, but saw only a silhouette. But what he did see was familiar. A tall, pointed, wide-brimmed slouch hat, the glint of black leather that made up a broad belt thrown over one shoulder, the shimmer of silver on the basket handle of the sword dangling in its sheath. Kane could even smell gunpowder, freshly tamped into the barrels of pistols, ready to launch primitive balls with the force to shatter the skulls of monsters.

"Solomon…"

Just a Puritan named for a wise king.

"And we share the same familial name. For what it's worth," Kane added.

The Puritan shook his head, clucking his tongue at

Kane's continued speech, before putting a gloved finger to his lips, gesturing for silence.

Focus.

Kane gritted his teeth and pulled, trying to separate his feet. Again he could feel the scrape of metal on bone as he tried to get off the petard he was hoisted upon. The drag of his flesh on the steel spear pinning his ankles against each other was an illusion.

A leather-clad palm cracked across Kane's cheek.

Focus!

Kane took a deep breath.

"What do you want me to focus on?" he muttered through clenched teeth. He was getting sick of being abused while stuck in no condition to return fire. "How about you help?"

Because I am merely a memory. In terms you would understand, I'm a gene, a chemical reaction based on a code buried deep within your DNA. I am your brain's efforts to escape this trap, your subconscious trying to give you a key that only you can turn.

Kane sneered, then thought back. There was something, some scrap of conversation, that nagged at his memory, but what felt like years of torture and mutilation had submerged it deeply.

Focus.

Kane wanted to spit into the memory's features, but he realized that would be useless. The Puritan was simply a memory, a false image, no more real than the "universe" that he and Durga had been hurled to, nor as truthful as his assumption that the silver threads were simply paths back home. Rather, they were leashes, held on to by an entity who ruled this…

Kane wanted to kick himself.

"I had to free Durga," he muttered, "and he was going to free me."

Focus.

"Kane...stop fighting!" Durga hissed. *"The more you piss it off, the more it hurts the both of us!"*

There was some kind of equation at work that he wasn't seeing.

"The two of us established that only by hurting each other could we escape from this tether," he said aloud. He looked down at himself, and there was no sign of the silvery umbilicus that had been the target of so much of his focus since he'd become trapped in this predicament. "And yet the entity holding this tether used it like a whip, a leash, subjecting it to all manner of forces that ended up hurting me all over, but not causing damage to the thread itself."

Kane began to pull in his arms and legs, drawing himself into a ball. Here, he was an entity of thought, and everything about him was under his control, malleable. He did as his subconscious wished, focusing himself, squeezing himself down.

"The mind is everything," Brigid Baptiste had told him, quoting an ancient religious figure called the Buddha. "What you think, you become."

It was that focus, that thinking. Each inch of self Kane could feel, could retain, could control, felt as if it had been ripped through miles of briars. Something had scattered him, filled his perceptions with lies and falsehoods. Now, he couldn't even determine whether anything over the past years of existence was real. He was lost, without anchor, and seeking out a solid piece of ground seemed impossible.

Anam chara, wake up.

Kane knew that voice. He knew those words.

Brigid Baptiste was summoning him, wresting him from the depths of his unbeing.

That was his anchor.

His *focus.*

By now, Kane had drawn himself into a ball of white-hot

anger. No more; they weren't going to keep him shredded, torn to pieces and helpless. The imagined wounds, the illusions pressed upon him of all the tortures, were cracking, shattering, flaking off of him like dead flesh.

Anam chara, wake up.

"I'm coming through, Baptiste," he grunted.

He felt warmth now. An electrical tickle to one side. A rush of air over him.

Brigid Baptiste was real. She was his anchor. His soul friend.

And so Kane pulled through, spikes of psychic energy spearing at him from all sides as he gathered himself back together, forcing himself into a living whole. She needed him. Grant needed him. All those people in the redoubt needed him, be they the local Zambians or even the lost and embattled millennialists.

Even Durga, who Kane was willing to suffer agonies to free.

Kane had no delusions that he was so vitally important, but he was a *part* of the effort, and here he was, "lying down on the job." It didn't matter to him anymore that he'd been laid low by a psychic trauma. He needed to break loose, get back to his body.

And then he remembered who the entity, the voidlike being who'd toyed with him, batted him around like a cat's toy, reminded him of. It was Kakusa's rant. Not word for word, but similar.

The void being was a prisoner, akin to that alien organism imprisoned by the Annunaki, a threat that was something other than human. And it had been riding along with the group, at least as far as Kane and Durga's separation and their initial conflict with each other.

That void was what had been at the core of the myths that Brigid had referred to, the demons imprisoned by Suleiman and the mighty staff Nehushtan. That same entity had attacked, knowing that Kane had a link to the artifact, trying to protect itself from the mythic weapon.

Kane pulled himself tighter. He fought to ignore the universe, even as hooks of mental energy lashed from the darkened expanse of emptiness about him, sinking into the surface of the psychic sun that he'd become.

Would Kane alone be able to shatter this hold?

The mind is everything. What you think, you become.

"Let go of me, demon," Kane growled. "Let me go, and I won't destroy you when I uncover your tomb."

The void being spoke again, its voice booming, but Kane no longer felt pain or pressure.

"You threaten me, human?" it asked.

Kane wanted to glare at the entity, to hold up a middle finger and spit in its face. But here, there was no true form, no body. He was a searing orb of fire, a blaze stoked by his anger and frustration at being jerked around and forcibly separated from those he loved.

"You're threatening *me?*" Kane countered. "Do you know who I've battled? Who I've defeated? Those who have called for my extermination and found themselves overcome?"

Suddenly Kane felt himself in a body again, but he knew it wasn't reality. Not unless he'd fallen asleep, clasping a fine Spanish blade from the sixteenth century.

"A fine form you've chosen for yourself," the void entity intoned. It was huge, and looking down upon Kane. About them, the terrain had altered, and they were once more on the shore of the Zambezi River, the sun burning in the sky, the falls releasing their roar of thunder.

Durga was beside him again, crumpled and battered, looking just like Kane had felt. Still, the Nagah prince drew himself to his feet, scaled lips curling in a sneer.

"You distracted her," Durga murmured.

"Her?" Kane repeated.

Those amber eyes glimmered for a moment. "She took a different tactic with me than you. It did. As a she. As Hannah, specifically."

Durga's hand filled suddenly with an odd-looking sword—long and rectangular, with saw teeth along each edge, and a blunt, ugly looking pry-tip at the end. "My Khanda."

"It failed with you?" Kane asked.

"It tried, but once you started putting up the fight—"

"Silence, you worms!" the void being roared.

Kane looked up at the monstrosity looming over them.

"You have been tested, and found annoying," the entity growled.

"So, smash us, almighty ink blot!" Kane bellowed in return. "Or are you just too damned afraid?"

There seemed to be a smirk descending across the countryside. "Then throw your frail little psyches into the fray, humans," the entity invited, seeming to spread its "arms."

Durga nodded to Kane and, grimacing, the two men lunged toward their psychic tormentor, blades drawn.

THE KONGAMATO PAWN glared at Brigid Baptiste as she aimed her pistol at the thing. It suddenly swung to one side in a blur, so quick that her shot missed. The bullet cracked against a tree trunk, and the creature was in motion. Luckily, Brigid was able to make out its shadow, thanks to the advanced optics installed within the faceplate of the suit she wore.

The beast moved quickly, bounding through the forest. Brigid held her fire, even dumping out the partially spent magazine and putting a fresh one in place. Her first few shots had either missed or struck thick muscle and bone designed to get hundreds of pounds of mammal airborne. Clearly, the pistol she carried was less than ideal for a brutish predator as this, at least when firing at its most heavily muscled and armored body parts.

Her mind raced through the anatomy of the creatures Grant and the others had brought back from their first encounter with the beast. The lower abdomen was similar to those of humans and other mammals, meaning that there was a main trunk line artery to the hind legs that branched off to feed each of those limbs. That was a traditionally weak area, and upon examination, she spotted a few good "landmarks" to aim for with either a firearm or a blade, which could cause rapid exsanguination. The head itself was big, heavy, but it had large eyes, nostrils and ears, meaning that she could shoot through its face or the side of the head in order to get to its brain. A shot to the forehead or the dome of the skull would be wasted, due to the high peak of muscle and bone that went along with those powerful jaws and inch-long canines.

That was one thing about Brigid's photographic memory. Once she got a good look at a creature, she could figure out its anatomy by extrapolating it against similar species. On her original examination, she'd determined that the jaw muscles of the kongamato were more than sufficient to provide a ton of bite force based on the sheets of muscle along the top of the skull and the thick ridge of bone that anchored them.

That bit of knowledge would help her direct her bullets to better effect, but there was no way she could fire without a decent target. The kongamato was dodging, darting sideways to keep her from getting a good sight picture so she could fire with effect.

Brigid cursed her luck, and realized that the entity in charge was aware that she still had a chance of fighting back. The kongamato's puppet master had enough fear for itself that it was reluctant to send the monster into fair combat with her.

That, too, was information the archivist could add to her quiver of advantages. Perhaps the possession of the mutant allowed it to feel the pain inflicted upon it.

And maybe the 9 mm rounds that had struck the creature hasn't been completely useless. After all, Brigid had never been hindered in combat with Nephilim or large, muscular men in the past with her TP-9. She scanned quickly back to the spot where she'd initially struck the creature, and the high-tech shadow suit optics picked up on droplets of blood, their infrared signature cooling, but still discernible from the background foliage.

Emboldened, she swung her attention toward tracking the bestial enemy. It was nowhere to be seen, which meant that it had somehow found a hiding spot, or was looking for some way to flank her. Brigid knew where the redoubt was, and took a mad dash toward it at a ninety-degree angle, her long legs propelling her over ruts, tangled roots and shrubbery in an effort to cover some distance. The tactic of rushing at an angle to her initial goal was intentional.

The malevolent intelligence controlling the kongamato was obviously trying to keep Brigid from rejoining her allies. Even now, she realized that the creature had let her off easily, using blunt swats that her shadow suit could protect against. The entity wanted her alive, perhaps to make use of her intellect, as others had attempted in the past.

The move away from her goal left the possessed animal dumbfounded long enough for her to pick up its bulk in the periphery of her vision. With a fluid movement, she pivoted and brought the sight of the small TP-9 to bear, firing off two more quick shots at the mass of muscle perched in the crook of a bough twenty-five feet off the ground. The kongamato released a shriek of pain, but even from this distance, Brigid could tell that her bullets caused little damage.

The thing's reactions were quick, but blood, glowing hot and yellow in her infrared filter, spattered against the trunk where it had rested. The creature spread its wings, glided twenty feet to the next tree, then lashed out with one arm, yanking itself out of sight even as Brigid sent a third shot after it. The bullet missed.

She let out a breath and turned, darting quickly through a thicket, bending low and cutting along a narrow game path that even her slender shoulders were almost too broad to squeeze through. Branches scraped her arms, splinters of wood stabbing, but the shadow suit fabric kept her from snagging on the undergrowth. Brigid had dropped onto her butt, using gravity to draw her down an incline, when the suit's optics went wild.

Something was moving at the bottom of the gully she'd dived into, and she paused, digging in her heels before landing at the edge of a churning stream. The optics were picking up millions of individual moving elements in one great crawling force, but Brigid's own sharp, canny mind clicked on the truth of them.

Genus Dorylus. Known by the Swahili speakers as siafu. Commonly also called "driver ants."

In central and southern Africa, the sight of a colony such as this, millions of them on the march, was cause for terror and retreat. Fortunately, Brigid had stopped herself just in time before stumbling into their column. She recalled the encyclopedia entries on the creatures. These old-world insects were blind, operating by an incredible sense of touch and smell, and inside her shadow suit, with its environmental seal, Brigid would be safe from either. Even the piezoelectric seam that kept the faceplate and hood connected to her suit wouldn't allow the tiny creatures under the second skin.

However, if she had crashed into the group, their sense of touch and vibrational sensitivity would have identified her as a threat, turning the relatively slow-marching horror into a teeming, hungry swarm. While they didn't possess the deadly tail stingers of their South American fire ant counterparts, the driver ants had jaw strength proportionally as strong as a kongamato, and the deadly insectoid soldiers would still bite and chew into human flesh, even with their bodies torn from their grabbing mandibles.

Brigid let out a scream of terror and pain, her mind formulating a plan even as she inched a little farther back from the stream of hungry, monomaniacal biomass beneath her. She hoped that her cry sounded sufficiently weak and helpless, and just to be certain, she slid her pistol beneath one buttock, so it wouldn't be visible. It was a risky maneuver, but she had to make the effort to bait the brawny kongamato and its dark passenger into attacking.

A sharp barking shriek split the air, a hammer of sound and pressure buffeting Brigid even through the environmental and audio dampeners on the shadow suit. Had she not been wearing it, her ears would have been left ringing, and even so, she still suffered a headache from its ultrasonic bark.

Almost immediately, the kongamato dropped from its position above her, landing on the opposite side of the gully. Brigid looked up at it and realized her instincts were right. The creatures were, in general, twice her mass, so while she herself had trouble slowing down while skidding on the gully's sloping side, the kongamato was unable to stop at all. It crashed to the ground, and though its hind claws sank into the dirt, its body weight took it skidding to the bottom of the gully.

Once there, it scrambled to its feet, eyes locked on to her, likely looking for her weapon. When it confirmed that she wasn't visibly armed, the corners of its mouth rose in a sneering grin.

And then the siafu's ferocious bites started drawing its attention. Thousands of jaws stabbed at the creature's flesh, and it thrashed violently.

"Noooo!" Its scream was agonized and unending as the swarming flood of driver ants attacked the kongamato in its midst. Brigid hated to do that even to a puppet of an inhuman intellect, but she needed to break the control it held on these creatures.

Swarms of ants rushed toward the bloody gunshot wounds she'd inflicted upon the beast, and in desperation the kongamato leaped, hurling itself back out of the gully. But it was too late. Siafu were all over it, snarled in its thick fur, their jaws sinking into flesh and tearing into skin. Its open wounds quickly became homes for hundreds of hungry ants burrowing into the exposed tissue and blood within.

The kongamato staggered and stumbled, moving without its former precision and grace. Brigid had driven the controlling entity from its mind. She'd reached for her TP-9, hoping to end the creature's suffering, when three more of the winged monstrosities dropped from the forest canopy above. Powerful, clubbing knuckles hammered into the skull of the suffering being, and the unmistakable crunch of shattering bones reached Brigid's ears.

The kongamatos were not going to allow one of their own to suffer.

They looked at the corpse, and Brigid remained still, frozen in place on the other side of the gully, shaded by trees and long grass. She didn't even dare take a breath, especially when a pair of bestial eyes turned and met hers—or would have had not the black, nonreflective faceplate been sealed to her hood.

Brigid watched as the trio of creatures bounded back to the nearest trees, hurling themselves up the trunks and higher, where they would have more mobility and freedom.

Brigid closed her eyes and let out a tense breath.

"Grant, the kongamato have overtaken me, and are now

between the redoubt and my position," she said through her Commtact.

"Copy that," Grant replied. "Unfortunately, we've got plenty of problems on this end now."

Brigid bit her lower lip. "Did they get through underground?"

"Not yet, but the lockup system on the main vault doors has failed, freezing them in the open position," he said. "Something is inside the computer system, and it's doing its damnedest to screw us up the ass."

Brigid scrambled to her feet, then gauged the jump to the other slope of the gully. "I'll try to help, but all I have is my TP-9."

There was a grunt behind her.

She whirled, heart hammering, to find a large form looming in the shadows just above her. She reached for her gun, but it skidded down the slope, landing amid the churning river of vexed siafu.

Unarmed, she looked up as the shadowy hulk reached out for her.

Chapter 20

Brigid Baptiste grimaced as she realized the gun she'd tucked against her thigh, in an effort to seem like bait, had dropped as soon as she reacted to the shadowy form above her. The figure blended into the foliage so completely that even the advanced optics built into her faceplate were stymied by the shape. Her attention was split between the gun falling into the stream of powerful-jawed killer ants at the bottom of the gully, and the presence of the figure above. so it took a few moments for her sharp mind to recognize that the latter was the same size and shape of former magistrate Edwards.

Rather than a heavily camouflaged kongamato or some other menace, the new arrival was there to assist her. Even so, she'd lost the TP-9. After seeing how the driver ants had swarmed the puppet kongamato, seeking out every possible opening, she didn't want to risk reaching down to grab her gun. She recalled that those jaws were so powerful, the locals sometimes used driver ants as "living stitches," making them bite the sides of a wound, then tearing off their bodies, the death grip of their mandibles holding for days until the skin could heal.

"Come on, Brigid, reach up!" Edwards commanded from above.

She complied and his brawny arm hefted her easily to his side. Domi was crouched nearby, hood down, her ruby-red eyes scanning the jungle around them.

"She's got better night vision than I do," Edwards said,

as if to answer an unasked question. "Plus I was tired of getting smacked in the face with branches."

"Why didn't you let me know you were coming?" Brigid asked.

Edwards tilted his head. "You were shooting at something. We wanted to flank whatever you were fighting, and didn't want to draw more attention to this spot."

"They all passed," Domi said tersely. "Between us and redoubt."

Brigid could hear the brittle tension in her voice. She was in full-on siege mode, and the effort it took her to use multisyllable words was almost palpable.

"Thanks for letting me know that Edwards and Domi were on their way to get me," Brigid mock-growled into her Commtact.

"Things have been moving way too quickly," Grant said. "I'm keeping both ends of this redoubt buttoned down. Word to Edwards."

The big ex-magistrate nodded. "What's up?"

"We heard your first two lines of traps go off in the tunnel leading to our back door," Grant told him. "That might just slow them down. How many did you leave?"

"Three lines," Edwards returned. "Trip wires to implode grens."

"So, that could have taken a good number out," Grant surmised.

"I don't think so," Brigid interjected. "The first group heading down that tunnel may have been unaware of a trip wire, but there is an intellect behind these things."

"It never goes easy," Grant sighed. The three people in the forest could tell that he was speaking under his breath, relying on vibrations conducted through his mandible to carry his words via the Commtact, rather than actual speech. They could also pick up the muted sound of sporadic but heavy gunfire, also carried by the communication device. "Domi, did they follow you up through the vent?"

"No," the albino girl answered.

Grant knew better than to question her awareness of that. Even so, both Edwards and Brigid swept the forest with the optics on their shadow suits, and ended up confirming Domi's supposition that they hadn't been followed.

"Want us back there?" Edwards asked.

"I'd like some extra bodies, but you should see the Zambians here. They have the 'front door' buttoned down tightly," Grant answered. "Brigid, do you think that this entity controlling the kongamato might be out there in the forest with you?"

"I don't know. I doubt it, if only because someone accessed the Threshold to deposit me out here," Brigid answered. "And then immediately dropped an intelligent kongamato on me."

"Nathan wasn't able to ascertain whether it was the Threshold in the room with you, Kane and Durga that launched you out there," Grant responded. "But then, it's not like a Sandcat. He touched its surface, but the motor seemed cold to him."

"And North hasn't been acting strangely?" Brigid asked.

"He's with me," Grant said. "No glazed eyes, no look of concentration."

Gunfire resounded, conveyed by the Commtact once more.

"I need you to see whatever happened to the Manosha militia," Grant said. "I'll have Bry send you GPS links to where they'd last been seen."

"You think they might have something to do with this?" Edwards asked.

Brigid nodded. "There are more players at this table, Edwards. I hate to say it, but we've stumbled into something a lot larger than Durga and his bat-winged army."

The silence both at their and Grant's end of the conversation was not made any more comfortable by the fading howls of the kongamato making their way to the redoubt.

THE ENTRANCE TO the redoubt had all manner of furniture thrown into a barricade, and the smell of hot metal seared Grant's nostrils. The Zambians were holding the line, their rifles chattering loud and hard, smoke streaming from hot muzzles and spent brass. One thing in the defenders' favor was that the vault doors, while massive, provided only so much room for the kongamato to try to get through, and it was still a bottleneck for the enemy forces.

As soon as the creatures appeared in the opening, they were immediately in the line of fire, and with limited room for them to maneuver, the automatic rifles of the Zambians tore into them with brutal, swift efficiency. As one soldier exhausted the ammunition in his magazine, he was promptly replaced by a fresh man with a full weapon, and the line was strong.

"You don't seem pleased with this turn of events," Lomon said to Grant as they watched the coordinated defense against the seemingly mindless foes. So far a dozen of the kongamato had fallen, and each had been torn to shreds by concentrated fire. The probes by the assaulting creatures were sporadic enough that the Zambians had managed to hold off from using the light machine guns.

Grant knew that the machine gunners needed to be disciplined and conservative with their ammunition. The fact that they had two hundred rounds in a belt was not as important as the fact that they could warp and damage the barrels of their heavy weapons in sustained fire. In this position, simply shooting until they ran out of ammunition was just a waste of the gun's deadly power.

Even the men with assault rifles worked in short bursts.

Lots of gunners and lots of guns wasn't license to shoot at anything that moved, and the Zambian soldiers had years of experience dealing with raiders and barbarians in the wilds around their city-state. Here, in a defensible position, they'd been able to set up a good counter to the kongamato, whose leaping and bounding was limited by the size of the redoubt entrance.

"I'm glad we've got things under control, so far," Grant answered the Zambian officer. "But the kongamato must know what kind of a defense is down here. Otherwise, they would have tried to surge on through. Using the corpses of their dead, they might even reach the defense line."

"And then we'd fall back, our second line providing cover fire," Lomon said. "But I can see where you're on edge."

"I'm used to being the one outnumbered, and everything right now is telling me that we *are* outnumbered," Grant admitted. "There's something we're not seeing."

"I can feel that, too," Lomon said. "Thurpa and the millennialists mentioned Gamal and the Panthers of Manosha. They are deadly."

Grant nodded.

"You think that the force that jammed the doors might have the Manosha militia on deck to do something?" Lomon asked.

"I'm used to things going sour. When it rains, it always pours. What's an army of vat-bred freaks without a force of maniacs with rifles backing them up?" he replied.

"What about Sela?" Lomon asked.

Grant smirked, glad that Lomon had noticed the other Cerberus warrior missing from the mix. "She's checking the back door, the one that Domi and Edwards found."

"And the tunnel systems linking this to other facilities in this network of redoubts," Lomon added.

Grant nodded.

"Any news?" Lomon asked.

"None yet. But she's reporting in regularly."

"Constantly, more like it." Sela Sinclair's voice came through the Commtact, audible through the vibrating plate attached to pintles on Grant's jaw. He smiled at her response. One thing about the Commact was that it could keep them in near constant communication, and thanks to the pickups on the devices, they could hear what the others were hearing.

"So what's up?" he asked, making a point of pressing the Commtact plate on his jaw.

"The door is jammed shut," Sinclair answered. "Edwards wedged it fairly tight, and the millennialists know their way around a welding torch."

"A few joints going to be enough?" Grant pressed.

"Probably not, but we've also got the hallway rigged with high explosives, and a couple of steel I beams bracing the door," she replied. "Still nothing on Edwards's third trip line."

Grant grunted in affirmation, then turned back to Lomon. "Just be ready. These things might have backup that can return fire."

"You're still operating under the assumption that an intelligent agency is controlling them," Lomon commented. He nodded. "Yeah. It's been quiet for the past couple of minutes. I don't like this. Not one bit."

Grant handed him a piece of paper. "That's the frequency you can reach me on. Keep me appraised. And stay well back from your front line."

"That's going to be hard. I'm a leader, and not from the rear echelon," Lomon retorted.

"In this case, I need you alive and talking to me," Grant said. "I have to check on something."

"Godspeed, Grant," Lomon offered.

He smiled. "Thanks."

THE WARLORD WATCHED as the shapes of the kongamato orbited lazily over the Zambian hydroelectric center, the one that hid the redoubt, and his lips turned upward in a mirthless smile. His enemy was surrounded, and they didn't know how badly they were outnumbered *and* outgunned. Had it just been the clone-bred beasts from the underground laboratory, or the armed men of the Panthers of Manosha, then the Zambians would have been set up for one of the greatest battles of their lives.

For years, warlord Gamal had sought the treasures of the preskydark era. He'd hunted them down. He'd murdered for the slightest of hint of their locations. Gamal's frustration was sated only by acts of slaughter, or the amassing of more weapons and power. Stockpiles of old rifles, the means to produce gunpowder for bullets and bombs—those were tantalizing tastes of what could be. The occasional finds of operating trucks and half-tracks that the Panthers of Manosha kept in operating condition were an appeasement, especially as he listened to the screams of torment as they raided small villages for metal and scrap that could be fashioned into crude replacement parts. Even so, half those trucks were drawn by tamed Cape buffalo, and a third of his men used single-shot muskets and were relegated to raking up used brass to reload their automatic rifles.

But Gamal pressed onward.

Let Harare and Zambia continue to live in a semblance of what the ancients had. Factories and manufacturing, utilizing kerosene and biodiesel and hydroelectric power, were all well and good for grass-chewing prey, but Gamal was a lion. He was a predator. And his desire was simple.

Nuclear power.

Then, one night, the russet-skinned angel had whispered in his ear.

Her name sounded innocent enough.

Neekra.

She came as lover. As prophet. As guide. As king maker. *They believe themselves well girded against your might, Warlord.* Her voice had been breathless, heady, intoxicating.

Gamal could almost feel those rose-petal-red lips brushing softly against the lobe of his ear, even though he knew that she communicated with him through mind, not body. She was about him, *in* him, and her presence warmed him.

"What of Kane and the snake man?" Gamal asked her.

Her answer was a kiss on his mouth. *They struggle to free themselves. They take up arms against me.*

Gamal nodded. "So your testing is nearly concluded."

Her giggle was infectious, bringing a smile to his lips, a tingle all the way down into his loins.

Neekra came as an angel, but Gamal knew the truth of her, having learned the name of such beings as a child, listening to the superstitions of his people. She was a succubus, a seducer. That was why she came to him as his guide, as his muse.

Neekra wanted her freedom. And to achieve that, she needed a man of strength and iron will.

Someone like Gamal, who had an army.

He wanted to feel jealous about her attention to the two foreigners, the strangers, but realized that even if she left him with only Africa, he commanded millions of square miles of empire. With Durga and Kane as her consorts in North America and the Orient, Gamal would still be king of a third of the world, especially as he could push up into Europe.

There might be some tension if Gamal's and Durga's empires bumped borders in the Middle East or Eastern Europe, but Neekra would be their court of appeal, and the succubus would appease any injured feelings.

"Is it time?" Gamal asked.

Send them, my love.

Gamal smirked. "And shall I send them your love, goddess?"

The image of her smile was indelible within his mind.

I have no love for those who resist me.

For a moment, that sounded hollow, strained.

Gamal raised the radio to his lips. "Send the bombers in."

GRANT FELT THE floor shudder beneath his feet even as he reached the conference room where Nathan was tending to Nehushtan, Kane and Durga. The young man had propped up the snake-headed staff and put both men's hands on its shaft, hoping that it might give them something, return their minds to their bodies. But the situation was discouraging.

"Oh, that was not good," Grant murmured, even as Nathan turned his attention to him.

"Was that an explosion?" the young man asked.

"Give me a moment," Grant said apologetically. "Lomon, come in. You there?"

Coughing came over the radio waves. "Barely. Something just blew up at the vault doors. I've got four dead and a half dozen wounded."

"Do you need help with evacuation?" Grant asked.

Lomon's voice sounded rougher, older than usual. "Anyone else would just get underfoot here. We've got our fallback plan in action. Laying down a lot of chemical smoke."

"What hit?" Grant inquired.

"We saw a kongamato bounce off the ground. He deposited something and we fired, but when our bullets hit, it exploded," Lomon answered. "Regular blast, and shrapnel."

Grant grimaced. "Sela? You heard that."

"I'll be up there with first aid," Sinclair responded over the radio. "We're…"

Her words trailed off into a grunt, and vibrations ran through the soles of Grant's boots once more.

"Sela!" he exclaimed.

"Door's holding," Sinclair answered, sounding as ragged as Lomon. "But they're using more than their damned muscles to breach the redoubt from below."

Her voice became muted as she shouted commands to the millennialists, waving them away from the tunnel entrance. Grant had been waiting for the kongamato to engage in a two-pronged attack, and he wasn't surprised by the creatures' use of explosives, especially in the wake of Brigid's description of one showing intellect and malice as it pursued her in the jungle.

"All points, fall back to secondary defense lines. Leave your charges set to blow," Grant ordered. "They might not make an immediate push, but we're dealing with an intelligence controlling these creatures now. They've adapted enough to use explosives."

"What are you going to do?" Lomon asked.

"Whatever I have to," Grant answered, ending the call.

He moved over to Kane. "Come on, you stubborn bastard. I need you to wake up, and to bring that snake face Durga back, too. We need access to the Threshold right now."

Kane grunted in his unnatural slumber. He was in his mind, battling. Even Durga seemed to be entering some form of consciousness, his eyelids fluttering in rapid eye movement, something Grant recognized as the dream state.

Nathan clutched both men's hands, keeping them pressed to the artifact. "Staff of Solomon and Moses, scepter of Israel, arm of the Lord, I pray, if you've ever in your existence listened to one of the Longa men, heed my plea now!"

Grant looked on as Nathan squeezed his eyes shut. There was no activity from the black-coated staff, but then again, you couldn't see the Commtact working even as it was implanted against your own jaw. Nathan opened his eyes and shook his head. "I've got nothing."

"The stick might be fighting something. They're already in conflict," Grant said, motioning to the two unconscious men.

"They're not waking up fast enough. And why do we need the Threshold?" Nathan asked.

"Because Durga knows where these things are coming from, and the command center that might be controlling them," Grant answered. "And Kane would go with him."

"And what about you?" Nathan asked.

"Bry, send through the interphaser to the mat trans," Grant said aloud.

Nathan appeared confused for a moment, then realized that he was speaking with Cerberus redoubt utilizing the cybernetic communicator on his jaw. "What's an interphaser?"

"It's like the mat trans, but it doesn't need a nuclear-powered redoubt and plasteel chamber to power it," Grant said. "It allows navigation across natural parallax points."

"Wormholes," Nathan translated.

Grant nodded.

"We still have *Star Trek* here in Africa," Nathan answered with a smile. "But because you don't have the coordinates…"

"I'm going to go out, pick up Brigid and the others, and we're going to see where we can land to do the most good," Grant answered.

"Can I come along?" Nathan asked.

Grant looked at Kane, who was still in distress. "Your job is protecting the ancient artifact, son. And making sure my friend wakes up. Someone has to leave a message with him."

With that, Grant bent over his war bag and pulled out a large, unseemly weapon.

"What the hell is that?" Nathan asked.

"This is a USAS-12 automatic shotgun loaded with one-ounce solid slugs. It's the closest thing to the marriage between an assault rifle and an elephant rifle you could ever come up with," Grant answered. "The shells are so big, only seven of them fit into a magazine that would normally hold thirty to fifty regular rifle rounds. And the slugs can punch through quarter inch steel as if it were paper."

"That sounds…terrifying," Nathan observed.

Grant fit a magazine into the big cannon. "Think about the kongamato, fighting with weapons and intelligence, in addition to all that strength and rage."

He stuffed a spare slug shell into the breech of the bulky cannon. A tap on the bottom of the magazine, and his expression brightened with a brief glimmer of hope.

"Time to battle some devils," he grunted. "Sela, is the interphaser here yet?"

His voice faded into the hallway even as he spoke on the Commtact, leaving Nathan alone with Kane and Durga.

Chapter 21

Durga raised his saw-toothed sword in a swoop, steel carving into tentacles, slicing them from the main arm of the horror projecting them at him. Kane moved swiftly, dodging other attacking pseudopods. Their touch burned his "skin" and yet Durga seemed to endure their touch for a little longer.

Kane brought the fine Spanish sword around, plunging it through the heart of the entity's log-sized arm, causing the being to withdraw from the two of them. It was a giant, standing at least twenty feet in height by Kane's estimation. And yet the two warriors seemed to hold their ground against it.

Durga dropped back, his scales smoldering where they had been caressed by the nebulous cold of the tentacles.

"That's got to sting," Kane said to him.

"Sting doesn't begin to describe it," Durga growled, his jaws clenched. He patted himself, grimacing, and the cold, smoky burns faded from his flesh. "Will to power, Kane. You're sitting here in that shadow suit, which can't be a lot of protection…."

Kane looked down at himself. Sure enough, he was clad in the black second-skin designed by the moon techs. "You're armoring yourself?"

"With will. Anger," Durga answered. "It still hurts, but I see myself as I have to be to win."

Kane nodded.

He concentrated, even as the void goddess lumbered

toward them, trunklike legs shaking the ground with each ponderous step. In a heartbeat, he was back in the form he felt most battle-ready, head to toe in the shiny black carapace of his magistrate armor. Except this time, rather than his protective shell being forged from polycarbonate and Kevlar, his armor was days of anger and frustration.

Kane surged forward, the silvery Spanish sword disappearing and taking the form of his old trusted, foot-long combat knife. The entity reached toward him, arm branching, swirling like rivulets of black blood in snow. The Cerberus warrior slashed with his knife, carving through grabbing, hungry limbs. The flicker of a thought and the knife became two Sin Eaters, drawn far faster than he could have in real life, and bolts of flame and thunder rippled up the thick center of the entity's arm.

The thing staggered as twin streams of Kane's realized anger and pain stabbed into it. It reached for him with another arm, those suckers stretching to seize him. Kane felt the cold burning on his skin, even through the armor, but in a way, it didn't hurt as much, and indeed, only served to strengthen his resolve. He was about to turn and launch an attack on the void being's other hand when Durga drove the blunt point of his sword into the entity's wrist.

The sky broke open as the thing threw its head back, ebony lightning crackling from where a mouth would have been. The sunny sky that they had been battling beneath had been invaded by thick, choking clouds dangling writhing vines of ebony. The tentacles fell as thick as rainfall, but Kane growled and swept out with his combat knife.

Durga wrenched his sword free from the entity's forearm, where inky blood sprayed like a geyser, then hacked with the saw-toothed edge of his Khanda. As jagged points met skin, Durga slashed, cut, sawed at the entity's limb. The sheets of tendrils threatening to engulf Kane, Durga squirmed in reaction, and the void beast was now the one in need of retreat.

Kane whipped around and slashed at the shadow limb, drawing blood and quivering hunks of gelatinous "flesh" with each hacking strike of the knife. Within a matter of moments, the black strings of insanity dangling from the clouds were withdrawn, recoiling from the two beings who had caused their master such agony.

The "hand" itself lay on the earth at their feet, tawny grass blackening with its blood, as if it were infected. Durga saw a flinch of reflex still in the severed bit, and kicked at it, stmping it into the mud.

The void entity, clutching its ruined limb to its chest, was becoming more and more defined. Sure enough, Durga had been correct about the thing being female, as the fuzzy aura seemed to rinse away in the return of sunshine. Kane could make out the curves, soft and full, but other than its figure, the rest was indistinct, featureless.

Kane glanced toward Durga.

"She looked even better than that," the Nagah prince said with a shrug. "Those curves are…"

"I don't need to know that," Kane answered.

He extended both hands, and the Sin Eaters appeared again, blazing thunder on a scale they'd never have been capable of in reality. The ground around the void witch shook, divots of earth and clouds of dirt exploding skyward as Kane's wrath-made will struck out at her. She squirmed now, on the receiving end of sound and fury, though unlike the Shakespearian quote, this signified Kane's resistance to all the manhandling he'd been through. All the games and illusions thrown at him were now his ammunition, the fuel for his fire, which flowed like lava oozing from the earth where he'd wounded it.

Molten red magma bubbled, shaking off sparks of yellow, making the grounded void witch step back, again and again. When the flaming earth blood touched one foot, her entire leg would flare, lit with a wreath of fire and pain, causing her to scream even more loudly, twisting as Kane continued hammering at her. Soon, he'd carved an entire lake of fire about her, and she stood on a central island, surrounded by seething lava.

Kane held his fire, seeing her contained.

"You're not going to kill it?" Durga asked.

"First you called her a 'her,' and now an 'it'? Make up your mind," Kane said.

Durga rolled his eyes and formed a rocket launcher. "Her. It. Semantics. It's been trying to kill us. Why not finish the thing off?"

Kane looked at the creature, trapped, held at bay by a molten magma moat. "You're kidding, right? We've got it trapped. Now let's…"

"Let's what?" Durga asked.

"The tethers. They're gone," Kane said. "There's no reason for us to be here anymore. We could just wake up."

"If it were that easy, we'd be gone right now," Durga countered. "Kill the bitch, or I will."

Kane grimaced. "No."

Durga pointed the rocket launcher at the ground. It was the same one Kane had seen carried by Durga's father in the memorial at the center of the Nagah city. "What?"

"No. I've got her beaten. She has no control over me," Kane told him. "You want to kill her, it's up to you."

"I already did my part. I caused her grievous injury. I severed her arm."

"With my help," Kane answered.

Durga grimaced in turn and opened fire, hurtling a spear of metal and thunder at her. The end result, however, was a fading phantasm that merely disappeared in a puff of smoke. "See? I can't touch her anymore. But you can!"

"That does not make any sense," Kane grumbled.

"We've severed most of her link to us. It's up to you to finish the job," the cobra man urged. "And that means finishing off the enemy on this plane."

Kane looked back to the void witch. He remembered his rough treatment at her hands. He remembered every torture, agonies that had been stretched over seeming years, across every inch of his body, and he was enraged enough to want to take revenge on that But he noticed the way she held herself, limbs curled protectively. She was trapped. Helpless.

Kane walked to the edge of the lake of fire. "What do I call you?"

The void witch seemed to shrink at his approach.

What?

"What should I call you? Because 'hey you' is rude, and 'void thing' is kind of impersonal," Kane said.

She'd decreased in height. Now she was only about twelve feet tall. She had more room on the crumbling islet, but that was fading quickly. Already her feet, dainty in relation to her other proportions, were getting closer to the edge.

You may call me "the queen."

Kane shrugged. "So why are we still here? What are you waiting for?"

She looked down at the flaming lake.

"Don't give me that. You can get away. This is a place built by imagination, thought," he said. To demonstrate his point, he began walking forward, and a bridge unrolled under his feet, each step meeting with its solid surface as he moved across the magma lake. "You could fly. You could stretch. You could do anything you wanted. What the hell?"

The queen looked down at him, then shrank to match him in height. Features, sensual and full-lipped, were now visible.

"Don't!" Durga spit.

Silence! You rule me not!

The Nagah prince lowered his hand, but his amber eyes glared in hatred at Kane as he stood face-to-face with the queen.

Her eyes glimmered like black glass, light playing on them, drawing Kane in just a little deeper. *You would spare me out of curiosity?*

"And because you stopped fighting," he answered. "However, if you don't want me to spare you…"

The queen's luscious lips turned up in a smile. *Perhaps I chose the wrong one as lover.*

Durga's ire was intense enough that Kane could feel its heat, even past the moat of lava behind him.

"Behave, Prince," Kane said aloud, not even bothering to look back at him. "I'm talking with real royalty here."

"You…"

The queen tilted her head, and Durga's complaints were stifled.

"You seduced him. You tortured me. You wanted to see which would show more mercy, didn't you?" Kane asked.

She nodded.

"Any particular reason? Maybe because you're a prisoner somewhere on this continent?" he asked.

What makes you believe that?

"You sound like someone else I met. Another prisoner. This one was at the bottom of the Atlantic Ocean, and he'd been imprisoned by Enlil, as well," Kane answered.

Those glassy eyes narrowed, full lips pursed. *You know your enemies and friends well.*

"Don't tell Baptiste, but I actually pay attention when she starts sharing legends," Kane answered. "This is where Solomon had his mines. This was the end of the world, where he'd chased demons and imprisoned them. You're one of those demons."

The queen stroked her hand across his chest. This time,

no bitter cold bit through his armor, frosting his skin. Indeed, she seemed much warmer. Gentler.

Enlil was a jealous god.

"Is. He's still around, though we've taken the piss out of him," Kane responded.

And you'd spare me?

"There is no real reason to fight. Let me go, and we never have to cross each other's path again," Kane replied.

She tilted her head.

"That's not going to work for you," Kane stated.

I am a prisoner. You are correct. Come find me, and I shall shower upon you the gifts of the heavens.

"I don't do the servant thing," he said.

She stepped back, but stopped as her heels touched the edge of her islet. One more step and she'd be swimming in magma. Her smile had turned to a frown.

"So that's why Durga came here," Kane said. "He wanted to walk again. To be whole. He wanted some power back, too."

"You think you know me?" the Nagah prince asked.

Kane turned. "Your coconspirator. But she wasn't quite satisfied with you, was she? Or maybe she needed more."

Her hand touched Kane's cheek. She was still in seduction mode, though. Her palm was warm, not bitter and frosty. *I need someone strong enough to break my tomb. And you've got a special edge, Kane.*

He frowned, looking at her.

She was smiling now.

"Nehushtan," Kane replied.

She nodded.

"The same weapon that imprisoned you," he added.

We could do amazing things together. You could take the Earth and return it to a golden age.

"With you as an all-powerful goddess," Kane he murmured. He shook his head.

Arrogant worm, she spat with a sneer.

Kane stepped back, onto the bridge he'd formed in this mental landscape. "Pick your battles, girl," he growled.

The magma suddenly erupted around them. She grew in stature, lunging forward, but thick tongues of burning lava arose between them. Even as the queen reached out, she released a screech of agony and rage. The sky crackled again, but her power was weakening.

She tried to escape, but a tidal wave, a wall of magma, rose behind her.

"You brought the fight to my mind," Kane said. "You know exactly how to end this, too!"

The queen snapped her gaze toward him.

"You know..."

"...WHAT TO DO!" Kane yelled as he sat up suddenly.

"Good grief!" Nathan spit, at the Cerberus explorer's sudden awakening.

Durga's eyes opened, as well, but he didn't sit up right away. Rather, he seemed to be taking inventory of himself.

Kane threw his legs over the side of the table, resting his elbows on his knees and letting his head hang. "Nathan?"

"Kane," the young African responded.

"How long have I been out?"

"About twelve hours," he answered.

Kane blinked, wiping the crust from his eyes.

"It felt longer," Durga said. Kane looked back over his shoulder and saw that the Nagah prince was gingerly lowering himself from the table.

Durga closed his eyes as his feet touched the cool concrete floor of the conference room. As most Nagah, he was barefoot, though the scales on the soles of his feet were as durable as any shoe leather. Kane could see how the man's fused toes flexed against the floor. A smile crossed his reptilian lips.

"You don't know how good it is to have feeling in your feet," Durga said. "After all of—"

"Don't push it, snake face," Kane grunted, letting his gaze settle to the floor between his knees.

Durga glared at him. "You'd…"

"You're the one who let Queenie into my skull, Durga," Kane snapped. "You let her torture me. Where are the others, Nate?"

"Grant took an interphaser to meet up with Brigid," Nathan replied.

"And where's Baptiste?" Kane asked, sitting up a little straighter. It was she who'd broken through his coma. Who'd summoned her *anam chara* from his unnatural slumber, helping him to fight back to the surface, back to consciousness.

"An outside force used the Threshold to transport her into the middle of the jungle," Nathan explained. "She's all right. If anything, she's out of the way of the kongamato assault. Domi and Edwards are with her, too."

Kane stood up quickly, and he saw the Threshold, the gemlike artifact, sitting in the corner of the conference room. "Grant wants me to follow, using that."

"Yes," Nathan said. "Actually, he wants you and Durga to go directly to the cloning facility."

Kane turned to the Nagah. "Cloning facility. In another redoubt?"

Nathan nodded.

Kane took a deep breath. "Catch me up in a hundred words or less."

They heard the sound of automatic weapons rattling through the doorway. Another explosion shook the floor.

"The kongamato are at the gates. The redoubt doors have been hacked and they're open. Grant says the warlord that Thurpa spoke of is still on the hunt. He wants you and

Durga to hit the clone facilities, and find the main control center, maybe turn them off."

Kane nodded. "Grab your rifle and Nehushtan. You've probably been sitting on the sidelines long enough."

Nathan's face brightened into a smile.

Kane addressed Durga. "You can operate the Threshold?"

"It's how we got here," the Nagah prince replied. "And I remember where the clone vats are."

Kane nodded. "What about the control element?"

Durga frowned. "I wish I knew. Makoba was taking care of it, but someone robbed it from him."

"You're certain it was stolen?" Kane asked.

Durga's eyes narrowed. "The millennialists aren't stupid enough to screw themselves."

"No. But Makoba is a local. Was he the one who set up your meeting with Gamal?" Kane inquired.

"That son of a bitch," Durga snarled. "I'll need some guns."

Kane pointed to a table in the back. "You can borrow my Copperhead and spare magazines."

He retrieved his Sin Eater, strapping the hydraulic holster to his forearm. The folding machine pistol was a comforting weight on him; his arm felt complete again. A mental command, a twitch of a muscle and the deadly weapon slapped his palm, his straight finger the only thing preventing the gun from firing instantly.

"You do realize that you're going to need a lot more than just a glorified Glock," Durga said.

Kane felt his jaw, and aside from stubble, was acutely aware that he was without his Commtact plate. He found it next to where the Sin Eater and its holster had lain. "I've done well enough before."

"This isn't the psychic plane, where that thing shoots out thunderbolts and meteors," Durga pressed.

"If we need more, I'll improvise," he growled. He picked up his belt of grenades and tied it about his waist. Thankfully, he was still in his shadow suit, which was akin to a second skin.

"Grant," he called, placing his Commtact on his jaw. "Read me?"

"About time your sleepy ass woke up," his friend grumbled.

"Oh, be quiet. How much have you had to complain about me in the past week?" Kane returned.

Grant chuckled. "If I wasn't sneaking up on an army of muties and African militiamen, I'd get out my diary and read off the last three pages."

"What's the news on that?" Kane asked.

"I'm looking at easily two hundred men. The kongamato are ignoring them, and there's one guy on the flatbed of a large truck. He's sitting on a throne, and he's wearing a headpiece that's a hell of a lot more clunky than Erica's SQUID controller," Grant replied. "Kongamato are dropping down, accepting satchel charges from the militiamen, and flying toward the redoubt."

"What's your plan?" Kane asked.

"Throw grens and shoot anything still standing," Grant told him.

Lomon jogged through the door. He reeked of gun smoke, and he had a fresh bandage on his neck where shrapnel had struck him. Despite his disheveled appearance, he remained straight and tall, and seemed unsurprised to find Kane and Durga walking around. He had with him a familiar duffel—Grant's war bag. "Sela was right. You're awake. Grant said you'd need this."

Kane smiled, clasping the man's hand in thanks. "Grant's in position to supply you with some relief," he said. "How bad is it here?"

Lomon shook his head. "The kongamato have been

bombing the entrance. My people are hurting badly. Nine dead. A dozen wounded. One of our light machine guns is out of commission because the barrel cooked off."

Durga nodded. "So it's up to us to pull your asses out of the fire. Are you ready to jump, Kane?"

Lomon blinked. "You're the one who put us in the fire, making deals with Gamal, awakening the kongamato...."

The Nagah prince sneered. "Spare me your indignation."

Kane gritted his teeth, looking at Durga, then turned back to Lomon. "We're going to take the artifact that brought us here and head to where the kongamato were born. Grant's going to take out their commander in the field."

Durga held the Threshold aloft. "Quit this room, unless you wish to abandon your men."

Lomon shook his head. "I'll leave that to you, Durga."

He lowered the artifact. "You'll try my patience now, human?"

Kane snapped his fingers. "Focus here! The kongamato will tear you in half while you're in a pissing contest with Lomon!"

Durga raised the great jewel once more. "I shall prove myself the superior, human. Then we can discuss your attitude."

Kane snapped his fingers again. "How much longer can you hold out, Lomon?"

"We'll hold this line to our last man. Every beast that falls here is one less to threaten Zambia," he answered.

"I'll make sure no more die," Kane responded.

Durga closed his eyes, tilting his head back. Energy crackled about the jewel, then plasma fog began enveloping him, Kane and Nathan Longa.

"Good luck," Lomon called.

Kane nodded even as the Threshold took him through a wormhole. "We'll need it."

Chapter 22

Grant wished that he had Kane by his side, but at least the man was up and about, communicating with him over the Commtact, and working as part of his plan. Later, they could discuss the entity that had interfered with Durga and him, figure out what it was.

Right now, however, Grant had split the Cerberus warriors. He and Brigid Baptiste were crouched in the long grass, after slipping as close to Gamal and his truck throne as possible. Nearer now, and with the benefit of their shadow suit optics, both of them could see that Gamal's apparently relaxed posture was not due to overconfidence. He was connected to a console of computer equipment on the truck, and the throne actually provided him with an elevated position from which to observe the kongamato as they swept down on the Victoria Falls redoubt.

"The computer picks up Gamal's mental impulses and translates them into radio signals. Those signals are then broadcast to the mutants," Brigid explained, her voice low, but amplified through the Commtact on his jaw. "He also appears to be in conversation."

"Any idea who?" Grant asked.

"An invisible someone," Brigid said. "I'm not a gambler...."

"Except when playing cards," he returned.

"I'm card counting," she replied. "No gamble whatsoever."

"So Gamal is shacked up with the entity that's been

hacking the redoubt, arranged for the stolen mind control device, and maybe was the one who waylaid Kane and Durga," Grant concluded.

"You are no longer the student, but a master," Brigid praised.

"A master at laying down mayhem," Grant said. "Domi?"

"Ready," she answered.

Grant had CAT Beta set up as a cohesive fire team in the trees overlooking the Panthers of Manosha camp. The three of them had brought along an arsenal from Cerberus redoubt that was designed for long reach and maximum destruction.

Instead of Copperhead submachine guns, Domi, Sinclair and Edwards were equipped with SIG AMT rifles, well suited to reaching out five hundred yards, so as to hit those hard-to-scratch spots in Gamal's base camp. As well, they each had separate grenade launchers, six-shot revolving launchers that would enable them to arc high-explosive shells hundreds of feet into the Panthers' lair.

Grant wished he and the others had been quicker, but even so, they were moving as fast as possible, while still staying undercover. Their only hope in protecting the Zambians in the redoubt was to strike with surprise, and to completely overwhelm Gamal.

"First target Gamal or his equipment?" Grant asked.

"Both," Brigid replied. She wasn't in a mood to mess around. She lined up her Copperhead on the African warlord. "You blow the hell out of his equipment."

Grant nodded. "Domi, make it rain."

As soon as he said the feral girl's name, a trio of hollow pops sounded in the distance. He knew what they were, and Gamal suddenly sat up, realizing, too, that some new racket was on the battlefield. Even as the first grenades took to the sky, Grant and Brigid adjusted themselves, still keeping low behind a thick berm of dirt, and opened fire on Gamal's truck bed.

Brigid's Copperhead spit a stream of lead at the African warlord, but even as her bullets reached the man, a sudden surge of lightning filled the air. Obviously, the "clumsy headset" that Gamal wore was more than simply a means of telepathically commanding the kongamato. Streaks of white-blue plasma sparked, punching each of her copper-jacketed slugs to the ground.

Grant's slugs thundered violently from the mighty USAS-12, and those, too, were intercepted by the lightning arcing from the headgear worn by Gamal, even though his aim was toward the technology. Grant got off only four shots, then let the automatic shotgun hang, reaching for an implosion grenade.

"Zap this…." he snarled.

Brigid moved quickly, putting her hand over his. "Implosion grenade. If he bounces it, it'll land back in our lap!"

Grant paused, then disarmed the gren. High explosives might have been a good choice, but throwing a hand grenade into Gamal's lap, for him to lob back, was not the best move.

Even so, Brigid knew that their efforts weren't for naught, as Gamal suddenly turned his attention toward the muzzle-flashes that lit the jungle not far from him. Hopefully, since he was just a normal human warlord, he wouldn't have the multifunctioning intellect to continue control over the kongamato and deal with an attack.

As well, his lightning field protected only him, in his throne truck. Grenades landed amid the Panthers of Mano-sha column, and explosions ripped across the night in a staccato string of violence and devastation. Militiamen screamed as detonations spread shrapnel among them. It wasn't an all-encompassing rain of thunder, but the rolling blasts of eighteen 40 mm grenades were more than sufficient to switch the force from its standby position to scrambling for cover.

As a result, there were suddenly no more men to hand off satchel charges to the kongamato, who now landed and looked around in confusion.

Brigid smiled, realizing that she had been right about their attack at least distracting Gamal. Now they just had to hope that his lightning field wasn't powerful enough to swat at opponents farther away.

Gamal stood, looking in the direction of the muzzle-flashes.

"Ah. Finally, the visitors from America make their presence known. How you got out of the redoubt with my fine beasts covering both exits, I shall have to ask. If you survive," Gamal called.

Grant brought up the big shotgun and fired off the rest of his magazine. Sure enough, the heavy slugs were intercepted by streams of ions, which flared when struck. The electrical field was more than sufficient to stop the shotgun's metric ton of kinetic energy cold, dropping the fat bullets to the ground.

"Did you think that I'd sit here, unable to protect myself?" Gamal asked.

Grant sneered, digging for a magazine on his bandoleer "Honestly, I thought you were counting on people laughing at that headgear, so hard that you could shoot them before they recovered, given how ridiculous you looked."

Brigid let the big man speak, moving away from him in a hope to get a better angle. She didn't know what weapon could be used to penetrate the umbrella of charged energy that protected Gamal, but so far, he was simply standing there, not directing thunderbolts at Grant.

The optics of her shadow suit suddenly picked up movement in the corner of her eye, and Brigid threw herself to the ground, moments before a swooping predator came close to slamming into her. She rolled in the grass, and realized that Gamal didn't need thunderbolts.

He had kongamato. And they were nearly as swift and accurate.

More of the creatures were coming down, in attack formation, wings spreading wide to slow themselves, adjust their aim and strike down the lithe, athletic figure who had dared shoot at their master. Brigid brought up her Copperhead and opened fire on one of them. The stubby submachine gun chattered, and while she managed to hammer about 20 rounds into his belly, literally blowing him off course, she'd taken so much time that the other two were able to land, bracketing her.

Brigid Baptiste was poised between two murderous beasts, knowing the instant she turned to destroy one, the other would be atop her.

KANE, DURGA AND Nathan Longa appeared inside a cavern with a towering roof. Kane blinked as he looked up, seeing that it was not a natural space. Gouges and scours of powerful drilling tools were evident on the distant walls, as well as the ceiling, some seventy-five feet up.

"All right. Now I'm starting to become more impressed with you hairless apes," Durga murmured.

"You haven't been in here?" Kane asked.

"No. The Threshold simply picked a spot close to where I remember being," he explained. "When I was brought here, I was up...there."

Durga pointed a scaled finger toward the far side of the domed roof of the cavern, at what seemed at first to be a white box. But as Kane squinted, he noticed that it was light burning through a row of windows.

"From the inside of that, this really didn't look that impressive," Durga noted. Around them were terrariums, chambers formed of plasteel with metal frames. Lights glowed within, and at the bottom of each were pools of greenish slop.

Nathan stepped closer to one, then jerked backward in shock as a kongamato wing sliced up from the surface of the strange solution.

"Nutrient baths," Kane said. He'd seen this sort of thing before, in places such as the Anthill and in Greece. These were cloning facilities, where creatures were bred en masse and aged to maturity quickly. Thanks to biological over-clocking, the animals created within could be born and sent into battle within the space of a week.

This was the same technology that the barons used to perpetuate their hold over the nine villes, utilizing presky-dark technologies to dominate North America.

Kane himself had been part of one of those technologies. The magistrates had been selected from the ablest men, and bred, as per animal husbandry, to produce a template of physical and mental capability. Lakesh had interfered with that process, manipulating Kane's genealogy so that there was more than a simple spark of duty and obligation to his fellow man.

Aside from the magistrate breeding and education, the barons had vehicles and guns. The traditional magistrate armor was so high-tech that it made Kane, Grant and Edwards into nearly bulletproof human tanks, armed with advanced optics, communications, and weapons that could wipe out the barbarian scum who would not submit to baronial rule. The life of a magistrate hadn't truly ended up as a continual life of being the barons living will, and as such, they had become lawmen, often protecting even the non-ville residents who lived in teeming shanty towns that sprouted in the shadow of the megalithic villes.

Kane had discovered the truth about the barons, their "advanced evolutionary state" and the need for fresh humans to provide organs and blood to keep them alive, through transplants and transfusions. That was how he'd become a hunted rebel. But now, in a world where the deepest seeds of alien Annunaki DNA sprouted the barons into their true, superhuman forms, places like this, and the now destroyed Anthill and Area 51, were no longer necessary to them.

But that didn't mean there weren't those who tried to manipulate them. In Greece, a silver-clad bitch named Hera Olympiad had set herself up as goddess, utilizing hordes of vat-bred muties to create an eternal state of war. And now Durga and the Millennium Consortium had been drawn in by knowledge of these vats. The kongamato would serve as an amazing army, and given some time, without Kane's intervention, they might even have built a new body for Durga.

Now, however, another force had control of the cloned hordes. Kane knew that it had to be the queen, that voidlike psychic entity that had tried to crush him and seduce Durga. There was another of the queen's seductees out there, and from Grant and Brigid, he presumed it was Gamal, leader of the militia called the Panthers of Manosha. Together, the queen and Gamal threatened a ragtag assembly of Zambian soldiers and millennialists in a facility connected to this one.

"There's a lot of these baths between us and the control room," Durga said.

"Then let's get moving," Nathan grumbled. He clutched Nehushtan, an artifact entrusted to the Longa family for generations, whose ownership was reputed to go back through King Solomon and Moses to the high priests of Atlantis, which put it firmly as an artifact of Annunaki or Tuatha de Danann origin. The staff had performed many miraculous deeds over the past few days, reaching into the dreams of Kane, enabling feats of great strength, agility and prowess, even bringing Nathan back from the point of death and returning the quadriplegic Durga to his prime, in fitness and strength. Kane was glad to have the stick on his side, though he remembered how it had drawn up memories of a prior incarnation, giving him doubts as to whether he ever wanted to wield the staff himself.

He took the lead, the other two men falling into line behind him. After Durga and Kane awoke from their queen-induced coma, Grant had arranged for weapons to be provided to them. Right now, Kane had his Sin Eater in its hydraulic forearm holster, ready to burst into action at the slightest thought. And thanks to Grant, he had backup for it—a deadly little Copperhead submachine gun, and a Colt .45 automatic, which he wore in a holster on his hip.

Durga had his own Copperhead, and Nathan had a Zambian militia rifle, a G3, as well as his own little Detonics .45 auto, a copy of which Durga also had. Each of the three men was also equipped with hand grenades and spare ammunition. It made for a lot of firepower, but as they moved among the "growing chambers," where newborn kongamato twitching in their nutrient baths, it suddenly didn't seem like such an overwhelming advantage.

"So far, it doesn't look…" Durga began.

"Shush," Kane snapped. "Don't tempt—"

"…as if we've been noticed," he finished.

Even as the Nagah prince spoke those last words, the three men heard the hydraulic hiss of chamber lids opening. With their seals broken, the nutrient baths and the organisms growing within filled the air with a nauseating stink.

Nathan started coughing uncontrollably. "That screwed us," he grumbled.

"Move!" Kane ordered, and the young man from Harare was at full speed an instant later, running with incredible grace and agility.

Sure, now Nehushtan's active, Kane thought as he dug in and followed as best he could. Durga was hot on his heels.

"I didn't know your superstitions had merit," the Nagah prince panted.

Kane grimaced. "Maybe start paying attention to me in the future."

Durga suddenly tackled Kane, ropy arms winding about his legs and forcing him to the ground in a graceless tumble. Kane was about to curse the Nagah when he saw the kongamato perched atop his growth tank, struggling to regain his balance after missing its attack. Kane extended his hand and the Sin Eater popped into his grip, finger hooked to catch the trigger. In a heartbeat, the machine pistol roared, spitting lead into the winged beast, holes blasting through its chest and conical face. The creature thrashed under the multiple impacts, then toppled backward, splashing into the green nutrient slop that had nurtured it to physical adulthood.

Durga pulled his .45 and fired at a second of the vat-bred kongamato, the handgun's message accompanied by the thunderous bellow of a fat slug parting the air. One shot, two shots, three and the second of the attacking beasts fell, but this one smashed to the floor, blocking their path between the breeder containers.

Kane pulled himself up, then reached out for Durga's hand. "Come on."

The cobra man's amber eyes flashed with momentary confusion, but he took the proffered help, pulling himself to his feet. Right now, surrounded by quasi-alien humanoids, the two men needed each other, so the spoiled blood between them had to be forgotten.

Suddenly, a flash of light split across the dome of the chamber.

"Longa reached the control room," Durga said. "And he's run into the security systems."

Kane narrowed his eyes. "Security?"

"Move!" Durga ordered.

The urgency in his voice made Kane turn on his heels and leap over the corpse of the fallen kongamato.

Nathan needed help, and fast.

JONAS GRABBED ONE of his fellow soldiers, using a handle built into the collar of the man's vest to support his weight, rather than grabbing an arm and potentially dislocating it. The kongamato's assault had died out, but the killer beasts had taken their toll. Utilizing hurled satchel charges and their natural agility, they'd managed to turn the opening of the redoubt into a hell zone of rubble and pain. Most of the injuries hadn't come from the overpressure force of the actual explosives, but from concrete and rebar hurtled at bulletlike velocities.

Lomon stayed at the front, after having taken a brief respite to tend to the newly awakened Kane and the snake man. He was busy sifting through the aftermath of the mayhem, looking for anyone who still survived, holding on by a thread. Just to make certain that he wasn't caught helpless, Lomon had his big G3 rifle.

Jonas handed off the injured man to a fellow soldier, who transferred him to a cot. Even as Jonas did that, he made sure to keep his eyes on Lomon. They had survived this conflict so far, but there was no guarantee that they'd make it to the end.

Shuka already had lost most of his right hand, fingers crushed beneath a falling section of roof. Jonas remembered his knife cutting through flesh, because the carpal bones had been smashed to splinters. Shuka had transferred his handgun to his left hand, and what was left of the other was wrapped up in gauze and strips of a blanket.

Blood was being lost by the gallon. Men had died, but nearly everyone among the Zambians had picked up an injury, be it a broken eardrum from overpressure, or lacerations from flying rubble. Jonas himself was limping, a length of rebar having struck him in the knee. Had it been head-on, he would have been speared right through the patella, but as it was, putting weight on his leg was painful.

He glanced back into the redoubt as he heard the sudden crackle of gunfire.

"What the hell?" he asked. Already he was moving quicker, hop-limping to the intersection where he'd heard the sound. He shouldered the FAL rifle, both hands on the weapon, ready to engage in combat. Something had come through the back way.

That would be the only reason there would be shooting back here.

Staggering along, he saw a four-legged shadow amble into the open. Even from this distance, Jonas could recognize the gorillalike arms and shoulders of the beast. The kongamato must have made it through the booby traps at the bottom of the redoubt.

Jonas snapped up the front sight and triggered two quick rifle rounds into the thing. High-velocity bullets smashed the creature's shoulder and jerked it to the floor, a mist of blood and tissue remaining in the air thanks to the explosive exit of the deadly rounds. Jonas turned back. "We've got a breach! Form a line!"

He continued limping forward, knowing that the surviving millennialists would be in desperate straits, if not all dead.

That was when he noticed Makoba, the giant who had been recruited to the consortium. Looking relatively healthy, with eyes agleam, he stood withhis AK-47 grasped in one massive fist.

"Makoba! Get over here now!" Jonas shouted.

The big African bandit-turned-gunman-and-guide broke into a jog, closing the distance between them.

"Are you all right?" Jonas asked.

Makoba looked down at him. The millennialist was a

full head taller, yet Jonas could see strands of metal glinting through the man's thick, nappy hair. "Why should I not be?"

"The kongamato. They must have made it in. You saw the thing I shot," Jonas replied.

Makoba glanced back at the bullet-shattered corpse in the corridor. He turned his head to look at Jonas.

Something felt *very* wrong about this.

"I'm out of ammunition for my rifle," Makoba said. "Do you have any?"

"Not for that," Jonas answered. He took a step back, not liking how the millennialist was crowding his personal space.

Makoba shrugged. "Fair enough. I'll take your rifle…."

Jonas blinked, then saw stars as a massive fist crashed into his cheek and jaw. Nerves misfired, sending him to the floor in a collapse of numbed meat.

Just before the Zambian tumbled into unconsciousness, he realized that the metal in Makoba's hair could have been the missing helmet Durga had lost.

The control device that turned the kongamato from a mindless horde to a trained, deadly weapon.

Jonas cursed himself even as blackness descended upon him.

Chapter 23

From their position "surrounding" the Panthers of Manosha column, Edwards, Domi and Sela Sinclair had been raining hell upon the enemy. Their rifles might not have been full-auto like the Copperhead submachine guns, but with the SIG AMTs, one shot per pull of the trigger was not an impediment. Big rounds would strike a man and send him to the dirt, dead or crippled, unable to take further delight in the horrors that the winged kongamato inflicted upon the Zambian force trapped in the Victoria Falls redoubt. Their opening salvo of eighteen nearly simultaneously launched 40 mm grenades had destroyed trucks, and wagons made from converted trucks. Cape buffalo that weren't torn to pieces by shrapnel snapped out of their harnesses and stampeded through warlord Gamal's militiamen, spreading even more chaos and death.

Sinclair tried to suppress a smile as a gunman screamed, impaled on the horns of one of the buffalo, legs kicking as he clutched his belly with both hands. She tried not to feel any humor at the man's grisly situation, but she was reminded of an old tradition from the twentieth century— the running of the bulls in Pamplona, Spain.

The phrase that threatened to make her laugh was "when you mess with the bull, you get the horns."

"It seems like if you mess with Cerberus, you get the horns, too," Sinclair finally allowed herself to say, even as she granted the impaled man a merciful end to his suffering with a bullet through his skull.

"I don't even want to know where that came from," Edwards grumbled. While Sinclair and Domi were nailing down the perimeter with quick, lethal shots against the militiamen, the brawny ex-magistrate was quickly reloading his grenade launcher. The process wasn't the fastest, but over the space of twenty rounds from a rifle's magazine, he was able to put the six grenades into the revolver chambers of his launcher. Once done, he shouldered the weapon, lined up his sights and fired his first shot.

This one was directed at the umbrella of energy that had stymied Grant and Brigid in their attacks. Even as the 40 mm shell spiraled toward Gamal's "throne," Edwards sought out the second of the targets he'd scouted. Thanks to flash suppressors on CAT Beta's rifles, and the low charge in Edwards's multishot launcher, the Panthers of Manosha were unable to spot the trio in the darkness. Add in the night camouflage of their black shadow suits, and the three of them were more than a match for an assembled army.

Edwards planted his next round in a knot of men who were closing on Domi's position. The shell landed in their midst, scattering them with the force that six ounces of high explosive could muster. Two out of six rose from that group, but they quickly went down as Domi played cleanup. So far, CAT Beta had the Panthers of Manosha on the run, staggered by firepower and precision.

Then Sela Sinclair saw the kongamato alight, surrounding Brigid Baptiste, and instantly brought up her SIG rifle, targeting the creature on the left. A squeeze of the trigger, a second in rapid succession, and the winged hulk jerked violently. It collapsed, dead, and Sinclair was glad she didn't have to rely on the tiny 4.85 mm rounds that the Copperheads spit.

Brigid saw the one creature fall, and then the second seemed to explode in a violent tic. Grant charged from the shadows alongside the Cerberus archivist, his automatic shotgun having put it down.

"Thanks for the save, Beta." Brigid said via the Commtact.

Edwards came over the line. "That field around Gamal is gren-proof as well as bulletproof."

"I figured as much," Grant replied. "Brigid, any ideas?"

"Nothing here," she said. She sounded breathless, but that was understandable, as she was trying to keep pace with Grant's long strides.

So far, the Cerberus warriors had scattered the Panthers of Manosha with aplomb. From his position under a shield of charged ions, Gamal seemed to have forgotten his human warriors and was summoning more and more of the winged hybrids into battle.

Sinclair winced as she heard a sonic bark. She looked up, realizing that the monsters were even more batlike than just possessing wings. Judging by their cries, the creatures were undoubtedly using echolocation, a natural form of sonar that took the place of eyesight. There were few shadows that such a cry couldn't peer through, and Sinclair realized that she was relatively exposed. Already, her optics were picking up four of the winged horrors changing direction.

They were all focused on her, and she grimaced, running even as subsequent barks chased her. The air erupted behind her, and Sinclair looked back to see that a gren had gone off in midair. Charred lumps of meat struck the ground about her, and the kongamato who hadn't been hit veered off in midflight. She shouldered her rifle and chased one down with her front sight. Bullets sliced through the night and into the thick muscle and bone of the flying vat clone.

It, too, spiraled, losing control and crashing into the ground, wings vainly attempting to pick up air currents to allow it to parachute with relative safety. Instead, it landed with an ugly, wet thud. Another of the flying things swooped around, wings angled back, until it was a living arrow, jaws wide and open and forming a perfect circle in Sinclair's view.

She turned the rifle and fired bullets literally down the creature's throat, feeding it hot pills of lead and copper at supersonic speeds. The kongamato stayed on course, its momentum far too great to stop. But instead of snapping its jaws shut, and tearing through Sinclair's shadow suit with its teeth, the thing simply crashed into her. The lifeless clone rolled off, and Sinclair grunted in pain. The impact had been lessened by the non-Newtonian properties of her suit, but even with that, the wind was knocked out of her and her ribs ached.

She rolled onto all fours, realizing that each moment she spent in this position was another that enemies of any sort could swoop in upon her. She fought, pushing against the ground with all her might, and was starting to rise when she felt a rush of air just past her shoulder.

The kongamato threw down all four limbs, halting its forward momentum, but required a second to recover its wits and strength to turn back toward her. The Air Force freezie had lost hold of the grip on her rifle when the first beast struck her, though the weapon was still attached to her by its sling. Unfortunately, she didn't think she had the time or speed to unsnarl the twisted shoulder strap.

Her hand dropped to her holster and she pulled her Beretta 92, triggering the gun even as its muzzle cleared leather, and firing with all the speed and precision of an Old West gunfighter. She missed the first two shots, but the next four slammed into the whirling kongamato, 9 mm rounds punching deep through thick muscle and bone. The fifth and sixth shots recoiled up into the monstrosity's face. Bones collapsed under their intrusion, and the beast toppled backward, its brains whipped into a fine froth.

Sinclair turned, scanning for other menaces flapping in the night, but the kongamato seemed to have their attention split in multiple directions. Domi was visible, her albino features and ruby-red eyes readily apparent to Sinclair's night-vision optics, and the feral girl was a ballet dancer of carnage. With one fist clenching her .45, the other her fighting knife, she dodged, then slashed at her opponents, utilizing every ounce of her savage strength and speed.

The little human whirlwind seemed to revel in this conflict, but Domi's bared teeth were a blend of both wild abandon of her civilization and a rictus of effort. As quick and strong as the albino girl was in comparison to most people, she was still only a third the weight of these things, and didn't have the same reach as they did. She was expending energy at a greater rate than the vat-bred predators.

Sinclair untangled her sling swiftly, bringing the SIG's stock to her shoulder and looking through its red-dot scope. Even as a kongamato's mass intercepted the holographically projected dot, she pulled the trigger, sometimes firing in anticipation. The big .30-caliber rifle kicked against her shoulder, and downrange the savage, winged predator in her sights jolted as if a hammer had struck it.

It wasn't much, but at least it was evening the odds for the deadly little ruby-eyed Domi. She took advantage of the momentary distraction at the death of one of their own, and lunged like a fencer, the point of her blade tearing open the throat of another kongamato. A third whipped its attention back to her, roaring in bestial rage, but Domi snapped her arm up and pulled the trigger on her Detonics. A thunderous boom preceded the collapse of that creature, its skull excavated by a .4-caliber slug.

This was war to the knife, Sinclair realized. All she could hear over the Commtacts were gunfire, grunts and rapid breathing as warriors fought bandits and monsters in the night-blackened forest.

With the realization that it was everyone for themselves, Sinclair sought out new targets with her SIG.

The dawn would rise over a blood-soaked battlefield, and only her skills could give her a chance to see the sun again.

NATHAN LONGA GLANCED back over his shoulder even as he pole-vaulted from the floor of the vat chamber to the window of the control room. The lights were on within, and there was a man present. But even as he was springing off the ground, thanks to the artifact Nehushtan, he realized that he'd abandoned Kane and Durga fifty yards back, and he was already thirty feet in the air. The ancient staff of Solomon had once again gifted Nathan with phenomenal physical ability.

The knowledge was unnerving, as he'd accepted that prowess without a second thought. He stiffened his legs, driving them forward with all his might, to strike the glass. Even as his soles connected with the window, a dull glow sheathed him, the energies of Nehushtan reinforcing his body against the impact, and Nathan could see the layer of heavy gauge wire sandwiched between two sheets of Plexiglas. He watched as cracks spread, branching out like tongues of lightning during a summer storm, before the glass buckled, shattered into cubes and imploded into the control deck.

And then Nathan was on the floor there, crouched and looking around. The shift between mental states was disorienting, and he wondered why that had happened. He should have been aware of his landing, but then he noticed the man in the control room, an armed African in a millennialist uniform, flattened against the wall, an unseemly dent where his rib cage should have been.

Some things, I will spare you experiencing.

It was the staff. It had blanked him out while he'd

crushed that man's torso with…some form of attack. He was about to question the artifact out loud when the door to the control deck slammed open. There were more millennialists, and they were firing their Calico machine pistols from the hip, counting on sheer volume of automatic fire to catch the intruder.

Nathan jumped, seeking cover behind a heavy computer console as bullets chased after him. He fumbled for the pistol in his holster, thumbing back the hammer even as he drew it. He swung around the other side, seeing the flare of the consortium gunners' weapons, bullets flitting through the air like bolts of fire. Nathan realized that Nehushtan had him accelerated again, and he was able to line up the sights of the pistol on one of the two gunmen. The Detonics boomed in Nathan's fist, and he rode the recoil, swinging to aim at the head of the other man.

The staff took over once more, dragging Nathan back behind cover with a reflexive jerk, as bullets ripped through the air that he'd occupied moments ago. The staff of Solomon had saved his life by a matter of inches, by the span of microseconds, and for that, the young African was grateful. Even so, he knew that he wasn't invulnerable. The stick had overridden Nathan's instincts and reflexes simply because, as quick as the artifact had made him, it still was not sufficient to keep him safe from a speeding bullet.

He heard cursing through the doorway, and knew that the surviving gunman had not arrived alone. Nathan peered around a corner, closer to the floor, because he assumed that his opponents would be looking at head level for signs of movement. He saw one of the millenialists holding something through the doorway, something large and complicated, and oddly phallic.

Get out now.

Nathan didn't require a second warning, and he charged back to the window he'd leaped through before. That he was now thirty feet in the air was not as much a concern as the sudden blaze of light filling the area he'd just been in. Another second of blackness, and then he was aware and alert once more, crouched on the ground, with Kane and Durga coming toward him in a full run.

"What the hell was that?" Kane shouted.

"The nearest I can make out, it's the heavy artillery version of an ASP blaster," Durga replied. "You survived."

"I got out before they could shoot that thing," Nathan answered. "There's a cache of alien weapons in this complex?"

"There's a lot of bad stuff that I hoped to use," Durga answered.

Kane pulled the pin on an implosion grenade. "Find something else to hope for, snake face."

With that announcement, he stepped out from under the shadow of the control deck and lobbed the miniature bomb through the window. A couple millennialists were already poking their heads out as the gren passed between them, and there was a sudden burst of curses and screams. When the implode gren detonated, the two consortium henchmen were ejected through the window like rockets, their severed torsos trailing clouds of blood in their wake.

The floor above cracked under the sheer force of the blast, and Kane grabbed both Durga and Nathan, tugging them into the open before heavy equipment not sucked up by the implosion collapsed through the severely weakened floor. Nathan glanced back in shock as he watched computer consoles rain down, exploding into sparks and shattered components.

"You're not the only one who likes to blow shit up," Kane said to Durga.

Amber eyes narrowed, staring daggers at the Cerberus explorer. "I know. Firsthand."

Nathan lifted his gaze, and through the cavity blown in

the floor above, saw that the doorway seemed clear. "We're not going to climb up there easily...."

Kane pointed to Nehushtan. "If you let me borrow it..."

Nathan thought about that for a second, but Kane seemed to have a plan in mind, so he handed over the staff.

Kane then seized Durga under one armpit and pushed him upward. The Nagah prince let out a snarl of dismay as he was hefted off the ground and tossed through the door that Nathan pointed out.

"Oh, no," Nathan murmured.

Kane wrapped his free arm around him. "You'll be fine."

And with that, Nathan was airborne for the third time in what seemed as many minutes.

WHEN THE SUBLEVEL hatch started to buckle under violent assault, Thurpa the Nagah moved back from the group of humans. His instincts were on edge, especially since the only other cobra man in Africa was Durga, and he was elsewhere. In a melee between the men of the Millennium Consortium and a throng of wild, bestial kongamato clones, Thurpa had little hope that the technocrats would hold their fire, nor care if they accidentally killed him.

Thurpa had been involved in a pissing contest with members of this group since the beginning, and the young Nagah had already felt betrayal from the prince who'd brought him here. About the only people he sensed he could trust anymore were topside. Even Sela Sinclair, who'd come down to check on the millenialists, had had to leave, going on a mission to flank the wild horde above ground, risking her life for the sake of *everyone* down in this redoubt.

Thurpa kept his eyes on the group, slipping into a shadow. His chest still hurt badly from the laceration he'd received from these very creatures. The wound shifted, but coagulant gel and powerful glue kept it shut, a gauze wrap padding it and keeping infection away. He was in less than ideal condition to engage in a close-quarters battle with the screaming, apelike winged demons. If the millennialists actually possessed a tolerance for anyone but their own, Thurpa might have felt it worthwhile to stand with them and fight, but their distrust informed his decision that any battle would end with two forces against him.

So when he saw Makoba fall back and set an explosive charge on their barrier, Thurpa was in shadow, watching in abject horror. He was about to say something when Makoba depressed the trigger, detonating the whole thing. The iron beam holding the hatch shut was cut in half, and the kongamato smashed the freed door off its hinges. Makoba threw himself against the wall and out of the path of the screaming monsters that hurtled through the opening.

Thurpa squeezed himself tighter into the niche where he'd hidden, but the senses of one of the beasts picked him up as soon as it barked out a sonar wave. Thurpa's ears rang and his chest injury throbbed violently, but he gritted his teeth, forcing himself not to scream out.

The clone monster hopped toward him, its activity hidden by the sudden surge of its brethren taking after the consortium contingent. Thurpa winced as thick limbs slammed into the wall on either side of his hiding place. The reflex made him drop the handgun he'd received. It bounced and skittered between the beast's hind legs, disappearing into the shadows.

The creature opened its lips, baring its fangs. Thurpa and the animal turned their attention to the sudden surge of screams and gunfire in the distance. The kongamato force had caught the millennialists, whose submachine guns simply weren't enough to stop the massed assault.

The kongamato looked back at Thurpa, a low growl rumbling in its throat. The thing seemed to relish the fear it caused him.

If it hadn't been for the battle of the consortium gunmen, Thurpa would have been focused on his fear, caught up in pure panic. As it was, the brief respite allowed him to remember his natural abilities. In a heartbeat, the Nagah opened his mouth, flexing his fangs and emptying his venom sacs into the face of his tormentor.

In his panic, Thurpa held none of his body's natural venom in reserve. He got the toxic spit everywhere, in the creature's eyes, his mouth, his throat.

Almost instantly, his opponent was racked with pain, but as the first of the venom drops hit the back of its throat, its tissues swelled up, hindering its ability to cry out. The thing thrashed violently, at once blind and voiceless, but that didn't give Thurpa the break he'd hoped for. The kongamato brought up a powerful arm and smashed it across the cobra man's chest.

Searing, incredible pain rolled through Thurpam, who collapsed to the ground, gasping for breath. The glue keeping his wound shut held, but only barely. Skin stretched, and one of his chest scales dropped to the ground, leaving an ugly, piebald patch on his skin, growing redder and redder with bruising.

Breathe, he told himself, clawing at the floor. Any moment, the blinded kongamato would start casting about, looking for him. It didn't need eyes or sonar to locate him, and those arms were as strong as ever. Thurpa pulled himself to all fours, willing himself to move toward his fallen pistol. His amber eyes scanned the shadows for the one equalizer he could hope for.

Claws reached down, digging into Thurpa's scaled shoulder even as his fingertips brushed the butt of the weapon.

As the sharp nails pierced the cobra man's skin, he picked up the object and swung it toward his attacker.

Chapter 24

Grant looked skyward and saw that the kongamato were scattering, shrieking rather than projecting their echolocation barks. A grim smile creased his lips as he realized that something was interfering with the creatures' concentration.

"Kane, you blew stuff up?" he asked.

His friend grunted an affirmation over the Commtact. "Of course. The winged beasts confused?"

"Naturally," Grant replied. "Keep up the good work."

"Naturally!" Kane responded.

Brigid emptied the contents of her Copperhead into a particularly tenacious kongamato who refused to take flight in fear and confusion. Maybe its injuries had angered it too much to want to retreat, but the thing finally succumbed to multiple bullet wounds.

The archivist looked to Grant. "I take it your plan is going fine?"

"Hell no," he said. "There's too many of these things around, Lomon is on the radio telling me that the millennialists turned on the Zambians, and Gamal is still alive. The destruction that Kane wrought gave us a temporary reprieve, especially since Gamal has a lot of machinery by his throne."

"So, his control of the animals is still an issue," Brigid mused.

"A distraction, but a useful one," Grant replied.

He stuffed another magazine of slugs into the big shotgun. "That energy field does a good job of stopping bullets cold, and doing the same to grens."

"Ionic plasma discharge. It doesn't allow the grenades to explode," Brigid noted. "I watched your first attempt, and then Edwards's efforts with his launcher."

"At least it doesn't send an electrical arc back along the route of the attack. Otherwise we'd be screwed," Grant mused.

"There's another thing I want to try," Brigid said. "Distract Gamal for a moment."

Grant nodded. He threw another grenade at the warlord's protective energy umbrella, and the weapon shot away as it struck a pencil-thin arc of ions. He then turned the big shotgun at Gamal and fired off three quick shots. The muzzle-blast made Grant an unmistakable target, and once more the warlord summoned his winged minions. The batlike horrors swung out of the sky, swooping toward the Cerberus giant.

Grant let the shotgun hang and snapped his Sin Eater into action. The signature machine pistol roared, spitting out slugs quickly. He needed a couple more shots on target than with the shotgun slugs, but the Sin Eater held more and could be aimed with much greater precision. Grant and his Sin Eater knocked three of the kongamato out of the air before a fourth slammed into him.

He held his ground, and the bullet-riddled kongamato bounced away from him. Grant turned toward Gamal. "That all you got, sucker?" he taunted the African warlord.

"All I have?" Gamal asked in return. "My queen has promised me unlimited power, the secrets of the gods. I have so much more at my command...."

Grant spotted Brigid sneaking up through the long grass. Thanks to the shadow suit, she was as hard to spot as a black cat, and the body-hugging material added to her feline grace and appearance. The militia had called itself the Panthers of Manosha, but so far, facing the Cerberus team, they'd been shown to be kittens, with Brigid taking on the stealth and cunning of a black panther herself.

"So, you have nothing," Grant said. His suit's optics allowed him to see Brigid, but Gamal didn't have any such eyewear. She produced a small handful of something, then lobbed it low.

Gamal sneered. "Pitiful…"

Grant realized that Brigid was going to try to come up through the truck's flatbed itself. The umbrella of ionic energy surrounded and protected the machinery, but those lightninglike fingers ended at the floor Gamal stood upon.

Hopefully, whatever grenade Brigid had tossed beneath the trailer would cut through the metal. If not…

The implosion grenade went off with a deafening roar, and instead of being hurled upward, the platform beneath Gamal bent down to the ground. The African warlord screamed as he was knocked from his feet. The machinery on the flatbed with him shook violently, rolling toward the sudden depression in the metal they rested on. Gamal scrambled, rushing to get out of the way of toppling consoles, but there was a brutal crunch, and the warlord broke into pained screams.

Grant didn't take any time to gloat over the fall of the Manoshan madman. The kongamato took the destruction of their control systems as a bad, bad sign.

The flying beasts let out a unified shriek of rage.

There must be at least fifty of the monsters left, Grant mused as he quickly reloaded his shotgun. "Find a way to burn these things' brains, Kane!" he growled.

MAKOBA SMILED AS he watched the kongamato surge from the underground tunnels, a dozen of the brawny, brutal beasts having slipped in the back door, thanks to his brilliance. Certainly the Millennium Consortium and Durga would consider this treachery, but Makoba was nothing if not set in his ways. He'd lived his entire life with minimal influence from whites, and he was damned certain that Africa was *not* going to give up its secrets to snake men from India.

Makoba, younger brother to Gamal, was going to be a prince of Africa.

He looked down at Jonas, who had expected him to arrive topside, having sealed off that entrance with high explosives. The man was unconscious, and Makoba had taken his rifle.

Lomon and the Zambians still in a mood to fight were farther down the hall, and Makoba concentrated, looking at the throng of kongamato he'd been given. At first, while they were coming to his side, they seemed confused, unmotivated. They milled around instead of moving at full speed. Makoba wondered if this was simply because they had feasted upon the surviving millennialists who had been assigned to him. They were covered in blood, with shreds of flesh stuck between their long teeth.

"Move, you morons!" Makoba growled. He ran his fingers through his hair, touching the control crown that he'd stolen from Durga. Gamal said that he'd be able to keep the creatures in line with them.

They'd been quick and brutal. The millennialists had died screaming and shooting. When the kongamato were done, there were only scraps and bones. Makoba felt a little disappointed that he hadn't seen Thurpa torn to ribbons by the snarling horde, but the annoying outsider was nowhere to be seen.

"Attack them," Makoba whispered, ifocusing as hard as he could through the control crown.

The beasts suddenly galloped forward, charging on all fours.

Except they were simply plowing through the battered Zambian soldiers, shoving them aside. Some were hurt by their passage, but the chaos, the carnage that Makoba wanted, was ignored. The creatures reached the shattered entrance of the redoubt and leaped upward into the night sky, taking to the wing.

"Come back. No! Come back!" Makoba shouted. "You're supposed to kill them all!"

Even as he bellowed at the fleeing kongamato, he clutched Jonas's rifle tightly in both hands, muzzle pointed in Lomon's direction.

Bad idea.

"Son, you'd best lower that weapon!" Lomon called out.

The ragtag Zambians turned their attention toward the man they'd known as a millennialist. Now, he stood over one of their own, Jonas, and had taken his firearm, calling out about having the mutants stay and kill them all. Makoba watched their eyes go from confusion and exhaustion to hard anger and determination. Those with the strength to sat up or rose to their feet, swiftly reloading their guns.

Lomon rushed to the front of the group, getting between his fellow Zambian militiamen and the consortium gunman.

"Look at the odds, Makoba," he shouted. "If you shoot, you'll be dead in an instant."

Makoba took a step back, then prodded the muzzle of his rifle into the stunned Jonas. "You attack me, I'll kill him. I swear upon my brother, I'll murder this little bastard!"

Lomon's glance of concern faded away. "If you do, you won't die from a gunshot wound. Hurt my friend, and I'll make your ending long, slow and painful."

Makoba looked down at Jonas. He continued to step back, but kept his weapon trained on him. "If you know what's good for you, you'll let me be."

"Really?" Lomon asked. "You call out to a group of

maniac beasts to kill us, attack one of my friends and expect me to leave you alone?"

The Zambian officer didn't press the point. He was hurting badly from all manner of dings and cuts. Chasing an armed, uninjured opponent was nothing that he cared to engage in. The battle with the kongamato and their satchel charges had wrought a hefty toll upon him and the others. While Lomon didn't have much attachment to the millennialists, the sight of Makoba alone meant that he'd betrayed them. The kongamato wouldn't have been the only ones that the big bandit brought with him. That meant the consortium contingent was gone.

Likely torn to pieces by the beasts who'd run out on Makoba.

If he let the marauder escape, the murders of those men would go unpaid for, as well. Lomon cursed his limits.

Then he saw a movement behind the gunman.

It was a hooded figure in the shadows, and it was carrying a length of rebar.

Makoba backed right into Thurpa. Sheer panic filled the man, and he pulled the trigger on his rifle. Only fear and providence had kept that stream of bullets from striking Jonas or any of Lomon's other fellow Zambians. Makoba whirled and tried to bring up the rifle, but Thurpa smashed him across the face with the knobby length of steel. The first stroke laid open the Manoshan Panther's flesh all the way down to white, gleaming bone.

A second stroke with the rebar, and Makoba toppled against the wall, clutching his throat, rifle forgotten in a clatter on the floor. Thurpa glared at the fallen figure, then dropped the rebar down to the ground, to support himself as a cane. His shoulders heaved, and even the rebar couldn't keep him on his feet for long.

"Get that man help!" Lomon shouted.

"Makoba?"

"Thurpa! The Nagah!" Lomon spit.

"He saved Jonas," Shuka added. "He's one of ours."

Lomon led the rush, picking the wounded Nagah up from his knees.

Even as he held the exhausted Thurpa, Lomon knew that there was a chance for this ragtag Zambian contingent.

BRIGID BAPTISTE SCAMPERED through the grass, moving as quickly as she could to the side of the collapsed, almost folded truck bed, looking for Gamal and his control crown. If she could get hold of the device, and the detonation of the implosion grenade hadn't destroyed the electronics, she could utilize it. There were still dozens of the kongamato flying around, but at this point, they were on a rampage of their own, no longer directed by the mental impulses of the warlord.

That didn't make anything safer for her or the other Cerberus warriors, but now, the kongamato were turning their attention and their hunger toward the carrion and wounded in the wake of their initial strikes. Men screamed and gunshots rang out as the creatures swooped down and plucked at the dead, the dying and those just running scared as hell. At least the focus was off her and Grant, but she couldn't see her friend for the darkness and the confusion.

That might have been a good thing, especially since that would mean Grant could be out of sight of the flying predators suddenly possessing free will and great hunger.

She reached the side of the wrecked flatbed and saw a massive form swing into view. Brigid was about to fire on him, but the faceplate suddenly outlined the form and threw up a green identify-friend-foe flag on the optics. It was Grant, and thankfully, her reflexes were slower than the technology she wielded.

"Brigid," he said. "Looking for Gamal?"

"Yes," she responded. "See him?"

Grant shook his head. "But there's a trail of blood. And I found this...."

He held up the headpiece that the warlord had worn. She could see that it was broken.

"Damn," Brigid grumbled. "I was hoping to use that.... Is the equipment all right?"

Grant tilted his head. Brigid stepped around, peering closer. There were field computers, bulky, heavily armored systems with green screens and keyboards. They had been meant to take a pounding, but both showed damage. The screen on one showed an error message, its hard drive having lost vast amounts of its programming as it had collided with the ionic field.

The other machine seemed to be in operating condition. Its lights were working, but its monitor had shattered, having struck a corner of the other console.

Grant looked around. "We need something to kill all these things, or sooner or later, they're going to overwhelm the amount of ammunition we have."

Brigid looked at the working device, then leveled her .45 at it. A pull of the trigger, and the keyboard and its guts were blasted to pieces.

"Why did you do that?" Grant asked.

"Because it's obvious we can't control these things from here. Gamal is gone, that control headpiece is broken, and there's no way we can jury-rig one screen to another," Brigid replied. "So, we remove these machines from the equation immediately. That way, there won't be any interference when Kane and the others find something."

She held out her hand. "Let me look at the crown."

Grant handed it over. "If anything, it looks like the tech we're using for the Commtacts."

"I'll call Bry and see if he can pick up anything on it," Brigid offered.

"Grant? Brigid?" It was a familiar, Indian-accented

voice, but it wasn't Durga's. Kane and the cobra prince had been out of contact for several minutes, meaning they could have gone deeper underground, or into an area where electronic interference was preventing communication.

"Thurpa?" Brigid asked.

"I've found Durga's control unit," the Nagah said. "Makoba took it."

"Where are you?" she inquired.

"With Lomon. I'm using his radio, since Grant keyed him to the Commtact frequency," Thurpa replied. "Makoba tried to control the kongamato, but he failed…."

"Presumably because Gamal had more powerful equipment," Brigid said. "Can you try to use it?"

"Yeah," Thurpa replied.

Grant looked to the tree line. The kongamato were avoiding it, because CAT Beta held down that area. Unfortunately, that reprieve wasn't going to last long.

"Okay, I've fit it on my head," Thurpa said over the radio. "What's your order?"

Brigid looked to Grant. "Anything from Kane?"

"I'll give it one more try," he said. "Bry, you read me? Can you boost the signal?"

Donald Bry, the computer genius back at Cerberus redoubt, was on immediately. "If we can't reach him, it won't because the satellites were too weak."

"Kane!" Grant shouted. Brigid tensed, flinching away from the stentorian bellow.

"Damn it, Grant, I kind of need my eardrums!" Kane answered. The signal was loaded with static.

"Well, we need a surefire way to deal with the clones," Grant countered. "What have you got?"

"Durga's located a self-destruct mechanism for the cloning facility," Kane replied. "It's a pretty simple fail-safe. Kerosene is released through sprayers, and then it's ignited by a timed charge."

"Kerosene," Grant murmured. "The clone facility will turn into a fuel-air explosive underground."

"Send them here!" Kane ordered.

DURGA GLARED AT Kane, not enjoying being manhandled like a sack of rice. But considering that the Cerberus explorer held the ancient artifact Nehushtan, and his strength had been boosted by a considerable degree, the Nagah prince held his tongue.

Kane felt almost disappointed. He wanted to get into a throwdown with his old foe. Or did he?

With the influence of the staff, and his adventures on the psychic plane, Kane still felt off balance. The power coursing through his veins could have been like a drug, and the influence of that unknown, voidlike queen could have spurred an even more intense rivalry with Durga. She sounded as if she was interested in getting Kane on her side, even after doing her best to crush and mutilate him with all manner of telepathic torture.

"More of those things are waking up," Durga said, pointing back the way they'd come.

"That's why we're up here, in a more defensible position," Kane countered.

Durga narrowed his eyes. "You want to treat me as a simpleton?"

Kane closed his eyes and took a cleansing breath. "No. But the queen seems to like competition. If we keep working together, if we find a way to destroy these things en masse, then she loses a major asset when she wakes up."

Durga paused, and Kane could see realization dawning. "She's upped our testosterone levels."

"Yes," Kane returned. "Why should I be pissed at you? You protected my ass down there!"

"And if you two don't stop arguing, I'm going to have to save you," Nathan said. Even as he spoke, he triggered his rifle, punching two shots into a newly awakened kongamato who'd grabbed the edge of the hole they'd jumped through.

Kane turned his attention back toward the vat chamber. Allthe lids were open, and the kongamato, slick and green from their nutrient baths, spread their wings tentatively. He plucked a grenade from his belt and lobbed it back down among the rows of vats, then grabbed Nathan by the shoulder and led him down the corridor. Durga stayed on their heels as the gren detonated, cracking the air like a thunderbolt.

Kane looked at the ground. His implosion charge had sucked up whatever weapon the remaining guards wielded, but there were still a few bodies strewed on the ground. He scanned the corridor, hoping to see a sign that would give him a destination. He glanced back to Durga.

"Do you know if there's a self-destruct in this place?" Kane asked.

Durga nodded. "But it's not going to be pretty."

"You've got the Threshold, so we can get out," Kane urged. "Where is it?"

Durga pointed the way, and the three men took off in that direction. They moved at a quick jog, not speeding up even as one of the vat clones appeared in the corridor behind them. Kane stopped and turned his Sin Eater against the creature, triggering a burst into it.

Even as the kongamato fell, another lurched through the door behind it. As the thing unleashed its ultrasonic bark, Kane winced, feeling the whine of the high-frequency sound moving across multiple waves, both what he could hear and what he could only feel as vibration stinging inside his skull. Kane fired the Sin Eater again, batting the creature down, before turning and racing after Durga and Nathan.

They finally reached a room at the end of the corridor, and all three of them swung the door, a metal hatch with a locking wheel in the center of it, closed. As the wheel turned, bolts an inch-thick slid into notches in the heavy steel frame. This door was a bulkhead, and it wouldn't be opened by anything less than a phenomenal pounding.

The only trouble was that the kongamato had proved that their strength was up to the task. There was no telling how long they would have.

Durga took Kane by the elbow and led him to a console. "This is the emergency shutdown for this facility," he said. "There's tanks of kerosene, which feeds out through sprinklers."

Kane nodded. "The makers of this knew what could go wrong if a clone batch got out of control. They saturate the facility with flammable fumes, light a spark…."

"This place looks as if it's got enough fuel to match a two-kiloton atomic warhead," Durga murmured into Kane's ear. "I don't know how much damage it's going to do to the whole complex…."

"Meaning that we blow this joint, we could take out the other redoubts," Kane concluded.

"Do you want to risk that?" the Nagah asked. "You might not be able to get home if the mat-trans chambers are knocked out."

Kane shook his head. "No problem there. We've got the interphaser to get home."

Nathan looked over the console. "But there is the problem that if we blow this up, Lomon, Jonas, Shuka and the rest of the Zambians in the redoubt across the way."

Kane nodded. "The explosion's overpressure will take the path of least resistance, going through any connecting tunnels. Our allies could end up crushed by the blast we intend to use to save them."

Durga smirked. "I remember an old saying, to save the village, we had to destroy it."

Kane glared. "I'm sure that Lomon and his men would

willingly give their lives to protect the rest of Zambia, but I'd like to save them."

"Then call and get them to move to a safe location," the cobra man suggested.

Kane spoke. "Kane to Grant, over."

He adjusted the pressure of the Commtact plate along his jaw. "Grant?"

Durga dropped his gaze, putting his hand to his scaled forehead. "We're too deep to call the others."

"Look for an intercom system," Kane ordered. "Maybe we can reach them...."

The hatch shook violently, as if a bomb had gone off on the other side.

Time was running out.

Chapter 25

The hammer blow against the steel hatch focused Kane, Durga and Nathan Longa as surely as a gunshot over their heads. The kongamato were here, and they began the savage effort of beating the door off its hinges. The three men could see the door shake, saw the iron rods flex under each impact.

"Intercom. Find one," Kane said.

The three spread out through the room, but there was nothing. The place was not much more than a suicide bunker. There was even a sprinkler above their heads, bearing the international symbol for inflammable, so it wasn't a fire-control device. Kerosene would spray down, most of the droplets so small that they'd vaporize before striking the ground, saturating the air with fuel, creating the perfect environment for a single spark to turn every cubic foot of atmosphere in this facility into an explosive charge.

Kane knew full well the scale of a fuel-air explosion. It was the same basic mechanism of the implosion grenades he used. The small hand weapons popped, releasing a sphere of microscopic, flammable particles that spread a radius of ten feet. A secondary explosion lit those particles, and the resultant flash of fire created a vacuum effect that gave the implode gren its nom de guerre. Durga had been right in stating that this self-destruct had near-nuclear levels of devastation.

"Grant, damn it, you'd better find a way to talk to me," Kane murmured.

He looked toward Nehushtan, the very artifact that had haunted his dreams, drawing him here to Africa. Since then, he'd been caught up in a war, meeting with old enemies such as the Nagah prince Durga, who'd been hunting through the wilderness in search of a means of restoring his body to health.

Well, at least the staff had solved Durga's predicament, though he and Kane nearly didn't survive it. As soon as the artifact worked its healing power on the cobra man, they'd come under assault by a psychic entity that plucked them from their bodies, trapping them in a dream state. Originally, they'd thought they were on a journey across the multiverse, but the truth was far more insidious. Durga had told Kane he was seduced by a succubus that called itself the Queen.

In the meantime, Kane himself had been put through tortures no man with a body could hope to survive. The only thing that kept him alive was the fact that it was a psychic state. No acid ate his flesh, no saw had hewn his limbs, no crucifix had hung him in a strangling position. Nehushtan had awakened the spark of an old memory in him, a DNA pattern of his heritage, from the artifact's owner in the sixteenth century.

The man had been called Solomon Kane, and he, too, had traveled Africa and the world, seeking to deal with dark forces. It was just a memory, not a true ghost, but it had focused him enough to fight the queen. That, and the whispered prayer of Brigid Baptiste for her *anam chara* to return to the waking world, had galvanized Kane to turn his imprisonment into a battle in the dreamscape.

Nehushtan had granted him other gifts, too. It was a tool of healing, and enhanced the abilities of those who held it, making Nathan Longa, its current caretaker, strong enough to battle kongamato in four-to-one odds and survive. It had given Brigid Baptiste the speed, agility and stamina to run a kilometer in thirty seconds to bring its healing powers to a badly wounded Nathan. And Nathan himself had mentioned how the staff guided him though dreams, his quest bringing him to this flash point at Victoria Falls, where two armies gathered.

One army had been Gamal and the Panthers of Manosha, a bandit force hired by Durga and the Millennium Consortium as their local guides. The other army was made up of clones of a creature known as the kongamato, a hideous blend of gorilla and bat, possessed of great strength and talons, the ability to fly, and the savagery to tear a man in half. Gamal was in command of these creatures now, and his forces assailed the surviving contingent of Zambian soldiers who had welcomed Kane and his allies. Somewhere, aboveground, Grant, Brigid Baptiste and the other warriors of Cerberus redoubt were engaged in a battle to protect the ragtag force.

Kane held out his hand for the staff. "Give it here."

Nathan looked to Nehushtan, then once more ceded it. "You're not going to try to throw me through the wall, are you?"

"No," Kane answered. He touched the haft of the black stick. Nehushtan, according to myth, was an object of brass, but in truth, it was made of orichalcum—an alloy whose secrets were at once dangerous and lost to antiquity. Kane squeezed the staff. "Please have the ability to boost radio signals, or else—"

"Kane!" Grant's stentorian bellow rocked Kane's skull through the Commtact. The signal was loaded with static, but at least now he was in contact with his friends.

"Damn it, Grant, I kind of need my eardrums!" he answered. Despite the complaint, he was glad and relieved to hear his friend's voice.

"Well, we need a surefire way to deal with the clones,"

Grant countered, crackles of white noise accompanying each word. "What have you got?"

"Durga's located a self-destruct mechanism for the cloning facility," Kane replied. "It's a pretty simple fail-safe. Kerosene is released through sprayers, and then it's ignited by a timed charge."

"Kerosene," Grant murmured. "The clone facility will turn into a fuel-air explosive underground."

"Send them here!" Kane ordered.

Thurpa's voice came over the radio waves. "I'll do what I can. Tell Durga I found his control crown. Makoba stole it."

Durga and Nathan, however, were both listening in. The communication signal was being translated by Nehushtan.

"Where is that traitor?" Durga asked.

"Dead," Thurpa answered.

Durga smirked.

"I'll send the kongamato home," Thurpa announced over the radio link.

Durga looked at Kane again. "You're certain you want to destroy this facility? There's no telling what kind of wonders are in storage in other parts of the complex."

"Grant, make sure that Lomon and the others get the hell out of their redoubt," Kane said. "When we set off the self-destruct…"

"I know," Grant answered. "Fuel-air-explosions are known for two things. Being almost as powerful as a nuke, and for the blast and fire to spread through systems of caverns, looking for every nook and cranny."

Kane glanced at the door. The kongamato had stopped hammering at it. Thurpa was using the control headset to send a signal to all the creatures. And maybe, just maybe, Kane's request to Nehushtan was making that possible.

"Durga still has the Threshold, right?" Grant asked.

The Nagah prince slipped the backpack he wore off his shoulders and removed the jewel-like artifact.

"Yeah," Kane said.

"The Threshold stays with us. It doesn't recall to the other side of the planet like your little toy." Durga seemed disgusted, his ire rising, but then he gave his head a shake, flexing the sheets of muscle that made up his cobra hood. "Sorry. The queen…"

"Get us ready," Kane said. He decided to take a chance. The rods clacked from where they were rooted, and the hatch swung open.

The corridor was empty, though the barks of the kongamato now permeated the air. And they were growing louder.

"Grant, are they gone from your position?" Kane asked.

GRANT LOOKED UP into the sky. The brutish winged horrors had taken flight. Thurpa's mental command had gotten through to the creatures, a simple urge that Thurpa understood all too well.

Home. The Nagah was an exile from his own underground home, the city of Garuda. That thought was similar enough to entice the kongamato to take to the wing. Half of them dived to a spot in a grassy clearing. The others were flying straight through the sky, back toward the facility where they'd discovered Durga and the millenialists.

Domi, Edwards and Sinclair had joined Grant and Brigid, and the feral girl pointed toward the clearing. "That's where the access hatch to the tunnels brought us up."

"So they're backtracking the way they came," Brigid mused. "What about the others? The ones Makoba let into the redoubt?"

Grant looked toward the Victoria Falls redoubt, but only two of the kongamato flew toward that entrance. The rattle of a light machine gun filled the air, and the beasts were swatted from the sky.

"Thurpa, can you keep track of them?" Grant asked after a few minutes, keeping watch whether the creatures wound their way to this battleground.

"I'm getting some feedback," the Nagah replied. "Oh, damn. Yeah, my sinuses are burning. My ears are ringing, too. They smell kerosene, and they're listening to each other. They're confused by the urge to go home...."

"They're in the complex," Kane announced. "Countdown is forty seconds."

Thurpa released a grunt. "Took off the crown. The kongamato are confused by the smell, but they feel safe now. Their bellies are full of meat, and they're in the caves where they were born."

The air came alive with electricity. Brigid felt her hair rise, lifted by the static charge. A few moments later, the mistlike form of a plasma wave fogged the space next to them. A battered Kane, Durga and Nathan Longa stood there. Durga wielded the Threshold device.

The cobra prince did not look happy. "I want Thurpa. Now."

Brigid and Grant kept an eye on the Nagah as they moved closer to Kane. The three entered a loose embrace, glad that they were back together again.

"Did you hear me?" Durga asked.

"He's with Lomon's men. And he's injured," Grant told him.

"Then heal him," Durga said to Nathan, who held Nehushtan.

"I'm not your servant," the young man from Harare said.

"You insolent..." Durga began.

The ground shuddered.

"Lomon?" Grant called over his Commtact.

"We're above ground," the Zambian officer answered. "We're safe, for now."

"Thurpa!" Durga growled.

The tremors continued, and a roar of thunder rose in competition with the rumble of the Zambezi River as it crashed down the Victoria Falls gorge. The access vent that the kongamato had flown through suddenly glowed brightly.

A jet of flame shot into the sky, superheated fuel energized by a spark burning and seeking an exit. The column of fire split the night, forcing all present to look away from it. It was so bright that they kept their heads down for several seconds, the afterglow still burning orange behind their eyelids.

The heat, however, was gone after a full second, the rushing roar of the flames as well.

The assembled travelers looked at each other with uncertainty.

"Lomon?" Grant called over the Commtact.

"We rode it through. No fire or heat from the vault doors," the Zambian officer replied.

"And Thurpa?" Durga pressed.

"You have another track for that mind?" Kane snapped.

"Grant, tell my prince that I resign from his service," Thurpa croaked over the Commtact.

"Nathan, you have your radio?" Kane asked the young guardian of Nehushtan.

He nodded, took it out and turned it on, switching to the Commtacts' common frequency.

"Repeat what you said," Grant requested. "He can hear you himself."

"Thurpa...come here—"

"Piss off, Prince." Thurpa cut him off.

Durga's amber eyes flared with anger.

"I've got people here who've shown concern for me. Unlike you," Thurpa added.

Durga was about to say something in response, then

turned his head, almost as if he were capturing a whisper in his ear.

The Threshold glowed, then plasma mist surrounded him and swallowed him, spiriting him away as if he'd never been present at all.

"Not even a goodbye?" Brigid asked. "I'm insulted."

Kane grimaced. "Good riddance."

"He should owe you his life," Brigid said.

"He saved my life when we went to the cloning facility," Kane answered. "Besides, I don't like holding debts. Let him go."

"We'll need to get back to Lomon and the Zambians," Nathan interjected. "There's quite a few men who'll need the power of the staff. And I suppose you'll take your interphaser back home...."

Kane shook his head.

Grant and Brigid locked their eyes on the Cerberus leader.

"We're staying. Durga was seduced while we were in our downtime," Kane explained. "Maybe he was in contact with the entity that trapped us even before I was put into a coma."

"You never explained what exactly happened during your nap," Grant said.

Kane grimaced. "There was a creature. It claimed godhood. It called itself the queen, and it pulled Durga and me from our bodies. We beat it, eventually. That's when we woke up."

"And you're concerned that Durga's going after her?" Brigid asked.

Kane nodded. "The bitch said she was imprisoned. Just like Kakusa had been."

Brigid frowned. She'd heard the story of the possessing entity, trapped at the bottom of the ocean in a facility called the Tongue of the Ocean, TOTO for short. That entity had the potential to unleash itself as a plague upon the world, despite being trapped in cephalopodlike individual bodies, psychically connected as a hive mind.

That there was such a prisoner here in Africa, able to reach beyond the walls of its tomb and effect Kane…

"Gamal mentioned a queen, as well," Brigid stated quickly. "She seems to be calling a lot of bad people to her side."

"Maybe it even had a conversation with North," Kane mused. "When we first saw her, she was a cloud around him."

Grant looked around. He then activated his Commtact. "Lomon, Thurpa, any sign of that weasel bastard?"

"None." Both men answered at once.

"We can't leave," Kane said. "We walk away from Africa, we'll lose Durga's trail."

"And how do we track this demon queen?" Grant asked.

Nathan tapped the shaft of Nehushtan. "It's been guiding me toward you. Toward the people who could figure out what threat woke it up."

Kane, Grant and Brigid watched as CAT Beta assembled and approached them across the battlefield. There weren't many remnants of the Panthers of Manosha, only guns, wreckage, and body parts left behind by engorged kongamato.

"We'll do what we can for Lomon's injured," Kane offered. "The six of us owe them that much."

"And a communication link to Cerberus," Domi added, jogging the short distance between her team and Kane's. "We've been listening to your conversation."

"You've been quiet about it," Grant commented.

"We'll be on call. An interphaser hop away, if necessary," Sinclair said. "After all, someone has to watch Cerberus and America while you three are running around on the Dark Continent."

Kane regarded herr, then frowned.

"Sela, this continent is a hell of a lot darker than anyone ever guessed," Kane finally announced.

The breaking dawn did little to lighten the mood as the Cerberus warriors made their way back to the battered Zambian contingent.

GAMAL OPENED HIS eyes. He remembered crawling through the grass, especially after pulling the pulped remained of his crushed foot from between chunks of machinery. The same energy field that protected him from incoming gunfire had done little to deal with damage on the underside of a heavily armored truck bed.

And now, he wasn't certain where he was.

All he could see were shadowy figures. There was little light with which to make out details.

It looked as if he was surrounded by men in hoods. And there were a dozen of them.

One stepped closer, crouching before Gamal as he fought his way to a seated position. A click, and a small LED light turned on, illuminating Durga's reptilian features. Gamal winced at the nearness of the Nagah prince, and his wicked smile.

The glow from his tiny torch seared Gamal's eyes. It took a few moments, but finally they became accustomed to the glow.

It turned out the men's hoods were not made of cloth.

They were all Nagah, just like Durga.

"Are you going to kill me?" Gamal asked.

Durga's wicked smile continued, unabated. "Neekra still has some fondness for you, despite your failure."

Gamal looked down. He saw his leg ended in a heavy, crudely wrapped bandage.

"Do not worry about your impairment," Durga said, standing once again. "Neekra will provide for you."

Gamal breathed a sigh of relief. "Really?"

Durga winced. "I'm sorry. I got that all backward."

Something cold brushed its fingers across Gamal's skull. Icy chill burned his scalp, digging into his brain. The Manoshan warlord suddenly began to thrash.

His screams filled the air, his skin changing from deep ebony to a ruddy, rusty crimson.

"You will provide sufficient biomass to take care of Neekra's impairment," Durga added.

Pain sliced through every nerve in Gamal's body.

"After all, what good is a queen who is simply a waking dream? Isn't that right, love?" Durga asked.

Gamal felt his lips move. But he heard a woman's voice speak.

"That is correct, my king."

Gamal wanted to scream, but nothing came out. His senses fell away, and the African warlord was no more.

In his place was a demoness.

"Now, let us hurry to my city, before this body burns out," Neekra said.

Durga nodded. "Yes, my queen."

* * * * *

*Don't miss the exciting conclusion
in NECROPOLIS, coming May 2014.*

The Don Pendleton's
Executioner®
AMAZON IMPUNITY

U.S. missionaries get caught in the crosshairs of a Brazilian drug cartel...

Sent to Brazil to take down one of the country's most powerful drug lords, Mack Bolan stumbles across two U.S. missionaries taken prisoner by the cartel. But while attempting to extract them to safety, Bolan learns that not everyone wants to be rescued. Suddenly Bolan is caught in a deadly game of cat and mouse—and the cartel soldiers are rapidly closing in on their prey. With his reluctant charges on the run, and a cocaine shipment already en route, Bolan is torn between destroying the trafficker's thriving business and saving American lives.

Available in March, wherever books and ebooks are sold.

GOLD
EAGLE®

GEX424

3 2953 01175192 4